JERSEY SWEETS

THREE-IN-ONE COLLECTION

JANICE HANNA

BARBOUR
PUBLISHING

Member of the
Evangelical Christian
Publishers Association

Printed in the United States of America.

Dear Readers,

I had the privilege of visiting the boardwalk in Atlantic City several years ago with my mother and sister, and saw first-hand the quaint, yet bustling area that has become known for its arcades, tourism and, of course, that sticky-sweet stuff called salt water taffy. There's really no other place on earth like the boardwalk. You get the salty smell of the Atlantic all mixed up with the scent of hot dogs roasting, kettle corn popping, and sugary delights of every kind. It was in this locale that I decided to place *Jersey Sweets*. How fun would it be, I reasoned, to write a series about a family-owned candy store (Carini's Confections) and set it on the boardwalk? And how much more exciting to create three sisters and imagine each one's own love story?

In the first book, *Salt Water Taffie*, I had the great joy of introducing the first of the Carini sisters, Taffie. Oh, how I envy her! Can you imagine working in a confectionary? Running the taffy machine? Serving up sweets all day long? Yum! In book two, *Cotton Candy Clouds*, I had the opportunity to share the story of the second sister, Candy Carini—the one who always has her head in the clouds. Of course, I had to make her a pilot. In *Sweet Harmony* I introduced the reader to the youngest of the sisters, Tangie, (short for "Tangerine," which happened to be the flavor of the month when she was born). In this quirky tale, Tangie, a Broadway-bound actress, moves to the town of Harmony, New Jersey, to become a drama director for a local church.

What a blast I had traveling across the great state of New Jersey—from Atlantic City, to Newark, to Harmony—getting to know the world of the Carini sisters. I can honestly say these three novels are the "sweetest" stories I've ever penned, (pun intended).

Janice Hanna

SALT WATER TAFFIE

Dedication

To Joe Marini—a fourth generation candymaker at Marini's Candy Shop on the boardwalk in Santa Cruz, California. Thanks for answering all my questions. And by the way. . .the taffy was great!

Chapter 1

I'll have a half pound of assorted taffies, hon. And don't bother with the fancy box. Just put 'em in a plastic bag, and I'll be on my way."

Taffie Carini glanced across the glass counter at her customer, a woman in her early sixties with wind-blown gray hair, and offered a smile. "Anything else?"

"No, I'm supposed to be watching my waistline," the woman responded with a wink. " 'Course, it's getting easier to see every day, so I don't know why I bother."

Taffie forced back a grin and took several steps to her right—beyond the maple fudge and tiny mounds of white divinity, past the homemade peanut brittle, the crystallized rock candy, and countless rows of caramel apples—to the large glass candy jars. She kept on moving beyond the colorful jelly beans and the jars of licorice, finally landing in the taffy section.

Reaching for a metal scoop, she measured out a half pound of taffies in a variety of flavors, then threw in a couple of extra pieces for good measure. After pressing a Carini's Confections sticker on the bag, she closed it with a twist tie, and then returned to the register and passed it over the glass counter to her anxious customer.

"Oh, honey, I can't resist." The woman's double chin became more pronounced as her lips curled up in a girlish grin. "Give me another half pound of the peanut butter–flavored ones. They're my favorite. I used to eat them all the time when I was a girl. My mama said they were responsible for some mighty big dental bills back in the day."

This time Taffie couldn't hide her smile. She'd visited the dentist on countless occasions as a child as well. But who could blame her? When your parents ran the most popular candy and ice cream shop on Atlantic City's busy boardwalk, you were bound to suffer a few casualties. . .er, cavities.

She made her way back over to the glass jar that held the peanut butter taffy and filled another bag, this time tossing in a good quarter pound more than necessary. Her parents wouldn't mind. In fact, if Pop hadn't disappeared into the back room to service one of the machines, he probably would have told her to double the order, just for fun.

"My parents used to come to this store when they were children," the woman explained as she fumbled for her wallet. "I think they must've known your mom and dad."

"Or possibly my grandfather," Taffie offered. "He's the one who opened the shop in the late thirties."

"Was his name Gus?"

"Yep." Taffie sighed at the mention of his name. Grandpa Gus passed away five years ago, but she still missed him terribly and so did the customers. Her parents insisted on telling folks he'd gone to "the sweet by-and-by," something that always brought either a sigh or a chuckle.

A sound at the window distracted Taffie from her work. She looked over to see three elementary aged children dressed in bathing suits, peering through the glass from the boardwalk outside. Their sticky fingers left behind imprints on the window she'd spent much of the morning cleaning. Still, who could fault them, especially since the stickiness came from the taffy she'd sold their mother just minutes before? Taffie gave them a wave and they skipped off, disappearing into a sea of tourists.

"Looks like I'm not the only one with a sweet tooth today." The woman slipped a ten-dollar bill over the counter. As she did, her gaze shifted to the name tag on Taffie's blouse. "Oh! Is that your real name?"

"Yes, ma'am." Taffie sighed. She got this a lot. "I'm Taffie Carini. And yes, my parents did it on purpose."

"How clever."

"Yes." Should she mention that her younger sisters, Candy and Tangie, had suffered similarly embarrassing fates? Having imaginative parents in the candy biz could be tough on a girl, especially a single girl in her late twenties. What sort of guy was going to take any of them seriously? No, the Carini daughters were destined to remain single. Loaded with sweets. . .just not the right kind.

"My husband and I don't make it back to Atlantic City often enough," the woman continued. "We live in the Midwest now. But I've still got salt water in my veins." She giggled. "I guess you do, too. Salt Water Taffie!"

Taffie did her best not to groan. She got this one a lot, too. Stretching out her hand with the woman's change, she smiled. "Have a sweet day."

"Have a sweet day, yourself!" The woman undid the twist tie on one of the bags and reached inside for a piece of peanut butter taffy. She unwrapped it and popped the whole piece in her mouth as she made her way back out to the boardwalk.

Taffie glanced across the confectionery—beyond the small round tables and white wrought-iron chairs—to the turn-of-the-century style soda fountain on the other side. She watched as her mother schmoozed the customers, young and old alike, serving up malts, sodas, sundaes, and banana splits. Yes, Mom certainly had a way with people. And in August, as the last of the summer tourists made their way up and down the boardwalk, she knew just how to draw them in from the heat. . .with the promise of ice cream and old-fashioned sugary delights of every kind.

The double doors opened and, like the waves rushing the shore, a new batch of customers flooded the shop. Taffie tried to stay focused as she measured out half a pound of this and a pound of that. The children giggled as they sampled the sweet treats. Their parents, with childlike excitement in their eyes, peered through the glass at the homemade goodies. And the old folks sighed with joy as they reminisced about the candies that made them feel young again.

Taffie loved watching this scene play itself out over and over again. In fact, she loved pretty much everything about her life at the candy shop. Well, everything except the financial stuff. But something about the look of pure longing in a customer's eyes made her happy.

She just had to wonder. . .would anyone ever look at *her* with that same sense of longing? Determined not to grow sad, she turned her attention back to her customers.

❧

"Ryan, are you still in the kitchen?"

"Still in here, Pop. Checking out this oven." Ryan Antonelli closed the door to the large pizza oven and turned to look into his father's anxious eyes.

"So, what's the diagnosis, son?"

"Busted heating element," Ryan explained. "We'll have to order the part. Shouldn't take long to arrive. A couple of days, maybe. Three, at most."

"Two days? Or three?" This time the voice came from his right. Mr. Petruzelli, owner of the pizzeria, entered the room with worry etched in his brow. "How will we stay in business if our main oven is down? What a mess!" He paced the room, muttering in Italian.

Ryan looked at his father and shrugged. Pop's expression spoke volumes. *Antonelli's Appliance Repair guarantees every customer will be satisfied, no matter the sacrifice.*

"Tell you what, Mr. Petruzelli," Ryan said as he tucked his flashlight back into his tool belt. "I'm headed to Philadelphia in a couple of hours. I've got tickets to see the Phillies play tonight. I'll go by the parts store before the game and pick up the heating element myself."

"Yes, that's right." His father patted him on the back, and Ryan could almost read the relief in his expression. "Tomorrow morning, bright and early, my son and I will come by to make the repair. That way you can open for business at the usual time."

"You promise?" Mr. Petruzelli asked, the wrinkles in his forehead relaxing a bit.

"I promise!" Ryan extended his hand and his customer took it, offering a friendly shake.

Mr. Petruzelli followed Ryan and his father outside, his words tumbling forth a mile a minute, undergirded by a hearty Italian accent. While Ryan loaded his tools in the van, the two older men took to chatting about the weather and the price of gasoline. He grinned as he watched his father at work. *You've still got it, Pop. You know just how to win over the customers, even after all these years.*

Not that his father had to try. No, Victor Antonelli's heart for the Lord came shining through in every situation. Ryan had witnessed it hundreds—if not thousands—of times.

He took his place behind the wheel, waiting until his father wrapped up with their now-happy customer. Then, with Pop onboard, Ryan pointed the vehicle toward Antonelli's Appliance Repair—the small converted office at the front of the family's house in Bungalow Park. Not much had changed in the disorganized office over the years. Pop still hadn't quite managed to stay on top of things. But who could blame him? He'd suffered more than his fair share of challenges.

Ryan looked over at his father and relaxed a bit as he spoke. "All's well that ends well."

"Yes." His pop flashed a smile bright enough to light up the boardwalk at night. "Son, you saved my neck back there. No telling what might've happened if we'd made Mr. Petruzelli wait on the part. Are you sure you don't mind picking it up while you're in Philly?"

"Don't mind a bit. What time should we meet in the morning?"

"The restaurant opens at eleven. How long do you think it will take to make the repair?"

"Maybe an hour and a half?"

"Let's say nine, just to be safe."

"Sure." Ryan shrugged. He would do anything to help his father, and the past year had proven that. Laying down his own wants and wishes, he'd come to Pop's rescue after the stroke, taking over most of the repairs. Thankfully, the recovery time had been minimal, and his pop was back at work. Now on a daily regimen of medications, he struggled to keep a healthy balance between work and rest.

Ryan did his best to carry most of the burden where the business was concerned. Sure, his older brother Luke helped out on occasion, but for the most part Ryan and his father tackled the commercial appliances of Atlantic City. . . together. There was hardly a business in town they hadn't become acquainted with. School cafeterias, day cares, hospitals. . . You name the business; they'd serviced it.

Not that Ryan particularly enjoyed his work as a technician. No, under better circumstances, he'd stick to working with business promotions. His marketing degree had hardly prepared him for repairing dishwashers, garbage disposals, and the like, but Pop needed him. And as long as Pop needed him. . .

"Who's going to the game with you, son?"

"Luke and Vic. Same as always." He loved hanging out with his older brothers—most of the time. Since Vic's recent separation from his wife, he'd been pretty sullen. And Luke, despite his twenty-nine years on planet Earth, still spent most of his time forgetting to show up for work. More often than not, he continued to act like an irresponsible teenager.

As if reading his thoughts, his father reached over and patted his arm. "You're the one I count on, Ryan. Sometimes I forget you're only twenty-seven. You're more mature than most your age."

"Thanks, Pop. But keep on praying for all of us. I have a feeling it won't be long before Luke and Vic realize they're not kids anymore."

"I'm sure you're right."

Ryan felt the usual twisting in his heart. Surely the Lord wasn't finished with his brothers yet. And surely He saw to the very depths of Ryan's heart. . .knew that his plans for the future didn't exactly include appliance repair.

At least, not for long.

Chapter 2

Taffie woke up early Saturday morning with a lot on her mind. Last night's business class at Atlantic City College, for example. Sure, she'd gone into the course with the best of intentions. After all, her parents would be retiring at the end of September, and with her sisters both away in school, running the shop would fall to her. She needed to learn the ins and outs of managing the business's finances, and also figure out a new marketing strategy for the winter season. Unfortunately, things weren't going as well as she'd planned. Last night's test score served as the biggest red flag so far.

Oh, if only she could skip all that financial stuff and just make candy and tend to the customers. Why did she have to do everything else, too? When would she work up the courage to tell her parents that she did not. . .*could not*. . .even balance her checkbook, let alone take on the family's finances?

Candy making she could handle. No problem. Operating the taffy pull? Sure. Customer service? Of course! But money? The very thought of lining up numbers in tidy little columns sent a shiver down her spine. She understood the purpose behind it, of course, but to actually do it? Well, that was another thing altogether.

Yes, delving into the world of finances was certainly stretching her.

Stretching, hmm.

She thought about the taffy machine at once. The family had been in the stretching business for years, hadn't they? And the results had always been sweet. Perhaps things would end well this time, too, if she just stuck with it. Oh, but how she wanted to give up!

Taffie rolled over in the bed and gazed at the slivers of early morning light peeking in through the bedroom window. For a second, she contemplated putting on her bathing suit and heading off to the shoreline before opening the shop. She needed to clear her head, to step away from things long enough to figure out if she had what it would take to run the place once Mom and Pop headed off to explore the great unknown in that new RV of theirs.

The great unknown. She pondered those words. They seemed to reflect her life. Her future, anyway.

Resting her head against the pillow, Taffie closed her eyes and spent a few minutes drawing in deep breaths. *Lord, this is Your candy shop. Not mine. Not my parents'. Yours. And I know that You know how to run it. I'm just asking. . .* She sighed as she wrapped up her prayer. *I'm just asking that You teach me the things I need to know so that my parents can get the rest they deserve.*

Off in the distance, a peal of thunder startled her back to attention. Looked like a dip in the Atlantic was out of the question. She dressed in her usual attire, pausing long enough to pull her long dark mane of hair into a ponytail. No point in styling it, really. A ponytail seemed to work best, especially in her line of work.

Still, as she examined her somewhat haggard appearance in the mirror, she had to wonder what had happened to the old Taffie—the one who used to care so much about how she looked—the one with the sparkle in her eyes and the natural glow in her tanned cheeks. This new version wasn't exactly improved.

She sighed and reached for her blush. Maybe she could paint over the frustration. Nope. Seconds later, the same reflection stared back at her, though her cheeks did appear a hint rosier. She tried a bit of coral-colored lipstick. *There. That's better. As long as I make sure my lips are curled up, not down.* Taffie quickly applied some mascara to her long lashes, then gave herself another once-over. *Not too bad. Not too bad.* Maybe now her parents wouldn't pick up on her frustrations. And maybe the customers wouldn't see her as a single twenty-something, still working in her parents' candy shop.

Not that it mattered. No one seemed to notice her anyway. Her customers only had eyes for one thing—sweets. She could show up for work in a frayed T-shirt and ratty old jeans with no makeup at all and no one would notice, as long as the apples were dipped in caramel, the strawberries coated in chocolate, and the taffy jars full of colorful delights.

Ah, well.

Taffie looked around the house for her parents, but apparently they'd already left. But why hadn't they told her?

By the time she climbed in the car, raindrops pelted the windshield.

Great. No telling what this weather would do to business. She was already concerned enough, what with summer drawing to an end. How would they go on wooing customers in the fall and winter, when things slowed to a grinding halt?

"You'll come up with something, Taffie," her pop had said.

Only, she hadn't. At least not yet.

She arrived at the store, surprised to find her father already there, dressed in a white undershirt and slacks. This could only mean one thing—one of the machines had gone down. Again.

"So, what's happened?"

"Oh, it's that main taffy machine." Pop reached for a bottle of water and took a swig. "One of the arms is locked up. Jammed tighter than a drum. Again."

"I'll look at it," she said. "I've always managed to get it freed up."

"I know, but this time I think we're going to have to call in the big guns. We're looking at a major problem."

"Nah. Let me take a look." Taffie made her way into the back room where the largest of their taffy pulling machines stood. Unlike the smaller one in the front window, this one was grander in scale and more complex in function. She'd managed to get it going several times in the past but had to admit, after nearly half an hour of trying, it appeared to be frozen in place this time. Nothing she tried seemed to work.

"Who should we call?" She turned to her father, unsure of what to do next. "It's not exactly under warranty. Grandpa Gus bought it in the thirties, didn't he?"

"Right. Let me think." Her father paced the room, offering up suggestions. "We obviously need someone who does machine repair."

"You mean, like office machines? Copiers. . .that sort of thing?"

He shrugged. "I don't know. I was thinking of someone who could get the parts we need from another machine. Might be expensive, though."

"Maybe we could find someone to make the part." Taffie thought about it for a moment. "But why don't we start with the obvious. . .get someone in here who knows about commercial kitchen equipment. Might be a stretch, but surely there are other commercial appliances that have similar functions."

"I don't know." Pop raked his fingers through thinning gray hair.

"We'll never know till we try." Taffie reached for the phone book and flipped it open, ready to solve this problem once and for all.

ⓢ

Ryan lifted his head out of Mr. Petruzzelli's oven to take an incoming call on his cell phone. "Antonelli's Appliance Repair."

The voice on the other end of the line caught him off guard. A woman. Upset. Voice trembling. "I, um, I wonder if you service. . . ?"

He didn't catch the rest. Must be poor reception. Ryan shrugged at his pop and mouthed, "I'll take this outside," then stepped toward the door.

The woman's voice came through a bit clearer from here. "So, you see, we've got quite a problem on our hands. If we don't get this fixed, we'll lose business. And this would be the worst possible time for that to happen. I can't stress how important this is."

He wasn't quite sure what problem she referred to, and tried to get a word in edgewise to ask, but she plowed ahead, talking about the upcoming slow season and the fact that she hadn't figured out how to market the products in her store enough to increase winter sales.

What in the world did this have to do with machine repair?

"I'm wondering if you can come by our shop this afternoon. I hate to ask on such short notice, but it's urgent."

She went on with her somewhat confusing explanation, and Ryan finally managed a few words. "Where are you again?"

"On the boardwalk. Carini's Confections."

"Oh, the candy store." Must be one of the commercial coffeemakers or industrial refrigerators. Hopefully a quick fix. Not that he minded working on a Saturday, but if he planned to take in a movie with his niece, as promised, he'd have to be home by six.

"I'm booked up for the next hour or two," he explained as he looked at Mr. Petruzelli's oven, "but I'll be there when I can."

"Thanks so much." He could hear the relief in her voice. "And if you're able to get the job done, we tip in sugar."

"Oh, um, okay. I get it. Funny. See you around noon."

"Just ask for Taffie."

Ask for taffy?

Ryan wrapped up the job at the pizza parlor, and Mr. Petruzelli, who obviously tipped in food product as well, insisted that he and Pop settle in for a large thick-crust pepperoni pizza, heavy on the mozzarella.

"Great stuff, Mr. P.," Ryan spoke through mouthfuls of food. "Best pizza I've had in years."

"It's that oven. Turns out a perfect pizza every time!" Mr. Petruzelli said with a beaming smile.

"They've had me on a special diet," Ryan's pop explained to the pizza owner. "So don't tell my wife I'm eating this, okay?"

"I promise." Mr. Petruzelli gave him a wink, then began tending to his influx of customers.

After dropping off Pop at the house, Ryan headed over to the south end of the boardwalk. He parked near one of the larger casinos and made his way around to the back—to the boardwalk, teeming with tourists, folks dressed in swimsuits, and children running amuck. Nothing much had changed over the years. Sure, he used to be one of those kids, racing up and down the wooden sidewalk in search of adventure. Today, he'd come for another reason altogether.

A few paces down, he located Carini's Confections. Ryan's excitement grew as he looked through the front window at the small taffy pull, loaded with a sticky pink mixture. Back and forth it twisted. He found himself transported back in time, to his childhood. How many times had he stood here in a wet bathing suit, begging his parents for money so that he could go inside?

This time he would enter the building for a different reason, and they would put money in his pockets. Not a bad deal. And maybe he'd still buy a half pound of vanilla taffy before leaving. It had always been his favorite.

Ryan glanced up at the sign above the door and smiled as he read the words. How Sweet Are Your Words to My Taste, Sweeter Than Honey to My Mouth! Perfect marketing strategy, and a pretty amazing way to share a spiritual message. He entered the store behind a mob of children and parents. The tantalizing aromas almost caused him to forget why he'd come.

Better stay focused. I've got a machine to fix. But what machine? He looked at the coffee bar. Everything appeared to be in working order. He glanced behind

the ice cream counter. Every piece of machinery was in use. No problem there.
Strange.

That woman on the phone. . .the one with the mesmerizing voice. . .what was it she told me to ask for when I arrived? Ah yes, taffy.

He joined the line of customers jockeying for position to get to the candy counter.

Ryan took in the sights and sounds while waiting. Overhead, a familiar melody played. Sounded like something he'd heard as a kid. What was that, again? After a bit of humming, he recognized "Sugar, Sugar." Clever.

As he inched his way up in the line, the scents nearly overwhelmed him. The shop smelled sweet. And talk about a visual overload! Somewhere between the candies, coffee, and ice creams, Ryan found himself toying with the idea of consuming a little of each. Or maybe a lot of each. Who needed a marketing strategy when the product spoke for itself?

He reached the counter in short order and looked over at something—or rather, *someone*—far more appealing than candy. In fact, he could scarcely get a word out, though not for lack of effort. He ended up stammering like a grade-school kid. "Hi. Um, I—I—was told to ask for taffy."

"What flavor, sir?" Her brow wrinkled and her beautiful brown eyes seemed to gaze into his very soul.

"Oh, they didn't tell me."

"They?" Now she looked genuinely confused.

"Someone called from your shop. I'm Ryan from Antonelli's Appliance Repair. I was told to ask for taffy."

"Oh!" Her face lit into a smile broad enough to light up the casino next door. "I'm Taffie! Taffie Carini."

She pointed at her name tag, and he felt his tongue stick to the roof of his mouth as he tried to give a sensible response. "I—I see."

The irony struck him at once. Taffy had always been a temptation. No doubt about that. But today, as he stared into the chocolate-brown eyes of one Taffie Carini, the idea of the old-fashioned version suddenly lost all its appeal. No, the only thing he wanted to wrap up and take home today. . .was the beautiful girl behind the counter.

Chapter 3

Taffie wondered why her ability to think clearly disappeared the moment Ryan Antonelli spoke his first hello. She'd never been struck deaf, dumb, and blind like this before—unless you counted that time in her third grade play when, fully dressed as a double-dipped strawberry ice cream cone, she'd frozen on stage in front of hundreds of her peers. She still laughed at the irony. This time around, however, she couldn't blame it on stage fright. No, she could only blame it on one thing. One shockingly handsome appliance repairman with the richest brown eyes she'd ever seen.

Coming to her senses, Taffie called for her mom to take over at the candy counter for a few minutes so that she could escort Ryan into the back room to examine the broken taffy machine. As her mother approached, Taffie tried not to stare at his thick dark hair. A girl could get a little envious of a guy with hair that great. And long eyelashes, to boot.

"Mom, this is. . ." Taffie blanked out, unable to remember his first name.

"Ryan," he interjected, extending his hand in her mother's direction.

At once, Taffie could read the expression in her mama's eyes: *We've got a keeper here, Taffie!*

Thankfully, Ryan turned back to Taffie and spoke again before her mom could say something aloud. "I couldn't quite make out your words on the phone," he explained, "so I'm not sure what I'm here to repair." Somehow, staring into his gorgeous brown eyes, Taffie couldn't remember either. Instead of responding like an educated businesswoman, she stammered a choppy, "O–oh?"

"So, I'm here to service a piece of equipment?"

Startling to attention, she tried to still her overanxious heart and offered a smile. "Yes."

They made their way through the crowd and entered the back room where the family's largest taffy pull usually filled the place with a melodic churning sound. Instead, the room stood silent. Pop looked up with relief in his eyes as Taffie and Ryan entered.

He approached, extending his hand. "Carl Carini."

"Ryan Antonelli."

Taffie watched the exchange, noticing the interesting similarities in the two men. Both had the same upper-East-Coast-meets-Italian-American dialect and dark hair, though Pop's had lately begun to gray. Both had a strong grip. And, as they dove into a lengthy discussion about their respective businesses, she noted that both talked with great zeal about putting their customers first.

At the first lull in the conversation, Ryan looked around, curiosity etched in his brow. "So, what am I here to fix?" he asked. Taffie's father led him to the taffy pull and his eyes widened. "Th–this?"

"Yeah," Taffie drew near, picking up on the scent of his cologne. "The arm is jammed. I've always managed to get it working again, but this time I think we're looking at a bigger problem."

"Bigger than you know," he said.

"What do you mean?" She gave him a curious look.

"I mean, I've never worked on one of these before. I wouldn't have a clue where to begin." He examined the machine more closely. "And we're not talking about something made this century. This thing's got to be. . ." He walked around it, taking it in. "Fifty years old."

"Seventy," her pop interjected, "but the age shouldn't matter. It's just a piece of machinery, like any other. Made out of the best possible materials, so it should last another seventy years, at least."

"At least," Taffie echoed.

"Well, it's not like any other machine I've ever seen or worked on." Ryan looked up, the sparkle in his eyes diminishing.

Taffie felt the energy slip right out of her, and she sat on one of the nearby wooden barrels. "Not exactly what I needed to hear today."

"Is there someone you can call?" Pop asked. "Surely you know lots of people in the appliance business. Maybe one of them. . ."

"Maybe." Ryan raked his fingers through his dark hair.

"We need to pray," Pop said. "The Bible says, 'You do not have, because you do not ask God.' Well, Lord, we're asking. . . ." He dove into an intense dialogue with the Almighty, right then and there, not pausing to warn anyone.

Taffie had grown up watching Pop chat with God in this fashion, but wasn't sure what their new appliance guy would think of it. To his credit, Ryan bowed his head and appeared to join in.

Pop, never one to pray with his eyes closed, paced the room, the tenor of his voice rising dramatically. "Lord, we ask for wisdom from on high. We don't know what to do, but we know that You do. You are the Creator of all things, so surely You know how to fix a taffy machine. Your Word says that our faith can move mountains. This taffy machine is our mountain, Lord, and we'd be grateful if You'd see fit to move it. Up and down and all around. Send us the person to accomplish that—we ask in Your Son's name."

Without so much as an *amen*, he ended his prayer and took a seat on a nearby barrel. Taffie watched as Ryan did the same. The men sat in silence for a few minutes, while Taffie bit her tongue. She wanted to speak but knew better.

Finally Ryan cleared his throat. "So, um. . .what next?"

Taffie released a sigh. How could she explain her father's somewhat fascinating views on faith to a total stranger? Carl Carini was of the opinion that if you asked the Lord a question, He was bound to answer. . .sooner or later.

Problem was, they never knew if it would be sooner or later, and Pop appeared to have a lot more patience than most. She'd seen him wait it out for hours before moving.

Ryan stood and began to pace the room. "Tell you what," he said at last. "I could call my older brother Luke. He's had some experience as a mechanic. I think that's what you're going to need—someone who can actually engineer the part."

"Yes, and amen!" Pop rose to his feet and clapped his hands together. "I knew the Lord would answer our prayer."

"Well, I make no promises. . . ." Ryan looked a bit flustered, but Taffie noticed the color returning to his cheeks. "But I'll see what Luke has to say. Just give me a few minutes to make the call."

"Son, take all the time you like." Taffie's father gave him a friendly pat on the back. "I'll fix you a coffee. What kind do you like?"

"Espresso would be great," Ryan said.

"And what about some candy to go with that?" Taffie asked. "Our taffy is the best in town." She led the way to the candy counter, gesturing for him to join her behind the glass case.

"Oh, trust me, I know." He flashed a grin and her heart melted. "I've been coming to Carini's since I was a kid. I've probably consumed a dozen pounds of vanilla over the years."

"Just vanilla?" She reached for the scoop.

"Well, um. . ."

"What?" She gave him a pensive look.

"I'm a creature of habit. What can I say?"

"So, vanilla all the way?"

"Pretty much."

"Wow." Taffie leaned her elbows on the counter and looked him in the eye. "So, you're telling me there's not one other thing in this place that appeals to you more than vanilla?" She gestured to the rows of candy, pausing as she noted the playful glimmer that came into his eyes. "What?"

"Oh, nothing." His gaze shifted and he quickly added, "I, um, I'm. . .stuck in my ways, I guess."

"It's just hard for me to believe you're not willing to branch out. Try something new." Taffie quirked a brow and before long, a smile lit his face.

"Tell you what. . ." He looked inside the taffy jars. "I'm taking my brother's seven-year-old daughter to the movies tonight, and she loves taffy in every flavor. Give me a little bit of everything." As the words "a little bit of everything" slipped from his lips, he glanced up at her with a smile, and for a second. . .a mere second. . .she nearly misunderstood his words.

Feeling the heat rising to her cheeks, she reached for a metal scoop and went to work filling the bag.

Ryan watched Taffie fill the plastic bag with candies. Her question, "So, you're telling me there's not one other thing in this place that appeals to you more than vanilla?" had almost caused him to fold like a deck of cards. He'd wanted to respond, "Yes, and she's standing right in front of me," but he'd somehow managed to bite his tongue.

Snap out of it, man.

He wasn't usually the sort to fall for a complete stranger. In fact, he wasn't the sort to fall easily, at all. Women—the ones he'd dated, anyway—had turned out to be more complicated than the machinery he repaired.

Taffie handed him the bag of candy and he took it with a grateful, "Thanks."

"Hope your niece likes it." Taffie reached up with the back of her hand to sweep a loose strand of hair behind her ear.

"I'm sure she will."

"I think it's nice that you're taking her to the movies. You must be quite a bit younger than your brother if he's got a seven-year-old."

"Yeah. I'm the youngest of three boys. Vic's the oldest. Then Luke. Then me. Vic runs his own Web design business, and Luke. . .well, he usually works with Pop and me."

"That's funny. I'm the oldest of three girls. My sister Candy is twenty-two. She's in flight school in Tucson. And Tangie's only nineteen. She's studying theater in New York."

"Wow." He gave her another look as he reached for a piece of vanilla taffy. "Tangie. Interesting name."

"Well, we have rather interesting parents, in case you haven't already noticed. And you probably picked up on the fact that they're older than most parents of twenty-somethings. They weren't able to have children for a long time. Mom was in her early forties when I was born."

"Ah." That answered one question.

"And as for our names. . .I guess when you've waited as long as they did for children, you can name them whatever you like. Tangie is short for tangerine, which happened to be the flavor of the month when my sister was born."

"I'll bet she takes a lot of grief over that." He paused to think about just how embarrassing it might be. Still, the quirky parents part he understood. . . firsthand.

"Um, yeah." Taffie gave him a winning smile.

Better come up with something clever to say. "Vic is the only one in our bunch who's married. So far, anyway. But, um. . ." How much should he divulge? After all, this girl didn't even know his brother. Didn't know that Vic and his wife had just separated. "Anyway, his marriage isn't the strongest," Ryan explained. "And Casey—their daughter—is caught in the middle."

Taffie's brow wrinkled as she responded. "That's sad. I've been blessed with parents who have the best marriage in the world."

He laughed. "I thought I held that claim to fame."

"Nope. It's mine." Again with the coy smile. The girl didn't realize what she was doing to his heart.

After a moment's pause, he remembered the reason for being here in the first place. "I'll call Luke now. Hopefully he can advise me on the repair." Ryan stepped outside the shop to get better reception and placed the call to his brother, quickly explaining the problem.

"A taffy machine?" Luke asked. "I don't have a clue how—"

"No, that's not the right answer," Ryan interjected. "I don't ask a lot from you, Luke, but this time I really need your help. We've got to figure out how to get this done. I don't care how. I don't care how much. But we've got to figure it out—and soon."

"What's her name?"

"W–who?"

"The girl. What's her name?"

"T–Taffie."

An awkward silence followed, then, "You've fallen in love with taffy?"

Ryan held back the laugh that threatened to erupt as he responded to his brother's question. "I guess you could say I have developed a sudden interest in the art of candy making. Let's just leave it at that. But get over here as quick as you can, okay?"

"Sure. Whatever."

As he ended the call, Ryan stepped back into the shop and then shifted his gaze to Taffie, who now waited on a customer. She glanced his way with a warm smile, one that very nearly melted his heart.

Ryan did his best not to let the corners of his lips give him away as they shared a glance. For whatever reason—nerves, maybe—he reached into the plastic bag, coming up with a bright pink piece of taffy. Ready to throw caution to the wind, he unwrapped it. . .and popped it in his mouth.

Chapter 4

Taffie kept a watchful eye on Ryan over the next twenty minutes or so, as he waited for his brother to arrive. She tried to tend to her customers with the usual zeal, but with someone as handsome as Ryan pacing back and forth, she found it a bit difficult. She accidentally measured out a pound of cherry taffy for a woman who asked for strawberry, and she overcharged another customer for a quarter pound of licorice. But who could blame her? Ryan Antonelli proved to be a formidable, but happy, distraction.

Her parents apparently found him likable, as well. They'd pretty much swept him into the fold. . .in a number of ways. Since his arrival, he'd heard her father's tale of how the Carini family had come to New Jersey from Italy in the thirties. Her mother then took to playing hostess, offering Ryan a hot fudge sundae followed by a caramel mocha frappuccino. All of this following the initial espresso and taffy, of course. If this repair took too long, he'd put on twenty pounds. Or send his blood sugar levels soaring.

Hmm. Taffie looked down at her midsection and sighed. She'd put on a few pounds over the past year, working with sweets, hadn't she? Oh well. Such were the woes of life in a candy shop. There would be plenty of time to focus on that later. Right now she needed to zero in on the broken taffy machine. If they didn't get it up and running, production would go down. If production went down. . .

She shivered thinking about it. Her parents wanted to travel in their RV, to leave the shop in her capable hands. If production stopped, everything else would eventually come to a grinding halt as well. She couldn't let that happen. And, with Ryan's help, she wouldn't.

Taffie looked past the throng of customers as she heard a voice ring out. "Hey, little brother. What's cookin'?"

She watched with interest as Ryan rose from his seat and moved in the direction of a fellow a couple of years older than himself. One with a swagger in his step and a crooked smile on his face. In many ways, the two men resembled each other, though she had to admit Ryan took the prize for good looks.

Seconds later her father greeted Luke with the usual Carini gusto. The three men stood in the middle of the busy shop, talking at length.

When the crowd thinned, Taffie made her way out from behind the counter to introduce herself. She wondered at the laughter in Luke's eyes as she spoke her name, and couldn't figure out why Ryan jabbed him in the arm.

What's up with that?

Unfortunately, she never had time to search for an answer. An incoming rush of customers sent her behind the counter once again.

The men ventured off into the back room to tend to the taffy machine. As the men walked away, she whispered a prayer that all would go well. Then, determined to stay focused, she waited on the next customer in line.

&

As Ryan followed Mr. Carini into the back room, he did his best to ignore Luke, who insisted on making verbal jabs.

"I get it, little brother. I get it. *Taffie.*"

Ryan turned and glared at his brother, then mouthed, "Cut it out."

There would be plenty of time to explain later. Not that he could explain it, really. Ryan's sudden fascination with a total stranger was nonsensical, at best. And Luke, of all people, knew him to be extra careful when it came to relationships. These days, anyway.

Mr. Carini led the way to the taffy machine. Luke took one look at it and let out a whistle. "Wow, she's a beauty."

"Even more impressive when she's working properly." Mr. Carini pointed to the stream of customers on the other side of the large window at the back end of the store. "Almost any day of the week you can see kids standing out there, just watching the different colors of taffy as they're being pulled."

"I was one of those kids," Luke said. A smile crept across his face as he added, "Carini's was one of our favorite places to hang out." He gestured to Ryan. "We were in here nearly every week. You've probably wiped our fingerprints off of that glass dozens of times."

"Or more." Ryan couldn't help the smile that rose up as he remembered. In his mind's eye, he could see himself as a boy, standing with his face pressed to the glass, his older brothers next to him. Watching the machine pulling this way and that, stretching the colorful candy, had fascinated him.

If he closed his eyes, he could almost see it working now.

Almost.

"Well, let's see what we can do." Luke ran his hands across the cranking mechanism, then leaned in for a closer look.

For the next hour or so, with Mr. Carini leaning over their shoulders, Ryan and Luke worked on the stubborn taffy machine. They finally managed to get it freed up—and quite a shout went up from the people on the other side of the glass the moment it happened—but even with that, things did not look good.

"You've got to replace the joint mechanism that links the arm to the base," Luke said, wiping his brow with his sleeve. "Otherwise the problem is just going to repeat itself. I don't know how it's lasted this long."

"Kind of like my arthritis, eh?" Mr. Carini flashed a smile. "Things get locked up over time."

Luke laughed as he responded. "I guess you could say that."

"Only you can't order new parts when your hips and knees go out," Ryan added.

"Sure you can," Mr. Carini threw in. "My dad had a hip replacement when he was in his seventies."

"Wait." Ryan looked up, as a particular memory flooded over him. "Was he the older man who used to run the store? The one with the white hair and the thick moustache?"

"Yep. Gus Carini. Do you remember him?"

"Of course. He gave me more free candy than any kid should be allowed by law."

"Yeah, that was my pop." Mr. Carini's face lit up for a moment. Then a more serious expression took its place as he turned to look at the machine once again. "He always knew just what to do. Whenever a problem came up, he found the solution."

"Sounds a lot like you," Ryan said.

"Like Taffie, too." Mr. Carini shifted his gaze to watch his daughter at work. "She's a fixer. Always has been."

"I think there's a little of that in all of us," Luke said. "And when you're in the repair business, that's not a bad thing."

Mr. Carini nodded. "I suppose. Though only the Lord can do the ultimate fixing, so we have to rely on Him."

Ryan threw in a quiet, "Amen."

"So, where do we get the part to get this thing up and running smoothly?" Mr. Carini asked. "And do you have any idea how long it will take?"

"If I could track down another model like this one for a reasonable price, would you be interested in buying it for parts?" Ryan asked. "That way you wouldn't have to go searching next time."

"I suppose that depends on the cost," Mr. Carini responded.

"It's that, or I try to build the part myself," Luke said. "Either way, it's going to be a process."

Mr. Carini raked his fingers through his thinning hair. "I see."

"Do you have a pen and a piece of paper?" Ryan asked. "I'll write down the manufacturer's name and the serial number."

"Sure thing. I'll be right back."

As Mr. Carini made his way through the crowd of people, Ryan did his best to sneak a peek at Taffie, who continued to work behind the candy counter.

"You've got it bad, haven't you?" Luke gave him a friendly pat on the back.

"Just met her a couple of hours ago," Ryan explained. "Not sure what's happening, to be honest."

"Well, I understand the attraction. She's a knockout." Luke gave a quiet whistle.

"There's more to her than that." Ryan continued to watch her, mesmerized.

"Look at how she connects with the customers. She was born for this."

"She's got a lot of energy. Probably from all that sugar." Luke laughed. "Remember how Mom used to have to reel us in after we'd swallowed down a bag of candy?"

"Yep." Ryan smiled as the memory flooded over him. "But what kid doesn't like candy?"

He peered through the glass once more at the beautiful woman on the other side. Something about watching her work brought joy to his heart. She dipped a metal scoop into the large glass taffy jar, then—for whatever reason—looked his way. As their eyes met, a hint of a smile graced her lips.

Then, as her cheeks flashed pink, she turned back to her work.

Chapter 5

Taffie arrived home from work a few minutes before six. Her cell phone rang as she pulled her car into the driveway. When she saw Tangie's number, she couldn't help but smile. She answered right away. "Hey, girl! You must be awfully lonely to be calling your big sister on a Saturday night."

"More lonely than you know." Tangie's familiar giggle seemed to bounce across the phone line. "I'm about twenty miles from home. Just pulled off the road to gas up and decided this would be a good time to call. I needed some family time this weekend."

"Are you serious? What about that off-off-Broadway show you were in? I thought you had two performances every Saturday."

"Yes, well, um. . ." Tangie's voice trailed off. "Let's just say it vaporized. So, I'm now free on the weekends."

"Till the next show comes along." Taffie smiled as she thought about her little sister's penchant for the theater. Tangie—who tended to march to her own drumbeat—had always been at home on the stage. She bounced from one show to the other, one part to the next.

"I guess." Tangie sighed in an over-the-top fashion. Nothing unusual about the high drama in her response. "But right now I don't want to think about theater. Or my classes, which start up again next week. I just want to come home and hang out with you."

"No problem there. You know I'm always free. Well, except for my business class, but it ends in a couple weeks."

"Meet any handsome guys in your class?"

"Nope."

"You're not dating anyone?" Tangie probed.

Taffie groaned before responding. "Um, no. When would I have time?"

"Hey, you've got to make the time, big sister," Tangie said. "I manage."

"You fall in love as often as most people change their clothes."

"Hey now. . . ."

"C'mon. Has there ever been a leading man in one of your shows that you didn't fall for?"

Tangie's boisterous laugh bounced across the phone line. "No, you're right. I've got a consistent record. But I somehow doubt the Lord is going to pair me up with any of the guys I've met in New York, at least the ones I've met so far. God's got a sense of humor, so I somehow suspect He'll bring me an engineer or a scientist or someone like that."

"You think?"

"I sometimes wonder if I could live with someone who's a polar opposite." Tangie giggled. "But regardless, God will bring the perfect person. . .for me. . . and for you."

"And for Candy, too," Taffie added. After a moment's pause, she said, "But you don't even need to be thinking about all of this yet. You're only nineteen."

"Twenty in a couple of months," Tangie reminded her.

As if that made any difference.

"Okay, okay." Taffie decided a change of subject was in order. "So, what do you want to do this evening? Go to dinner or just hang out at the house in our pj's and talk about all the guys I'm not dating?" Funny, but as she said the words, Ryan's face flashed before her.

"Let's go see a movie. Have you seen the previews for that new romance?" Tangie asked. "The fairy-tale one? It looks so cute."

"Ugh. Do we have to see a romance?" Taffie asked. "What about something action packed? There's a great new movie about—"

"C'mon, Taffie. I hardly ever get to spend an evening with you. Let me pick the movie, and you can pick the restaurant. Okay?"

Taffie pressed back the smile and quickly chimed in with her agreement. They ended the call, and she made her way inside the house, ready to shower and change into a comfortable pair of jeans and a T-shirt.

Tangie arrived in short order and managed to convince their parents to join them at the movies. "It'll be a blast," she said. "And we'll do dinner out afterwards. Mom deserves a break from the kitchen."

"I could use a night off, especially after the day we've had at the store," her mother interjected.

"No joke." Taffie quickly filled her sister in, telling her about the broken machine. "Thank goodness we found someone who's able to help us," she explained. "Otherwise, I don't think any of us would feel like going out tonight."

Tangie grabbed her hand and gave it a squeeze. "God always provides." She gave Taffie a wink. "Now, if I could just talk Him into bringing you a husband, I'd feel a lot better about leaving you alone at the shop while I pursue my dreams."

"There are a thousand things I'd rather have you pray for," Taffie assured her. "So, put the husband prayer on the back burner for now, okay?"

"For now." Tangie quirked a brow. Thankfully she let the subject drop as they climbed into the car to leave.

Taffie did her best to steer the conversation in a different direction as they traveled toward the theater. All the while, images of Ryan Antonelli kept reappearing. She couldn't get his beautiful eyes or his warm smile out of her mind. At once she scolded herself. *Stop it. I'm not living out one of my sister's goofy romance movies. I live in the real world.*

Unfortunately, it appeared to be a world without romance. . .at least so far.

When they arrived at the theater, Tangie led the way through the mob of people inside to look for seats. Her buoyant zeal as she pushed through the crowd reminded Taffie of the kids in the candy shop. *I wish I could be more like that. . .more carefree.*

She looked around the packed theater, stunned to find it full to the brim with popcorn-eating, soda-drinking children, teens, and women. "Don't tell me we're going to have to sit in the front row."

"Aw, come on." Tangie looped her arm through Taffie's, her face awash with joy and childish pleasure. "It's not so bad. We can pretend we're kids again. Remember when we used to sit in the front row just for fun? The theater would be half-empty and we'd still do it. . .just because."

"I remember when you used to talk me into it. And it was never much fun. I always ended up with a stiff neck and a headache by the end of the show."

"Don't be such a killjoy. C'mon." Tangie led the way down to the front.

As they reached the lowest level of the theater, Pop looked back up at the crowd, then shook his head. "Am I the only man in this place? Maybe I should go see something else while you ladies—"

"Don't be silly." Tangie scanned the other theater-goers, then pointed. "Look. There's a guy right there—with that little girl."

Taffie's heart leaped into her throat as she looked across the front row, directly into the eyes of Ryan Antonelli.

He smiled as he rose to his feet to greet them. "Hey, are you following me?"

Taffie felt her cheeks warm at the very idea. *I hope he doesn't really think that.* "I, um. . .it's just a coincidence. I promise."

She couldn't help but wonder at the look of disappointment in his eyes.

"After all," she was quick to add, "you didn't even tell me what movie you were seeing."

"True."

Off to the side, Tangie elbowed her in the ribs and whispered in her ear, "You know him?"

She quickly made introductions. "Ryan Antonelli, this is my sister, Tangie." A smile lit his face as he said, "Tangerine!"

Tangie groaned, then muttered, "Nice to meet you," before taking her seat.

Her mother greeted Ryan with an affectionate hug, as if they'd known each other for years, then began to rant and rave over the little girl with dark curls who now stood next to him.

Ryan snapped to attention and introduced his niece. "This is Casey, everyone. She, um, she picked the movie. I'm just here because I, um, I. . ."

"Right, right." Taffie tried not to laugh at the look of embarrassment on his face.

Casey giggled, then shared her thoughts on the matter with a boisterous,

"You're gonna love it!"

"I doubt that," Ryan said with a shrug, "but it'll be worth it, one way or the other, as long as I get to spend time with her." A look of sheer joy came over his face as he pulled Casey into a warm embrace. Taffie looked on with a sense of warmth flooding her soul.

Her mom leaned in and whispered, "He's a keeper," in her ear.

Taffie's cheeks warmed, and she turned to give her mother her best cut-it-out look.

The previews began and everyone took their seats. Everyone except Taffie. She looked around in horror, realizing the only empty seat was the one right next to Ryan. She groaned internally. *Oh man. I sure hope he doesn't think I set this whole thing up.*

With a forced smile she took her seat, determined to enjoy the show.

❧

Ryan couldn't have planned this evening any better. As Taffie settled into the seat next to his, he did his best to focus on the screen. But how could he?

"Uncle Ryan?" Casey whispered loud enough for others to hear.

"What, honey?"

"I like her."

"Like who?"

"The one with the candy name. Is that why you brought me the taffy? 'Cause of her?"

Ryan smiled, then put his finger to his lips. "The movie's starting."

He settled back in his seat, half-embarrassed for having been caught at a chick flick and half-excited to have landed in the seat next to the woman who had consumed his thoughts most of the day. Had the Lord arranged this, perhaps?

The movie—a musical comedy—moved forward with ease. Despite his efforts to the contrary, Ryan found himself laughing on several occasions, and smiling as the hero and heroine came together in the end. Not that life was really like that. No, you couldn't believe what you read in books or saw in the movies. Real life was much more complicated. And even though the fair maiden in the seat next to him appeared to be a true heroine in every sense of the word, he was certainly not swashbuckling-hero material.

As the movie wrapped up, a love song played overhead. He glanced out of the corner of his eye at Taffie. Something about her made him want to slay giants. If he could just get that machine fixed, that would be a great start. Maybe then he would. . . Nah. He would never be like that guy in the movie. Not if he tried for the rest of his life.

Casey sprang from her seat, eyes filled with wonder. "Thank you so much, Uncle Ryan! That movie was awesome!"

"I have to agree." Taffie rose to her feet with a childlike grin. "I'm not usually into the fluffy stuff, but that one really made me smile."

"So, what did you think, Mr. Carini?" Ryan looked at the older gentleman, curious to see his response.

"It was okay." He shrugged. "I just don't understand all that singing and dancing. Seems so. . .improbable. One minute people are walking down the street, acting completely normal, the next they're bursting into song and dancing all over the place. Life isn't really like that."

As if to prove him wrong, Tangie started singing along with the love song that continued to play overhead as the credits rolled on the screen. She extended her arm in an invitation for her father to dance, and his somewhat sour expression changed right away.

"Well, when you put it like that. . ." He took his daughter in his arms and started turning her in circles.

"Me, too!" Casey squealed.

If you can't beat 'em. . . Ryan bowed, and Casey responded with a curtsy. He took her in his arms and began to spin her round and round. Pretty soon, movie-goers turned to watch, and before you knew it, several others in the theater were responding with applause.

"Okay, that's enough of that." Ryan felt his face grow hot.

He released his hold on Casey, and she reached for her midsection, moaning in dramatic fashion. "I'm *starved*, Uncle Ryan. Where are we meeting everyone for dinner?"

"Yes, what's for dinner?" Mr. Carini asked, bringing his dance to a halt. "I'm with Casey. I'm starved, too."

"Dad, we can't just interrupt their plans." Taffie shot her father a look, but Ryan did his best to smooth things over.

"Sure you can. I'm meeting up with my parents and my sister-in-law at that new place just around the corner—Three B's Burgers. They claim to have the biggest burgers in the state, and I'd like to find out firsthand."

"A burger would hit the spot," Mr. Carini said with a nod. "We'll meet you there."

"But. . ."

Taffie gave Ryan an apologetic look, but he attempted to put her mind at ease once more. "I'm glad you're coming. And I'm sure our families will enjoy getting to know each other." He leaned in close to whisper, "Besides, we're more alike than you know."

"Oh?" Her brow wrinkled.

"You're about to find out for yourself."

Casey reached for his hand, and Ryan led the way out of the theater and toward the parking lot. Somehow, that little song and dance number with his niece had done something to his heart. Set him free in some way. He felt like bursting into song right now, in fact.

Maybe when the crowd thinned. . .he'd do just that.

Chapter 6

As she slipped into the backseat of her parents' car with her sister at her side, Taffie's thoughts tumbled a thousand different directions. First the movies. Now dinner. Would Ryan think they were following him? She didn't have time to contemplate the question for long before being met with a barrage of questions from her overly anxious youngest sister. Tangie leaned in close and, like a detective on the hunt, started the first round of questioning.

"So, what's all this about you not dating? That guy is amazing."

"I'm not. Seriously. I just met him today." *But you're right. He is amazing.*

"Obviously you two have eyes for each other."

"We do?"

"Taffie. . ." A scolding sound came into her sister's voice. "I study acting. I know when you're pretending. You can't fool me."

"I–I'm not trying to fool anyone. I just don't know what you're talking about."

"Sure you don't." Tangie leaned back against the seat and gave her a know-it-all smile.

Taffie rested her head against the window and stared outside as her father pulled the car out of the theater parking lot. She pondered her sister's words. Despite her admissions to the contrary, something about Ryan did tug at her heart. But why? And how, after only knowing him one day, could she feel anything for him? Sure, things like that happened in movies—like the one they just saw, for instance—but love at first sight in the real world? Simply didn't occur. At least not in her world.

Not that she minded the idea. No, a real romance would be great, especially after so many years of waiting. For whatever reason, she just wondered if she'd ever be the princess in the story. More often than not, she took on the role of the overlooked, moderately-nice-looking-but-not-exactly-pretty sister.

Thankfully, she didn't have time to give this idea more thought because their father pulled the car into the crowded parking lot of Three B's and hollered, "We're here, Carini family! Burgers, fries, and shakes—it's on me tonight, ladies." He reached over and gave Mom a kiss on the cheek, and she grinned in response.

"We can't stay too late," Taffie said. "I've got to be early to church in the morning to get things set up for kid's church. And I've still got to get my lesson

31

ready when I get home tonight."

"We'll get you home before the car turns back into a pumpkin, I promise." Her father looked back at her with a wink.

Good grief. Did that movie actually get to Pop, too?

Once inside, Ryan met them with Casey at his side. "My parents were just around the corner at the appliance store. They should be here any moment."

True to his word, the couple—about the same age as Taffie's parents—entered the restaurant, faces alight with joy. They took one look at Casey and swept her into their arms, speaking blessings over her as if she'd just achieved sainthood. What would it be like, Taffie wondered, to have a child to pamper? To whisper words of love in her ear and to feel her soft words echoed back in your own? She didn't have time to give it much thought. Mrs. Antonelli greeted her mother with a warm hug, as if they were long-lost friends, then gave Taffie a hug, as well.

Minutes later, as the two families gathered around an extra-large table, voices layered on top of each other, much like the children's in the candy store. Taffie observed it all with a smile. She liked Mrs. Antonelli right away, and apparently so did her mother. The two women were like twins separated at birth. They chattered a hundred miles a minute.

And the two fathers. . .well, the resemblance was almost uncanny. They both sported thinning hair, sparkling eyes, and vivacious voices. Like the women, they couldn't seem to talk fast enough. Turned out the families—several generations back—were from nearby Italian villages. Go figure. And both families had undergone spiritual transformation in the seventies. Just one more thing they had in common.

Ryan caught her eye from across the table. "You enjoying this?"

"It's. . .crazy. Who would've known? Next thing you know, they'll be telling us we're distant cousins."

"Hope not." He gave her a wink and her heart skipped a beat. For once speechless, she shifted her gaze to the menu.

Not that she needed to worry about keeping the conversation going. Casey, it turned out, provided constant chatter and unending entertainment for everyone at the table. The youngster hollered across the crowd, "Grandma, you missed the bestest movie in the world! You would've *loved* it."

"Would I?" Ryan's mom looked up from her conversation with Taffie's mother, clearly unaffected by her granddaughter's table manners. "What was it about?"

"It was about a prince and a princess and they were in love." Casey clasped her hands together at her chest and pretended to swoon. "They danced and they sang and it was so romantical!"

"Sounds like my kind of show," her grandmother said. "Right up my alley. I love those happily-ever-after movies. They touch me. . .right here." She put her hand to her chest and smiled, then turned to her husband and gave him a kiss on the cheek. "Of course, I've already got my prince, and he's mighty charming. Your grandpa won my heart thirty-six years ago, and he still has it."

Mr. Antonelli leaned over and planted a kiss on his wife's lips—right there, in front of everyone. Taffie glanced at Ryan and noted his cheeks as they turned crimson. He stared at the menu, but the edges of his lips curled up in a smile.

"I think that's so sweet." Tangie sighed. "I want a marriage like that."

"All you have to do is find your prince," Casey's eyes took on a dreamy look. "And he will sing to you—and tell you that you're the most beautiful woman in the world—and then you will get married."

"Oh, that's all there is to it, huh?" Tangie gave her a knowing smile.

"Of course!"

As Casey began to sing one of the songs from the movie, Taffie turned to her younger sister and laughed. "She reminds me of you when you were her age. No doubt she'll end up on the stage, acting and singing."

"Hey, there's nothing wrong with that!" Tangie shrugged in her usual playful way.

"Only, I don't want to act on Broadway." Casey wrinkled her nose. "I want to be in the movies, like that girl we saw in the movie tonight. She's my age and she's already famous."

"You're going to be famous, eh?" Tangie grinned, then whispered, "Been there, done that," in Taffie's ear.

Casey nodded. "Oh yes! Did you see her clothes? And her hair! She probably lives in a big house in Hollywood and doesn't have to go to school." A dramatic sigh erupted and everyone laughed in response.

"There's a lot more to life than being famous, kid," Ryan said. "Like homework, for example. Which reminds me. . .doesn't school start next week?"

"Yes." Casey groaned. "But *please* don't ask me about math again, Uncle Ryan. Not tonight. I'm having too much fun."

Taffie gave her a sympathetic gaze. Now *this* she could relate to. "You struggle with math?"

"Yes." Casey dropped her forehead down into extended palms and let out an award-worthy groan. "I'm terrible with multiplication."

"Just wait till she gets to fractions!" Tangie laughed. "They were always my downfall."

"I hate fractions!" Casey shook her head back and forth, her brown curls bobbing every which way.

Out of the corner of her eye, Taffie watched as a lovely woman—probably in her early thirties—neared the table. Everything about her spoke of beauty and glamour. Her perfectly styled hair. Her polished nails. Her impeccable makeup job.

"Wow." Tangie leaned over and whispered in her ear. "Who is that?"

As if in response to her question, Casey rose to her feet and yelled, "Mommy!

You're here. Am I staying with you tonight, or with Daddy?"

The woman's face suddenly contorted as her daughter's words rang out for all to hear. She put a finger to her lips, then whispered, "Use your inside voice, Casey. We're not announcing our. . .situation. . .to the masses. Not yet anyway."

As the woman took her seat, Ryan made introductions. "Ladies, this is Mallory, my sister-in-law. She's obviously Casey's mom."

"Is Daddy coming tonight?" Casey asked, looking back and forth between her mother and her uncle. "I can't wait to tell him about the movie. It was so great, Mom. A love story with lots of singing." Casey erupted in song once again, and for a moment Taffie thought Mallory might shush her, but the woman's lips eventually turned up in a smile. Funny, how a child could have that effect on a grown person—even one with a somewhat sour disposition.

"I talked to your father a few minutes ago, and he's on his way," Mallory explained, her face still tight. "He can't stay long because he's got some work to do on the computer tonight." Under her breath she added, "Like that's ever going to change."

Taffie observed, for the first time all night, how Casey's demeanor shifted. Sad, really, how a child could be so impacted by the adults in her life. Just as quickly, the youngster perked back up. Before long, she was cracking jokes and back to being the center of attention.

Still, Taffie couldn't help but think that Casey was covering up for the pain of her parents' separation. Out of the corner of her eye, Taffie caught a glimpse of Mallory. The woman, though perfectly made up on the outside, carried grief in her expression. How sad would it be, to marry someone, only to have that relationship disintegrate after just a few years? If only life could really be as simple as the movies. Then everyone—including innocent kids like Casey—would have a chance at their happily ever after.

❧

With a smile that went all the way down to his toes, Ryan observed the interaction between Taffie and the other members of his family. If the Lord hadn't led the Antonellis and the Carinis together, who had? Surely they were destined to meet. Funny, how a broken taffy machine had been the source of their meeting.

"So, you work on appliances?" Tangie posed the question to Ryan.

He drew in a sigh, then, just as quickly, looked up to make sure his father hadn't seen or heard his reaction. No point in upsetting anyone. Not tonight anyway. "I've worked for my dad for the past couple of years. But I studied marketing in school. I really want to. . ." He stopped himself, just short of speaking the truth. He really wanted a business of his own, something he could be passionate about. He wanted Luke to do the right thing—to step up to the plate so that Pop wouldn't have to work alone.

Thankfully, Tangie took the conversation and began to run with it, telling him about her most recent show in New York. He was happy for the diversion. Happier still that all her animated conversation gave him a chance to focus on the one thing he wanted to focus on. . .Taffie.

Out of the corner of his eye, he took in her beautiful face, her dark hair—which she wore differently tonight than at the store—and her whimsical smile. He'd seen that same look of happiness on her face as she'd waited on customers. And now, with her family gathered around, she was clearly in her element.

For that matter, so was he. Ryan couldn't remember a time when he'd ever felt so at home. His parents chatted with hers, lost in some conversation about RVs and traveling to see the wild, Wild West.

"So, your pop owns his own business." Taffie turned her attention to Ryan. "What about your mom? Does she work?"

"She used to work as a party planner," he explained. "You should've seen the theme parties she pulled off when we were kids."

"Sounds like fun."

"Sure was. But it's been years since she's done that. She's great at a lot of things. Her cooking is out of this world. But"—he increased his volume to make sure his mother took the bait—"if you want to see her come to life, ask her about her dog." Ryan leaned back in his seat and crossed his arms at his chest, waiting for the usual response from his pop.

"Oh?" Taffie looked across the table at his mother, whose eyes lit up at once. "You have a dog?"

"Dog, my eye." His father shook his head. "It's a fourth child."

"Only more expensive," Ryan threw in.

"Snickers is not that expensive," his mom argued. "Besides, she's worth every penny."

"Snickers?" Taffie repeated, her brow beginning to wrinkle.

"She's a schnoodle," Ryan explained. "Half schnauzer, half poodle."

His mom's expression brightened. "I just love to pamper her. She goes to the Doggy Spa occasionally to have her hair and nails done, and the vet bills are a little higher than most dogs because she has some rather, er, peculiar allergies."

"Peculiar is putting it lightly." Ryan laughed. "She's allergic to grass."

"Wow." Taffie laughed.

"And dust mites," he added. "And my father's deodorant."

"Hey, I switched brands," his father threw in. "Didn't want Snickers to suffer on my account."

"Heavens, no," Ryan said. "The dog will never suffer, not with all the attention she gets. They're even using a new fabric softener because Snickers was allergic to the sheets on their bed. Heaven forbid the dog would sleep on the floor. And Mom makes Snickers's dog food. Homemade. From scratch. That mongrel is definitely more like a child than a dog."

"Well, now. . ." His mother gave him a stern look. "My boys are all growing up and leaving me. I need someone, er, rather. . .some*thing* to occupy my time. It's hard to be an empty-nest mother." Her eyes filled with tears, and Ryan watched in amazement as Taffie's mother slipped out of her chair and went to the other side of the table to wrap her in a warm, I-hear-you-sister embrace.

For a moment, no one at the table breathed a word. When the women finally loosened their hold on each other, they apologized for the emotional outburst, dried their tears, and handed the conversation back to the others. Ryan didn't quite know what to make of it. He rarely saw this side of his mom.

"Wow." Taffie looked at him and smiled. "We all seem to bring out the best in each other, don't we?"

"No kidding," Ryan echoed. "It's weird, isn't it? Like we've all known each other for years."

"Like we were destined to meet." Taffie's eyes locked onto his as she gave voice to the words he'd been thinking and feeling all night long.

He would have said something in response, but suddenly found his tongue stuck to the roof of his mouth. This time, he couldn't blame it on the taffy.

Chapter 7

O n Monday afternoon, Ryan rushed to get to Carini's before they closed for the day. He got hung up in traffic and found himself arriving just as Mr. Carini locked the door.

"I'm too late." He groaned, holding up the part his brother had spent all day working on. "Sure you don't want to let me in?"

"Oh dear." Mrs. Carini looked down at her watch. "We have a Sunday School party to attend."

"What about Taffie? Is she—"

"Taffie's got a business class tonight. She won't be home till after nine." Mr. Carini sighed. "Would it be too much to ask you to come back tomorrow?"

"If you can wait, I can wait. I've got to work with my pop until after three, but I can come then."

"That would be great."

He noticed that Mrs. Carini carried a box in her hands. "Taking candy to the party?"

"Oh yes." She laughed. "Our pastor is something of a sugaraholic. Not a good thing, since he's recently been diagnosed with diabetes. So I take him some of our sugar-free candies, just to put a smile on his face."

Ryan joined them as they walked toward the parking lot. "So, Taffie tells me you two are nearly ready to retire."

"That's right." Mrs. Carini's face beamed.

"What will you do? Work in the yard? Travel to Europe?"

Mr. Carini laughed. "I know it's hard to believe," he said. "Most people our age want to go to Europe, to travel the world. Our families are from Europe, and we've traveled back and forth for years."

"It's the rest of America we want to see," Mrs. Carini explained. "In all the years we've lived here, neither of us has been west of the Mississippi."

"Wow. Are you serious?"

"Yes. Our whole lives are wrapped up in our children and that candy shop." A look of longing came into her eyes as she spoke. "But we've seen the Grand Canyon in pictures."

"And Mount Rushmore. And the redwoods of northern California," Mr. Carini added.

"We want to see them up close." Mrs. Carini sighed. "As much as we love candy making, we also want to spend part of our time traveling."

"We bought a used RV last spring, and I've been fixing it up," Mr. Carini explained. "We plan to head west sometime next month, but we're waiting to see if Taffie comes up with a plan to bring in new business before we do."

Ryan nodded in understanding. "Oh, I'm sure she'll do fine. You've all done such a great job with Carini's over the years. Everyone in town knows you've got the best candy on the boardwalk."

"The best in the country, you mean!" Mrs. Carini laughed.

"Of course!" Ryan agreed.

"Well, what can I say? Candy gets in your blood. There's just no better way to explain it." Mr. Carini spoke with a faraway look in his eyes. "My pop was a candymaker and his father before him. In Italy, of course." He shook his head, as if remembering. "There's something about the smell of sugar. And the look on a child's face when he sees something sweet. . .there's no job in the world greater than sprinkling sunshine in someone's eyes."

Ryan tried to remember the last time he'd seen a client with joy radiating from his or her face. Mr. Petruzelli—the pizza shop owner. *Hmm.*

"This is how I look at it. . ." A peaceful look came over Mrs. Carini as she spoke. "We're believers. We love the Lord wholeheartedly. We want to serve Him and have prayed about how to accomplish that. Some might look at our candy shop and ask, 'How is that a ministry?' We see it as such because God draws the people in, and we spend time sharing His love with them."

"I would imagine candy is a great door-opener," Ryan said.

"Always has been," Mrs. Carini said with a smile. "All you have to do is read the Bible to see that. Think of all the scriptures about honey—and the sweetness of God. Candy has always been a special treat—something served up on only the nicest of occasions. Now it's not so rare."

"The dentists are happy about that, no doubt," Ryan added.

"No doubt," Mrs. Carini said, "but sugar isn't all bad! Think of how it's used to bring people together, after all. A man will give his sweetheart chocolates to show that she's precious to him. Hosts serve decadent desserts to their guests as a special gift. I can't help but think that God knew what He was doing when He gave us sweets. That's what we are to Him after all. . .precious."

"Wow." Ryan paused a moment, then looked Mrs. Carini in the eye. "Have you ever contemplated preaching, Mrs. C.? You teach a great lesson."

She laughed. "I teach a women's Sunday school class every Sunday morning at Grace Community Church. But I'm afraid you might feel a little out of place with the older women in the room."

"Maybe, but it might be worth it, just to sit in on a teaching with such depth." He offered her a playful wink and her cheeks reddened.

"Aw, go on with you. I just do what comes naturally."

I just do what comes naturally.

The words ran deep. Was he doing what came naturally? Repairing appliances? Not really. If he had to admit the truth, what came naturally would be stepping up to take the bull by the horns. Owning his own business. Using every tool available to promote it. Managing the details. Not fumbling around with heating elements and broken dishwasher disposals.

Lost in his thoughts, Ryan almost missed Mrs. C.'s next statement. He managed to catch the end. "The safest place to be is in the center of God's will."

"Yes, but how do you know you're there?" He turned to her for the answer.

"There's a peace that passes understanding. It's the only way I know to describe it. When you're in that place, you feel safe. And right."

"That's not to say you won't have problems," Mr. Carini threw in. "This shop has been God's will for our family for years. And we've had our share of problems. That's why we're a little hesitant to leave right now, before we've got things resolved."

"Resolved?" Ryan paused before asking the next question. "What sort of problems. . .if you don't mind my asking?"

"Don't mind at all," Mr. Carini said with a shrug. "Here's the primary thing— it's hard to keep the doors open during the winter. The products we sell are mostly summertime specialties."

"Even with the coffees?"

"Yes. Most of our sales come from candy and ice cream. Summer treats. After years of only keeping our doors open in the summer, we tried a winter run. But we couldn't seem to draw in the customers, so we ended up closing just after Thanksgiving. When this boardwalk falls silent. . . ," he pointed out to the shore, "then the people don't show up. Oh sure, the casinos are full. But we haven't figured out how to draw those customers into our shop like we do the kids in summertime."

"What else is going on?" Ryan asked.

"Well, we're not as computer savvy as we should be," Mrs. Carini added. "We should be selling a lot more through our Web site. But getting the word out across the World Wide Web takes time."

"And it's time we don't have," Mr. Carini threw in. "We're all so busy right now. But if we could up our Web traffic, then we could increase sales during the off-season. And if we could find a way to run specials online, then we'd probably do a lot more shipping, which would be great."

Ryan paused to process the information he'd just received. *Is that why you've brought me to this family, Lord? Do you want me to offer my services to help them out?* An idea took root, one he couldn't seem to let go of. Maybe he'd never own his own business. Maybe he'd go on working with appliances forever. But perhaps. . .just perhaps. . .the Lord had opened a door for him to use his marketing skills on the side. What would it hurt, anyway?

He glanced over at Mr. Carini, took note of the pride in his eyes as he talked about the candy store, and made his decision. He would do whatever they needed him to do. And he would do it with joy leading the way.

ॐ

With books in hand, Taffie crossed the campus, the night sky crowding in around her. Tonight's business class, though tough, had gone better than expected. If she could just ditch the guy with the blue-streaked hair. He seemed to be drawn to her, and yet he refused to stop making fun of her name. Why did she always find herself the brunt of so many jokes? And what could she do to stop it?

As she neared the brightly lit parking lot, Taffie slowed her pace and thought about the class. She'd somehow muddled through tonight's lessons. And finally, though she hated to admit it, the numbers in the columns were actually adding up.

Not that she enjoyed it, even when things worked out on the spreadsheet. Now, she'd rather toss the idea of managing the shop's finances out the window. If only she could do that and still give her parents the freedom to drive cross-country in that new RV of theirs. She drew in a deep breath and made up her mind to make it through her last few classes.

Locating her car among the rows and rows of vehicles proved to be a bit of a challenge. She finally managed, and climbed inside, then leaned her head back against the headrest and sighed. After a few moments of deep breathing, Taffie turned on the car and turned up the volume on the radio. She caught the tail end of a worship song, one about God's greatness. Instead of slipping the car into gear and pointing it toward home, she took a couple of minutes to drink in the music. Afterward, she leaned her head against the headrest once more.

"Lord, I know You're big enough to handle every problem. I don't know why I keep taking things into my own hands, anyway. I usually just mess everything up. But, God. . ." She looked out the window, up into the starry expanse. "God, I really, really don't have a plan of action to promote the business. My heart just isn't in it." She exhaled deeply, realizing the truth of it. Was this going to turn out to be a battle of wills—hers against God's? Or did the Lord have something—or someone—else in mind?

All these things she contemplated as she slipped the car into gear. . .and pointed it toward home.

Chapter 8

On Tuesday afternoon around three, Taffie stood at the front window of the shop, staring out at the skies. She recognized the ominous color from years past. "Pop, come look at this."

As he gazed upward, a look of concern seemed to sweep over him. "Hmm. Doesn't look good."

"Did you hear anything on the news about an incoming storm?" she asked. "I've been so busy, I haven't been paying attention."

"Yes, there's a storm creeping its way up from Virginia. But I don't think they're expecting it to do much damage."

She peered outside once more, unconvinced. The usually bright colors of the shops around the boardwalk were clouded over, the gray skies hanging eerily low. Off in the distance, the tide did its usual late-afternoon thing, but with more force than usual. The white peaks on the water made her wonder if something of a greater magnitude was about to blow ashore.

"Do you think we should board up the windows?" Taffie turned back to her father. "Something about this doesn't look—or feel—right."

"Hmm." He stood beside her, staring outside. "I don't know. From what I saw on the news, it's going to pass over pretty quickly. I think we'll be okay. I'll just close the shutters."

"Do you ever worry about hurricanes hitting Atlantic City?" Taffie turned to Pop with her question. "When I think about what keeps happening along the Gulf Coast. . ." She gave a little shiver. "I sometimes wonder how Atlantic City has been spared." She stared out at the beach once more. "All we have are piles of sand. No levees. No seawall. Nothing. And we're at sea level. It's just scary."

"We can't live in fear," her father responded, "but I have to admit, the thought of getting hit by a big storm occasionally crosses my mind, especially on days like today. All the buildings are so close to the shore. Too close. Thank goodness the waters of the Atlantic are colder than the Gulf of Mexico. Otherwise, I think we'd see more activity."

Taffie shook off her concerns. "From what I hear, it's not likely a big one will ever hit Atlantic City. By the time a storm reaches us, it's usually fizzled out or stays offshore."

"Oh, I don't know. I remember the big storm in '62," Pop said. "Tore up a section of the pier and destroyed thousands of homes. Thankfully the shop didn't suffer much damage. Your grandpa always said there was a guardian angel looking out for Carini's."

Taffie thought about that for a moment. "Maybe he was right. We've been really blessed, especially when you consider how close we are to the water."

"We're going to be fine, honey. And trust me, there are plenty of other things to worry about, if you've got your heart set on worrying." He flashed a smile. "But I'd suggest focusing on the good things."

"Good things." She thought at once about her business class and her inability to come up with a plan to get the shop through the winter months.

"Did I mention that Ryan Antonelli is on his way over here with the part for the taffy machine?" Pop interjected. "Should be here any time now."

"No. Really?" Yikes. Did she have time to slip into the back room and touch up her makeup?

"Yes, and I have it on good authority he wants to learn how to run the taffy machine, once we get it back up and going."

"No way. He told you that?"

"I read it in his eyes." Pop winked, and then headed back into the shop.

"Sure you did." Taffie took another look at the darkened skies and prayed Ryan would arrive before the storm did. Then, determined to remain in good spirits, she stepped away from the front window and went back to her place behind the counter of the candy shop.

a.

Two storms were brewing at once as Ryan headed back to the boardwalk area—one in his heart and mind, the other in the Atlantic. He needed to get back to the candy shop before high winds blew out the electricity in the area.

As Ryan made his way toward the car, his cell phone rang. He recognized Mallory's number right away. Her words sounded rushed, almost frantic. "Ryan, I hate to ask this, but I'm tied up in a meeting at work and need someone to pick up Casey from school."

He glanced at his watch and did his best not to groan out loud. Not today, of all days. "What about Vic?"

"He's on a deadline with a new client. They're paying him double to get their site up and running quickly. He could go, but with our current situation, well. . ."

He knew she would've finished the sentence with "we really need the money now that we're living apart," so he saved her the pain. "Say no more. I'm only five minutes from the school right now. Will you call the office and let them know I'll be picking her up instead of you?"

"Already done."

"I'll have to take her with me to my next repair job, but I'll bring her home after."

"No problem. And thank you. I'm so grateful."

As the skies continued to darken overhead, he pulled into the parking lot of the elementary school. Rows of cars made maneuvering the parking lot next to impossible. *I'll just have to wait it out.*

About ten minutes later, after inching his way forward, Ryan finally located Casey. She waved and bounded toward his work van. "Uncle Ryan! I'm so glad you came and got me. Can we get ice cream before you take me home?"

"Actually, I'm headed to the candy shop on the boardwalk," he explained. "And they've got the best ice cream in town. Want to spend the afternoon with your old uncle Ryan, watching him fix a broken taffy machine?"

"Will that girl be there?" Casey's eyes sparkled as she posed the question.

"She'll be there. But you've got to promise not to play matchmaker. Or suddenly burst into a love song or anything crazy like that. You don't want to embarrass me, do you?"

"Why not?" She giggled. "I like embarrassing you."

"Obviously. But not today. Today. . ." He looked up at the gray skies. "Today, I just need to get my work done and get out of there before the storm hits. So, you can have some ice cream and visit with Taffie and her mom. I'm sure they'll treat you like the princess that you are."

"I'd like that." Casey flashed a wide smile, revealing an incoming tooth.

The traffic headed toward the boardwalk was lighter than usual. More folks seemed to be moving away from the shore than toward it. *Hmm. Might be a bad sign. Maybe they know something I don't.*

Regardless of the weather, he had to make it to the shop before it closed for the day. Had to get the part installed. The Carinis had done without their primary machine too long, already.

After parking the van, he walked around to open Casey's door. "Stick with me, kid." He took Casey by the hand and, despite the winds that now blew every which way, took off running. They arrived, breathless and red-cheeked, at Carini's Confections just as Mr. Carini put the CLOSED sign on the door.

"Not again." Ryan groaned. "I thought for sure I'd get here before you closed up shop."

"Oh, we're going to stick around and watch you work your magic," Mr. Carini explained. "But with the storm headed inland, it just made sense to go ahead and put up the sign. We haven't had a customer in nearly an hour. Folks are shying away, and I don't blame them."

"I see." Ryan entered the store on Mr. Carini's heels.

"Taffie!" Casey hollered out in her usual joyous way. "You're here."

"I'm here." Taffie's face lit in a smile. "And so are you. This is a special surprise."

"Uncle Ryan picked me up from school today."

"Do you mind that she's here?" he asked. "I thought maybe she could hang out with you and your mom while I replace the part on the machine."

"Mind? Are you kidding?" Taffie's broad smile brought a rush of joy to his heart. "In case you haven't figured it out by now, I love kids."

"Yes, I figured that out, which is exactly why I didn't mind bringing her. And besides"—he grinned—"I have it on good authority she's starving for ice cream. rocky road, to be precise."

"We just happen to have the best on the boardwalk!" Taffie assured him.

"The best in the country!" Mrs. Carini's voice rang out from the other side of the room. Ryan looked over and discovered her standing behind the espresso maker.

Mr. Carini took another peek outside before throwing in his two cents' worth. "We might be the best ice cream and candy store on the boardwalk, but not for long, if we don't get busy. C'mon, son, let's go fix that machine."

Before heading into the back room, Ryan looked out the front window. The skies overhead were an odd yellow gray. Not a color he saw very often. And even from where he stood, he took note of the rollicking waves.

"You go on now and get that machine up and running," Mrs. Carini said. "No point in standing around waiting for the skies to clear. God's got this storm under control."

Funny. He wasn't sure how to take the word *storm*. And if Taffie's mom—the whimsical candymaker-turned-espresso-aficionado—had her way, he'd have the taffy machine fixed long before the rain started.

A crash of thunder convinced him otherwise. Within seconds, a streak of lightning lit the place from the outside in. Yikes.

Casey clapped her hands together. "Ooo, a storm! I *love* storms!"

"Me, too," Mrs. Carini agreed. "But they're better when you spend them with a friend. So, come on back here behind the counter and help me scoop up some rocky road."

"Really?" Casey's eyes widened.

"Well, of course," Mrs. Carini said. "What good is a storm if you don't spend it eating ice cream?"

Casey squealed her delight and disappeared behind the ice cream counter just as Ryan slipped into the back room. Off in the distance, he caught a glimpse of Taffie's sparkling eyes and wide smile. She mouthed the words, "Thank you," and he nodded in her direction. His heartbeat jumped to double time. Something about that girl just sent him reeling. Perhaps, when this was all over with, he might work up the courage to ask her out.

Right now. . .well, right now he had to slay a few dragons.

Chapter 9

Ryan celebrated alongside the Carini family as he and Carl Carini got the taffy machine up and running. Almost immediately, he started packing up his tools. Storm clouds hovered and the night skies beckoned. He needed to get Casey home. . .and quick.

"What? Leaving so soon?" Mr. Carini's smiled shifted into a frown. "No way! You two stick around and we'll make a little taffy. It's time to introduce both of you to Carini's candy world."

The man's enthusiastic response put Ryan in mind of Willy Wonka. Taffie's father truly did have sugar running through his veins. But what about the storm? Should Ryan mention they probably only had minutes before it hit?

"Follow me, kiddos." With the wink of an eye, Mr. Carini led the way to the cupboard, pulling out bags of sugar.

Ryan and Casey watched in awe as Taffie and her father went to work mixing up corn syrup and sugar in a huge metal pan on the stove. With a deep sigh, Ryan realized he probably wouldn't be going anywhere, at least for a while. Then again, as he watched Taffie at work, he didn't really mind.

"We'll add a bit of water to this mixture, and a pinch of salt." Mr. Carini made quite a show out of tossing in the white grains of salt.

"Oh!" Casey pulled a lollipop out of her mouth. "Is that why they call it salt water taffy?"

Mr. Carini turned to her, eyes wide. "You mean to tell me you're an Atlantic City native and you don't know the story of how salt water taffy got its name?"

Casey's brow wrinkled in response. "No, sir."

"Well, then. You watch close and I'll tell it as we go."

Casey pulled up a stool and sat on it, watching as the mixture in the pot was stirred. Ryan stood next to her, drinking in every moment. Every now and again he caught a glimpse of Taffie out of the corner of his eye. She was certainly in her element now. In fact, she seemed to know just what to do and when to do it.

"I'm going to tell you a very tall tale," Mr. Carini's eyes sparkled with excitement. "The stuff fairy tales are made of."

"Ooo, I love fairy tales." Casey giggled, then stuck the lollipop back in her mouth, her gaze focused on the Wonka-like fellow who stood before her.

"This will be the tallest tall tale you ever hear," Mr. Carini explained with great whimsy. "So hold on to your hat. I'm about to take you on a candy-land adventure!"

❧

Taffie tried to hide the smile that crept up as her father told the story. She'd heard it a thousand times, of course, though the listeners were usually just small children like Casey, not folks in Ryan's age group. Still, she never tired of the legend—more fiction than fact.

Her pop's face lit up as the story began. "Back in the 1880s—or so the story goes—a terrible storm blew into Atlantic City."

"Like this one?" Casey pointed beyond the glass to the window at the front of the store. With the shutters pulled down, it was hard to tell what the weather was up to outside. Just then a peal of thunder clued them in.

"Like this." Pop grinned. "The waves were vicious, frightening even the locals. A merchant by the name of David Bradley owned a candy shop not far from where we're standing now. Sold many of the same products we sell today."

"Wow. A candymaker." Casey's eyes widened. She stuck the lollipop back in her mouth and listened attentively.

"Anyway, the storm was mighty and the waves high. They crashed ashore, putting all the shops underwater, including Bradley's candy shop. The man thought his business was drowned in the sea, thought there was no hope for his soggy candies."

"Wow. Really?" Ryan asked.

"Have we mentioned that this is a tall tale?" Taffie whispered, leaning in his direction.

"Shush, Taffie. Now, would I lie to you, son?" Her father gave him a stern look, then continued, turning his attention to Casey. "Anyway, the following day after the waters went down, a little girl about your same age came prancing into Bradley's shop, looking for something sweet to nibble on. Bradley, in a state of despair, offered her a few pieces of the waterlogged delicacies, but told her to watch out for slivers of jellyfish and other sea-life buried inside."

"Icky!" Casey squealed.

"Yes, very. He called it salt water taffy because it had been soaked in salt water from the Atlantic. Inspiration from on high, I believe."

Taffie rolled her eyes, but said nothing. She continued to stir the bubbling pot of corn syrup and sugar.

"Then came the best part." Her pop rubbed his hands together, clearly delighted with the end of the tale. "A candy store owner's dream."

"What happened?" Casey sat on the edge of her stool.

"The salt water taffy tasted wonderful! And the idea caught on! Folks came from north, east, south, and west to buy Mr. Bradley's salt water taffy. Before you knew it, other competitors sprang up, and Atlantic City became known as the home of this confectioner's delight. And poor Mr. Bradley..."

"What about him?" Casey asked.

"Forgot to copyright the name *salt water taffy*. So, alas, it was stolen."

"Mm-hmm." Ryan pursed his lips, then asked, "So, all of this came about because of a terrible storm? Water washing into a store? A man selling soggy candy?"

"Oh yes."

"I'm sorry, but that tale sounds a little fishy, Mr. C."

"Fishy? No way! Salty, sure!" Pop slapped his knee.

"Would you like to hear the real story now, or are you happy with that rendition?" Taffie asked. "Because there's a more boring tale, sure to satisfy your curiosity, but certainly not as much fun."

"I'm all ears." Ryan turned her way, and for a moment, her heart kicked into overdrive and she couldn't think straight. What was it about him that sent her reeling? Best get to the story.

"Taffy has been sold in Atlantic City since the 1880s," she explained. "People used to believe that bathing in the sea was good for your health. Doctors would send patients to the seashore for medicinal purposes."

"To cure what ailed 'em, eh?" Ryan grinned.

"Right. Theory being that salt water made you healthy. So adding the words *salt water* to the candy, which had been around since the 1880s—even without the fishy story—made it sound. . ."

"Healthy?" Ryan laughed. "So, taffy was billed as health food?"

"Exactly. Boosted sales. Even back then, smart business owners knew what to do to draw in a crowd." She sighed. "I guess I have a lot to learn from them."

"Taffie is making up that story, I tell you!" her father insisted. "She's pretty good at stretching the truth." He pointed at the machine, then smiled. "Get it? *Stretching* the truth?" He erupted in laughter and Casey joined him.

"Very funny, Pop." Taffie released an exaggerated sigh and rolled her eyes. Some jokes she would have to live with forever, it seemed.

Ryan looked back and forth between Taffie and her father, finally letting his gaze rest on Mr. Carini. "If I have to be completely honest, I think I like his story best. Sorry."

"Yeah, me, too," Casey echoed.

Taffie shrugged as she responded. "Most people do. It's the stuff legends are made of." She gave her pop a wink, and he responded with a boyish grin. Then, as she turned to look at Ryan—the hero who'd swept in to fix their machine, the man responsible for getting their business up and running once again— Taffie came to a quick conclusion. . . .

He was the stuff legends were made of.

&

Ryan observed the interaction between father and daughter with a sense of wonder passing over him. Someday. . .someday he would have a daughter who looked at him with such love and respect. Right now, he had other things to do. He'd never considered taffy making, but could not escape the inevitable.

"We're ready to let the candy cool." Taffie prepared a large work area on a marble table, then, as the mixture on the stove stopped its bubbling, she poured it out.

Ryan stared in confusion at the gooey mess. "Doesn't look like much."

"Not yet. Just wait."

As the concoction cooled down, they swapped stories about life in Atlantic City. Before long, Taffie checked the taffy and discovered it was just the right temperature. Ryan watched in wonder as she lifted into her arms the block of what now looked like putty, and began to wrestle with it. "How much does that weigh?" he asked.

"Probably forty pounds or so." She shrugged. "But I can handle it."

"Obviously." She was definitely strong, no doubt about that.

"Wow, you're like Wonder Woman!" Casey interjected.

"Why, thank you!" Taffie put the somewhat buoyant mixture onto the pulling machine and turned it on. The machine, now running like a champ, stretched the sheer, yellowish blob over and over again. Suddenly it began to change colors, turning a fabulous white color with a terrific sheen.

"The air circulates, making it softer," Mr. C. explained. "It's almost like elastic at this point."

"It's in a continual state of change," Ryan observed. The parallel between the taffy and his own life hit him squarely between the eyes. *I'm in a continual state of change, too. But I'm not as pliable, that's for sure. I probably need to work on that.*

"Yes, and it's softer to the touch now, too," Taffie added.

"Now comes the fun part," Mr. Carini said. "What flavor do you like?"

"Well, I, um. . .I like the vanilla, myself."

"Vanilla?" Mr. C. eyed him as if he'd just landed in a spaceship. "No vanilla for my guests. Let's go with something more exciting than that. What about you, Casey?"

"I love banana!" Her voice carried a hint of a squeal.

"Banana it is, then." Mr. Carini turned to Ryan. "You will add the flavoring and the color, young man. It's high time you learned to do this for yourself."

"It is?" *Why?*

"Now, take this banana flavoring. . ." Mr. C. showed him exactly how to add it to the sticky mixture. At once, the room filled with the scent of bananas.

"Mmm." Casey closed her eyes and drew in an exaggerated breath as a peal of thunder sounded overhead.

"Now what?" Ryan asked.

"After it's mixed in really well, we add the yellow coloring."

Minutes later, the shiny white mixture had turned a slippery looking yellow.

Bright yellow. Banana yellow.

"Now we feed it into the cutter and wrapper. I'll show you how." Mr. Carini led the way. "You will operate the machine."

"M–me?" Ryan stammered. "But I—"

"You work with appliances, boy. You can do this."

What followed could aptly be described as a midair collision. Ryan couldn't seem to control the speed of the cutting and wrapping with the same precision as Mr. C. He ended up with shreds of taffy—now almost plastic-like in feel and texture—and bits of paper floating through the air. All the while, Casey laughed at him, pointing and giggling with great glee at his misfortune.

Taffie eventually snapped off the machine and took his place. He watched in dazed curiosity as she got the process going again. Then, with her father's help, he slipped in alongside her and they worked together, finally getting the job done.

Afterward, Mr. Carini clapped his hands. "You two are remarkable together."

I believe we are, at that.

"Yes, well, remember. . .many hands make light work," Mrs. Carini said, entering the room. She gazed at the yellow pieces of taffy and added, "You didn't do all that work just to stare at it. Have a piece, Ryan. And you, too, Casey."

He hesitated, if only for a moment. Sure, he liked bananas all right. But in taffy form? What if he took a bite and hated it? Could he control his expression to avoid hurting feelings? He'd never been very good at that sort of thing.

To his great delight, the piece of banana taffy brought a smile to his face. "Man." He chewed it up and reached for another. "That's not what I was expecting at all. It's not strong. Just the perfect amount of banana."

"It's yummy!" Casey agreed, as she snatched a second piece.

"Your mama's going to have my head for feeding you so much sugar." Ryan groaned, then looked at his watch. Six thirty? They needed to leave. . .right away.

"You did a fine job adding the flavoring, son," Mr. C. patted him on the back.

Mrs. Carini bit into a piece, then looked at Ryan with a smile. "You're quite the candymaker. Maybe our families have more in common than we know." She hesitated, looking back and forth between Ryan and Taffie. "Or maybe this is all part of a grander plan."

"Grander plan?" He reached for his tool belt, but the sound of thunder stopped him in his tracks. A shocking flash of lightning followed and then a shriek from Casey. Seconds later, the lights went out and the candy shop stood in utter darkness.

Ryan stared around, trying to get his bearings. Above his head, he could hear the rush of a shrill wind and the sudden pelting of raindrops. Or was that hail? And to his side, Casey whimpered in fear.

"Doesn't look like anyone's going anywhere for a while," Mr. Carini said. "So, let's all settle in and make ourselves at home."

Off in the distance, a flashlight came on. The illumination lit up one startlingly beautiful face—Taffie's. She smiled in his direction, then called for Casey to come and join her. Ryan watched through the shadows as his niece slipped across the room and into Taffie's welcoming arms, then he reached for his cell phone to call Mallory.

Chapter 10

Nearly an hour later, Casey dozed off in Mr. Carini's recliner in the back office. Ryan joined the Carinis around one of the small tables in the shop for a bite to eat.

"I always keep lunch meats and cheeses in the fridge," Mrs. C. explained as she placed a paper plate down in front of him. "We eat lunch here most every day. We'd better eat it up quick, before it goes bad."

Ryan bit into the tastiest ham and cheese sandwich he'd ever eaten. "Mmm. This is awesome. Best meal I've ever had on the boardwalk."

"Hardly." Mrs. Carini laughed. "But we're happy you're sharing it with us."

"Speaking of food, have you been to that new seafood place a couple of doors down?" Taffie asked. "I've been dying to go. I've heard great things about it."

"Oh, Luke told me about it. Said they've got wonderful service and good food," Ryan said. "I've been wanting to go, myself." In fact, if he used his imagination, he could almost taste the lobster now.

"Well, you two kids should go check it out sometime," Mr. Carini said. "Tell us if it's any good. Then maybe we can all go. Both families, I mean."

"I–I'd like that." Ryan paused a moment, wondering if Taffie realized that he was asking her out. *Am I asking her out?* "W–would you like to go with me, Taffie?"

"I. . .well, sure."

Though he could barely make out her face in the shadows, Ryan felt sure he saw the look of contentment in her eyes. He certainly heard it in her voice. *Lord, I could spend the rest of my life sitting right here. With her.*

A flash of lighting caused the direction of the conversation to shift. "I hope the power isn't out too much longer," Mrs. Carini said. "That ice cream is packed hard, but we're going to lose it all if the storm lingers."

Mr. Carini, in his now-familiar way, began to pray aloud. "Lord, we thank You for unexpected time together—always a gift—and we praise You for sending Ryan to fix the taffy machine. Oh, and thank You for Luke, who made the part. Now, Father. . .we ask that You send this storm on its way so that we can get back to the business You've called us to. And, Lord, if it's not too much to ask, could You protect our ice cream? Use Your supernatural freezing abilities to keep it solid till the storm passes?"

Everyone at the table echoed his "amen," then sat in silence awhile. Ryan knew by now what they were doing. Waiting on the Lord. He didn't mind waiting. Not with Taffie so nearby, anyway.

"I remember a storm that hit when I was a kid," he said, finally. "I was about Casey's age. It scared me to death. I don't know why, but I've always been afraid of lightning."

"Not me," Taffie's voice had an easy sound to it. "In fact, I love it when it storms outside. It's especially great at night, right about the time I'm climbing into bed. There's something about the sound of rain tapping at my window—"

Just then a clap of thunder ended the sentence for her. Another flash of lightning followed, its white rays sending slivers of light through the shutters at the window.

"Whoa." She laughed. "Maybe I don't love it *that* much."

"I love that scripture in Isaiah—the one about how we can go through the waters and not drown," Mrs. Carini threw in. "Lets me know that I can go through storms and make it, with God's help." She paused for a moment, then the tone of her voice changed. "I've already learned from personal experience that it's true. About three years ago I went through the worst storm of my life."

The room grew eerily silent and Ryan's curiosity increased.

"I was diagnosed with cancer," she finally explained. "Went through months of chemo and radiation."

"Oh, I'm so sorry." He didn't ask for details and she didn't offer them.

Her voice softened further. "Thank God for my family. They were my life support. Well, that and my faith. We never stopped praying."

"Prayer is the answer," Mr. Carini said.

"And Mom is really strong." Taffie's voice broke as she shared. "Every time I showed up at the hospital, she was more concerned about whoever happened to be in the bed next to her than about herself. We spent hours praying for people we'd never even met before."

"I'm not the only one who's ever suffered," Mrs. Carini replied. "And what would be the point of being in a place with that many hurting people and *not* praying for them? I knew I was there for a season, so I connected with as many folks as I could. And prayed for as many as I could."

"Amazing." The thunder rolled overhead. "What about you, Mr. C.?" Ryan asked. "You haven't told us your take on storms."

"I faced my share of them as a child," Mr. Carini explained. "Most were not the kind like we're experiencing tonight, but in the way of persecution because of my heritage."

"Oh?" This struck a chord.

"Yes, I was called names. Hurtful names."

"I heard a few of those myself, growing up," Ryan acknowledged. Kids could be so ugly at times.

"Actually, what I went through was nothing like what my pop experienced," Mr. Carini explained. "He came over from Italy in the late thirties, just before the Second World War, and was so proud to be an American. As I said, he opened the candy shop right away and had a steady flow of customers. But just a few years later, after Italy declared war on the U.S., people weren't always friendly to him. With all the tensions in Europe, a lot of people treated him like a foreigner."

"My grandparents told me stories about all that when I was young," Ryan said. "In fact, my grandfather was in an internment camp for a year or so when he was in his teens."

"Didn't happen to the same extent that it happened to Japanese Americans," Taffie's father explained. "But several hundred Italian Americans were held in military camps. Thank God my pop wasn't one of them. He managed to keep the store going. But he had to carry an identity card that labeled him as a resident alien. Worst of all, the Italian language was nearly lost here during that time. Italian Americans were afraid to speak anything but English for fear of persecution. They just wanted to fit in—at any cost."

Ryan nodded. "Personally, I think the Italian language is the most beautiful in the world."

"Ooo, I agree," Taffie said. "I still love it when my mom gets excited about something and dives in, forgetting she's not speaking English."

At once Mrs. Carini began to explain, in perfect Italian, just why she loved the musical sound of the language. Ironically, Ryan understood every word. Just one more thing they all had in common.

"My pop has worked hard to make sure my brothers and I had hefty doses of Italian," he said with a grin.

"Your parents raised you right." Mr. Carini laughed. "So, you'll have to make sure your children learn the language as well. Promise?"

My children? Funny, until earlier tonight, Ryan had never thought of himself as a father. Sure, he helped out with Casey, but. . .kids of his own?

Sitting here, in the dark, with the Carini family surrounding him, he came to a startling reality. If he could find a wife half again as good as any of these people, his children were bound to be wonderful.

❧

Taffie listened intently as Ryan talked with her parents. He had such an easygoing way about him. Comfortable. Sure, it could be because they had so much in common. . .but there was more than that. She sensed something deeper.

"Your mother told me you're very active at your church," Taffie's mother said, breaking the silence.

"Yes. I lead worship for the singles ministry."

"You sing?" Taffie tried to make out his face in the shadows. "Really?"

"I do. And I play the guitar, too."

"Tangie is the singer in our family," Taffie said. "And Candy is amazing on the piano. I've never really had any musical abilities."

"Not true, not true," her father reminded her. "Remember in the fourth grade. What was that contraption your music teacher made you play?"

"The recorder?" She laughed. "Pop, I was terrible, even on the recorder." After a moment's pause, she shifted her attention back to Ryan. "Do you sing contemporary worship songs at your church? They're my favorite."

"Yep. Sure do. We throw in an occasional hymn, just to mix it up. But we've got a pretty young crowd—mostly people in their twenties and thirties. So, most of them were raised on contemporary music."

"I like those songs," Taffie's mother interjected, "but I love the old standards, too." At once, she began to sing, " 'Tis So Sweet to Trust in Jesus," her lyrical voice turning the candy shop into a sanctuary. When she finished, Taffie could scarcely breathe. Something about her mother's voice ringing out across the darkness sent shivers up her spine. . .in a good way.

"That was gorgeous, Mrs. C.," Ryan said. "So, you're not only a Bible study teacher, you're a vocalist as well. I can see you now, traveling from state to state in that RV of yours, entertaining folks at RV parks all over the country."

"Great idea!" Pop interjected. "And I'll bring my harmonica."

Taffie groaned. Pop and his harmonica.

"Maybe you're on to something there, Ryan," Taffie's mother said. "I do love to sing. That particular song came to mind because of the candy store. We're always playing music overhead that has the word *sweet* in it. Or *sugar*."

"Oh, right," Ryan said. "I remember now. You were playing 'Sugar, Sugar' the first day I came in."

"Marketing strategy," Taffie's pop explained.

"Oh, you should hear the rest of our repertoire." Taffie laughed. " 'The Candy Man.' 'Big Rock Candy Mountain.' 'Lollipop.' And then we have our spiritual numbers: 'In the Sweet By and By,' 'Sweeter as the Days Go By.'" She laughed. "It gets pretty sticky in here sometimes."

"But the customers love it," her pop interjected. "So we keep it up."

"Terrific idea." Ryan laughed. "You folks sure know how to run a business."

Taffie squirmed in her seat, afraid the others might sense her discomfort. *If only he knew how much I don't know.*

Just then, the lights flashed back on, nearly blinding everyone in the place. "Whoa!" Taffie's eyes finally adjusted and she glanced at Ryan. His gaze met hers and they lingered a moment, neither Taffie nor Ryan speaking a word.

"Praise God!" Taffie's mom's voice rang out as she checked out the ice cream. "I do believe we've avoided a calamity. It was that prayer of yours that did it, Carl. The ice cream is saved!"

"Amen!" Pop shouted. "What say we celebrate by eating some?"

The noise—and likely the lights—served to awaken Casey. She came bounding from the back room, rubbing her eyes. "Did someone say ice cream?" Her expression, filled with innocence and wonder, took Taffie back to her own childhood.

Ryan looked at his watch and groaned. "Your mom is going to kill me."

"What about this?" Taffie offered. "We've got sugar-free ice cream. Maybe she could have a small scoop?"

"Please, Uncle Ryan? Please!"

"Just a tiny, tiny scoop." He sighed. "How in the world can I argue with her? Look at that face."

Everyone turned to look at Casey, who gazed back at them with sleepy eyes. Taffie had to conclude, the little girl had somehow wriggled herself into everyone's heart.

Turning her attention to Ryan, Taffie concluded something else. . . .he had wriggled his way into her heart as well. And she might just celebrate the fact with a double scoop of rocky road.

Chapter 11

Ryan hated to see the evening come to an end, but as he glanced down at his watch, he realized the late hour. "It's almost nine o'clock." He looked at Casey with a sigh. "She should be home in bed."

"I was asleep already, Uncle Ryan," she reminded him. After a lengthy yawn, she added, "Besides, I don't have any homework tonight."

"I'm sure she'll doze off the minute she gets in the car," he reasoned aloud. "That's how I was as a kid."

"Me, too." Taffie laughed. "To this day, I have a hard time staying awake when someone else is driving."

"Remind me to do all the driving then." He paused, realizing what he'd said. *Now she knows I want to spend time with her. Lots of time.* Instead of allowing embarrassment to overcome him, he laughed and turned back to Casey. "Ready to go, kiddo?"

"If we *have* to." She raced to Mrs. Carini, giving her a hug, then did the same to Mr. Carini. She finally landed in Taffie's outstretched arms.

"We loved having you here, honey." Taffie ran her hand across Casey's tousled hair. "Come back and see us anytime."

"Ooo, I would love that!"

Ryan faced Taffie. "Would you. . .would you mind walking me to the door?" His courage nearly failed him as the question eased its way out.

"Of course." She stepped alongside him and they made their way toward the front of the store, their conversation easy, as always. Casey tagged along behind them.

"I had a great time here—with you and your family," he admitted. "In some ways it's just like being home. And in others. . ." Under the glow of the iridescent light overhead, he stared into her rich brown eyes and almost stumbled over the next few words. "In others, it's so much better. When I'm with you"—he gestured back to her family—"all of you. . .I'm completely comfortable. It's like I've discovered a part of myself that I never knew existed."

"I think that's the nicest compliment I've ever heard." The edges of Taffie's lips curled up in a smile. "But you make it easy. I don't think you realize just what a nice guy you are. Children love you. Adults love you. I. . ." She stumbled over the next few words. "I—I think you're great."

"Thanks." He took hold of her hand and her cheeks immediately turned crimson. "I want to spend more time with you. Do you really think you can take an evening away from the business stuff to go out for seafood? Maybe this coming Saturday night? We could go out to see another movie after."

"Can I come, too?" Casey jumped up and down at his side.

"Not this time, honey. Uncle Ryan wants to take Taffie out on a date."

"Like that guy in the movie!"

"Well, sort of."

Casey crossed her arms at her chest and gave him a knowing look. "When your date is over, you have to sing to her. And kiss her, too."

Ryan slapped himself in the head. So much for trying to accomplish this in front of a seven-year-old. He glanced over at Taffie to gauge her response. She offered a coy smile, which warmed his heart.

"So, with all this singing and kissing in our future, do you think we should see another fluffy romance?" Taffie quizzed him with humor sparkling in her eyes.

"Um, no. Something practical. Something we both agree on."

"In that case, you've got a deal." She gave his hand a squeeze, then reached to give him a warm hug. "I can't wait."

Casey rolled her eyes as she shared her thoughts on the matter. "You two are *so* boring."

Ryan did his best to ignore her, keeping his gaze fixed on the one woman who now totally consumed his thoughts. Right now, the way his heart felt, he *could* burst into song. And kissing her? He fought the temptation with every breath. "I'll call you on Saturday afternoon to settle on a time," he said. "And, Taffie. . ."

"Yes?"

"I—I think you're as sweet as your name."

❧

As Taffie watched Ryan walk out the door, her heartbeat escalated. She'd seen the look in his eye. Longing. The same look in the eye of every child begging for candy. Finally! Was it really possible?

She practically floated on a cloud all the way back into the shop, where her parents met her with childlike grins on their faces.

"W–what?" She played innocent.

"You know what!" Her mother's eyes sparkled. "He likes you. And we like him. He's great, Taffie."

"He is pretty great." Her face warmed at the admission, so she turned away for a moment, pretending to busy herself.

"You two are a match made in heaven. I can just see my grandkids now—your smile, his great hair. Your love for people, his great singing voice. . ."

Taffie groaned as she turned back to face her mother. "Mom, don't marry me off just yet. We haven't even had our first date yet. And besides, things aren't always as easy as they seem on the surface." As she spoke the words, a chill came over her. No, things were not always as easy as they seemed. Take running the shop, for instance.

"Seems like he's got a good head on his shoulders," her pop said. "But can we talk about your love life on the drive home? I'm worn out. I'm ready to get out of here."

"Of course." Not that Taffie wanted to chat about her pending love life with her parents, but she was ready to get home. A bubble bath sounded mighty good. And she had a sudden urge to write in her journal—something she'd been lax in doing over the past few weeks.

Thoughts of Ryan tumbled through her head as she helped her parents clean up the store. She pondered the evening's events. No doubt God had ordained every moment. Taffie smiled as she thought about Ryan's trying to handle the taffy wrapper. His clumsy antics made her laugh. Maybe his skills didn't lie in candy making, but she could see the excitement in his eyes as they'd talked about the business end of things. She'd have to pick his brain. He seemed to have a lot of expertise in that area.

As her father turned out the lights, Taffie stood in darkness for a moment, reflecting back on the words Ryan had spoke earlier. . .also in the darkness. All that stuff about leading worship at his church. *The boy has hidden talents!* Somehow, just knowing he could carry a tune made her want to try. She warbled out a few notes of "Sugar, Sugar," but stopped cold as her mother looked her way. "What?"

"I don't recall ever hearing you sing alone before, that's all. And you're not tone-deaf, Taffie. You've got to stop saying that."

"Really?" She tried a few more bars. This time her mother joined in, harmonizing. From out of the darkness, the sound of a harmonica playing almost caused Taffie to stop singing. Instead, she increased her volume. The Carini family had a full-out concert, right there at the front door of the candy shop. "Sugar, Sugar" filled the air.

Taffie couldn't help but think it was the first of many love songs yet to come.

❧

As Ryan pulled his car into his older brother's driveway, he glanced in the backseat to find Casey fast asleep. "Go ahead and sleep, you little matchmaker, you." He turned off the car and opened his door. A stirring at the front door of the house caught his attention. Vic approached the car.

"Hey." Ryan stepped out of the car, then looked at his brother with great curiosity. "You're. . .home."

"Yeah. I'm home."

"So, are you and Mallory. . . ?"

"We're thinking about it. Tonight we're on again. Maybe tomorrow we'll be off. Who knows." Vic shrugged. "To be honest, I'm so tired of the back and forth stuff."

"Me, too." This time the voice came from the backseat. Ryan reached for the handle and opened the door, watching as Casey—eyes now wide open—unfastened her seat belt. "Daddy! You're home!" She practically flung herself in her father's arms. "I had so much fun tonight. I learned how to make taffy, and I ate lots and lots and lots of sugar!"

"Hmm. I see." Vic turned to give Ryan an inquisitive look.

Ryan put his hands up in self-defense. "Not my fault. I did my best to curb the sweets. But when you're stuck in a candy shop with a seven-year-old, you're lucky to get out alive. That's all I've got to say on the matter."

As if to echo his words, Casey groaned. "My tummy hurts. I don't feel so good."

"Mm-hmm." Vic swept his daughter into his arms. "C'mon in the house, baby. Your mommy will make it all better."

Ryan watched the interaction between father and daughter with a hopeful sigh. Maybe, just maybe, this time things would work out between Vic and Mallory. Maybe God, in His infinitely supernatural way, would make everything better.

Chapter 12

The following Saturday morning Ryan picked up the phone to call Taffie. When she answered, something caught him off guard. Was she...singing?

"Taffie, is that you? This is Ryan."

"Oh, I uh..."

He heard the strains of music in the background and couldn't resist asking the obvious. "Were you singing?"

"Who, me? I, um, I don't usually..."

"Sure sounded like singing to me," he said. "And on key, at that. So what was all that stuff about your not being able to carry a tune in a bucket?"

"Not sure what's going on," she confessed. "I guess I was singing along with the overhead music and didn't even realize it. Strange, huh?"

"Yes. And very suspicious, though I'm sure Casey would have plenty to say about it. She would probably cast you in her next movie."

"No doubt. And Tangie would try to put me in one of her plays." She laughed, temporarily breaking the tension. "But I can assure you, I couldn't act my way out of a paper bag."

A momentary silence followed, just long enough for Ryan's nerves to kick in once again. Time to give his reason for calling. "I, um, just wanted to check in with you. What time should I meet you at the shop?"

"Five would be fine. I'm looking forward to it."

"Me, too." Should he say how much? Nah, better leave it at that.

They ended the call, and Ryan spent the rest of the morning and the better part of the early afternoon working alongside his father to repair a commercial refrigerator at one of the city's larger restaurants. Afterward, dripping with sweat and completely exhausted, he headed home to take a shower. Casey met him at the door of the house. Her eyes lit up the moment she saw him.

"Uncle Ryan!"

"Hey, pip-squeak. What are you doing here?"

"Grandma is watching me. My parents are on a *date*."

"Really?" Ryan had to smile at that idea. "And what do you think of that?"

"I think it's romantic." Her smile broadened...for a moment. "But..."

"But what?"

She shrugged and led him by the hand into the living room. "They still fight a lot. I heard them last night really late. They thought I was sleeping, but I wasn't. They were so loud."

"I'm sorry, baby." He reached to give her a hug.

"I'm—I'm scared. Do—do you think my daddy's gonna leave again?" Her eyes filled with crocodile tears.

Ryan sighed. He hated this part. "I hope not, honey. But we'll pray about that. I know that God is bigger than any problems your parents are facing. Want to pray with me?" When she nodded, he took her by the hands and prayed a simple but heartfelt prayer.

Afterward, Casey looked up at him with a confident smile. "I feel better now."

"Me, too."

Her eyes twinkled as she asked, "Are you still going on your date tonight, too?"

"Yes, but no singing. And definitely no dancing. I've got two left feet, you know."

"You do?" She looked down, clearly confused.

Ryan laughed, wondering if he should explain that statement or just move on. *Nah, just move on.*

"Uncle Ryan?"

"Yes, baby?"

She paused for a moment and her eyes glistened as she asked, "Even if you don't sing and dance, you're still gonna kiss her, right? Like the prince in the movie?"

"It's just our first date," he argued. "A gentleman would wait until later."

Casey released an exasperated sigh. "You're never gonna find a wife, Uncle Ryan. And I'm never going to get to be a flower girl."

"Ah." Realization struck. "Is *that* the real issue here?"

"I'm getting old."

"Old?" He gave her a curious look.

"All my friends have already been flower girls, but I never have. And everyone knows flower girls have to be little. I'm still pretty short, but I won't be forever, so you have to hurry up."

"Ah. Well, kiddo, I'll see what I can do about that, but I can't make you any promises but this one: If and when I *do* get married, you can be a flower girl."

"I'm gonna look pretty goofy if I'm, like, twenty or something. I guess I'll just have to be a bridesmaid." Casey rose from the sofa and skipped off into the kitchen.

Ryan thought about her words as he showered. Was he looking for a wife? Was that the plan? He hadn't really thought about Taffie as wife material before, had he? In fact, he hadn't given much thought to marriage at all, not with the problems going on between Vic and Mallory. No, right now marriage seemed more like an illusion of some sort. All smoke and mirrors, but not real.

On the other hand... He allowed his thoughts to shift as he got dressed. His parents had a strong marriage. So did Taffie's. Maybe Vic and Mallory just needed to take a few lessons from the older generation.

At four thirty, Ryan bounded down the stairs, headed toward the front door.

"Stop right there, mister." His mother entered the room, beaming like the late afternoon sunshine. "I hope you don't think you're blowing in and blowing out that fast. You didn't even say hello. And now you're not saying good-bye?"

"Sorry, Mom. I'm just—"

"I know, I know." She chuckled. "Casey told me. You have a date with Taffie." Her eyes reflected genuine curiosity. "Though why you never told me, I don't know. I remember when you used to share the details with good ole Mom. Now I have to hear the juicy tidbits from a seven-year-old."

Ryan sighed. "That's just it, Mom. There are no juicy tidbits. I want to be careful about all this. I really like Taffie. A lot. But we haven't even been on our first date yet, and Casey's already got us married off. She's got her heart set on being a flower girl. Can you believe it?"

"Pink."

"E—excuse me?"

"Casey is hoping you'll choose pink for your wedding color. She wants you to know she looks best in pink. Cotton candy pink. Not hot pink or anything like that. And by the way, she wants to carry pink sweetheart roses and wear a tiara with lots of sparkles in it."

"Good grief." Ryan sighed, ready to stop the conversation as quickly as possible. "I'll keep that in mind. But for now, I'd just like to have a quiet dinner with a really nice girl from a great family. No pressure. And no wedding bells. No pink roses. And definitely no tiaras."

His mom put her hands up in the air, feigning innocence. "I'm not saying another word. Go. Have a good time. But don't think you're sneaking in here late tonight without giving me details."

"I feel like a kid again."

"Well, you should. It's been a while since you've been on a date. Now, skedaddle."

With an unexpected smile on his lips, Ryan turned and skedaddled...all the way to the car.

❧

"Mom, can you and Pop do without me now?" Taffie looked across the shop at her mother.

"Um, sure, honey." Her mom looked up from serving a chocolate malt to a customer. "Go ahead and get ready."

Taffie slipped out from behind the candy counter and made her way to the office in the back of the store, where she located her change of clothes. Looking at the beautiful pink blouse and black slacks, she had to smile. People always said she looked great in pink. Well, her mom and sisters always said she looked great in pink, anyway. Maybe Ryan would think so, too.

She rushed to the ladies' room, where she changed out of her work clothes, then worked to transform herself. A little makeup, a few minutes with the curling iron, and before long, she was good to go. Taffie gave herself another once-over in the mirror, startled at how changed she looked from just a few short minutes ago. Or was it just the sparkle in her eyes? Possibly.

Why not sparkle? Just the idea of spending time alone with Ryan made her smile. In fact, every time she thought of him, a delicious sense of joy rose up inside her. Surely tonight she would get to know him better, find out for sure if he was the sort of guy she would want to. . .

To marry? Strange, how the words flew into her mind. Not even one date yet, and she was thinking of marriage? Odd, but not really, in light of her upbringing. What was it Pop always said? "Don't waste your time dating 'em if they're not the sort of fella you'd want to marry." Consequently, her dating life—if one could call it that—had been very limited. There just weren't a lot of guys out there she'd want to spend the rest of her life with.

Till now.

Just the thought of a "happily ever after" with Ryan reminded Taffie of the fairy-tale images in that silly movie they'd seen together. Had it really only been a week? Were the people on the screen singing and dancing their way into her heart?

Taffie eased her way back into the store, noticing an incoming rush of customers. Could she—should she—really leave her parents alone without help? Her pop took one look at her and let out a whistle. "You look like a million bucks, kid. That Ryan is one lucky fella."

A handful of customers looked at her with curiosity. She drew in a deep breath, then turned her attention to a woman ordering ice cream. As she scooped up a beautiful round ball of toffee almond delight, her thoughts drifted to Ryan. For some reason, she felt like a silly schoolgirl, waiting to see if the boy she had a crush on might look her way.

Well, nothing wrong with feeling young, right? And it wasn't like she was given over to flights of fancy, like the girl in that movie. No, she had a good head on her shoulders and was a hard worker, to boot. Rarely thought about things outside of work and church, and certainly never focused on boys. . .er, men.

Minutes later, just as the clock struck five, Ryan entered the shop. She watched from a distance as his gaze went first to the candy counter. When he didn't locate her there, he turned toward the ice cream area. The minute their eyes met, Taffie's breath caught in her throat. She took one look at him in that sharp-looking dress shirt and slacks, and found herself caught off guard by his looks. He'd been handsome in his work attire, and nice-looking in his jeans and T-shirt that night at the movies, but the sight of him in that blue shirt sent her into a tizzy.

"Ryan." She finally managed his name. "I'm nearly ready." She turned back to a customer, filling the order. All the while, he looked on, his eyes sparkling.

She finally broke away from the crowd, and turned to her parents with a smile. "I'll see you guys later. Have fun."

"No, *you* have fun." Her mother winked, then went back to work.

Taffie followed Ryan to the door, which he opened for her. After they stepped out onto the crowded boardwalk and took a few steps, he paused for a moment. "Do you mind. . .I mean, would you mind stopping for a minute?"

She paused, then turned to look at him. "Everything okay?"

"Yes. I just wanted to say"—his cheeks turned a rosy color—"that you look. . .wonderful."

"Thanks." Taffie fought to keep the edges of her lips from curling up as she drank in his sweet words. "Pop always says, 'Powder and paint make a girl what she ain't.' It's amazing what a little lip gloss and mascara can do."

Ryan shook his head. "No, it's not the makeup—though that looks great, too. You're just like a. . ." He paused for a moment. "A scene from a movie."

"Yikes." She slapped a palm against her forehead. "Romantic comedy or action suspense?"

He gave her a knowing look, but said nothing.

"What? You're not going to tell me?"

"No." He shrugged. "You're going to have to guess."

"Well, it had better be action suspense, that's all I have to say. 'Cause I've had just about enough of all that musical comedy stuff."

"Mm-hmm." He slipped his arm around her waist and gently led her through the ever-growing maze of people.

A few seconds later, as Taffie's heart danced its way into her throat, they arrived at the restaurant with the words HIGH SEAS above the door. Just one step inside and her senses were overwhelmed with the smell of fried fish and the sound of clinking silverware. She looked around at the fish motif and smiled. "I like this place already. I'm a sucker for a themed restaurant."

"Yeah, me, too." He followed her gaze. "We'll have to come back with our families. Soon."

Is that another date you're asking me out on, Ryan Antonelli? 'Cause I just might have to say yes.

As if in response to her ponderings, he flashed a playful smile, then melted her once again with his brown eyes.

The hostess seated them in short order and left them to review the menu.

"What looks good to you?" Ryan asked.

"Mmm. Everything. I skipped lunch today."

"Busy day?"

"That's putting it mildly." She felt a wave of joy wash over her as she contemplated the business the shop had done today. "It's nearing the end of the season, so folks are coming into the shop in droves to buy taffy." She gave the menu a thorough read. "But I've had my fill of sweets. I want some real food."

"Lobster?"

"Mmm. Maybe." She glanced at the price on the menu and stopped cold, pointing at something that caught her interest. "Or maybe something else. I'm a shrimp cocktail fanatic. And salmon. I love salmon."

"I love a girl who loves salmon." Ryan's cheeks turned red the moment he said the words, but he didn't take them back. Taffie's heart swelled with joy. *Well, then. I'll order the salmon.*

The waiter reappeared and they placed their orders. Then, as a goofy love song played overhead, Taffie turned her attention away from the food. . .and to the handsome man who sat across the table. What a night this was turning out to be.

Chapter 13

Ryan spent every moment of his time in Taffie's presence completely relaxed and drawn into her easy conversation. As they ate, they talked about their families, their dreams, and their faith. Specifically, he told her the story of his wandering away from the Lord as a teen—how he'd almost let the most important decision of his life fade to the background as he searched for fulfillment in other ways.

She responded by telling him about everything she'd gone through during her mother's cancer struggle. . .primarily, how she'd nearly given up on God.

"Isn't it funny. . .or rather, sad, that we claim to have all the faith in the world one day, then plummet the next?" she asked. "I mean, God has done so many wonderful things in my life over the years. He healed my mom, for instance. In spite of my lack of faith. And yet I turn around just a few days—or even hours—later and forget."

"I'm the same way." He paused to think about some of the issues that had arisen after his father's stroke. "I think I get so self-focused at times. And I'm like you, at least from what I've observed so far. I'm a fixer. And not just appliances." He sighed. "I want to make everything right for everyone."

"I hear ya." She gazed into his eyes and they had a moment of quiet recognition.

"But we're not *called* to fix everything," Ryan added. "And I'll be the first to admit I can't go on much longer taking care of the business for my dad. I don't mean that out of a lack of respect; it's just not what I'm called to do."

"In some ways, I'm just the opposite," Taffie explained. "I don't mind staying at the shop. I'll work there for the rest of my life. I love the candy making, the people, and all that. But when I look at the whole business end of things. . ." She shuddered. "It stops me cold."

"We're a fine pair, aren't we?" Ryan reached across the table and took her hand, then gave it a squeeze. "But God has all this figured out. We just have to trust Him." After a few moments of embarrassing silence, he released his hold on her hand and shifted into lighter conversation. The time passed all too quickly, and before he knew it, they'd finished the meal. After Ryan took care of the check, he glanced at his watch, stunned. "Whoa. It's almost seven o'clock."

"Oh?" Taffie gave him a what-does-it-matter look.

"The movie. We'll never make it."

She laughed. "Want to hear something funny? I forgot all about the movie. To be honest, I was having such a good time talking that it slipped right out of my head."

"Yeah, me, too." They paused to gaze into each other's eyes for a moment, neither saying a word.

"I have an idea." Her eyes lit up as she spoke, making them prettier than ever. "Let's just watch the sunset out on the boardwalk."

"And maybe play a few games at the midway?" he suggested.

"Skee-ball?" Taffie's excitement seemed to grow.

"Sure. Why not." He rose from his seat and walked to her side of the table, then pulled out her chair.

"Thank you, kind sir." Taffie rose with a flourish, then gave a little curtsy, her cheeks turning pink.

"Wow." He grinned. "That was very. . .dramatic."

"Good grief." She slapped herself on the forehead. "I have no idea what's wrong with me tonight. It's got to be that movie. Or Casey. Something's had an effect on me."

"I don't mind a bit." Ryan bowed at the waist, hoping to look as dashing as the prince in the movie. "But we must make haste." He placed his hand on the small of her back and gently led her out of the restaurant, enjoying their closeness. Once outside, the glare from the setting sun nearly blinded him.

Taffie gazed upwards and mumbled something he didn't quite understand. When he asked her to repeat it, she looked at him, embarrassed. "Oh, I was just saying *tangerine*. That's what Tangie always said when we were kids. Whenever the sunset was more orange than red, she'd call it tangerine. When it was more red than orange, she called it raspberry."

"So, it's a tangerine sky." He gazed up again. He glanced at his watch and gasped as he realized how much time had passed. "We'd better get a move on if I'm going to beat you at skee-ball."

"Beat me, eh?" Her posture changed immediately. "I'll have you know I'm the Carini family champ. No one can even come close. So I'd watch my words if I were you."

"Ah. Now I see what I'm up against." He paused to stare into her eyes. He saw what he was up against, all right. But it had nothing whatsoever to do with skee-ball. His heart was slipping away in pieces, like the snippets of taffy paper floating around the room the other night. He didn't want to snatch them back. No, he was having far too much fun watching things progress.

Working their way through the crowd, they finally arrived at the arcade. With a groan, Ryan looked through the mob of people at the skee-ball machines. He hadn't expected so many kids. "Do you mind waiting?" He looked at Taffie, who simply smiled.

"Of course not. It's going to be worth the wait when I win the prize."

"Win the prize?"

She pointed up at the large collection of stuffed animals hanging on a rack overhead. "I want that one."

He followed her pointed finger to the fluffy white dog in the third row. "Wow. That looks just like Snickers."

"No way."

"Yes way. So, if you want a challenge, you're on. I'm going to win that. . .and give it to my mom."

"You wouldn't dare."

"I would." He did his best not to laugh.

"In that case, the challenge is on."

Like the Red Sea parting, the crowd in front of them dissipated, and Ryan stepped forward to a skee-ball machine. Taffie took the one next to him. He dropped coins in the slots on both machines, and the battle began.

Approximately thirty minutes and thirty dollars later—after much whooping and hollering from both Taffie and the ever-growing crowd around them—Ryan had to admit defeat. The white pup, which he could've purchased at the store for less than ten dollars, was now snuggled in Taffie's arms. The look of sheer contentment on her face made his defeat less painful.

As they turned back toward the boardwalk, Taffie leaned in and whispered, "Thanks for letting me win. I think the crowd actually thought you were trying."

"I—I was!"

"Okay. Whatever. But thanks, either way. I love my puppy." After a moment's pause, she added, "I think I'm going to name him Vanilla."

"Vanilla? A little boring, don't you think?"

She turned to give him a pensive look. "But vanilla is your favorite, right?"

Okay, she had him there. But he was finally ready to branch out, ready to try new things.

"Want to play any other games?" Ryan asked, gesturing around the midway.

"What? You don't mind if I whip you in something else? Won't hurt your pride?"

"Just because you're good at skee-ball doesn't mean you can pitch." He pointed to a booth with milk cans. "Are you game?"

She flexed the muscles in her right arm to show off. "Just so you know, lifting those mounds of taffy has given me a great pitching arm. Check this out." She flexed her muscles and a couple of passersby let out a whistle.

Ryan sighed. "Ah. Well, never mind then. Don't think my manly pride can take another defeat like the last one."

With a giggle, Taffie turned her attention back to the crowd. "I wish it was like this year-round. The people. The noise. The excitement. But this is the last weekend of summer, and before long, everyone will be gone." Her expression changed right away, and he noticed the somber tone in her voice. "I always get a little sad at this time of year. Can't seem to help myself."

"Why don't we sit awhile and talk," Ryan suggested. "Losing twenty-five skee-ball games in a row took all the wind out of my sails. And I happen to know of a great bench, just outside the best candy shop on the boardwalk."

"The best candy shop in the *world*," she corrected him.

"Yes. The best in the world." As they turned toward Carini's Confections, Ryan looped his arm through Taffie's, feeling so carefree his feet might just take to dancing. She looked up with a hint of a smile, and for a moment—a brief moment—he expected her to burst into song.

With one arm looped through Ryan's and the other holding the stuffed dog, Taffie walked toward the candy shop. She did everything in her power to still the exaggerated pounding that went on inside her heart. Could Ryan hear it? She sure could. In her ears. Her wrists. Her neck. Everything inside seemed to have sprung to life when he slipped his arm through hers. She tried to balance these feelings against the sadness that had swept over her so suddenly at the mention of the summer drawing to an end. She shouldn't get this worked up in front of Ryan, not about business problems, anyway.

And yet, as she gazed up into his eyes—eyes filled with loving compassion—she wondered if, perhaps, the Lord had finally sent someone she could confide in. Someone who might just understand. And possibly help.

They reached the bench just as the last of the evening crowd disappeared. With the glow of the lamplight overhead ushering them on, they took their seats. Ryan slipped an arm around her shoulder, and Taffie found herself comfortable with the fact. She held the prized puppy on her lap and gazed out at the water. "I love it out here at night," she said with a sigh. "I used to sit out here as a kid and close my eyes, just listening to the waves."

They both sat in silence for a moment, doing just that. Ryan finally broke it with a question. "So, you've grown up with the candy shop as part of your daily life?"

"In the summers, yes. It's so much a part of me. I don't know how I could be happy anyplace else."

"And yet. . ." He drew her a bit closer, and she found herself at ease, snuggling up against him. "You're worried about what's coming next with the business?"

She fought the temptation to tell him everything at once. "I'm just a little concerned about the off-season. My parents are leaving soon, but they want me to come up with a plan to bring in customers while they're gone."

"Right. They mentioned that."

She sat up straight and looked him in the eye. "They talked to you about this?"

"Only in passing."

She relaxed a bit. "Well, I've stretched my brain about as far as I can stretch it, and just can't seem to come up with a workable plan. Not a realistic one, anyway. And to be honest, every time I think about it for any length of time, I just start feeling sick inside. I'm so worried I'll take this business they spent their lives building and run it into the ground."

"What?" His brow wrinkled. "But I've seen you in action. You're great with the customers and you clearly love the product. What's the drawback?"

"I'm not business minded, and I'm not great with the whole being-in-charge thing." Taffie groaned. "My sister Candy is better suited for all that, but she's busy with flight school out in Arizona. Not that I'm complaining. She was meant to be a pilot. I wouldn't take that from her for anything. And Tangie. . . well, you met Tangie. I love her, but she's no help at the shop. She's always flitting off to be in this show or that show. And if she's not on the stage, she's in school. So that leaves me. Just me. And it's not that I don't want to help. I do. But sometimes I resent the fact that I'm left to run the whole show. I'll have to hire someone else to help me, of course. That's a given. But who? And when? I don't have a clue how I'm going to do this."

"Can you just tell your parents?"

She shook her head. "You don't understand. They already have the RV. They're leaving in a month. This has been a dream of theirs for as long as I can remember." She shook her head. "Anyway, enough about all that. I don't want to talk business tonight." She gazed into his eyes—eyes filled with compassion—and smiled. "If it's all the same to you, I just want to talk about other things."

"Fine with me."

Determined to change the direction of the conversation, Taffie finally came up with a question. "So, have you lived in Atlantic City all your life?"

"Born and raised."

"Crazy, that we've been this close and never met."

"Oh, I'm sure we saw each other as kids. Remember, I told you my parents used to bring us to the beach all the time. We were in Carini's dozens of times over the years."

"Just weird that you can grow up in the same town with someone and never meet at all."

"Well, look at this place." He gestured to the many buildings surrounding them. "Seems like every week a new building goes up. And the tourists are coming."

"Not always for the best reasons." She squinted against the lamplight and focused on one of the larger casinos.

"All the more reason God has planted you and your family right here." His brow wrinkled. "Hearing your mom talk about your candy shop as a ministry really put things in perspective for me. It's true, what she said. People are drawn into your shop because of the sweets, but what you guys give them—through your words, your actions, the overhead music, and the scripture above the door—is the love of God."

"Well, I guess, when you put it like that. . ." Taffie shook her head. "It just worries me sometimes. I want to have children one day, and I'm not sure this is the best possible environment."

"Oh, I know. But there are a thousand things to love about Atlantic City, especially the boardwalk area. History was made here. This is the world's first-ever boardwalk, you know."

"I know, I know." She laughed. "Now you sound like you could work for the chamber of commerce or something. And the excitement in your voice reminds me of Pop when he tells that goofy taffy story."

"Maybe I *should* work for the chamber of commerce." His eyes lit up. "I sure don't mind getting excited about the things I love. I enjoy marketing. Love promotion. Love getting people excited about people, places, and things."

"Well, you're good at it." She gave him a pensive look. "So, go ahead. Sell me on Atlantic City. Tell me how you're going to draw people here, even during the slow season. I could use the encouragement."

"Really?" He leaned forward and looked into her eyes.

"Yep." Taffie leaned back against the bench and waited for the show to begin.

Chapter 14

Ryan rubbed his hands together, excited by the possibility of sharing his thoughts about his hometown. "There are so many great things about this city; I hardly know where to begin." He paused a moment to get his bearings, then used his most professional voice. "What about this? All four miles of Atlantic City's beaches are free to the public. You don't get that just everywhere. Some places you have to pay to be on the beach. And here, the sand is snowy white."

She shrugged. "Not sure snowy white is completely accurate, but it's close. What else?"

"The very first Miss America was crowned in Atlantic City in the 1920s." He snapped to attention, remembering something else. "Oh! And the game of Monopoly was created using the names of the streets in Atlantic City. Not everyone knows that."

"True, true." She didn't look terribly impressed. "But you still haven't sold me. Why would I want to come to Atlantic City? I can play Monopoly at home in Timbuktu, and the Miss America pageant is no longer held here."

"Well. . ." He stared out at the coastline, deep in thought. "Because there's something in the air here." He rose from the bench, contentment washing over him as he spoke. "The smell of salt water gets in your veins. Rejuvenates you. Reminds you of why you're alive. And when you're on the boardwalk, it's like stepping back in time. You're reminded of the simplicity of summer holidays of the past. And when you venture into Carini's Confections"—he gestured up at the sign above the store—"you cross the threshold into the days of yesteryear."

"Yesteryear?" Taffie giggled. "Is that a word?"

"It is now." He shrugged. "But that's the thing. People want to be reminded of what life was like when they were young. When things were simple. Before they had bills to pay and problems to deal with. That's what Carini's is all about. It takes you back to a carefree time."

"True, true. . ."

"And that's what your candies do, too. Just biting into a piece of that taffy"— he closed his eyes—"you can almost feel the sun on your face. You can taste the salt water in the air. You're transported back to your favorite trip to the beach as a youngster, walking hand in hand with your father, picking up sea shells. Listening to the lapping of the waves against the shore. Feeling the presence of

God in the vastness of the waters." He grew silent and an odd sense of wonder came over him.

For a moment, neither of them said a word. Taffie finally responded with a soft, "Wow."

Ryan gazed at her with a smile. "Didn't mean to go off on a tangent like that, but you get the idea."

"I do." She chuckled. "I also see that your promotional skills are completely underutilized."

"Yeah." He joined her on the bench, then released a sigh. "It's not that I dislike working with appliances." He raked his fingers through his hair. "Actually, yes I do. That's my father's dream. And he's so good at it. He's always worked at keeping Antonelli's Appliance Repair a key player in Atlantic City. I don't want to be a disappointment, and carrying on the family business has been so important to him, especially with so many competitors springing up."

"I understand that part, trust me. Letting down your family is. . ." She shook her head. "Well, there's a lot at stake. I get it." Taffie's gorgeous eyes locked into his.

"It's complicated, isn't it?" He drew near and slipped his arm over her shoulder once again, cradling her. They sat in silence for a moment, staring up at the night sky.

Ryan listened to the sound of the waves as they lapped the shoreline in the distance. "Some things are always the same," he said with a sigh. "The tide, for instance. It goes in and out. No one has to tell it to behave. The sun rises and sets. My dad is just like that. Reliable. Steady. Unchanging."

"My parents, too."

"In some ways, I'm jealous of them," he admitted. "They figured out what they wanted to do and they're doing it. Me. . .I'm still trying to figure out what I want to be when I grow up."

"Me, too."

"We *are* a fine pair, aren't we?" He stared into her eyes, and she looked back with tenderness in her gaze.

"We are," she whispered.

In that moment, with the stars beckoning and the waves singing something akin to a love song, Ryan wrapped Taffie in his arms. She gazed at him with anticipation, her fingertips tracing the edges of his cheek. Seconds later, they shared the sweetest kiss imaginable. Ryan's heart merged with hers the moment their lips met. *I was made for this moment. For this woman.* He wanted to sing. To dance. To laugh. Instead, as unexpected passersby interrupted their privacy, he startled to attention.

Taffie began to giggle. Then, with a contented sigh, she rested her head against his shoulder. Ryan planted feathery kisses on the top of her head, then held her in his embrace.

Until reality hit.

He'd kissed her. *Kissed* her.

What in the world would he tell Casey if. . .or rather, *when*. . .she asked?

⤫

Taffie closed her eyes and relaxed in Ryan's arms. Oh, what a blessed night. It really had been something like a fairy tale. Ryan was Prince Charming, and she. . . Well, what she lacked in princess material, she made up for in joy. Surely God had arranged every second of this fabulous evening. Otherwise, why were her toes tapping? Why did her heart want to erupt in glorious song? So, life really was like one of those goofy romance movies after all. . .when you found the right person.

Hmm. So much for action-suspense flicks. From now on, it was romance all the way. She lingered, deep in thought. So many things about tonight made sense. Being in Ryan's arms. The things he'd said about the shop. Even his speech about Atlantic City. The man was a walking billboard. A marketing guru. He'd certainly given her a lot to think about with his enthusiastic dissertation.

Her eyes popped open quite suddenly as realization set in. "You know, you're right."

"About?" His brow wrinkled.

"Everything. We've been trying to get people interested in candy. Been trying to sell them on sweets. What we need to do is market our products to the masses to draw them back to that quieter, simpler time."

He stared at her, confused. "Wait a minute. I just kissed you, and now you're back to talking about marketing?"

"Oops." She stared at him, warmth creeping its way into her cheeks. "Sorry. Not sure how that happened. But, Ryan. . ."

"Yeah?"

"Ryan, something about being with you makes me want to succeed. I want to be the best I can be."

"Same here." He reached for her hand and kissed the back of it, then looked into her eyes.

"I can do this," she whispered, looking up at the CARINI'S CONFECTIONS sign. "With God's help, I can do this."

Chapter 15

On Monday morning, Taffie arrived at the store, deep in thought. Despite her best attempts, she couldn't stop thinking about Ryan. The joy in his eyes. The sweetness of his kiss. The comfort of his embrace. She'd pondered all these things from Saturday night till now, and she doubted she'd be able to stop anytime soon. He'd made plans to come by the shop later today, and her heart swelled with anticipation. Oh, if only she didn't have to wait!

Just as she reached into her purse for the key, a middle-aged man in an expensive suit approached. "Excuse me. Are you a member of the Carini family?"

"I am." Before using her key to open the door, she paused to look into his eyes. Though completely businesslike in appearance, something about him caused a shiver to run down her spine. "Can I help you?"

He extended his hand. "My name is Paul McKinley. I'm an attorney representing the owner of the new Gold Dust Casino. Likely you've heard about the project. We'll be breaking ground in a few weeks."

She'd heard, all right. Taffie bit her lip to keep from sharing her opinion on the matter. All Atlantic City needed was another casino. She'd had her fill of them, to be honest. Why the city saw fit to allow another one in this already crowded area was beyond her.

"I wonder if you might have a few minutes to chat." He smiled, but for some reason, she didn't feel like returning the gesture.

"I, um. . ." She started to press the key in the lock, but realized he might try to follow her inside the shop, so she hesitated. Taffie could think of nothing worse than being stuck inside the shop with someone who sent a chill up her spine at first meeting. No, best to stay outside in clear view.

"Have I come at a bad time?" He glanced down the empty boardwalk and she suddenly realized he must have deliberately picked the early morning hour to approach her. Clever.

"No, I. . ." She glanced at the key in her hand, trying to make a decision.

"I promise I've not come to bring you anything but good news. If you're willing to talk inside, I'd be perfectly comfortable with the door open. If not, I don't mind standing out here."

She hesitantly opened the shop, leaving the door ajar. After putting her purse behind the counter, she gestured for him to sit at the closest table. Before taking his seat, he reached to pull back a chair for her. Somehow his gesture didn't feel as genuine as Ryan's had on Saturday night at the restaurant. Still, she couldn't help but wonder what this fellow was up to. Surely he was here with something specific in mind. He had a determined look about him.

He got straight to it, scarcely pausing to catch a breath. "We've acquired the adjoining property, as you probably know. And, as I mentioned, ground breaking will take place soon. Still, my client has approached me with a proposition, one I've been asked to present to your family."

"A proposition?" For whatever reason, a sinking feeling came over Taffie. Whatever this fellow had to say couldn't be good. She took a seat across from him and braced herself, all the while trying to look as if she didn't have a care in the world.

McKinley put his briefcase on the table and snapped it open. "My client has had his eye on your property for some time now. He understands that Carini's is a landmark here in Atlantic City and wants to see your company succeed, but he also sees that the candy shop sits empty at least half the year. Or more."

Taffie did her best not to groan aloud at that last part. Even the casino owners were taking note of the fact that the shop couldn't keep a steady stream of customers. What next? Would the newspapers run an article, rubbing their noses in it?

McKinley pulled some papers out of his briefcase and thumbed through them. "After considerable thought, he has asked me to present you with an offer to purchase your property."

"P–purchase our property? But. . .Carini's isn't for sale. My grandfather bought this land in the 1930s, and it's been in the family ever since."

"Oh, trust me, I know the history of your store." Mr. McKinley fished through several pieces of paper, finally coming up with one that shared the value of the land and the building on it. "I've been researching this area for months now. I could tell you pretty much anything you wanted to know about most of the shops on the boardwalk—those currently operating, and even the ones that have been bought out by larger corporations."

So could I. Not from research, but from personal experience.

"I know all this must come as quite a surprise." He gave her what could best be described as a rehearsed compassionate look. "But my client is prepared to offer you three times what your property is worth. I doubt you will ever see an offer like this again."

"Three times?" Though she wasn't particularly good with numbers, this one had no trouble registering. If they sold the shop, her parents could both retire in style. And she could. . .

Hmm. She wasn't sure what she could do. Her whole life was wrapped up in this candy store.

"As I mentioned, my client is well aware of the impact Carini's has had on this community, and is prepared to do more than what I've already stated."

"O–oh?"

Mr. McKinley offered a genuine smile. "I think he's hit on a brilliant idea, one you're going to love. He would like to offer you a spot inside the new casino—rent free—to put your store. A place where you could do business year-round. You would draw a whole new clientele."

No doubt.

"Since the casino will generate business during the winter months as well as the summer, you won't ever have to close your doors. In fact, you can stay open twenty-four hours a day, if you like."

"T–twenty-four hours a day?"

"Best of all, the Carini's name would live on. We would technically own the property, of course, but you could manage the store. A percentage of the goods would go to the casino, but the rest you could pocket. And with the crowd from the Gold Dust so accessible, you could keep the shop open for years to come. Keep it in the family."

The way he phrased things sounded so. . .unnerving. A heaviness came over Taffie at once. She knew, of course, what her parents would say. They had tolerated the casinos, at best. And Grandpa Gus. . .why, he'd turn over in his grave at the idea of his store being purchased by a gambling hall owner.

Taffie rose to her feet, ready to give this fellow his first hint. "Mr. McKinley, I appreciate your stopping by. And I'm sure your client is making a generous offer. But Carini's isn't for sale. Never has been, and—as long as I'm in charge, anyway—won't be. At least not under these conditions."

He gave her a pensive look, then pressed the paperwork back inside his briefcase. "Clearly I've surprised you with the offer. You'll need time to think about it." He snapped his briefcase shut, then shifted his gaze back to her face. "My client is prepared to give you a week to respond. During that time we would be happy to draw up the plans for the new candy shop. We have the best architects in the business." McKinley looked around the shop. "They could take the basic idea of the store and improve on it, several times over."

Improve on it? Taffie felt her nails drive into her palms. She counted to ten and whispered a Lord-please-help-me-not-to-put-my-foot-in-my-mouth prayer. She finally felt released to speak. "Mr. McKinley, I don't expect you to understand this, but we can't possibly do business with a casino. It flies in the face of everything we stand for as Christians. And to think that Carini's might actually be housed inside a. . .a. . ."

"Ms. Carini, you make it sound like a house of ill repute." McKinley erupted in laughter. "The Gold Dust is going to be a high-end hotel and casino. Exquisite. And it will draw people from all over the world. Your shop would be filled from sunup till sundown with a steady stream of customers."

Taffie shook her head, unable to form words. She did her best not to spout

out the thoughts in her head. How could she make him understand? Grandpa Gus had loved the idea that the candy shop sat so near the casinos—near enough the Carinis could reach out to people with God's love. Offer them sweets as an incentive, sure, but offer them the gospel message, as well. In a simple, safe environment. A place away from the crowd, where they could sit awhile and get their bearings.

"I think you're going to need to let me discuss this with my mom and dad." Taffie shook her head. "Though I can pretty much guarantee you what they're going to say. As much as they want to see Carini's live to see another fifty or seventy years on the boardwalk, I can't imagine they would agree to your terms."

He clutched his briefcase with a determined look in his eye. "Ms. Carini, I'll swing back by in exactly one week. I'd like to arrange for your parents to join us, if that's possible. And my client will want to be here, as well."

"Well, as I said—"

She never got the chance to finish her sentence. Mr. McKinley put his hand up. "No. No decisions today. Think on it. Plan that dream vacation you're going to be able to afford, once this land is sold."

She stopped cold, unable to continue. Not that she wanted to. No, all she wanted to do was usher this fellow back out onto the boardwalk so that she could get on with her day. . .and forget all about his so-called offer.

✥

Ryan picked up his cell phone and punched in Taffie's number. He couldn't wait to see her again. She'd wound her way around his heart, and every time he thought of her, a song came to his lips. He found himself humming, even when working. More than once, his pop had questioned him about it.

The phone rang several times. He half-expected it to click over to voice mail, but Taffie answered with a brusque "Hello?"

"Hey, Taffie. It's Ryan."

"R–Ryan. . ." For whatever reason, her voice broke. "I–I'm glad you called. But. . . ."

"What? Bad time?"

"Oh, Ryan. . ." She groaned. "I've got the biggest mess on my hands." She spent the next few minutes filling him in, and before long, he felt the same sense of frustration. How dare that attorney confront her alone. . .without her parents there! Everything inside Ryan balked at the very idea.

"Can't you just turn him down? Tell him he's crazy? They can't make you sell your store, after all."

"Right. But there's more to it than that. He was right about so many things. We're struggling to keep the shop open in the off-season, anyway. And he had a good point. If we moved locations, we'd have a crowd year-round."

"Taffie, surely you're not seriously thinking about. . ."

"No, no. Of course not. I'm just scared, Ryan. I'm already on a strict time-table, what with my parents leaving so soon. And now, with this guy breathing down our necks, it just feels like an added pressure to prove I can make a go of this."

"And you can. You will. Remember what we talked about?"

"I don't know. I need a plan of action. Something specific. I've got to come up with a workable strategy soon. And I have to tell Pop about Mr. McKinley today. He'll flip. But as soon as he's done flipping, he'll ask if I've come up with any ideas to keep the shop going. And I haven't."

"I'm going to help you with that. Remember? I'm your guy."

"You are."

They both paused for a moment as the realization of what he'd said sunk in. An unexpected enthusiasm rose up inside him. "In fact, that's one of the reasons I was calling. I want to meet with you about a plan for the shop. I've given this a lot of thought, Taffie. And I've prayed about it. I really think I'm supposed to help you through this. In fact, I think that's why the Lord brought us together."

"Y–you do?"

"Well, that, and. . ." He didn't say the words, though they threatened to leap from the tip of his tongue. "I care about you. And I want to spend more time with you."

"I want to spend time with you, too," she whispered.

"What are you doing tonight?"

"I have a class." She groaned. "The numbers stuff is finally starting to make a little sense. You don't know how close I came to giving up a few weeks ago. But I'm glad I stuck with it. Now I've only got a couple more classes left."

"You can do everything through Him who gives you strength," he said. "Remember?"

"Well, yeah, but. . ."

"Taffie, don't sell yourself short. Stick with it. I can help you through the marketing end of things, but keeping the books. . ." He laughed. "Not my strong suit."

"Okay." He heard her release a sigh and imagined the look on her face. His thoughts shifted to the color of her eyes. The funny way she held her mouth when she was upset. The way her nose tipped up on the end. For a moment, Ryan found himself lost in his imaginings—so much so that he almost missed her next line.

"I'll do my best," she said.

"Great. And I'll come by today on my lunch break. Will your parents be at the shop then?"

"Yes." She paused. "And Ryan, I can't tell you how grateful I am for all your help. God knew what He was doing when He sent you here. I don't think it was an accident that I called you that day."

The pounding in his heart almost stopped him from responding. "Oh, I don't either. In fact, I can truly say—for the first and last time in my life, probably—that I'm glad to be in the appliance repair business." He let out a laugh, and within seconds she joined him.

"We're a mess, aren't we? Both of us in businesses we're not sure about."

"You're perfectly suited for your work, Taffie," he encouraged her. "I've never seen anyone with better customer-service skills. And when I saw you pick up that thirty pound mound of taffy—"

"Forty pounds," she corrected him.

"Forty pounds. . .I knew I'd found a jewel."

She laughed. "So, what happens next? Are you going to write me a song? Come up with some sort of choreography we can do? Waltz around the candy shop. . .that sort of thing?"

"Nah." He laughed. "None of those things. But I might just write a praise song. For some reason, I feel like thanking God today. In fact, it's number one on my priority list."

"I just hope I feel like praising Him after telling Pop about Mr. McKinley." Taffie's voice wavered. "Pray for me, okay? He's not going to be happy."

"I'll pray for you. But tell him what I said. . .that I'm going to help. I'll see you in a few hours. Don't give up the ship."

They ended the call moments later, and Ryan leaned back in his seat, thinking through their conversation. Minutes later, as he ambled to the work van to make a service call, he found himself humming a happy tune. Pretty soon, the words tripped over his tongue. "Sugar, Sugar" had never sounded so good.

Chapter 16

Later that morning, Taffie told her parents about the visit from Mr. McKinley. Afterward, she watched her father with a heavy heart as he paced the back room, muttering, "Who do these people think they are? They've already swept in here and torn down most of the quaint little shops I knew as a kid. And to replace them. . .with what? More casinos? More places for folks to lose their money?"

"I know, Pop."

"We own this property, free and clear. No mortgage. And I pay my taxes. No one can drive a man off of his own land." He slipped off into a ranting spiel, marching back and forth. "My pop would roll over in his grave. Can you even imagine what he would say?"

"I can imagine." Taffie drew in a deep breath.

"Are all the stores going to eventually sell out?" He gave her a pensive look. "Get swallowed up by the bigger corporations? Is that what's happening? No independently owned stores anymore? No mom-and-pop shops? Everything owned by the big names, and those big names funded with gambling dollars?" He paused to draw in a deep breath and Taffie noticed the tears in his eyes. She moved in his direction, hoping to console him.

"Pop, I'm in total agreement. We won't let them intimidate us."

"Right." His response was weak, at best.

"But?"

Her father shrugged his shoulders. "We'll never sell out. I can promise you that. It was your grandpa's dream to keep Carini's in business for many generations to come. I can envision your children working here. And your grandchildren."

Taffie paused to think about that. She could almost see her daughter or son waiting on customers, chatting about the family's history.

Pop's words interrupted her thoughts. "I've got to wonder how long we can go on if we can't keep the store open year-round."

"Don't you worry about that." Taffie garnered up her courage to speak. "Ryan and I are working on a plan, one we hope to share with you soon."

"Before McKinley comes in here again?"

"Yes. Today at noon, to be precise. But Pop, promise me this."

"What?"

"Don't lose heart. And don't worry. Carini's is the best thing that ever happened to Atlantic City. Ask anyone."

"Except the casino owners."

Taffie turned to face her father. "No, that's not true. Till now, they've all been on our side. And most still are. This is just one man, who happens to want our property so that he can build on it. The others will go on supporting us. And sending us customers. And promoting us. I know they will. And this fellow will, too. Eventually. Grandpa Gus's dream of reaching out to people with God's love will live on."

Taffie's father went to work at the stove, mixing up a batch of taffy. "I think I'm just tired, honey. Been at this a long, long time. And. . ."

"And what?"

He turned and sighed. "I know you have sugar running through your veins. More than your sisters, for sure. I can sense it. But you. . ."

What about me?

"Sometimes I feel like you're just here out of obligation, and I feel guilty about that. Would you be off pursuing your dreams if I hadn't bamboozled you into staying?"

"Pop." Taffie took a seat. "You didn't bamboozle me. I love the shop. I love candy making. It's in my blood. I can't speak for the other girls, but I love most everything about being here. Only one thing concerns me—the business stuff. The kind of things we're dealing with today. But when it comes to the customers. . ." Taffie couldn't help but smile. "When it comes to the customers, I'm in my element."

"You are, at that." He shrugged. "And honey, God has a plan for the rest of it. I know He does. One that does not involve selling out to a tight-fisted casino owner with an eye for someone else's property."

"Amen." She whispered the word, feeling the truth of it all the way down to her bones. With the Lord's help, they would get through this. Well, the Lord and one very handsome appliance repairman.

∂

Ryan wrapped up a repair job at eleven forty, then headed to the boardwalk to meet with Taffie and her parents. He was half-tempted to call and check on his father. Pop had stayed home this morning, complaining of not feeling well. The first repair job had gone well without him, but Ryan was concerned. He'd have to remember to phone home after visiting with the Carinis. Right now, he had a thousand ideas for the candy shop, rolling around in his brain. He couldn't seem to control them.

Minutes later, he stood inside the candy store, the Carini family sitting in rapt awe as he spoke. "I've been giving this a lot of thought." He paced the room, ready to lay out a plan of action; one he hoped would breathe new life into Carini's Confections.

"Like what?" Mr. Carini sat on the edge of his seat. Ryan could read the anxiety in his expression.

"Well, as you've mentioned, your business does well during the summer. You've been trying to work double-time to increase summer sales so that you can lay low during the off-season."

"Right."

"What if the off-season didn't have to be an off-season? What if you could bring in the same amount of money year-round?"

"I don't know. . ." Taffie didn't look convinced. "Remember, I told you we tried to keep the shop open through last year's winter season without much luck."

"Well, hear me out. I've been thinking you should work from holiday to holiday, drawing in customers with different products during different seasons. I asked my mom for some suggestions. She's really good at this kind of thing."

"Your mom?" Taffie smiled. "Keeping it in the family?"

"Of course!"

"What did you come up with?" Taffie's mother asked.

"Well, think about it. It's August now. Almost September. Most of our sunbathers have already headed back to school, back to work, and so forth. But fall is coming, and with the fall comes all sorts of possibilities." Excitement grew as he laid out his ideas. "There are so many different types of candies—and coffees, for that matter—that make me think of fall. Think of what they serve at fall festivals. . .popcorn balls, caramel corn, candy apples, and so forth. You could decorate the window with fall colors and promote a new coffee flavor each month, something to draw in an older crowd. That's what you need to get through the off-season, anyway—an older clientele."

"Never thought of that," Mrs. Carini said. "But you're right. We count on the kids during the summer, but it never occurred to me that we could keep things going without them during the winter."

"Well, speaking of winter. . ." Ryan smiled with anticipation. "Wait till you hear what I'm thinking of for the Christmas season. Along with coffees, you could serve wassail and hot apple cider. And you could put a huge Christmas tree in the window, decorated with the seasonal candies and cookies you're featuring. My mom suggested old-fashioned ribbon candy, and some sort of homemade candy cane. Maybe a new flavor each Christmas. And think of the possibilities with the taffy. Focus on Christmas flavors—cinnamon and peppermint. You could drape the tree in garland made of wrapped taffies. . .or even the ribbon candy."

"Wow, you have been thinking ahead." Taffie's face lit up in a smile. "What else were you thinking?"

"Well, if you really want to go with something different, why not chocolate fondue? You can provide all sorts of things for dipping—marshmallows, pretzels, dried fruits, cookies. And over in the coffee area"—he gestured—"why not sell Christmas-themed coffees and flavored hot chocolates? Keep it looking and sounding like grown-up fun. So what if the children don't come? If you provide Internet access—and that's something I've been wanting to talk to you about, anyway—you will attract business people who are looking for a nice, quiet seaside setting where they can check e-mail, work on projects, and so forth."

"Internet." Mr. Carini shook his head. "What is the world coming to. . . people coming to a candy store to work."

"Nothing wrong with that," Ryan said. "They've got to work someplace. Why not let them take care of their business in a fun, safe environment, where you serve them themed sweets for every season? And speaking of which, I have so many ideas for Valentine's Day. I've been thinking about all the chocolates you could sell, and how we could promote them on the Web site. You know that Internet traffic is your best bet for surviving the coldest months."

"Hmm. The Web site. . ." Taffie shook her head. "It needs a lot of work."

"I know, but that's Vic's specialty. He'd be amazing at getting it up and running like a true marketplace. He could add a shopping-cart feature. He's also great with getting the site into the bigger search engines, which would be helpful. Before long, if things go the way I think they will—the way I pray they will—you will be shipping candies all over the country, especially during Christmas and Valentine's. So, if things slow down at the store, you'll still be plenty busy shipping sweets all over the country. All over the world!"

"Wow! You're full of ideas." Mrs. Carini gave him a confident look.

"What about this one?" He grinned. "It's just something I'm rolling around in my head. Tangie is an actress, right? And a singer."

"Right."

"What if you offered singing valentines? People buy a box of chocolates and for an additional small fee, their loved one gets an impromptu visit from Tangie, dressed in tuxedo, white shirt, and red bow tie, crooning a love song?"

"Heavens! Great idea!" Mrs. Carini exclaimed. "I think she'll love it."

"If she can work it into her schedule," Taffie added. "But she never passes up an opportunity to perform, so I think she'd like it."

"And it will be a good way to put a little cash in her pockets, too." Ryan nodded, trying to remember what he'd left out. "But if it doesn't work out for her to do it, why not Taffie? She's got a great voice."

"Who. . .me?" Taffie paled. "I can't imagine. . . ."

"Just think on it." He shifted gears, unable to control his enthusiasm. "Oh, I wanted to tell you my ideas for Easter. Why not design a specialty Easter egg every year? The Carini's Easter egg. You could have an unveiling in your front window—kind of like the big department stores do at Christmas. Make it something the locals anticipate, especially the children."

"I love window design," Taffie said. "Sounds like fun. And I like the surprise element."

"Me, too," her mother echoed.

"What about Easter baskets, all made up with homemade goodies?" Ryan suggested. "Have you ever done that before?"

"No, to be honest, we usually don't open the shop till mid-April, and Easter is already past. But I think it's a good idea. Wish we'd thought of it sooner."

"They could be shipped, as well. You could target folks who grew up in Atlantic City, but now live elsewhere. Give them a piece of their past in an Easter basket. That sort of thing."

"Yes, and what about an Easter egg hunt for the kids?" Mrs. Carini threw in. "That might be fun. And maybe we could plan a special time where the kids could come and decorate their own candy eggs. If we promoted it, we could fill this place with children."

"Yes, and I've been thinking about the building, itself," Ryan moved from one area of the room to the next, taking in every square inch of it. "The colors in here need to be punched up a bit. That said, I think the different areas of the shop need to look vastly different. On the adult side"—he pointed to the coffee area—"you could do something really cool and sleek. On the kid's side"—he pointed to the candy counter and the ice cream area—"play off the colors of the taffy. Bright colors. Interesting designs. And give them something to do while they're here. List on your menu or on the walls, the names of famous people who've eaten here. And what about candy trivia? People love that sort of thing. It would be conversational."

"Ryan, you surprise me." Tears sprang to Mrs. Carini's eyes. "This is all so much to take in, but I know you're right. We've just done things the way we've always done them. But it's time to look ahead."

"Oh, that reminds me. . ." He looked at the candy counter. "I notice you sell a few sugar-free items, but I think you'd draw a more adult crowd if you came up with a few more. And the packaging. . ."

"What about it?"

"Taffie and I were talking about this not long ago. When people come to Carini's, you're taking them on a journey back in time. So your packaging needs to have an old-fashioned vintage feel to it. Same with your Web site. I'll talk to Vic about it, but I feel sure he can come up with something that's just right."

Taffie shook her head. "Ryan, you're amazing."

"I have a thousand other ideas," he said with a shrug, "but I don't want to overwhelm you. You can offer specialty candies for weddings, bridal showers, baby showers, that sort of thing. Promote yourselves to the hotels, even. They're always hosting corporate events. And then there's Veteran's Day."

"Veteran's Day?" Mr. Carini looked at him in dazed curiosity.

"Sure. Why not pick a certain candy to sell for that month, and give a percentage of your proceeds to the Veteran's Hospital? That way, the people wouldn't just be eating candy—a personal pleasure—they would be giving back in some small way, as well."

"Ryan, you are a wonder," Mrs. Carini said. "But I have to say I'm absolutely exhausted, just listening to your ideas. My head is spinning."

"I only wish I could do more." He took a seat, wishing he could speak his heart. If he had his druthers, he'd quit the appliance repair business altogether and just help people with things like this. He'd— Just then, his cell phone rang, interrupting his thoughts. Ryan glanced down, recognizing his pop's number at once. He answered to discover another repair job awaited.

With a heavy heart, he turned away from the excitement of untapped dreams... and toward his more dismal reality.

Chapter 17

After leaving Carini's, Ryan pointed his work van in the direction of Mama Mia's Italian Restaurant on the south end of town. Pop had mentioned a walk-in refrigerator in need of repair. Not a small job. And from what his father said, a complicated situation, one he couldn't tackle alone, particularly since he wasn't feeling well.

As Ryan contemplated what lay ahead, he felt the joy leak out of him, much like air out of a balloon. Working with Taffie and her parents on a plan of action had been exhilarating. But now. . .

Well, now he had to get back to the real world.

He arrived at the restaurant in short order and found his pop in a quieter-than-usual mood as they worked alongside each other. "I missed you this morning," Ryan said after several minutes of silence from his father's end. "Feeling better now?"

"Not really." His pop gazed at him with tired eyes. "It's times like this I truly don't know what I'd do without you."

Ryan drew in a deep breath to keep from saying anything he might later regret.

"Had a hard time sleeping last night," Pop continued. "Just worn out today. And I woke up with a terrible headache, which isn't helping any."

"What's up with that?"

The wrinkles in his father's brow deepened. "I hate to admit it, but I've been worried about Vic and Mallory. Your mom told me they're talking about separating again." He rubbed at his brow, then shrugged.

"No way." At once Ryan's thoughts shifted to Casey. Poor little thing. Would she ever know the peace of mind that a solid parental relationship would bring?

"I don't know what's wrong with that brother of yours," Pop said with a sigh. "I didn't raise him to put his own needs above those of his family. Not sure where he came up with the idea that he's the one that matters most. And why he's turned his back on his faith." Here, Ryan's father's eyes misted over. "It's beyond me. Surely he can see that God is the only one who has the answers to these sorts of problems."

"I know Vic is going to come around. We can't stop praying." Ryan did his best to muster up a smile. "And I know you, Pop. You take the same fix-it mentality you use in the appliance business and apply it in other areas of your life. I'm the same way. But in this case, it's truly between Vic and God. There's nothing you can do but pray."

"That's why I couldn't sleep last night," his father explained. "Your mom was a little, well, weepy. I'm surprised you didn't hear us from your room upstairs. We ended up having quite a prayer meeting."

"Ah. No, I slept like a log. But I did notice your light was on before I headed up to bed. Sorry you woke up not feeling well, though."

"Oh well. I'll sleep better tonight."

They went back to work, finally locating the source of the problem. "We're going to have to come back tomorrow to wrap this up," Ryan said. "I'll stop by and pick up the parts we need. What time tomorrow morning, Pop?"

"I guess. . ." His father tried to stand, but stumbled. He reached for his right leg, shaking it. "S–strange. Must've f–fallen asleep." Finally aright, he seemed to falter.

"Pop?" Ryan looked his way, alarmed. "You okay?"

"W–what? I–I–" His dad looked dazed, disoriented. "I'd better s–sit down a m–minute. Stood up too f–fast or something. M–mighty dizzy."

Ryan's heart leaped into his throat as he guided his father to a chair. Something was up, for sure, and it was more than a simple case of exhaustion or a headache.

"Pop, I think it'd better—" He never got to say the words *call 911* before his father slumped over in the chair. Ryan reached out to grab him before he slid to the floor. Everything seemed to be happening in slow motion. "Pop? Pop!" When no response came, Ryan called out to the restaurant manager, who appeared in a flash. The fellow took one look and went into a panic. Ryan thrust the cell phone into the man's hand, stammered, "Call 911!" then promptly began to pray. "Oh God. . .please help my father!"

&.

Taffie waited till the crowd cleared at the end of the afternoon to pick up her cell phone to call Ryan. She could hardly wait to thank him for his kindness earlier in the day. Oh, and what amazing ideas he'd had! She and her parents had already talked through many of them, coming up with a plan.

She punched in his number and waited in anticipation to hear his voice on the other end of the line. When his voice mail kicked in, she sighed. Oh well. A message was better than nothing.

"Hey, Ryan. Just wanted to say thanks for all your suggestions today. You've definitely put the rainbow back up in the cloudy sky for my parents. And I can't even begin to tell you how happy I am. And how hopeful. I, um. . . I'm so happy God brought you into our lives." She glanced at the clock, then continued. "Listen, I'm going to be in class after I leave here, but I'll be done around nine. Give me a call tonight, if you can. When McKinley shows back up with his client, I want to be fully prepared to explain our plan of action. In fact, I'd feel better if you were here with us when they came. If you don't mind, I mean."

She paused a moment, wondering if there was enough recording time left to sneak in a final phrase or two. "Have I told you how much I appreciate you? I—I think you're great. And I—" A beep suddenly ended the call and she hung up, feeling like a giddy schoolgirl as she thought through what she might've said: *I think you're the best thing since rocky road. I think you put the dream in Dreamsicle. I think I could write a song right here and now, and dance around the room, making up my own choreography as I go along.*

After a deep, heartfelt sigh, she went back to work. A few minutes later, as she closed up the shop, her mother approached. "You're singing again."

"I am?" She paused to think about it. "Yeah, I guess I was. Didn't even realize it. What was I singing?"

" 'Big Rock Candy Mountain.' " Her mother pointed up to the speakers in the ceiling. "It's been playing for the last couple of minutes, but you're louder than the music."

"No way."

"Yep. Just thought it was worth mentioning. Falling for Ryan has brought out your musical gifts. He's right about that singing valentine thing. You could do it, no problem. We just have to come up with the right songs."

"Oh, I don't think I—"

"You know, I can hardly wait to see what happens after the two of you get married and start having children. You'll probably end up in Nashville, cutting an album together."

"Mom." Taffie laughed. "You're funny. And who said anything about getting married? Ryan and I are just—"

"Perfect for each other."

"Well, but he's—"

"An amazing man of God who cares about his faith, his family, and my daughter."

"Mom." Taffie couldn't hide the smile. "You're quite a matchmaker."

"With your sisters both away in school, who else do I have to match up?" her mother asked. "Besides, this time I've hit the nail on the head. Ryan is perfect for you."

"Well, I can't say that for sure yet," Taffie acknowledged, "but I can say he's been good for all of us. Those ideas of his were clever, to say the least."

"Clever enough that Pop and I are already talking about our trip. I've told him to start packing. We leave in three weeks."

"Okay, so tell me all about it." Taffie took a seat at the table, finally ready to hear her parents' plans in detail.

"Ooo! Hold on and I'll get the brochures." Her mother disappeared into the office, returning a few minutes later with a manila envelope stuffed full to the brim.

Just then, Pop entered from the back room. "Finished that last batch of cherry taffy. Guess I'll call it quits for the day." He looked at the brochures and his eyes began to sparkle. "Are you two talking about what I think you're talking about?"

"Yep." Taffie's mother grinned and gestured for him to sit beside them. "I'm telling Taffie about our trip out west to see the cowboys."

"Cowboys?"

"Well, modern-day cowboys." Her mother pulled out a brochure for a museum in New Mexico. "Ruidoso. It's one of the towns with several RV parks. And you should see the place we're going to be staying at when we get to Bryce Canyon."

"Bryce Canyon?"

"Utah," her father explained. "We'll stop by the Grand Canyon on the way, but from what we've heard, Bryce Canyon is even more breathtaking, especially as the sun is setting."

Her mother pulled out another brochure, this one with an exquisite photo on the front. "If a picture paints a thousand words, then what do you have to say about this?"

"Wow." Taffie had never even imagined anything so beautiful, and told them so.

"And then there are the redwoods in northern California, and the Lewis and Clark Expedition Trail in Idaho, Montana, and Washington." Pop's voice grew more excited with every word. "And we're talking about hitting a few Indian reservations along the way."

"There's this place in Washington State that does historical reenactments," her mother explained. "Doesn't that sound like fun?"

"Um, sure." Taffie leaned back against her seat. "I just have one question."

Both parents looked at her at once, echoing, "Yes?"

"Are you ever coming back?"

Her mother laughed. "Well, sure. For the wedding. I wouldn't miss it for the world."

"Wedding? Is there something I need to know? Has Candy met someone?"

"No, silly."

"Tangie? 'Cause if she has, remember, she's fickle. She might say she's in love today, but—"

"Taffie, I'm talking about you and Ryan. Dad and I have been praying, and we're convinced he's the one for you. So, we'll be home in plenty of time for the wedding, but we think it would be better if you planned it for next summer sometime. That would be most convenient for us."

"Mom." Taffie dropped her head in her palms and began to rant—a la Broadway style—about her mother's ability to twist the conversation back to marriage. "There's not going to be a wedding anytime soon, so don't get your hopes up. He might be the right one for me, but. . ."

"But what?" Pop reached over to kiss her on the cheek. "If he's the right one, he's the right one. You two go together like. . .like marshmallows and almonds in rocky road."

"Like. . .like mint and chocolate chip," her mom threw in. "Like peanut butter and chocolate."

"Stop, stop! I get it!" Taffie laughed. "I'm going to put on ten pounds, thinking about how perfect Ryan and I are for each other."

"He would still love you anyway,"

Love? Who said anything about love? Taffie flashed a smile, then got back to closing up the shop, humming a happy tune.

Chapter 18

Ryan paced the hallway of the emergency room. His mother leaned against the wall, exhaustion showing in her red-rimmed eyes. In the two hours since their arrival, his father had been examined by countless doctors. "How long is this going to take?" His patience wore thinner as each minute ticked by.

His mother's tears were the only response he got. He reached over and slipped an arm around her shoulder. "I'm sorry, Mom. I need to stay calm, I know."

"You're doing fine, son. In fact, I don't know what I'd do without you boys. I could never make it through this alone."

"You won't have to."

"I just feel so. . .guilty." She dissolved into tears, then finally came up for air with an explanation. "His blood pressure was elevated last night, and I insisted on talking about Vic and Mallory. I think I got him worked up." She dabbed at her eyes with a tissue. "This would never have happened if I had just rolled over and gone to sleep. I should have known better."

"We don't know that, Mom. And besides, you can't hide things from Pop. He had to have known things between them were bad again. You can't slip anything by him."

"I know, but—"

"There are no buts. We just move forward from here," Ryan said. "We'll get through this as a family."

"You're just like your pop," his mother said. "Wanting to make everything right again."

Even when I can't. Even when things are totally out of my control.

Just then, Vic and Mallory rounded the corner. Together. A sense of relief washed over Ryan right away. Now, if only they could lay their differences aside to walk through this valley without fighting with each other, perhaps they could present a unified front as a family.

"How is he?" Mallory's wrinkled brow and tear-stained eyes showed her concern.

"He's had another stroke. That's all we know for sure. Worse than the first one," Ryan said. He wanted to add *much worse,* but didn't, because he wanted to keep his mother's spirits up. In his gut, however, he feared the worst. Pop had pulled through the first one, but this one was bad.

"Did he ever come to?" Vic asked.

Ryan shook his head. "No. They've taken him for an MRI and have already drawn blood. Lots of it. And you wouldn't believe how many doctors they've sent in to examine him. It's been like a revolving door in his room."

"What are they thinking?" Vic took a seat, and looked up with concern in his eyes.

"They're suspecting a blood clot that blocked the blood flow to his brain." Ryan shrugged. "But we don't know for sure yet. They're still running tests."

"Anyone heard from Luke?" Vic asked.

"He's here. He went to get a soda."

"Who's watching Casey?" Ryan's mother asked.

"My mom," Mallory explained as she sat down next to Vic. "And she'll keep her all night, too, so we're not in any hurry to leave. We can stay here with you." She looked up at Vic hesitantly. "At least, I can."

"I can, too," Vic added. He drew near to Mallory and gave her a look that could almost be described as endearing. He reached over and took her hand, giving it a squeeze. "We're in this. . .together."

&

Taffie curled up in bed with her journal at her side. She tried not to fret over the fact that she'd now left two messages on Ryan's phone and he hadn't returned them. On the other hand, it was Wednesday night. Surely he'd spent the evening at church, leading worship. Likely he'd call her in the morning.

Just then, the phone rang, startling her. She reached for it, her heart racing a mile a minute. Just before answering, she glanced down at the caller ID.

"Candy!" She answered with joy leading the way. "I can't believe it."

"Believe it. I finally slowed down long enough to call."

"How are things in Tucson? Are you jetting all over the world?"

"Hardly. But I am inching toward the goal. I'll have my pilot's license soon. Then comes the hard part. It's a tough road to go from private to commercial, but I'm determined."

"What are your plans?"

"After I get my commercial license, I hope to eventually get hired on with Eastway so that I can fly out of Newark. That way I can stay close to home. Being here in Arizona makes me feel like I'm on the other side of the world. And I'm so busy, I can hardly stop long enough to check my e-mail or make a call. I miss my sisters."

"Aw. I miss you, too. And you know Tangie. She misses us when she's not in love with whatever leading man she happens to be starring alongside."

Candy laughed. "You've hit that nail on the head. But speaking of falling in love. . ."

"What? Have you met a handsome pilot or something?"

"Well, a few." Candy laughed. "But everyone is so focused on the task at hand, there's little time for romance. Besides, that's not where I was headed."

"What? Something about Tangie I need to know?"

"No, goofy. Mom tells me *you've* met someone."

Aha. The real reason for her call. Taffie groaned. "She's a snitch. I wanted to tell you myself."

"Tell me about him. All she said was you two were a match made in heaven. Then she mentioned something about how she's finally going to get to see Pike's Peak and Rocky Mountain National Park."

Taffie sighed. "Yeah. They're leaving on their extended tour of the western United States in a few weeks if Ryan and I can set this new plan in action for the shop." She proceeded to tell her sister all his suggestions. She paused and explained each one in detail, remembering the look on his face as he'd shared his ideas. What progress they'd made in just one day.

"It all sounds great," Candy agreed, after hearing the particulars. "But you haven't told me about *him* yet. What's he like? Mom says he's a keeper, and I know what that means. He's got a good relationship with the Lord. But that doesn't tell me anything about what he looks like."

"Oh, Candy." Taffie paused, trying to figure out where to begin. "He's tall, dark, and handsome."

"As in, Hollywood handsome?"

"Well, yeah, but not Hollywood self-absorbed. He doesn't even seem to realize how great he is."

"But he is?"

"Oh yes. He's one of those people that the love of God just shines through. You can see it in his eyes. He's the real deal. Oh, and get this. He's the worship leader at his singles group. And he has the most adorable seven-year-old niece. You should see him with her. They're great together. And his parents. . ." She went off on a tangent about how similar their two families were. Before long, Candy was laughing.

"Well, you'd better claim him quick, or I'm going to grab him up when I get home."

"No you're not."

"Kidding. But seriously. . .what happens next? It's not like in high school where you could say you were going steady. You're not wearing his class ring or anything like that."

"No, but I feel like a kid when he's around, that's for sure." Taffie couldn't seem to stop the giggles. "And I sing now."

"You do not."

"Yeah, I do. Love songs. Worship songs. Mom says I sing all day at the shop, but I don't really think about it."

"Well, you know what the Bible says," Candy reminded her. " 'A cheerful heart is good medicine.' So, you must have a cheerful heart."

"And it's just what the doctor ordered," Taffie admitted. "I guess I was ripe for this and just didn't realize it. I'd put my love life on the back burner to handle things at the shop." She considered telling her sister just how burdened she'd been with taking over the store, but opted not to. Why put a damper on things now, when she was finally starting to see that light at the end of the proverbial tunnel?

Candy's voice interrupted her ponderings. "So, the doctor ordered up a tall, dark, and handsome male to cure the blues, huh?" She laughed. "Looks like I'm due for a trip to the doctor myself. I've been mighty lonely out here. All this talk of good-looking guys is making me a little jealous."

"Well, come home and see us sometime," Taffie responded. "Ryan has a single brother."

"Hmm. Don't think I want to be fixed up on any blind dates, thank you very much. But I will be there for the wedding. I understand we're wearing pink."

"Wait, wedding? Pink?" Taffie sat straight up, puzzled. "What are you talking about?"

"Mom said Ryan's niece called her on the night you two went on your first date and told her she wants to wear pink at the wedding."

"Good grief. Are you serious? Casey actually called the shop?"

"Yep. Told Mom she's got her heart set on cotton candy pink. And something about a tiara. I understand she was even specific about the length of her gown. So, keep all that in mind as you make your plans."

"Plans? What plans?" *Right now, I can't even get Ryan to answer my calls, so don't jump the gun with this whole wedding thing.*

"Oh, I've got to go. Got a call coming in. But take care of yourself, sis. And take care of Mom and Dad before they gallop off to meet the cowboys. Give them my love."

With that, Candy was gone. Back to her fast-paced world of flying hither, thither, and yon.

And Taffie. . .well, as she rolled over in the bed, she pondered the many things Candy had shared. Had Casey really called the shop and insisted on pink? If so, why hadn't Mom said anything? And did everyone think they were a match made in heaven. . .after just one date?

Did she?

A dozen thoughts rolled around in Taffie's mind at once. . . .

Cotton candy pink dresses.

Singing valentines.

Salt water taffy.

Specially designed Easter eggs.

Bryce Canyon under a setting sun.

A sweet-as-sugar kiss from a handsome appliance repairman.

Hmm. All such lovely thoughts. With a love song consuming her heart, Taffie finally drifted off to sleep.

Chapter 19

Ryan walked the hallway outside his father's hospital room, and prayed. In the days since his father's stroke, the news had gone from bad to worse.

"It's going to be months before your father is himself again," the doctor had warned. "Your family needs to gear up for a lengthy recovery."

Lengthy recovery. Even now, as he paced, Ryan couldn't imagine what they would do. Already, he was behind on repairs. With Luke's help, he could probably get caught up, but who would stay at the hospital with Mom? Vic and Mallory had been great, coming and going as much as possible, but with both of them working—and with Casey to tend to—they wouldn't be able to make sure Mom's needs were met, at least not full-time.

Ryan continued to walk back and forth as he mentally replayed every instant of that awful day at the Italian restaurant. *I should have seen the signs. Should have acted quicker once I realized what was happening. Instead, I. . .*

He shook his head, then gave himself a mental scolding. *I should've told Pop to rest. To go home. To let me take charge.* Instead, he'd been so busy thinking about his love life, so overwhelmed with excitement about the Carinis' new business plan, that he'd completely overlooked his father's physical issue. And now that issue would have life-altering effects. Ryan forced back the tears as he contemplated the severity of the doctor's words: "When the stroke occurred, blood flow to the brain was interrupted. Brain damage took place during that critical time period."

Brain damage. Just the words sent him reeling. Business issues aside. . .would Pop ever be the same? Would he laugh with them and be able to share in family get-togethers? Could he play with Casey and any grandchildren yet to come? Would he be able to get around the house? Make it up and down stairs?

"Son? Are you all right?" Ryan turned as he heard his mother's loving voice. He noticed Dr. Loring standing next to her.

"Oh, I'm. . .I'm just thinking."

"I was hoping to have a few words with you both," Dr. Loring explained. "There's a room just down the hall where we can talk."

Ryan nodded, then followed in silence behind his mom and the doctor. They'd already had two or three of these conferences with various doctors. Had something else happened?

As they settled into chairs in the tiny conference room, the doctor began to speak. "Your father will have a long haul. The paralysis on his right side could last for weeks. Or months, even. His ability to speak has been affected, as you've noticed. The muscles in his tongue and palate are weakened, but a speech therapist will help with that."

"So, he'll talk normally again?" Ryan asked.

"I can't guarantee that." The doctor gazed at Ryan and his mother with compassion in his eyes. "I don't want to give you false hope. Mr. Antonelli has been through a life-changing event. And while it's possible he could make a full recovery, it's more likely he'll only come back to about the two-thirds point."

"Two-thirds?" Ryan raked his fingers through his hair.

"What sort of disabilities?" his mother asked, her face turning pale.

"Some will be more obvious than others," the doctor explained. "The speech issues will take time. But long-term complications could include behavioral problems, memory problems, and even emotional issues. We've seen patients in his age group struggle with serious mood swings, even after physical issues dissipate. They cry without warning or laugh uncontrollably. They truly have no control over these behaviors."

Ryan took note of the tears that welled up in his mother's eyes as the doctor spoke. He fought to keep them from rising in his own.

"We'll keep him here in the hospital a few more days to make sure he's out of danger, then we'll transfer him to a rehabilitation facility."

"Rehabilitation facility? For how long?" Ryan's mom spoke, tears leaking out the corners of her eyes.

"Likely several weeks. But even after he returns home, Mr. Antonelli will be on a daily regimen of medications, physical therapy, diet, and so forth. I can arrange for a physical therapist to come to your home. He or she will play an integral role. We really are talking about a lengthy process here, and I need you to be prepared for that." The creases in the doctor's brow deepened.

"What about his work?" Ryan asked. "Will he ever. . ."

The doctor thumbed through his paperwork before asking, "Your father is self-employed, is that right?"

"Yes." Ryan swallowed hard.

The doctor shook his head. "As I mentioned before, I don't want to get your hopes up. If I give you the worst-case scenario, then you'll be pleased when things go better. At this time, I'd suggest early retirement."

"Early retirement? But how will he. . . How will he pay the bills? If he stops working, the money stops coming in. If the money stops. . ."

Doctor Loring looked at Ryan's mother, gently placing his hand on her shoulder. "The best thing for him right now is TLC. He needs his family. He doesn't need any additional stresses of any kind."

He doesn't need any stresses of any kind.

The words played themselves out over and over again as Ryan left the conference area and returned to his father's room once again. It ripped his heart out to look at the man—once so strong—who lay still and quiet in the bed, strapped to IVs. Ryan reached down and kissed his ailing father on the forehead, then whispered, "I love you, Pop."

Then, overcome with emotion, he dropped into a chair and began to pray.

❧

Taffie tried one last time to call Ryan. She couldn't understand his silence over the past few days. Had she somehow offended him? Her mind reeled as she thought back through their last conversations. No, they'd ended things on a positive note. So, why the silence on his end? Didn't he realize Mr. McKinley would return in just a few days to confront her family? Didn't he know she needed to solidify a plan of action before then?

Taffie felt sick at the sudden possibility that something had happened to Ryan. It wasn't like him not to call. With that in mind, she pulled his business card out of her wallet. . .the same one he'd given her that first day. She located the company's e-mail address and quickly composed a note to send him. *If this doesn't do the trick, I'm going to drive to their office.* She looked at the card once more, taking note of the address. *Hmm.* Looked like their office was in a residential area. Might be awkward if she showed up at his house, looking for him. Would that be too forward?

She began to pace, thinking things through. He'd kissed her. Kissed her. And told her that he cared. Surely he wouldn't mind if she showed up at his place of business, after all they'd been through together. Besides, they had unfinished business to take care of. Her parents wanted a solid plan of action. And they wanted her to hire Ryan as a marketing consultant. But none of that was possible if he wouldn't communicate with her.

She paced the shop and began to pray. For what, she wasn't quite sure. But Taffie knew in her heart that something prayer-worthy had transpired, and she wanted to be quick to respond.

"Lord, I don't know what's going on, but You do. I ask for Your will to be done—in my life and in Ryan's."

Her desire to fix the situation slowly dissipated. Surely, if she could just continue to trust God with the unknown, He would reveal His perfect will.

Oh, if only her impatience didn't get in the way!

Chapter 20

Ryan left the hospital with a heavy heart. He glanced down at his cell phone, noticing he'd missed several calls. Listening to his many voice messages, he couldn't help but groan. Seemed every place in town needed a repairman. Why now? The timing couldn't possibly be worse.

Determined not to let his emotions get the better of him, he pointed the van toward the parts store. He'd better get a move on. Get back to business. What else could he do?

He continued listening to the voice messages as he drove. Buried between a frantic call from the owner of Mama Mia's and a request for service from a local day care, Ryan found a message from Taffie. Just the sound of her voice lifted his spirits. Somehow, in the midst of the chaos, he'd forgotten to call her.

His heart ached, thinking about it. He immediately punched in her number and waited for her to answer.

"Hello? Ryan?" Her voice—sweeter than anything he'd heard in days—gave him reason to hope again.

"Taffie, it's—it's me. I'm sorry, I—"

"I've been so worried about you. I called several times and even sent an e-mail."

"I'm sorry. I've had my phone on mute for the past three days, and haven't been near the computer to check my e-mail. I—"

"What's happened?"

"It's my pop. He's had a stroke. A bad one." A lump rose up in Ryan's throat, making it difficult to continue. Though he'd never been one to cry—especially in front of a lady—he couldn't seem to control the tears.

"Oh, Ryan. I knew something had happened. I just knew it. Where are you right now? Are you at the hospital? What can I do to help?"

"I'm just leaving. I have repairs waiting. I'm going to try to squeeze in as many as I can over the next few days while Pop's in the hospital. But they're going to transfer him to a rehab, and once that happens. . ." He drew in a deep breath, not knowing how to continue. He had no idea what would happen at that point. What did you do when life was abruptly interrupted by tragedy? Pop's last stroke had been minimal in comparison to this. Why, he'd scarcely been out of work for a couple of weeks that time around. This time. . .no, he wouldn't think about that.

"Have you called your church?" Taffie asked.

"Yes. Pastor Billings has been at the hospital with us through the worst of it, and several of my friends from the singles ministry have stopped by. And my mom's friends. . ." He shook his head. "They're putting together a committee to bring food by the house, that sort of thing."

"That's what the church is for," Taffie said. "I'm sure the minute my mom finds out, she'll be right there with them, so prepare yourself. She's liable to become your mother's closest companion. At least, until my parents leave on their trip to the wild, Wild West."

"That would be great. But. . ." He paused for a moment. "I miss you."

"I miss you, too." He heard the catch in her voice. "And we're going to get through this together. What time do you think you'll be back up at the hospital? I want to come and be with you. I'm free in the evenings."

"What about your class?"

"It ends this week. And guess what."

"What?"

"I'm finally getting the numbers thing down. Pop's been working with me in his spare time, and it's starting to make sense. I might not be a marketing strategist, but I think I can take care of the books. . .eventually, anyway."

As soon as she spoke the word *Pop*, a lump rose in Ryan's throat. Would his pop ever be able to work again?

"A—are you there?" Taffie asked.

"Yes. Sorry, I was just thinking about my father. I've been so worried about him."

"He's going to pull through this, Ryan. We won't stop praying until he does. And I'm going to be there with you. I—if you want me to be."

"Oh, I want you to be." How he'd made it through the last three days without her now seemed an impossibility. In that moment, Ryan made up his mind. . . he would never walk down another road without her. Not if he could help it, anyway.

&

The minute Taffie closed up the candy shop, she headed for the hospital. All the way there, she prayed for Ryan's dad. Though she tried not to think about it, an occasional fear would try to take root in her mind. *What if something like this happened to one of my parents? What would I do?* Just as quickly, she fought to shove those troublesome thoughts aside.

Still, life was full of unexpected things—good and bad. And it all seemed mixed up together. For whatever reason, her mind shifted to the taffy mixture she'd stirred just hours prior. A mixture of sugar and salt, glycerin and cornstarch. Talk about opposing tastes and functions. And yet they somehow combined to create the perfect candy. Could life, with all of its goods and bads, end up just as sweet? Even when there were valleys to walk through. . .like the one the Antonellis now faced?

At once, she thought of Ryan, tried to imagine what he must be thinking, feeling. Her heart ached for him. On top of everything else, he had to go on with the business. Suddenly, all her prior worries about taking over the shop dissipated. In light of what Ryan was going through, her situation seemed easy. How could she possibly complain about anything work-related when he and his family faced such troubles?

Taffie arrived at the hospital in a prayerful state of mind and quickly made her way to the ICU area. She was relieved to discover Ryan had added her name to the visitors list. After checking in with the nurse, she tiptoed into the tiny room. Oddly—except for Mr. Antonelli, who lay quite still and silent—she found it empty. With the curtains drawn, the place was dark and still. Taffie inched her way toward the bed, noting the various IVs and monitors. A shiver ran down her spine as she contemplated his current condition.

She reached out a hand and placed it gently on his shoulder, then began to pray. "Lord," she whispered, "there are so many things I don't understand, but I trust You. Father, I pray for healing for Mr. Antonelli. Touch him, Lord. And be with his family."

The words no sooner escaped her lips, than she heard a sound behind her. She looked back to see Mrs. Antonelli with tears in her eyes. Taffie reached over and gave her a warm hug.

"I'm sorry I didn't come sooner," she whispered. "I just found out."

"The past few days have been such a blur. I'm sure we've overlooked calling so many people. We did remember to call the church, but I can't imagine who we might've left out."

"How are you doing?" Taffie asked.

The older woman shook her head. "I wish I could say I was a pillar of faith, but I'm—I'm struggling."

"Nothing to be ashamed of, there," Taffie said. "My heart goes out to you. And my mom wants you to know that she and Pop will come up tomorrow while I'm at the store. They want to help. And they're praying, of course. They've even called our church to put your husband's name on the prayer list."

"Thank you so much." Mrs. Antonelli walked to the edge of her husband's bed and gazed at him, then reached for a tissue. Dabbing her eyes, she bowed her head, and her shoulders began to shake as the sobbing—completely silent—began. Taffie drew near and reached for her hand.

"He's been in and out of consciousness. Wakes up long enough to gaze up at us, then falls back asleep again. But at least he's making progress. The doctors say it'll be slow going, but we're going to be here, to walk with him through this."

"Of course you are." Taffie gave her hand a squeeze. "And if ever there was a family that could pull together. . .well, I know you Antonellis have an amazing bond, and that's more important than ever now. Remember what the Bible says: One person can put a thousand to flight; two, ten thousand. Imagine, in a family your size, how many battles you can win. . .as long as you stick together."

"I know you're right." Mrs. Antonelli reached to wrap her in a tight hug, and they stood together for a moment until the door swung open and Vic and Mallory entered the room.

Mallory took one look at the two of them and her eyes widened. "Has something happened?"

"No, no." Mrs. Antonelli shook her head. "Don't fret. I'm just having a moment."

After a few minutes of quiet conversation, Mallory gestured for Taffie to join her in the hall. Once there, she poured out her heart. "I don't know what's going to happen to Mama Antonelli if he doesn't make it," she whispered. "And it's breaking my heart to watch this. For both of them."

"It's going to be a long haul, but she's a strong woman. God is going to see her through this." Taffie tried to sound reassuring.

"I know." Mallory took a seat on a nearby bench and leaned her forehead down into open palms. "Watching her makes me see just how much she loves him. It's amazing, really. She's—she's taught me so much about unconditional love. I've never seen anything like that. Ever. I—I want to be like that."

"You can be," Taffie said.

"I don't know," Mallory said. "I've got a stubborn streak a mile long. And I'm used to getting my own way." She shrugged and looked up, defeated. "It's been a long time since Vic and I have really focused on each other. We're both so. . . selfish."

"Our parents are from a generation that really understood sacrifice," Taffie explained. "I watched my grandpa pour himself out for others every day of his life. My pop's the same way. And my mom. They're just givers. And even though I haven't known Ryan's parents a long time, I can tell they're the same. You and me. . ." She sighed. "We were raised in a different day and age. We're part of the me-myself-and-I generation, hard as that is to admit. We're inundated with messages about living to please ourselves."

"Feels good in the moment," Mallory confessed, "but living for yourself doesn't work long-term. Ask me how I know. At the end of the day, you feel pretty empty. Especially when the person you love isn't there to walk you through it."

Taffie sat down next to her, working up the courage to ask a question. "Are you and Vic still separated?"

Mallory shrugged. "He's back at home, and we're going through the motions of being married—as much for his mom's sake as Casey's." Tears began to trickle down her cheeks. "We're together in the same house, but we're not a couple. Does that make any sense? We're like two strangers. Roommates.

Nothing more. Things are just. . .cold."

"Wow." Taffie nodded, though she had to wonder how such a thing was even possible.

"I'm tired of pretending." More tears coursed down Mallory's cheeks. "Tired of acting like everything's okay when it's not. And when I see Mama Antonelli—how she dotes on Vic's dad. How she loves him with every fiber of her being. . ."

"You want that for yourself?" Taffie asked.

"I—I do." Mallory nodded, then began to sob uncontrollably.

Just then, a male voice interrupted their private moment. "What is it? Is it Pop? Has something happened?"

Taffie looked up and saw Ryan standing there with fear in his eyes. She started to explain, but Mallory jumped in ahead of her.

"I'm sorry, Ryan. I was just confiding in Taffie." Mallory dabbed at her eyes with a tissue, then gazed with great kindness at Taffie. "I don't know why I poured all my problems out on you. I hardly know you."

"She's easy to get to know." Ryan joined them on the bench, reaching to take Taffie's hand. "And to know her is to love her."

Taffie looked at him, stunned. Did he just say *love*?

The word must've jolted Mallory, too. She looked at him with a hint of a smile through her tears. "*That's* what I'm talking about," she whispered. "I want to know what *that* feels like. I want it to be real. You can only go through the motions so long before reality hits."

"I'm going to be praying," Taffie assured her. "I know that God is in the restoration business. If you and Vic both seriously want Him to renew your relationship, He will do it. But you have to decide. . .once and for all. Make up your mind."

"Make up my mind?" Vic now stood in front of them with confusion etched in his brow. "What are we making up our minds about?"

"To fall in love all over again." Mallory looked up at him with a sheepish grin. "The happily-ever-after kind."

The tightness in his face seemed to melt away as she stood and wrapped herself in his arms. In that moment, as Taffie watched the couple embrace, her heart flooded with joy. If she could have choreographed a victory dance, she would have done so—right then and there.

Instead, she turned to face Ryan, who slipped an arm over her shoulders and drew her close. She rested in the comfort of his embrace, reflecting on his earlier words: *To know her is to love her.* Overwhelmed with joy, she reached up and pressed a gentle kiss on his cheek. In that moment, the reality of her feelings for him registered.

So this is what it feels like. . .to be in love.

Chapter 21

On Monday morning, just before ten o'clock, Taffie and her parents prepared themselves for the expected visit from Mr. McKinley and his client—the new owner of the Gold Dust Casino. They'd spent the better part of the weekend putting their plan for the candy shop down on paper. Not that they needed to show it to anyone, but it helped solidify things in Taffie's mind. She felt better, facing Mr. McKinley with a clear focus.

At five minutes till ten, Ryan arrived, looking winded, but happy.

"You made it." She raced to give him a hug, and he responded by holding her close, then planting a kiss on her brow. "How's your dad?"

"They're moving him to the rehab tomorrow. Then the real work begins." He looked around the shop. "I'm on time?"

"You are. They're not here yet." She pulled out the paper with the plan he'd helped put together, and he glanced over it, then nodded.

"Carini's has bright days ahead. Just don't let them convince you otherwise, okay?" Ryan looked deeply into her eyes and she sighed—partly at his reassurance, and partly at the joy of knowing she could stay wrapped up in his embrace forever.

"Okay." Taffie whispered, and then kissed him on the cheek.

His face turned pink, but he quickly recovered and greeted her parents. They welcomed him, as always, with open arms and hearts. Taffie still relished the fact that her mom and pop had fallen for Ryan like they had.

At ten straight up, McKinley arrived, briefcase in hand and an elderly man at his side. Taffie couldn't help but wonder at the fellow's age. His yellow white hair and stooped physique took her by surprise. She'd expected a young, intimidating fellow—one with a steely-eyed glare. Someone tall and muscular. This man didn't appear the sort to steal anything from anyone. McKinley treated him like a king as he made introductions. "My client, Mr. Bruno."

"Frankie Bruno?" With a shocked expression on his face, Taffie's pop stared at the man. "Frankie, is—is that you?"

"It's me." The elderly man cracked a smile, his white moustache bobbing a bit. "Surprised you recognized me after all these years, Carl."

Taffie looked back and forth between the two men, confused. "Pop? You know this man?"

"Knew him as Uncle Frankie most of my growing up years," her father explained. "Your grandpa Gus's best friend." He gave Mr. Bruno an inquisitive look. "I heard you were doing well for yourself, but had no idea you were. . . well, that you were building casinos."

"Didn't start out that way," Frankie explained. "After my wife passed away, I found myself with too much time on my hands. My arcades were doing well, so I decided the next rung on the ladder would be the casino world."

"Ah." Taffie's Pop grew silent, staring at the older fellow with continued puzzlement on his face. He pulled a couple of the tables together and gestured for everyone to sit.

"So, you own the arcade?" Taffie asked, pulling up a chair. "Bruno's?"

"That's me."

"Bruno's is a landmark. . .like Carini's." Ryan's words were laced with curiosity. "I grew up going to Bruno's. Followed by a trip to the candy shop, of course."

"Bruno's will live on," the older man said. "But I've got my eye on a bigger prize these days. Hoping I could talk you Carinis into coming along for the ride."

Taffie opted to change the subject. "So, you're a native of Atlantic City?" She gave him an inquisitive look. Surely a man such as this would understand the importance of keeping the history of the boardwalk alive and well.

"I grew up here," Mr. Bruno explained. "Opened the arcade at about the same time your grandfather opened the candy shop." He looked around, his eyes sparkling. "Not much has changed at Carini's over the years."

Nor should it have to. She wanted to speak the words, but kept them to herself.

"I came into this store nearly every day in the forties and fifties," Mr. Bruno explained. "Consumed more sugar than most, thanks to your grandpa."

"You knew him well?" Taffie shook her head, still trying to put the pieces together in her head.

"There was a time when we were best friends. And my boys played with your father when he was little." He gazed at Taffie's father. "Do you remember my boys, Carl? David and Tony?"

"Of course." Taffie watched as her father rose to his feet and began to pace the room. "But, Bruno. . .you of all people knew my pop. Better than most. Knew his heart for this shop."

"Of course."

"Well, why would you try to take it away from us? Don't you realize this place meant everything to him?"

"I don't want to take it away." Frankie's eyes filled with what almost looked like compassion. "But I see what's become of the place. Your business is dwindling. It's just a matter of time before—"

"No, Mr. Bruno," Ryan interjected. "It's not just a matter of time. Carini's Confections is here for the long haul."

"Watch and see," Taffie threw in. "Go ahead and build your casino. We'll still be here."

"I don't mean this unkindly," Mr. Bruno said, turning his attention to Taffie's father, "but your pop was never a shrewd businessman. Always giving away more product than he sold. And giving money to the church. . .never made much sense to me. He had the perfect opportunity to make lots of money with Carini's, but he let his generosity get the better of him."

"It was never about the money for him." Taffie's father explained. "It was about the people. About relationships."

"About ministry," Taffie's mom threw in.

Mr. Bruno laughed, his aged voice cracking as he spoke. "You Carinis and your goodwill gestures. And all that God-talk. . .never made a lick of sense to me. Why trouble folks with all that talk about faith and such?"

Taffie caught a glimpse of the shock in her mother's eyes, but bit her tongue. No point further upsetting their guest with Grandpa Gus's ministry philosophy. Maybe the Lord would give them an opportunity to reach out to Mr. Bruno in the future, but today was not that day.

"I gave Gus my ideas and he refused them," Frankie continued, shaking his head. "I never could convince him to do the right thing."

"The right thing?" This time the words came from Ryan, who was starting to sound more than a little perturbed.

"Progress." Bruno's compassionate look morphed into something else altogether. "There are those of us who are looking at the future of Atlantic City, and then there are those who want to live in the past."

"It's not a matter of living in the past." Taffie's spine stiffened with each word. "We're perfectly capable of keeping up with the changing times. But we will not compromise who we are or what we believe. So you can take your offer, Mr. Bruno. . ."

She bit her tongue before continuing.

"What my daughter is trying to say," Pop interjected, "is that we're trusting God with the future—the future of both Atlantic City and Carini's Confections. We're looking to Him for direction. He knows far more about progress than any of your so-called experts."

"Only, *His* progress usually takes place in the heart," Taffie's mom was quick to throw in.

"So, you see, Mr. Bruno," Taffie explained, "we're perfectly happy right where we are."

"Not only that, you're about to see a year-round crowd at Carini's Confections," Ryan explained, the excitement in his voice intensifying. "This shop's business is about to double. Or triple. Just watch and see."

Go, Ryan! Taffie looked at him, her heart swelling with joy. In her mind's eye, Ryan was every bit the swashbuckling hero. No movie superhero could begin to compare.

"Humph." Mr. Bruno stood. "Foolishness must run in the family. Can't see as there's any use continuing this conversation." He looked over at the candy counter, his eyes narrowing. "You, um, you still sell strawberry taffy?"

"Of course." Taffie watched as her mother shifted gears.

"Best in town." Mr. Bruno's eyes twinkled.

"Best in the *country*." Taffie's mom went behind the counter and filled a small bag, then placed it in his hands. The older man reached for his wallet but she gestured for him to keep it in his pocket.

"This one's on us, Mr. Bruno," she explained. "And as for your comment that Gus gave away more than he should. . .well, at least he taught us the value of giving instead of taking. That's a lesson some have yet to learn."

Go, Mom!

Mr. Bruno shook his head, but accepted the gift. He muttered something under his breath to Mr. McKinley, and the two headed toward the door together.

When they were well out of view, Taffie looked at Ryan, stunned. "Did you just tell him we're going to double our business over the next year?"

"Actually, I think I said triple." His face turned red. "Hope I'm right."

"Of course you're right." Taffie's pop headed to the back room. "But in order for that to happen, I'm really going to have to further your education. Come with me, son. I'm going to teach you everything you ever wanted to know about running a candy shop."

ta.

"R–running a candy shop?" Ryan's eyes darted back and forth. "But I. . ." How could he tell Mr. Carini that he would likely be taking over his father's business? That he barely had time to travel from repair to repair? That any marketing he'd be doing for the Carinis would likely be done in the wee hours of the night after the real work was done?

Taffie looked his way, alarm in her eye. "Pop, I don't think this is the best time. Ryan's pop is still recovering, so his obligations are there. Not here. Besides, Ryan just offered to help us with the marketing, not the candy making. That's my specialty."

"I suppose you're right." Mr. Carini shrugged. "But whenever you change your mind, just let me know. There's nothing like stirring up a batch of taffy to get you in a happy frame of mind. In the meantime, get back up to the hospital. Tell your pop we're praying for him."

"And give him this." Taffie's mom rounded the corner with a large bag of candies. "Make sure he shares with your mom. And with Casey."

"Of course."

"Oh, one more thing, son." Mr. Carini placed a hand on his shoulder, and Ryan turned to look his way.

"Yes, sir?"

"Remember that conversation we had a while back. . .about fixing things?"

Ryan tried, but the memory eluded him. "When?"

"That day your brother was here. We talked about people who always try to fix things."

"Oh yes. That's right. I remember."

"Well, just remember this, son. There are some things in life that only God can fix. So, don't take hold of the reins unless He tells you to. Not everything rests on your shoulders, after all."

"Thank you for the reminder." Ryan reached over to hug Taffie's father. As he did, the strangest feelings came over him. *Will Pop ever be able to hug me like this again?*

He pushed aside that question for the moment, then took Taffie by the hand, leading her out to the boardwalk. Once there, he turned to her, his heart heavy.

"Are you worried about your pop?" she asked, reaching over to slip an arm around his waist.

"Mm-hmm. A little. But he's better today than he was yesterday, and better yesterday than the day before. Every victory is a major one, even the little things. It's strange. The physical therapists are having to reteach him things he learned as a kid." Ryan did his best to shake off his worries. "But in some ways, he's his old self. I still see glimpses in his eyes. And in spite of everything, he's still got his sense of humor."

"Really?"

"Yes. Last night Vic and I were sitting in his room, talking. We thought he was asleep. Vic started telling a story about something that happened when we were boys—about a fishing trip we all took together. All of a sudden, Pop's eyes popped open and a smile as wide as the Atlantic lit his face. Then he fell right back asleep. But I could tell he wanted to say something. The idea of fishing together was enough to get him excited."

"That fishing idea really hits the mark," Taffie said. "You boys should give him something to aim for. Tell him you're all going to go fishing together when he's well enough, like you did when you were kids."

"Wow. Great idea." Ryan leaned over and gave her a soft kiss on the lips. "Speaking of fishing. . ."

"What?"

"I think you did a great job of tossing that Bruno fella back in the water. You didn't take his bait, and I'm proud of you."

"No, I'm proud of you," she said. "It takes a strong person to stand up to someone like him. You are strong, you know. All of you Antonellis are."

"Including my brothers," he explained. "I had a long talk with Vic the other day. He and Mallory have agreed to get counseling. They've never done that before. But our pastor is going to be meeting with them once a week. They really want to make this work."

"I could tell that the other day," Taffie said. "And I'm so glad. Casey needs a stable family."

"I've never known anything but," Ryan said. "My parents are the epitome of love. Always have been. That's exactly the kind of marriage I want to have." He paused and gazed at Taffie. He wanted to add, *the kind of marriage I want to have with you*, but knew the time wasn't right. Not yet.

Still, as he gazed in Taffie's beautiful brown eyes, as he held her in his arms and pondered the possibilities, Ryan prayed it wouldn't be long before the Lord opened that door. When that moment came, he would gladly walk through it.

Chapter 22

In the weeks after Ryan's father was transferred to the rehab hospital, his family celebrated numerous milestones in his recovery. Yes, there were many obstacles ahead, but countless miracles had already taken place. Ryan didn't take a single one for granted. Luke had come to his senses and started helping out with the family business. Pop's illness seemed to have matured Luke. Or scared him. Still, Ryan was happy for the help. And then there was the big one. Vic and Mallory appeared to have reconciled. Truly reconciled. Mallory's countenance had changed completely, and Vic. . .well, Ryan could hardly believe the change he'd seen in his brother. Their father's near brush with death had motivated Vic in a number of ways.

It had motivated Ryan, too. Though he wasn't completely content with the idea of repairing appliances, he'd made his peace with it. He would do whatever it took to make sure Pop's needs were met. And, besides, much to his pleasure and surprise, Ryan had still found a little time on the side to venture out into marketing. The work with Taffie and her family had motivated him in a number of ways. Maybe. . .if he would just hang on awhile longer, he could jump start Atlantic City PR—a company focused on marketing the city's local businesses.

In the meantime, his days were filled with trips back and forth from job to job, rehab to home. . .and, of course, to Carini's, where he spent every available hour with the woman who now captured his heart. Oh, the joy that flooded over him as he and Taffie walked quietly along the water's edge, celebrating the influx of fall customers at Carini's. How good it felt to walk with her hand in his. He would be happy to do so. . .for the rest of his life.

The final Thursday in September, just as Ryan wrapped up a job at a local restaurant, he received a call from his mother. Her words surprised him. "Pop wants to chat. Can you stop by the rehab after you wrap up your last job of the day?"

"Talk? About what?" Ryan's curiosity almost got the better of him. And though his father could manage a few words of conversation, they were slow and strained. Usually Mom did most of the talking when they were together.

"He wants to share some things about the business. But don't fret. Just get here when you can."

"Okay. I'll see you around five fifteen."

As Ryan worked, his thoughts continually drifted to his father. Was he worried about the job Ryan was doing in his absence? Curious to see if they were bringing in new customers? *Stop worrying. God's got this under control.*

At exactly five fifteen, Ryan entered the rehab and wound his way through the many hallways, till at last he came to Pop's room. He found him sitting up in bed, eating a small container of ice cream.

"If I'd known you were in the mood for ice cream, I would've stopped at Carini's," Ryan said.

His pop's eyes lit up as he managed, "R–rocky r–road."

"Yes, I know. It's your favorite." Ryan laughed. "But it looks like you're enjoying that vanilla, so keep it up."

He took a seat in the chair by the bed. "Where's Mom?"

"C–coffee."

"Ah."

As if she'd been standing in the wings awaiting her cue, his mother entered with a Styrofoam cup in hand. She came to him and placed a kiss on his forehead. "Thanks for coming. I know Pop's anxious to talk to you."

"About?"

"Well. . ." She glanced at his pop, then smiled. "I think he'll want me to do most of the talking, actually. But I know just what to say. We've had this speech planned for weeks, long before. . .well, before the stroke." She gave him a reassuring look.

"What is it, Mom?" Ryan sat up on the edge of his chair and tried to calm his nerves. "What's happened?"

"Calm down, son." She paused, then began to spill her thoughts. The words flowed quickly. "Your father and I have been so grateful to you for everything you've done over the past year or so. Since his first stroke. The business would have folded back then, if not for you."

Ryan rested his arm against the edge of the chair. "Well, you both know I would do anything to help."

"Y–yes." The word came from his father, who managed a crooked smile.

"We do," Ryan's mother echoed. "But that's just it. Even before this stroke, Pop and I had been talking about a plan of action. He has wanted to sell the business for more than a year now."

"S–sell the business?" Ryan looked back and forth between his parents, confused. "Who would you sell it to?"

"M–Martinson's."

"Martinson's?" Their chief competitor?

"They made an offer months ago," his mother said. "But your pop was afraid to take it because he knew how much you loved the business and he didn't want to hurt you."

"L–loved the business?" Ryan slapped himself in the head and he turned to his father. "They made an offer? A good one?"

Pop's eyes widened as he slowly nodded.

"And you turned them down?"

Another nod.

"When we turned them down last year, your father decided he could probably handle working at least a few more years. But now. . ." She shook her head.

"I–I'm. . .t–tired." Pop's eyes misted over.

"He's ready to rest. Relax. And Bob Martinson came by the other day to visit."

"Oh?"

"He made a second offer. Even higher than the first. We've. . .well, we've decided to sell. It's really the best thing. We could use the money, and your father needs a break. Still, we've been so worried about how you would take this news. We've known since you got your degree just how much running a business has meant to you."

"I–I'm so s–sorry, s–son." A lone tear trickled down Pop's cheek.

Ryan stood and began to pace the room. "Pop, I love you. And you know I love working alongside you. You're the most amazing man I've ever known, and I enjoy spending time with you. But. . ." He paused for a moment, garnering the courage to continue. "I don't enjoy repairing appliances."

His mother glanced over at him, stunned. "Y–you don't?"

"No." Ryan shook his head. "With my marketing degree, I can do so much. I have so many ideas and plans—but I've never been able to get worked up about commercial appliances. Not sure why."

"R–really?" Pop's eyes held a hopeful look.

"Really." Ryan leaned over and took his father's hand. "And I can't believe I managed to convince you that I was happy being a repairman. I was so afraid your feelings would be hurt if you found out I didn't love the things you loved."

His mother's brow wrinkled. "Ryan, we've raised you boys to follow after God. And He will lead you all into the various businesses you're supposed to be in. It never occurred to me that you might be working out of obligation."

Ryan swallowed hard and tried to figure out how to respond. Of course he'd been working with Pop out of obligation—ever since the first stroke. But to say so now just sounded. . .callous. Cold.

Thankfully, he didn't have time to respond. The door to the room swung open and Casey entered with a broad smile on her face. "Grandpa!" She squealed, then bounded toward the bed. Ryan grabbed her and planted a kiss on her cheek before she could pounce.

"Hey, you!"

"Uncle Ryan. I need to talk to Grandpa." She scrambled out of his arms and made her way to the side of the bed, where she began to fill everyone's ears with chatter about her day at school.

At that same time, Mallory and Vic appeared in the doorway, hand in hand. Ryan looked over at them with a smile. He could see the peace in their expressions. For some reason, Mrs. Carini's words came flooding back over him. *The safest place to be is in the center of God's will.*

The center of God's will. Hmm. All those years of repairing appliances when I really wanted to do something else. I wanted to spread my wings and fly. And now...

All at once, a peace that passed all understanding swept over Ryan as the truth registered. He'd been faithful in the little things...and it looked as if the Lord was about to shift him into something much, much bigger.

With a smile on his face, he excused himself to make a very important phone call.

ꝏ

Taffie sprinted down the stairs, ready to bid her parents goodbye. They'd spent the better part of the afternoon packing up the RV and now, finally, the time had come. Her mother and father would ride off into the sunset. Literally. They would head west to Philly to spend the night at an RV park, then continue onward...westward...over the next several months. Of course, her mother still insisted they'd be back next summer for the wedding. Not that anyone was actually getting married.

Just as she reached the bottom of the stairwell, Taffie's cell phone rang. She pulled it from her pocket and smiled as she saw Ryan's number.

She answered with "Hey, I was just thinking about you."

"Same here."

"What's up?" She continued on her way to the front of the house. From here, she could hear the racket from outside. Half the neighborhood had turned up to bid her parents farewell.

"I have some news." Ryan's voice carried an unexpected level of emotion. Had something gone wrong? Taffie found herself distracted as both of her sisters rushed her way.

"Hurry up!" Tangie hollered. "They're ready to go."

"Pop's not going to leave until he says good-bye to everyone who's ever bought candy from him," Candy argued. "So, no rush. Most of Atlantic City is out there, saying good-bye, anyway. Take your time."

As her sisters disappeared through the front door once again, Taffie did her best to focus on Ryan, who continued to talk on the other end of the phone. She missed part of it, but heard something about his father's business.

"I'm sorry, Ryan. What did you say?"

"My pop."

Her heart plummeted. Surely something hadn't happened to his father. Not now, when things were going so well with his recovery! "W—what about him?"

"He's selling his business."

"Selling his business?" Taffie practically squealed with delight. For weeks she'd prayed that God's perfect will would be done in Ryan's life, particularly as it related to his work. While she'd admired his amazing work ethic, she could read the truth in his eyes. He really longed to be doing something else entirely.

"Pop is selling the business to Martinson's on the first of October. No more appliance repairs in my future."

"Well, except one," she prompted.

"What do you mean?"

"I mean, there's no guarantee our taffy machine is going to hold up forever. Now that you know how to fix it. . . ."

He laughed. "I can promise you this. . .if anything breaks at the shop, I'll take care of it for you. But don't tell your friends. My future is in marketing, not repair jobs."

"Oh, I don't know." She smiled, thinking about it. "I'd say you've done a fine job of repairing a great many things." She dove into an explanation of how he'd played a major role in fixing the future of Carini's Confections, and how he'd helped to repair his brother's marriage, as well.

She heard a horn honking from his end of the phone and it startled her. She'd assumed he was at the rehab. "Where are you?"

"I'm in the car on my way to your house."

"Seriously?"

"Of course. I wouldn't let your parents leave without telling them good-bye. And besides, Casey made a card for your mom. I should be there in a couple of minutes."

"Hope they're still here. I've never seen two people more anxious to travel."

She opened the front door and stopped short when she saw the mob of people. Squinting against the sunset, she made out her parents. Pop handed out bags of candy to folks and Mom. . .well, Mom hugged neck after neck. Taffie ended her call with Ryan, then bounded toward her parents, half-saddened and half-energized. The moment had finally come.

Drawing near her mother, Taffie found herself with tears in her eyes. "It's just not going to be the same around the shop without you. But I promise to do my best."

"You've always done your best and then some." Mom gave her a warm hug. "And I have a feeling you're going to have a lot of help."

"Oh?" Taffie followed her mother's gaze to Ryan's car as he pulled up to the curb. "Ah, I see."

She watched with joy flooding over her as he made his way through the mob to her side. It was just like a scene from that movie—when the hero appeared from out of nowhere to save the day. Sure, Ryan wasn't dressed in regal attire, and he certainly didn't come wielding a sword. But with the sun setting behind him, he almost carried an angelic glow.

Nah. It had nothing to do with the sun.

He greeted her with a kiss as sweet as candy, which she returned willingly. Then he gave her mother a warm hug and handed her a homemade card. "It's from Casey," he explained. "She's already missing you, and you're not even gone yet."

"I'm going to miss her, too." Taffie watched, stunned, as her mother's eyes filled with tears.

Pop appeared at her side and shook Ryan's hand. "Take care of this girl of mine," he said with a wink.

"That's my plan." Ryan slipped an arm around her waist and drew her close.

Taffie and her sisters spent a few quiet moments sharing their good-byes with her parents, then, with as much fanfare as a king and queen, the Carini clan leaders climbed aboard their RV and headed off into the sunset.

Standing there with the raspberry sunset settling in around her, Taffie had to admit there was something rather poignant about the fact that her parents were finally heading off on their way. The strings had been cut. She was on her own.

As if reading her mind, Ryan drew her close and planted kisses in her hair. Her heart swelled with joy. *No, I'm not alone.* The Lord—and a very handsome marketing guy—would walk with her. . .every step of the way.

Chapter 23

The winter months passed—one holiday to the next. Just as Ryan predicted, Carini's Confections thrived during the autumn season, and did even better at Christmastime. The winter brought in an older crowd, but Taffie didn't mind. In fact, she could hardly wait for Valentine's Day. Not only had she created a new product called "Carini's Rose"—a delicate chocolate, rose-shaped candy made specifically for the holiday—she had also agreed to participate in the singing valentines project.

What in the world had gotten into her?

Ah yes. Love. Love had motivated her to sing, to dance, to smile twenty-four hours a day. Love had left her dizzy and gleeful, silly and carefree. She could hardly think straight these days. Her whole life had morphed into a romance movie. Not that she minded. No, sir. In fact, she rather enjoyed it.

On the morning of February fourteenth, Taffie arrived at the shop and changed into her tuxedo attire, ready to get to work. Just as she made her way behind the coffee counter, Tangie appeared in the doorway, her cheeks flushed from the cold.

"Brr! It's freezing out there!" She came inside and gave Taffie an admiring look. "I can't believe you're doing this. You're going to—to sing."

"I am." Taffie grinned, unable to hide her joy. "But we couldn't have managed our orders without you. I'm so grateful you took a day away from school. You're saving my neck. Even with three of us participating, we almost have too many orders to cover. I almost asked Mallory if she would join us."

"Is she a singer?" Tangie's brow wrinkled as confusion set in.

"She is now." Taffie gave her a wink. "Love will do that to you. But I think we can manage. And Ryan's mom has agreed to stay at the shop, tending to our other customers while we're out."

Just then, Ryan made his entrance from the back room. He looked dashing in his black tuxedo, white shirt, and red bow tie. Tangie let out a whistle. "You clean up real nice."

"Thank you." Ryan bowed at the waist, looking every bit the royal prince.

Taffie's heart swelled as she looked at him. Seeing him in a tuxedo made her head spin. She forced herself to stay focused on the task at hand. There was much work to be done, after all. She pulled out the paperwork, showing a total of thirty-three orders for singing valentines. "Eleven apiece," she informed the others.

"Whoa." Tangie's face lit up. "You've really gotten good at this marketing thing."

"Blame it on him." Taffie pointed at Ryan, who shrugged.

"What can I say? I'm having the time of my life. My new PR firm is doing great. Business at the shop is growing every day. I can't believe how blessed I am."

"No, I can't believe how blessed *I* am," Taffie whispered. She gave him a light kiss on the lips, and his cheeks turned crimson.

"You two are something else." Tangie groaned. "To be honest, I'm jealous of you. It's Valentine's Day and you have each other. I've got. . ." She released a loud sigh. "No one."

"What about Joe?" Taffie asked. "That guy you told me about last month?"

"Joe? Oh yeah. Well, he moved back to Sheboygan when the show closed. Go figure."

"You're going to find your Prince Charming," Taffie reassured her. "Just don't get ahead of God."

Tangie offered up an exaggerated sigh, then went into the office to change into her tuxedo. Before long, Ryan's mother made her entrance, and the three songbirds were ready to hit the road. They agreed to meet back at the shop at five o'clock. After all, the first annual Valentine's Day Karaoke Extravaganza at Carini's was to begin at seven o'clock that evening. The place would be full of song-filled lovers, young and old.

As they left the candy shop, Taffie thought about all that had transpired in such a short period of time. God had truly stretched her. . .in more ways than one. Ironic. Not that she minded. No, looking into the chocolate-brown eyes of Ryan Antonelli, the only thing she minded was being away from him for the next several hours.

Well, no time to fret over that right now. Not with so much work to be done. With a song in her heart, she headed off on her way to belt out some happy tunes. If the situation called for it, she might even throw in a little choreography.

❧

As Valentine's Day progressed, Ryan thought about Taffie at least a thousand times. As he sang to a young couple at a local restaurant. As he crooned a tune for an elderly couple in their front foyer. As he surprised a young woman at her workplace. Everyone responded well to the singing valentines and the accompanying chocolates, but his heart still ached for Taffie. He wanted to sing. . .to her. And he would, before the day ended.

At five thirty, just as he wrapped up the final order, Ryan headed back to the candy shop. He pulled a slip of paper from his pocket and read the words over and over again. He couldn't forget these lyrics. To do so might change the outcome of his life.

He pulled into the parking lot nearest Carini's at a quarter of six, but didn't leave his car right away. Instead, he spent a few minutes in prayer, asking God to lead him. With so much on his plate, he certainly needed the Lord's guidance.

Ryan entered the shop and saw his mother at the coffee bar, serving up flavored coffees and hot chocolates to customers. Vic and Mallory had arrived with Casey in tow. Even Luke showed up to help out with the karaoke equipment. Ryan grinned as he noticed his father and Casey, seated near the front of the room. He walked over to his father and gave him a warm hug. "Glad to see you, Pop. Happy Valentine's Day."

"H–happy Valentine's D–Day." His father smiled a now-familiar crooked smile.

"I'm gonna sing a song tonight, Uncle Ryan," Casey said, her eyes sparkling. "I've been practicing all day."

"What song?"

"I can't tell you. But you're gonna love it!"

"If you're singing it, I'm sure I will." Ryan gave her a kiss on the top of the head. "Anything you sing will be wonderful." He looked around, curious. "Anyone seen Taffie?"

Tangie appeared from behind the candy counter with an explanation. "She's running late. She called about fifteen minutes ago to say that things went so well with the singing valentines that she got a couple more orders. So, she'll be at least an hour or more."

"No way." Ryan's heart plummeted. "Are you sure?"

"Yeah. Why?" Tangie gave him a curious look.

"Oh, nothing."

Several minutes later, the evening crowd started to trickle in. Before he knew it, over twenty people had signed up to sing in the Valentine's Day Karaoke Extravaganza. All love songs, of course.

Ryan started off the evening's festivities promptly at seven, but nothing felt the same without Taffie. Sure, folks were buying all sorts of goodies to munch on while they listened to wannabe singers croon love songs. But Ryan's heart just wasn't in it. . . . Until exactly 8:02 p.m., when the love of his life walked through the door. He took one look at Taffie—her lopsided ponytail, red bow tie all askew, and exhaustion etched on her face—and his heart sprang to life. After giving her a gentle kiss on the cheek, she went back to the office to change clothes. He was surprised to see her return in a beautiful red blouse and black slacks. No work attire tonight—not on Valentine's Day. No, tonight would be a night neither of them would soon forget.

He hoped.

A few minutes later, just after an elderly man sang a Frank Sinatra standard, Ryan took to the microphone. "I know I'm not on the schedule," he explained, "but I have a song I'd like to sing to someone very special. It's a valentine I wrote just for her." He picked up his guitar and swallowed hard before strumming the first chord.

From the audience, Taffie looked his way, clearly confused. Her cheeks flamed pink as he began to sing the song he'd worked on for days:

You're God's precious gift, my sweet valentine;
The love of my life, but will you be mine?
Forever I'll hold you, forever we'll be
One in His sight, if you'll just. . .marry me.

A gasp went up from the crowd as he sang the last line. He forced his attention to the woman he'd written the song for. From her chair, she stared at him in complete stunned silence, eyes filled with tears. Ryan stopped strumming the guitar long enough to gaze at her with a heart filled with love. He gestured for her to join him on the stage and she came. . .albeit slowly, hesitantly. When she stood next to him at last, he knelt down on one knee and a nervous chuckle erupted from the audience.

From out of the crowd, he heard Casey's lyrical voice, "You go, Uncle Ryan!"

He didn't let that stop him. Reaching into his pocket, he came up with the tiny box that held the beautiful princess-cut diamond. He knew it would be a perfect fit.

If she would just say yes.

❧

Taffie's hands shook uncontrollably as she stared down at Ryan. At least, she *hoped* it was Ryan. Through the tears, she couldn't quite tell. There, in front of everyone, he shared his heart. He asked her to be his. . .forever. The whole thing reminded her of a movie she'd once seen. A fairy tale.

Perhaps life really *was* like that, after all.

As he slipped the exquisite ring on her finger, she could hardly breathe, let alone speak. She finally managed an emotional, "Yes!" then pulled him to his feet.

Who cared if the world looked on? She didn't. No, as he leaned down to kiss her, nothing mattered. Nothing at all. Just the two of them.

Well, the two of them and Casey. . .who'd taken to dancing around the room and singing a corny love song at the top of her lungs.

Chapter 24

The twentieth of July dawned with one of the prettiest pink skies Taffie had ever seen. East Coast sunrises had always taken her breath away. But pink? Ironic, in light of the color of the bridesmaids' dresses.

Before she even had a chance to ponder the fact, the door to her bedroom flew open.

"Why are you still in bed?" Tangie demanded. "We've got so much to do!"

"It's barely seven in the morning." Taffie laughed as she double-checked the time. "The wedding's not till two."

"But we've planned a special breakfast. Then we have to get our nails done," Candy argued. "After that, you've got a ten thirty hair appointment. Then we've got to come back here and get dressed before Pop drives us to the beach. So, c'mon! Get out of bed."

Just like they did when they were little, Tangie and Candy climbed atop her bed and began to jump on it until she finally gave in. "Okay, okay! I'm coming."

Their mother appeared at the door, a scolding look on her face. "Don't make me tell you to get off that bed."

With sheepish looks on their faces, Tangie and Candy left their perches and raced for the door.

"Wait till you see what we've made for breakfast!" Candy called out as they left the room.

"French toast! Your favorite!" Tangie added.

As they disappeared from view, Taffie kicked back the covers and rose from the bed. Her mother entered the room with a smile. "Excited?"

"Mm-hmm. I could hardly sleep last night. And I had the craziest dream. Ryan and I were working in the candy shop, and he came up with an idea for a new flavor."

"Oh? What was it?"

"That's the goofy part." Taffie yawned. "I can't remember for the life of me. I just remember telling him it was a great idea."

"Funny. But put the business stuff out of your mind today, honey."

"Oh, trust me, I will! Oh, and Mom. . ."

"Yes?"

"I'm so glad you and Pop made it back from your trip in plenty of time for the wedding."

"Don't thank me just yet." Her mother sighed. "I still have to talk your father out of wearing that cowboy hat he bought in New Mexico. He's got his heart set on it."

Taffie laughed. "I'd say let him wear it, but I'm not sure it'll fit the beach wedding theme."

"Don't worry. If he won't give up on the idea, I'll hide the hat someplace at the shop." She gave Taffie a wink, then left the room with a playful smile.

With excitement building, Taffie began to prepare for the day. She looked at her reflection in the mirror, groaning as she saw the wrinkles on her cheek from the pillow. "Hope I can get rid of those before I walk down the aisle."

Not that it was really an aisle. No, the plan to get married on the beach had been hers. Ryan had willingly gone along. And the idea to host the reception at the candy shop was a given. Where else could they celebrate in such a comfortable setting? Her sisters and Mallory, now a wonderful friend, would make the best bridesmaids ever. And, of course, Casey would look radiant in her pink flower girl attire, complete with glistening tiara.

One more quick glance in the mirror and Taffie rushed to take her shower. All the while, she prayed, not just about the day ahead, but about the life ahead. Her praises seemed to flow as steadily as the water from the faucet above. How blessed she felt. And how excited!

For some reason, the scripture verse that hung above the door of the shop swept through her mind: *How sweet are your words to my taste, sweeter than honey to my mouth!* The familiar words made more sense today than ever. The Lord had done such an amazing work in her life over the past year. And truly today would be the icing on the cake.

Oh, if only Grandpa Gus had lived to see all of this. He would've celebrated in grand style. And he would have loved Ryan, too. Of that, she was quite sure.

After finishing her shower, Taffie ate breakfast with her family, then dressed in capris and her I'M THE BRIDE T-shirt, and made her way out to the car with her sisters in tow. Before long, they were all seated at the nail salon, where Mallory and Casey joined them. They chatted like they'd done a thousand times before. Only now, the situation was completely different. Today—with pink nails and a flowing white dress—she would become Mrs. Ryan Antonelli.

Giggles nearly erupted as she thought about it. Suddenly all the work that had gone into preparing for her and Ryan's big day seemed to escape her memory. All she could think about—all she could imagine—was taking that first step toward her Prince Charming. The first step toward the rest of her life.

&

"Having trouble with that?"

Ryan stopped fidgeting with his tie as he heard Vic's voice. "I've never been very good with ties. Good thing I don't have to wear them very often, right?"

"I guess so. Let me help you." Vic drew near and started working on it.

Afterward, he stepped back and sighed. "I'm hoping you'll forgive me for something."

"Oh? What's that?"

Vic shrugged. "I've set a terrible example for you. As a husband, I mean. I know you'll do a better job of it. You've always been so. . ."

"What?"

"Selfless." Vic sighed. "You've always been the sort to put others first, and that's critical in a marriage. It's a lesson I've had to learn the hard way."

"But at least you've learned it. And I have it on good authority you're doing a fine job with putting others first," Ryan said. "So don't be so hard on yourself. You and Mallory are great examples to all of us. When I look at you, I know it's possible for God to mend even the toughest situations. I also see that you're both great parents. That speaks volumes."

"Um, speaking of which. . ." Vic flashed a suspicious smile.

"What?"

"We, um. . .we're going to have a baby."

"No way!" Ryan slapped his older brother on the back. "Congratulations! Does Casey know?"

"Not yet. We wanted you and Taffie to have your big day. We'll make our announcement soon, don't worry."

"Well, I think it's amazing." Ryan chuckled. "I can almost see Casey now, bossing around a little brother or sister."

"No doubt. I'm hoping for a boy so I can take him fishing with his grandpa."

"Speaking of which, thank you so much for making all of the arrangements for last Saturday." Ryan reflected on the boat trip they'd taken last weekend with their father. "I could tell Pop had the time of his life. And Casey. . .she's a natural with a rod and reel."

A rap on the bedroom door caught Ryan's attention. He looked over to see his mother peeking in.

"Almost ready?" she asked. "It's nearly time to go. Don't want to be late to your own wedding. Pop and Luke are getting anxious."

"I'm ready." Ryan turned to look at himself in the mirror once more. He smoothed out a loose hair and straightened his tie, then smiled. "This is the best it's gonna be."

"No." His mother entered the room with a gleam in her eye. "It's just going to get better from here."

Ryan smiled as he caught her meaning. "I know you're right, Mom. It's only going to get better from here."

a.

"Aunt Taffie, do you like my dress?" Casey twirled around for Taffie's approval.

"You look beautiful, honey. You're the prettiest one here."

"Hey, I heard that," Tangie said with a wink.

"Me, too," Candy echoed.

Mallory leaned down to kiss Casey on the forehead. "She does look angelic, though."

"Aunt Taffie is the prettiest of all." Casey giggled. "She looks like a princess in her wedding dress."

"Do you think so?" Taffie turned a bit to show off the beautiful Grecian gown. "It's not as elaborate as most wedding dresses, but it's perfect for the beach."

"You look like a million bucks, kid." Pop reached over and kissed her on the cheek.

"Just like the lady in that movie," Casey echoed.

Taffie peeked out from behind the makeshift wall, waiting to hear the music. Finally, she heard the strains of Vivaldi's "Four Seasons." Off in the distance, across the sand, she saw Ryan and his brothers take their place near the pastor under the beautiful white gazebo, which Mom and Mrs. Antonelli had decorated with pink sweetheart roses just this morning.

"It's time," Taffie whispered to her father, who stood nearby, a sad look in his eyes. "A–are you all right, Pop?"

"Mm-hmm." He sighed. "It's just so hard to believe you're grown-up enough to get married." He turned to the other girls. "Before you know it, you'll all be married, and I'll be. . ."

"Old?" Casey interjected.

"Thanks a lot, kid." He patted her on the head, and she quickly readjusted her tiara.

Tangie snorted. "Well, I, for one, won't be getting married anytime soon. I've got a Broadway career to think of."

"And now that I've got my pilot's license, I have to stay focused on my work," Candy admitted. "So, no weddings in my future. And least not for a long, long time."

Taffie couldn't help but smile. God, in His own unique way, had shown her how to merge her business life and her personal life. Surely her sisters would eventually learn the same lesson. . .in His time.

But now, business was the last thing on her mind. No, the only thing driving her at the moment was the desire to sprint across the sand and land directly in Ryan's arms.

Instead, she drew in a deep breath and waited patiently.

"Do you remember what to do?" Mallory asked Casey as she pointed her toward the aisle.

"I've been practicing since Valentine's Day!" Casey jumped into place, then began to take calculated steps. As she took her first few steps, Taffie could hear her whispering, "Right, together, left, together."

When Casey reached the midway point, Mallory set off on her journey toward the gazebo. Taffie noticed Vic's beaming face as he watched his wife. Their reignited relationship truly warmed her heart.

"Almost my turn." Tangie gave her a wink, then took her first step toward the aisle. She turned back long enough to whisper, "Break a leg, sis," before heading off on her way.

Finally it was Candy's turn. She whispered, "I'm so proud of you," gave Taffie a hug, then began her journey to meet the others.

With tears in her eyes, Taffie turned her attention to her father.

He took her by the arm and whispered, "Are you ready, sweet girl?"

"I'm ready."

As they took their first few steps, Taffie looked beyond the rows of white chairs—filled with friends and family—to the front, where Ryan stood waiting. He looked every bit as handsome in his beach-friendly suit as he had back on Valentine's Day in his tuxedo. And the look in his eyes. Oh, such longing! Joy overwhelmed her as she gazed at the man who'd captured her heart. The one God had hand-delivered and wrapped with ribbon and bow.

Just as she got thoroughly caught up in the moment, Pop leaned over and whispered, "I keep forgetting to tell you something."

"Oh?" She tried not to slow her gait as she responded in a whisper.

"Ryan had a great idea for a new taffy flavor."

"Taffy? Pop, do we really have to talk about this right now?" She tried to keep her pace steady, but found it more difficult with each step.

"Wedding cake."

"What?" She almost stopped walking altogether as confusion took hold. "Wedding cake?"

"Yeah. Great idea, don't you think? He said the marketing possibilities are endless. Just think of it."

"But why are you bringing this up now?" she whispered, trying to keep in step with him.

"I made the first batch this morning." Her father reached into his coat pocket and pulled out a piece, then gave her a wink. "Tastes just like the real thing. Want a piece?"

"Um, maybe later."

He slipped the candy back in his pocket just as they approached the midway point of their journey down the aisle. Taffie turned her attention to her husband-to-be. He gazed at her with love in his eyes, a love so sweet she wanted to sing, wanted to dance, wanted to. . .

Hmm. "Pop, hand over the taffy."

He pulled it out once again and unwrapped it, never missing a step. Taffie popped it in her mouth and took her first bite, mesmerized by its creamy sweetness. It tasted almost as good as actual wedding cake. *Mmm. Yummy.* "Great stuff." As they neared the front of the aisle, Taffie leaned over to whisper, "We've got a keeper here, Pop."

Now, turning her complete undivided attention to the man she loved, the one she'd waited for all her life, Taffie repeated the words with a giggle. "Yep. We've got a keeper."

COTTON
CANDY CLOUDS

Dedication

To my sister-in-law, Stacey Hanna, a high-flyin' pilot who somehow manages to keep her head out of the clouds.

Chapter 1

Fasten your seat belt, please."

Candy Carini pushed aside her daydreams and looked up into the eyes of the flight attendant. After a cursory nod, she snapped the seat belt tight, then turned to look out the window once again. For as long as she could remember, she'd loved sitting in the window seat. Of course, her favorite place to sit these days was in the cockpit. And once she made it through the interview process at Eastway, she'd be making most of her flights from that position. If things went as planned, anyway.

As the plane taxied toward the runway, the woman in the seat next to Candy reached into her oversized purse and pulled out a piece of gum, which she extended in Candy's direction. "Would you like one?"

"Oh, sure." Candy reached for it, offering a polite smile. "Thanks. It really helps my ears during takeoff."

She unwrapped the gum and popped it into her mouth, then leaned her head against the seat and shifted her gaze out the window once again. The plane eased its way into line behind several others, and the waiting game began. In the meantime, the flight attendant began the usual safety spiel. . .a little too animated, to Candy's way of thinking. The perky blond had clearly given this speech a couple thousand times or more.

"I don't like this part," the woman next to Candy said as she pressed her purse back into place under the seat in front of her. "I guess I'm just impatient."

"Me, too," Candy agreed. "But it's like everything else in life. Good things come to those who wait." Take today, for instance. She'd had her share of waiting. Boarding her first flight in Phoenix early this morning. Making the connecting Eastway flight in Chicago a couple of hours later. And all to get to New Jersey. . .to see her family and, hopefully, acquire a new job. Yes, her patience had certainly been tried. But it would all be worth it.

"I guess you're right. Never thought of it like that." The woman went on to introduce herself as Wanda Kenner, adding, "I'll just be glad when we land in Newark. I've been missing my grandbaby something fierce. I don't get to see her nearly often enough."

Candy certainly knew what it felt like to be separated from family. She'd lived the past couple of years away from her parents and sisters.

Minutes later their 747 reached the head of the line. In the seconds before takeoff, Candy felt the usual sense of exhilaration. That feeling—that awesome, powerful feeling—reminded her once again of the call God had placed on her life: the call to fly. Since childhood she'd dreamed of soaring above the clouds, and now that dream was actually becoming a reality.

The roar of the engines sounded, and the plane began its inevitable journey faster, faster, and faster until the front end tipped up, skyward. Within seconds, the back wheels lifted and Candy found herself leaning back against the seat whispering, "We have liftoff!"

"Excuse me?" Mrs. Kenner looked at her with furrowed brow. "Were you talking to me?"

"Oh no. I was just—" Candy laughed. "Just talking to myself, really. After the takeoff. Nice and smooth."

"Ah. Wish they were all like that. The last time my husband and I came to see our grandbaby, we had the most terrifying takeoff. And the landing was worse." Mrs. Kenner proceeded to share the details with heightened enthusiasm. "We got two landings for the price of one that day."

Candy couldn't help but smile at the woman's sense of humor. "Good thing you can laugh about it," she said.

"Well, I can laugh now, but not at the time." Mrs. Kenner fanned herself with her hand. "It's a miracle we're still alive. Really."

"Wow." Candy smiled. In the days leading up to getting her pilot's license, she'd struggled through a few rough takeoffs and landings. Thankfully, she'd seen great improvement over the past few months while flying smaller planes in Arizona. Now she'd turned her sights to piloting bigger planes for Eastway. Just the idea of flying out of Newark brought a smile to her face. How wonderful it would be, to be back in Jersey once again. Close to family. Close to home.

Candy gazed out the window once more. Billows of white clouds now wrapped the plane in their embrace. The backdrop of deep blue sky behind the wispy clouds nearly took her breath away. Something about the contrast of colors always put her in mind of creation—God speaking the heavens into existence. She could almost hear it now. "Let there be light!" And there was light.

Just then, a voice came over the speaker. "Good afternoon, ladies and gentlemen. Welcome aboard Eastway Airlines flight 1403 from Chicago to Newark. This is your captain, Darren Furst. Not second, first."

A few of the passengers chuckled, but Candy rolled her eyes. Just then, the plane jerked a bit and Mrs. Kenner's eyes widened. "Oh dear."

Candy's gaze shot to the window once again. She expected to see heavier, darker clouds looming, but nothing significant jumped out at her. Certainly no reason for a rocky flight.

"Just a little turbulence, folks," the captain continued. "Keep those seat belts on until we tell you otherwise. And by the way. . .once the seat belt sign goes off, we ask you to please limit your walking to *inside* the plane, not out. When passengers walk on the wings it tends to affect our flight pattern."

A handful of passengers chuckled, but Candy did not. Turning back to the woman, she pursed her lips. "His comedic skills are great, but this isn't a stand-up show." *He needs to pay more attention to his flying skills and leave the comedy to folks on TV.*

"I've seen a lot of rocky takeoffs." Mrs. Kenner shrugged. "I'm sure he's a fine pilot."

Candy nodded. "Well yes, but—"

"We'll be flying at an altitude of thirty-five thousand feet," came the voice over the speaker, interrupting her thoughts. "Our expected arrival time in Newark is 5:52 p.m. The weather in Newark is a warm eighty-eight degrees with some broken clouds. We're hoping they'll have them fixed before we attempt to land. Now, settle back and enjoy your flight."

Candy did her best to do just that. Ignoring the chuckles around her, she reached for her MP3 player, pressed in the earplugs, and scrolled until she found the perfect worship song. *Ah. Much better.* With the soothing melody playing, she could almost relax.

Almost.

About three-quarters of the way into the song, as they continued their ascent, the plane began to tip to the right and then the left. The woman next to her reached into her purse again, pulling out a pill bottle. "I need an airsickness pill. This flight is really making me feel queasy."

"Me, too. But I'll skip the airsickness pill. They make me loopy."

"I do have to wonder about that pilot." The woman's brow wrinkled as she swallowed one of the pills with no water. "He's got to be a novice. Either that or we've got some really rough weather ahead." She fastened the top back on the bottle and put it in her purse.

"I can't do anything about the weather, but it does make me wish it was my turn in the cockpit." Candy shrugged.

"You mean you're a pilot?" The woman gave her an admiring look. When Candy nodded, she added, "Good for you, honey. These days, women can be anything they set their minds to. When I was a girl, only men had jobs like that." She laughed. " 'Course, when I was a girl, men held most of the jobs, period. I think it's wonderful that young women today are getting out there. . . fulfilling their dreams."

"Oh, women have been flying for ages," Candy explained. "There's a great organization called Women in Aviation. I'm a member. And there's another group specifically for female pilots called the Ninety-Nines that was formed in 1929." She went on to tell the woman all about the group, and how she hoped to join after she got hired on at Eastway.

"So, your job with the airline looks hopeful?"

A smile teased the edges of Candy's lips. "Yes, I'm headed to Newark for my final interview. I took the FAA check ride last year. Passed it with no problems."

"Check ride?"

"Private pilot certification. Scary process, but I made it through."

"So you're ready to go."

She shrugged. "Well, it's not that easy. You've got to have a minimum of 250 flight hours under your belt to take the check ride. I had that. But getting my commercial license didn't mean I could fly for one of the airlines. Most require more than a thousand flight hours, and 250 of those have to be in IMC."

"IMC?" Mrs. Kenner looked confused.

"Instrument meteorological conditions. So, I've been in Arizona, building up my time flying for a cargo carrier. I worked for a little while as a skydiving pilot, too, but that was more for fun."

"Skydiving?" Mrs. Kenner grinned. "I know you probably won't believe this, but I've always had the desire to jump out of a plane." She looked out the window as the plane gave another jolt. "Not today, of course. Unless that pilot doesn't get his act together." After another jerk, she added, "Somebody hand me a parachute."

Candy laughed. "I don't think we're quite ready for that yet. And from the looks of things, this isn't ideal jumping weather."

Mrs. Kenner leaned back against her seat and closed her eyes for a few seconds until the bumpy flight straightened itself out. When things had finally settled down, she opened one eye and peered at Candy. "So, you have enough hours to work for one of the airlines now?"

"Well, a regional carrier like Eastway," Candy explained. "Not a major airline. But eventually I hope to fly for one of the bigger companies, maybe even transatlantic flights." Just the idea sent a shiver down her spine. . .in a good way.

"Of course."

"Eastway just makes sense for now, since they fly out of Newark. My family lives in Atlantic City, and I like the idea of being so close to home again." Candy went on to tell the woman about her family's candy shop on the boardwalk. Then she reached into her bag and produced a clear plastic bag of saltwater taffy in a variety of flavors. She extended it toward the woman. "My mom's always sending me sweets from our shop. Have one."

"Oh, saltwater taffy! My favorite!" The woman grabbed the bag and stared at the label. "Carini's Confections. They're on the south end of the boardwalk, right?"

"Right."

"I remember visiting that store when I was just a girl. There was a wonderful man who ran it back then." She took a light red piece of the taffy, quickly unwrapped it, and popped it into her mouth.

"That would be my grandpa Gus." Candy smiled at the memory of her grandfather. "He passed away several years ago. My parents took over the shop, but now they've retired. They're gone several months a year, traveling in their RV. My older sister, Taffie, runs the store now."

"Taffie?" The woman spoke around the wad of candy in her mouth. "Well, if that isn't clever." She paused a moment to focus on chewing. "And your name is Candy," she said after swallowing.

Candy sighed. "Yes. But don't say that too loudly, okay?" Even after years of being away from home, she still cringed at the thought of their names. Taffie, Candy, and Tangie. The three Carini sisters.

"I think it's cute." The woman gave her a wink, then licked some of the stickiness off her fingers. "So, are you going to get to see your family while you're in Newark?"

"Yes, I can't wait. My sister Taffie just got married, a little over a year ago, and she's expecting her first baby. I was there for the wedding, of course. And I've been back once since. But mostly I've been raking in the hours I need back in Arizona. That's a long way from Atlantic City and my family. It's been worth it, but I sure miss them."

"Do you mind if I have a second one?" The woman held the bag up. "That last one was a strawberry, and I see a yellow one in here I'd like to try. Banana, right?"

"Yes." Candy offered a reassuring smile. "And take as many as you like. Once I get back home, I'll have access to everything in the store. Not that I need the calories."

"Calories?" Mrs. Kenner laughed. "Don't know why you're fretting over that. You're as slim as they come. Now me, I'd put on five pounds a week if I worked there." She bit into the banana taffy and a childlike smile followed. "Hmm. Maybe ten. This one's good."

"Yes, it's one of my favorites, too." Candy turned her attention to the clouds outside the tiny window. From here, they looked like soft white tufts of cotton candy.

She cringed, thinking of the nickname her parents had given her as a little girl. *Cotton Candy*. Oh, how she'd disliked that name as a child. But now, all grown up and staring at the powder blue sky, she had to admit Pop was right about one thing: his familiar words, "Cotton Candy, you've got your head in the clouds again," certainly rang true. Not that she minded from this angle. No, having her head in the clouds was a good thing from her current perspective.

Her eyes grew heavy, and before long she found herself drifting off. Dreams of piloting through a storm made for an uneasy sleep. She awoke to wheels touching down and the sound of the pilot's voice. "Welcome to Newark. Looks like they got those broken clouds fixed, so we were able to land with no problem. We hope you enjoy your stay, and thank you for traveling with Eastway."

Candy groaned, then reached for her purse to touch up her lipstick.

The captain came back on for one final word to the passengers. "Folks, make sure you get all of your belongings before exiting the plane. Anything left behind will be distributed among the flight crew. Please do *not* leave your children."

Several passengers laughed aloud at that one. A family in the row in front of Candy teased their son, then laughed.

Mrs. Kenner looked over with a shrug. "His jokes are growing on me."

Candy shrugged. *No comment.* As soon as the FASTEN SEAT BELTS sign went off, she rose and stretched to get the kinks out. The line slowly moved forward toward the front of the plane. She followed along behind Mrs. Kenner, who chatted the whole way.

As they approached the front door, the same blond flight attendant greeted her with a pleasant "Have a good day." Candy nodded and looked to the woman's right. She recognized the pilot's uniform right away. Her gaze shifted to his badge. CAPTAIN DARREN FURST. The comedic pilot. He was taller than many of the pilots she'd flown with, and considerably more handsome. His dark eyes and hair distracted her for a moment, then the line of people shifted forward once again.

He gave her a polite smile, adding, "Thank you for flying with us," as she passed.

She returned the gesture with a polite nod.

"Well, there you go, honey," Mrs. Kenner whispered in her ear as they continued on their way out of the plane. "He might not be the world's best comedian, but he sure makes up for it in looks, doesn't he?"

Please tell me he did not hear that. Candy turned back to give him one final look. No, the captain's focus had shifted to the people behind her. Convinced he hadn't overheard them, Candy said her good-byes to Mrs. Kenner and set her sights on the great outdoors.

Chapter 2

D arren yawned and stretched, happy to be free of the confines of the cockpit. Though he loved his job, he felt cramped at times. He'd started the morning in Newark, flown to Chicago and back again. A pretty typical schedule these days, and one his seniority made possible. Others who'd worked less time with the company didn't have it so good. Many who were based in Newark didn't get to see as much of the town as they'd like, due to their hectic schedules.

" 'Night, Captain." His copilot, Larry Cason, patted him on the back as he passed by. "Get some rest."

"Mm-hmm."

Larry paused. "You got anything special planned for the Fourth of July?"

"Who, me?" Darren shrugged. "My family's all on the West Coast, remember?"

"Ah. Right." His eyes lit up. "Well, why don't you come to my place? My wife's inviting her sister, and she's single."

Darren groaned. "Remember what happened the last time you tried to fix me up with someone?"

"Yeah." Larry smiled. "I had no way of knowing Abby was so clingy. But Chelsea's not."

"Chelsea?"

"She's really sweet. Maybe a little young for you, though. She's only twenty-one."

Darren groaned. "Um, no thanks. I don't think the age gap would work."

"Hey, don't be so hard on yourself." Larry gave him a funny look. "You're not as old as you act."

"Thanks a lot."

"No, seriously." Larry scrutinized him. "You act like you're in your forties, but I know you're a lot younger. What are you, maybe thirty-two?"

"On my next birthday." Darren shrugged.

"Okay, Grandpa. Well, maybe I won't fix you up with the twenty-one-year-old, but that doesn't mean you have to curl up in a ball and pretend your dating days are behind you. What have you got to lose, anyway?" Larry's laugh rang out as he made his way off the plane. "See ya later, Gramps."

"Gramps." Darren groaned, then pondered Larry's words —*What have I got to lose?*—as he turned back to the cockpit to grab his belongings. As he prepared to leave the plane, someone called his name. He turned to see a

familiar flight attendant. "Hey, Brooke. What's up?"

"Not much. Just wanted you to try this." She handed him a piece of candy. Saltwater taffy.

"Candy?" He gave her a curious look. "What's up with this?"

"It's taffy. Just thought you'd like a piece. One of the passengers gave me this bag." Brooke lifted up the plastic bag with a CARINI'S CONFECTIONS sticker on the side along with a picture of the boardwalk in Atlantic City.

"Good stuff." He reached for a piece. "So, taffy's a big thing in Atlantic City?"

She groaned. "How long have you worked for Eastway?"

"Four years." He spoke around the mouthful of sugary stickiness. "How come?"

"You've lived in Jersey for four years and haven't figured out that the boardwalk in Atlantic City is known for its saltwater taffy?"

"Never been to the boardwalk." He shrugged and reached for another piece and unwrapped it. "Guess I'll have to go someday."

"I'll ask Jason to plan a trip for our singles ministry," she added. "Would you go with us if we did?"

"Sure. Why not?"

"Okay. And while we're there, we'll take you to Carini's Confections. They've got the cutest little candy shop on the boardwalk."

The words *cute* and *candy* sounded pretty girlie. Still, the taffy tasted good. He couldn't argue with that.

"I'm still getting to know the Newark area," he said with a shrug. "And all of the surrounding places."

"Yeah, Jason told me you haven't even been over to Ellis Island yet. Or the Statue of Liberty."

"I know, I know. I'm just so. . ."

"Busy?"

"Yes." *And distracted. What's the point of going places if you have no one special to go there with you?*

Brooke continued chatting, and Darren tried to stay focused. However, he found himself stifling a yawn. He'd like to get home and out of this uniform. It seemed to be swallowing him up today.

"Hey, I have an idea." Brooke's eyes flashed. "Jason's picking me up. We're going to dinner at that new steak house he's been telling everyone about. Why don't you come with us?"

"You seriously want me to horn in on your date? No thanks." Though Darren valued Jason's input into his life—both as friend and singles pastor at his church—he couldn't imagine interrupting a date with the guy's fiancée. Even if the fiancée happened to be a co-worker and friend.

"But there's something we want to talk to you about." Brooke pouted, then flashed a sly smile. "I've got an old friend from college I want to introduce you to."

"Oh no." He put a hand up and took a small step backward. "Not another blind date. I thought I made that plain after the last one."

"I promise it won't be like before. This one's closer to your age, and she works in D.C. In fact"—Brooke leaned in to whisper—"she's the campaign manager for Paul Cromwell. You know who he is, right?"

"Doesn't ring a bell."

"Prominent senator from Texas, known for his conservative stance on several controversial issues. He's on FOX News all the time. And CNN, too. There are rumors Andrea's going to become his chief of staff in a few months, so we're talking big stuff here." Brooke winked. "I know how conservative you are. You two are politically perfect for each other." She jabbed Darren in the arm and he groaned.

"Oh, great. Is that how we're choosing mates now. . .according to their political stance? Is that how you and Jason fell for each other?" He put on his best newscaster voice and said, "And now, ladies and gentlemen—broadcast live from Newark, New Jersey—an interview with Brooke Antonelli and Jason Kaufman, political romanticists. They're here today to tell you the story of how they met during a nationally televised debate over opposing solutions to rising gas prices."

He shifted his gaze to Brooke, who laughed. "Actually, Jason and I have differing opinions on that," she said. "You know me. I'm a nature lover. I want to save the animals and their nature preserves. But Jason. . ." She laughed. "Well, he just wants to know why he has to pay through the nose for gas just so that the caribou can have the extra space to roam around. He says they're not going to know the difference anyway." She sighed. "He didn't take well to that SAVE THE CARIBOU sticker I put on my car."

Darren laughed. "You've got a soft heart, even when it comes to animals. That's one of the things Jason loves most about you. I know, because he told me."

"Aw."

Darren paused before adding, "Yes, but I have the opposite problem. I have yet to meet a woman with a soft heart. Most of the ones I get close to turn out to be edgy. Harsh. No soft edges at all. And a woman with political ambitions?" He shivered at the very idea. "I can only imagine. Give me a sweet woman. That's all I'm asking for. . . . Well, that and she has to have a great relationship with the Lord."

"She's out there. I know it." Brooke gave him a sympathetic look. "But don't be surprised if God brings you someone with some spunk, Darren. After all, you're as soft as a marshmallow. If you fell for someone just like yourself, where would the fun be?"

"Fun?" Darren snorted. "So, I should look for someone who is my polar opposite?"

"No, I'm just saying you don't have to have everything in common to love someone. And I'm not saying that's how you should choose a mate, per se. You ask God for His perfect will and go from there. But you'll never know if she's the one for you if you don't at least meet her. Her name is Andrea Jackson, by the way. My friend who works for the senator, I mean. She's great."

Darren groaned. "Okay, so when is this date you're setting up? And where do I take this politically-conservative-Andrea-person? Not a fancy restaurant, I hope. Someplace quick. Fast food. Then if things don't work out, I can scoot on out without hurting her feelings."

"You're such a man." Brooke rolled her eyes as she reached for her bag. "You're not taking her out for fast food. And you don't even have to go out with her at all, if you don't want to. But if you don't, you'll be missing out on an evening with a great woman. Did I mention she's a knockout, and she loves the Lord? She also does a lot of public speaking and heads up a ministry that reaches out to children in inner-city housing projects."

Okay, he had to admit. . .that last part held some appeal. Not that he minded her political leanings. They jived with his. It just seemed odd to date a woman that someone else had picked out for him. Made him feel incapable of doing it on his own.

Brooke continued, oblivious to his thoughts. "Andrea's about as close to ideal as you're gonna get, next to me. And I'm already taken." She gave him a playful wink.

Darren followed her, his rolling bag clop-clopping behind. *Ugh.* Broken wheel. He had to remember to pick up a new bag.

And while he was at it, he'd pick up a new love life, too. The one he had right now. . . ? Well, it just didn't appear to be working.

Chapter 3

Candy walked along the boardwalk at sunset, each step drawing her closer to her family's candy store. When she caught a glimpse of the sign, her heartbeat quickened. *Thank You, Lord. Feels so good to be home.*

She entered the shop and found a handful of people lingering inside. Hmm. Not bad for an evening crowd. Then again, her older sister, Taffie, had been telling her about the family's boom in business for a while now. *Things are really hopping around here.*

From across the counter, she watched as Taffie helped a customer with his order. Caramel apples, to be precise. And a half pound of taffy. Candy could judge the weight of the bag from here. Years of working in the store had made her an expert.

She shifted her gaze to the other side of the store where Taffie's husband, Ryan, dished up chocolate ice cream—or was that rocky road?—and chatted a mile a minute with the customers. Nothing had changed there. He'd always been a social person, and excellent with customers. And his marketing skills had really turned things around at Carini's.

A customer pressed past her, then offered up a rushed apology. Candy nodded but didn't say a word. She didn't mind the crowd a bit. No, now that she'd returned to the place she loved most, she simply wanted to drink in the experience. To let the sweetness that hung in the air permeate her heart. To allow her mind and her somewhat overactive imagination to reel backward in time, to the many, many years she'd spent playing and working alongside her parents and sisters in this familiar place.

Oh, what sweet memories. Literally. As a youngster, she'd loved walking along the edges of the candy case, staring at the delectable goodies inside. They still wowed her. She glanced at the rows of creamy maple fudge and the tiny mounds of white divinity. Her mouth watered as she took in the rows of sticky caramel apples and the rock candy. "Mmm." She could almost taste it all from here.

And the sounds! There was still something about the joy in the customers' voices that made her grin. Who could blame them? Candy always made people happy.

Candy always makes people happy. Her mind tumbled backward in time again. She could almost hear Grandpa Gus's jovial voice as he teased her out of a childish sour mood. *"You have the privilege of living up to that name, honey.*

As much as you are able. . .make others happy. Just remember that happiness—real happiness—only comes from above, so stay tapped into the source and you'll do just fine."

She'd done her best through the years. These days she did little to stir the waters, even when they probably needed stirring. Peaceful. That's what Mama called her. She often wondered if peaceful equaled passive.

The crowd eventually thinned and Taffie caught sight of her. She came rushing toward her with a broad smile. "You're here!"

"I'm here." Candy threw her arms around her older sister and gave her a tight squeeze. "I've missed you so much."

"Not half as much as we've missed you." Taffie rubbed her tummy and smiled. "This little one is happy to know his or her auntie Candy is sticking around this time and not high-flyin' her way to some other part of the country." Her brow wrinkled a bit as she added, "You are sticking around, aren't you?"

"If Eastway will have me." Candy shrugged. Inwardly, she wondered what might happen if she didn't get the job. Instead of dwelling on that possibility, she dove into a conversation about her upcoming interview.

About two-thirds of the way into the conversation, Ryan approached from behind the ice cream counter. He let Candy finish, then gave her a brotherly hug. "Glad you're home. How's my favorite sister-in-law?"

She gave him a pretend warning look. "Better not let Tangie hear you say that. You know how jealous she gets." Indeed, her youngest sister was very much the baby—in many respects. She thrived on being everyone's favorite.

Ryan laughed. "Well, when she returns from the glitz and glam of her off-off-Broadway show, I'll say it to her. But you're here now."

"Thanks a lot." Candy laughed. "Anyway, I'm going to wrap up the interview process in Newark tomorrow, and find an apartment there just after." She turned to her sister with a question. "Want to come apartment shopping with me? Are you feeling up to it?"

"The morning sickness ended weeks ago," Taffie said. "I'm so much better now. But before you go searching for a place to live, we have something to tell you. Or rather, something to run by you."

"You do?" Candy looked back and forth between her sister and brother-in-law. "What is it?"

Ryan gestured for her to sit at one of the small tables nearby. "I've got a cousin named Brooke who works as a flight attendant for Eastway," he explained. "She's rooming with a couple of other flight attendants at a fairly new apartment complex in Newark. She says it's a great place. Not too far from the airport, but not close enough that the planes keep you up all night."

"She's great," Taffie added. "I met her at the Antonelli family reunion a couple of months ago. I told her all about you, and she said to give you her number if the Eastway thing worked out. Told me they were going to be looking for a new roommate to share apartment costs in July. And it's July. So, what do you think?"

"Well, I think I have to think about it." Candy smiled. It certainly sounded like more than a coincidence. "So, it's in Newark. That's good."

"Yes, and I really think you'll like Brooke. She's our kind of girl." Taffie offered up a reassuring nod. "And her fiancé, Jason, is a great guy. We met him that same night. He's the singles pastor at their church in Newark. They told us all about it. Said you'd love the church. They're getting married in a few months, by the way."

"Wow." Candy thought about that a moment. "Do you go on being a singles pastor when you're married? Wouldn't that knock you right out of a job?"

"Oh, I don't know." Ryan smiled. "I led worship in our singles ministry before we got married and went on doing so after."

"Yes." Candy looked at her sister's slightly expanding midsection with a smile. "And before you know it, your baby will be grown-up and ready to find his or her perfect mate."

"Bite your tongue!" Taffie laughed. "Let's don't rush things, okay?"

"Okay, okay!" She put her hands up in the air. "But you'll see what I mean. Time seems to be flying by."

They all grew quiet for a moment. Ryan finally broke the silence. "I can tell you one thing. I'll probably go on leading worship when the baby's that age. In fact, I might just go on singing and praising God till I'm a grandpa. You know me."

"Yeah, I know you." Candy nodded. Ryan had such a heart for singles. The candy shop stayed filled year round with young adults, especially now that they offered specialty coffees and Christian karaoke night.

Before long they were caught up in conversation about the good old days. Candy laughed through several of the stories, particularly the ones that focused on her middle-child syndrome.

"I'm over that now," she assured Taffie. "I promise. I'm not the insecure little girl I once was. Something about flying helped me overcome all of that."

"So, you're okay with being stuck in the middle?" Taffie teased.

"I can think of worse places," Candy said. "So, yes. I'm okay with being stuck in the middle."

Funny, sitting here in the candy shop, she felt completely comfortable. She just had to wonder if she would go on feeling this comfortable once she faced the fine folks at Eastway Airlines.

❧

Darren rambled through the empty rooms of his house, wondering what it would feel like to actually have people in those rooms. In the two years since he'd splurged and purchased the home in Bridgewater, he'd had a few friends over. Even hosted a barbecue on the deck. But what he longed for—ached for, really—was a wife and children. People he could love who would love him in return. He wanted to fill the house with laughter and music. Anything other than the weighty silence or the occasional hum of the dishwasher.

He wanted the very thing he'd also longed for as a child, but never really had. A normal family. With an overbearing mother and a passive father, he'd missed out as a kid. It wasn't asking too much to see some degree of normalcy now, was it?

Oh, he wouldn't come out and admit his desire for the married life to his friends and co-workers. Why do that, when he'd managed to convince them he hoped to stay single forever? Yes, he'd done a fine job of making them believe he loved his current situation. If only he could convince himself.

He walked through the living room, stopping at the large empty aquarium. Maybe one day he'd actually buy a fish. In the meantime he had all the goods. Castle. Rocks. Food. You name it.

Someday.

Darren walked through the large kitchen to the back door. Sliding it open, he stepped out onto the wooden deck—a deck he'd built with his own hands. Off in the distance, the three oak trees he'd planted last summer were finally starting to look like something more than scraggly twigs. Hopefully in a few years they'd stand tall and sturdy.

Through the crack in the door, he heard his cell phone ringing in the house and scrambled to catch it before it went to voice mail. He'd been secretly longing for the call from Brooke about her friend Andrea. Unfortunately, the voice on the other end of the line was decidedly male.

"Darren?"

He recognized his friend Gary's voice right off and responded, "Hey, what's up?"

Gary's next words totally threw him. "I got a written warning, man. Eastway's doing everything they can to get rid of me."

"Wait. . .are you serious?"

"Yes. But this time I've got the union on my side. And we're pretty sure we know what's really happening here. Eastway is dropping employees right and left because of the increase in fuel prices. They're just using my warnings from last month as an excuse. No one's job is safe." Gary went on and on, anger lacing his words. Darren tried not to let his friend's emotions spill over on him, but he found it difficult. *"No one's job is safe"?*

"But it doesn't make sense," he said. "You've got seniority. You've been with the company two and a half years." Sure, Gary had received a verbal warning, and then a write-up. . .all related to his volatile temper and attitude with the crew several weeks prior. But he seemed to be doing better, of late. Why would they let him go now?

"Two and a half years isn't long enough, apparently," Gary said. "Rumor has it anyone who's flown for Eastway for less than three could be asked to go."

"Something about this just doesn't sound right." Darren raked his fingers through his hair, growing more frustrated by the moment. "I heard Eastway just hired a couple of new pilots this past week. Why would they yank your job away and give it to someone else?"

"One word. Females."

"W–what?"

"They're trying to meet their quota of women. I'm guessing Eastway has to keep a certain ratio of male-female pilots. Somehow they got off-kilter. I'd be willing to bet those new hires were women. So, decide for yourself."

"That's the most absurd thing I've ever heard." Darren began to pace, trying to make sense of this. "Quotas are a thing of the past. And the union would never stand for it. So, if there's even a hint of sexism, they're going to get to the bottom of this."

"I'm counting on it. But even if they skirt the issue—pun intended—Eastway still won't be in good shape. Not with fuel prices so high."

Fuel prices were high, sure. Airlines everywhere were cutting back. Some had even started charging for baggage. And meal services were almost non-existent, especially for regional carriers like Eastway. But. . .letting pilots go? Something about that just wasn't right.

He finally voiced the inevitable question. "So, do you think I'm next?"

"You?" Gary laughed. "You've been with Eastway longer than most of us. What's it been? Four years?"

"Four and a half."

"Right. And your record is clean as a whistle. I wouldn't imagine you'll be going anywhere."

Darren breathed a sigh of relief but knew he couldn't celebrate just yet. Nor would he want to, with his friend facing a job loss. No, what he really wanted to do was head up to the Eastway offices and give the higher-ups a piece of his mind. He wouldn't, of course. It wasn't in his nature. What was it Brooke had said, again? Ah yes. *You're soft as a marshmallow.*

Soft as a marshmallow.

As the frustration took hold, Darren wished—just this once—he had the courage to toss his marshmallow mentality right out the window.

Chapter 4

Just one week after arriving home in New Jersey, Candy moved into the crowded two-bedroom apartment in Newark with Brooke Antonelli and two other Eastway flight attendants. She loved her new place almost as much as she loved her new roomies. Brooke, Lilly, and Shawneda each surprised her with their uniqueness and their outgoing personalities. In some ways it felt like being with her sisters again.

She'd no sooner dropped her final load of boxes in the front hall than Lilly grabbed her hand. "You're going to be sharing a room with me. Hope you're okay with all the colors. I love color."

Candy followed along behind the petite Asian beauty until they entered the bedroom to the right of the living area. She'd seen the space a few days earlier, of course, but was still amazed at the effort that had gone into decorating it. The bright orange walls took her breath away. Literally. "You—you've done a great job in here."

"Are you okay with the bedding? It's a little bright."

"I love it." She looked at the orange and teal comforter and smiled. No, it wasn't what she would've picked out for herself, but why not expand her horizons? *My life could use a little color.*

"Good thing we already had the extra twin bed, right?" Lilly grinned. "My last roomie—Reagan—went to work for Continental. She's in Houston permanently now."

"Right. A friend of mine from Arizona just went to work for them."

"Male or female?" Lilly asked.

"Male." Candy smiled as she thought about Russ, her old flying buddy. Her smile was followed by a few moments of reflective thought. Seemed like all the pilots she knew eventually parted ways. . .each heading off to his or her own airline. Were there any long-lasting relationships in this business?

"Did I hear someone talking about men?" Shawneda, the oldest of the roommates, entered the room and plopped down on Lilly's bed, making herself at home.

"Oh, we were just talking about a friend of Candy's," Lilly said.

"Boyfriend?" Shawneda's brows elevated slightly. "Tell me everything. Don't leave out even one teensy-tiny detail." She stared up at Candy, apparently ready for a lengthy romantic tale.

"No, you don't understand." Candy shook her head. "I'm not dating anyone right now. I was just talking about an old friend of mine who's based out of Houston now."

"Houston!" The tone of Shawneda's voice changed. "Girl, I'm from Texas. Maybe you could tell from my accent." She went into a descriptive story about life in the South, and had the other girls laughing within minutes. All questions about Candy's love life faded to the background.

The doorbell rang, interrupting Shawneda's dramatic story about a horse-riding adventure she'd gone on when she was sixteen. All the girls looked at the door with surprised expressions on their faces.

"Were you expecting anyone?" Lilly asked.

"Not me," Candy said. "No one even knows I'm living here yet. . .except my family. And they're in A.C."

"A.C.?" Shawneda's puzzled expression almost made Candy laugh.

"Atlantic City." Lilly rolled her eyes. "Seriously, Shawneda. You're not in Texas anymore."

"I know, I know." The bell rang again. "I didn't invite anyone over," Shawneda said. "I'm not in a company frame of mind tonight. Too tired. Just give me a bubble bath and a good book."

"Me, too." Lilly shrugged.

"Maybe Brooke will get it," Shawneda said with a yawn.

Seconds later, Candy heard voices at the front door. Male voices. She followed along behind Shawneda and Lilly.

Brooke stood in the open doorway, squealing as two handsome guys entered.

The taller one reached to sweep Brooke into his arms. "Sorry I'm so early. But I was anxious to see you."

Candy watched this interaction with a smile. *Aha. This must be the fiancé.*

As if to answer her question, Shawneda said, "Oh, it's just Jason." With a wave of her hand, she headed to the kitchen.

"I heard that, Shawneda!" Jason called out. "I love you, too."

"Yeah, yeah. . ." Her voice trailed off as she disappeared into the other room.

Candy shifted her attention to the other man. . .the one standing next to Jason. He looked a little uncomfortable. She tried not to stare, but something about him felt familiar. Tall. . .about five eleven. Dark wavy hair. Deep blue eyes. Nice build. Hmm. *Where have I seen this guy before?*

His taste in wardrobe was nice—button-up shirt with tie. Great slacks. All in all, he was very well put together. He glanced her way and nodded, his blue eyes gazing into hers.

"It's going to take me a few minutes to get ready," Brooke said. "Do you guys mind just making yourselves at home?" She turned her gaze to Candy and Lilly. "Would you mind keeping them entertained? Please. I won't be long."

"Oh, I, um. . ." Candy tried not to stumble over her words, though she felt a little put-on-the-spot. "I–I'm Candy."

"Jason." The fiancé extended his hand. "And this is my best friend, Darren Furst."

"Aha!" She snapped her fingers as the realization set in. "You're a pilot."

"I am." A smile lit his face, and she took note of two strategically placed dimples. Very nice. *His flight comedy might not be great, but he's got a winning smile.*

"You work for Eastway."

"Yes." He gave a hint of a smile. "How did you know that?"

She did her best acting job as she said, "Good afternoon, ladies and gentlemen. Welcome aboard Eastway Airlines flight so-and-so from Chicago to Newark. This is your captain, Darren Furst. Not second, first."

Lilly laughed. "Sounds just like him!"

Darren groaned and slapped himself on the forehead. "I don't know if I should be flattered or offended. I can't believe you actually remembered that."

"Well, I'm—" She never got to finish because Shawneda reentered the room with sodas in hand. She passed them off to the guys and before long a conversation ensued.

Candy spent the next few minutes taking in Darren. In person—dressed in street clothes—he looked like a regular guy. Nothing pretentious about him. And, as they talked about the singles ministry at the church, his love for the Lord came shining through. In fact, it was evident in both his conversation and his kind manner.

So, what had ruffled her feathers that day on the plane? Had she really judged him based only on his voice? Or was it her bias against male pilots, in general, that prompted such a knee-jerk reaction. *Ouch. Can't believe I really admitted to that. I have an issue with male pilots?*

She'd tucked the idea away for months, but—being honest with herself—she'd struggled with the way the guys in flight school treated her. And she'd suffered more than her share of jokes as a skydiving pilot, too. The male pilots didn't always treat her with the respect she deserved, but she'd pushed their comments aside and moved forward. Was her knee-jerk reaction to Darren on the plane last week rooted in something deeper, perhaps?

Candy knew the statistics, knew what she was up against in this industry. She already had several things working against her. . .age, for one. Most new hires were twenty-seven to forty-two, and she'd just turned twenty-three. Many had more flight hours. Still, she felt she had what it took to be competitive. And she certainly knew what it meant to be patient.

"Are we all best friends now?"

Candy looked up as she heard Brooke's happy-go-lucky voice ring out. "S–sure."

"Well, that's great." Her new friend flashed a winning smile, then checked her appearance in the mirror on the wall. " 'Cause I want you to come to dinner with us."

"Come with you?" Candy shook her head, stunned by the idea. "But. . .I can't."

"Of course you can." Brooke sat next to her on the sofa. "We're all friends here. And we all work for the same company." Gazing lovingly at Jason, she added, "Well, all but Handsome here."

"Sure, come with us," Jason said. "It'll be great."

Candy sought out Darren's eyes, to see his reaction. She saw nothing but friendliness and encouragement there.

"I—I guess," she said finally. "Just let me change my blouse. I'm not dressed to go out."

"We'll wait," Brooke said. "Just hurry, okay? I'm starved."

As she changed into her favorite pink blouse and capris, Candy thought about Darren. He had that boy-next-door look about him. Shame washed over her as she realized how she'd judged him before even getting to know him.

"Sorry about that, Lord," she whispered. "I'm gonna keep an eye on that from now on."

While she was at it, she might just keep an eye on the handsome pilot, too.

&

Darren did his best to pay attention as Brooke went on and on about her upcoming wedding plans. However, his thoughts kept shifting to the young woman to his right. She must be a new flight attendant. He'd have to ask Jason later. But Brooke's words, "We all work for the same company," left little other meaning. Still, she didn't have that same bubbly personality that so many of the flight attendants had. There was a quietness about her, almost a reserved nature.

At a break in the conversation, he turned to her. "So, you're Candy." When she nodded, he said, "I don't think I ever heard your last name."

"Candy Carini," Brooke explained. "Remember? I told you all about Carini's Confections on the boardwalk in Atlantic City? They're famous."

"Well, not exactly famous. Though I can say my parents had the right idea by making sure they put God at the center of their careers, no matter the obstacles." Candy's cheeks turned a pretty shade of pink and she shrugged. "We've been in business a long time. We have longevity on our side. And now we're finally on the Internet. That helps."

At once his thoughts sailed back to the saltwater taffy Brooke had given him on the plane. "Oh, right. I remember now. You gave some candy to Brooke on a flight a week or so ago."

"Yes, that's right." After a moment's pause, she added, "Isn't it funny how the Lord works? I didn't know either of you back then. Now I'm rooming with Brooke and we're all fellow employees." Another smile lit her already-beautiful face and caused her eyes to sparkle. "I just got hired on."

He wanted to ask for more details, but the waitress appeared with their food. By the time they'd been served, his thoughts shifted back to the candy shop. "So, tell me about this name of yours. Candy from the candy shop?"

He watched with a hint of a smile as she sighed. "Yeah. My parents are funny like that. And trust me, I've heard every joke in the book, so you might as well save yourself the time and trouble."

"Taffie says they call you Cotton Candy." Brooke gave her a teasing look.

"Um, yeah. And thanks for bringing it up." Candy's cheeks turned a deep crimson. "I'll never live that down."

"Well, I won't be making fun of your name or anyone else's." Darren gazed into her dark brown eyes and offered a sympathetic look. "If anyone knows what it feels like to have a name that people make fun of, I do."

"True, true." She grinned. "Furst, not second." After a brief chuckle, she asked, "So, where are you from? And where did you train?"

"Oh, I'm from Southern California. Went to San Diego Flight Training School. Pretty well known."

"Sure." Candy's eyes lit with recognition, making her all the more beautiful. "I've heard a lot about them. Do you know about Double Eagle Aviation in Tucson?"

"Sure." He nodded. "One of the pilots I flew with last week got her wings at Double Eagle about six years ago."

"Her? It was a woman?" Candy smiled.

"Yeah." He shrugged. After his recent conversation with Gary, it might not be the best idea to get into a lengthy chat about women in the industry, particularly female pilots. Not that Candy would mind, most likely. Most of the flight attendants didn't really care if their pilots were male or female, as long as they kept the plane in the air when it was supposed to be in the air.

"Women are making inroads at the airlines," he said, and then shrugged. *I'll just leave it at that.*

"Hey, don't get Darren started on women." Jason laughed. "I think he's just sensitive. We've been trying to find Mrs. Right for him for ages now, and so far it's been a no go in every situation."

Darren shrugged. "I just don't see the purpose in dating. Maybe I have a different view of things. I guess I'm a little old-fashioned."

"Not at all." Candy looked at him and shrugged. "I think dating is a waste of time, too. It's almost like you're trying people out, one at a time. Seems kind of. . .odd."

Brooke giggled. "It's funny, hearing Darren talk about women at the dinner table. Usually it's the other way around with pilots. When they're flying they talk about women, and when they're with a woman, they talk about flying."

Jason laughed long and loud at that one. Darren felt the tips of his ears heat up, something he could never seem to control when embarrassed. He'd have to talk to Jason later about making him the brunt of every joke, especially in front of someone as pretty as Candy.

Brooke changed the direction of the conversation at that very moment. He breathed a sigh of relief as she started talking about a passenger on a recent flight, one who'd given her fits over a spilled soft drink.

Though he tried to pay attention, he found his gaze shifting back to Candy. The name suited her. She was sweet, through and through.

Hmm. Sweet. What was it he'd said to Brooke that day on the plane? *"Give me a sweet woman. That's all I'm asking for."*

Maybe. . .just maybe. . .the Lord had dropped one in his lap.

Chapter 5

Candy spent her first days at Eastway training on crew resource management and learning everything humanly possible about the aircraft. This gave her some time to get adjusted to the idea that she now belonged to a family. . .a very large family with eclectic brothers and sisters.

Not that she minded. No, being grafted into this new and strange place felt like an adventure. And she couldn't balk at the idea of a solid paycheck. Sure, there would be school loans to pay off in a couple of years, but she didn't have to fret over them just yet. By the time they came due, she'd be earning higher pay, anyway.

On Tuesday, after a particularly long day, Candy found herself walking through the Eastway terminal, waiting on Brooke's flight to arrive. They'd agreed to meet at the gate and then ride home together. Knowing she had over twenty minutes to kill, Candy stopped at a gift shop and purchased a soft drink, then strolled the long hallway near the gate, looking at the photographs on the wall. She'd seen them in passing a couple of times before but never paused long enough to actually take them in.

Candy stopped and looked at a photograph of Amelia Earhart, then read the information underneath. THE NINETY-NINES IS AN ORGANIZATION OF FEMALE PILOTS FOUNDED IN 1929 BY 99 LICENSED WOMEN PILOTS.

"The Ninety-Nines." *Lord, thanks for the reminder.* Many of her friends in Tucson had joined when they got their wings. She'd put it off, promising herself she would make it a priority as soon as she got her first gig with a real airline. *And now I can join.*

Candy couldn't hide the smile, as she looked at the next photo of a female pilot from the 1940s. The text under the photo inspired her. OVER 5,000 LICENSED FEMALE PILOTS FROM THIRTY-SIX COUNTRIES HOLD MEMBERSHIP IN THE NINETY-NINES. *Wow.* A shiver ran down her spine. *And soon I'll be one of them.*

One by one, she read about the inroads females had made in the industry. By the time she reached the last photograph, Candy convinced herself she not only needed to join the Ninety-Nines, she should link arms with other female pilots in the area to do something special. Maybe a banquet of some sort. They could invite someone of notoriety to speak. *Hmm. I'll have to think on that.*

Candy glanced at her watch. Brooke's flight still wasn't due in for another eleven minutes. She turned her attention to the wall on the opposite side of the hallway. The faces of several Eastway pilots greeted her, their smiles broad and inviting.

Soon. . .my picture will hang here, too.

She made her way down the line, taking them all in. One after the other, they held her interest. Sure, most were men. She figured that. But, when she reached the end of the row, she realized she'd seen photos of only three female pilots in the bunch. What was up with that? Looked like the percentage was lower than she'd thought. An uneasy feeling gripped her as she thought it through. Just as quickly, she released that feeling to the Lord.

You gave me this job. I know I can trust You with it.

Candy paused when she reached the photo of a familiar handsome pilot. Captain Darren Furst. She stared at his features for some time. A passenger rushed by and bumped up against her. "Sorry about that!" he called out as he sprinted toward the gate.

"No problem." She turned back to face Darren's photo, examining him from his dark wavy hair down to his broad shoulders. His bright blues eyes caught her attention, as always. Her father always said you could tell a lot about a person by looking into his eyes. She gave them another look. Yep. Warm and inviting. And his smile was genuine.

"A penny for your thoughts."

Candy turned around as she heard Brooke's voice. "H–hey. You're early."

"Mm–hmm. Whatcha lookin' at?" Brooke's eyebrows elevated mischievously.

"Oh. . ." Candy gestured down the wall, trying to look nonchalant. "Just trying to get to know my fellow pilots. I've met a few of them in person."

"Like this handsome fellow." Brooke pointed at Darren's picture, and Candy did her best to look sufficiently disinterested.

"Oh, Darren? He's worked for Eastway longer than most. Interesting."

"He's the best." Brooke took her by the arm, then whispered, "I've known him for ages, and he's really the cream on top of the coffee. Unlike some of the others. But then, you're going to give them all a run for their money."

"What?"

"Nothing." Brooke gave her a wink. "I'm just saying that you're going to be every bit as awesome. And that's a good thing."

"This isn't a competition, Brooke." Candy turned to face her. "And I sure don't want it to turn into one. Things are hard enough for female pilots as it is, without any comparisons."

"Oh, I know. I'm not saying that. And I love Darren. He's the best. I'm just glad Eastway came to their senses and hired on a few more women. Things were pretty out of balance before, that's all." She flashed a bright smile. "Let's get out of here, okay? I'm starving."

"Me, too." Candy nodded. "I skipped lunch today."

"Shawneda's cooking. She's making Texas barbecue. Brisket, to be precise. And I think she said something about southwestern beans and some sort of potatoes. Are you game?"

"Sounds great."

As they left the hallway, Candy's gaze shifted back to Darren's photo one last time. She felt a little foolish, like a child with her hand caught in the cookie jar.

Oh well. She'd come to Newark to fly planes, not fall for handsome pilots. There would be plenty of time to think of her love life later. Right now she had bigger fish to fry.

෧

On Tuesday evening Darren ended a long day of flying and made the drive home, completely exhausted. He'd barely made it through the door when his cell phone rang. Determined to get out of his uniform before dealing with anything important, he made the decision to return the call after he'd had a bite to eat.

After changing clothes and fixing a sandwich, he finally reached for the phone, ready to return the call. When he saw Jason's number, Darren relaxed. Thank goodness. Nothing work related. He punched the Send key, leaning back against the sofa with the sandwich in hand.

"Well, hey there." Jason laughed. "Thought maybe you were avoiding me. Did you listen to my message?"

"Message? No, sorry. Didn't even realize you'd left one. I just saw that you'd called." He went on to explain his exhaustion and his long day.

"Ah, okay. Well, Brooke put me up to this. You remember that friend of hers she told you about—the one who works for the senator?"

Darren perked up right away. "Andrea." He took a bite of the sandwich and listened to his friend's words.

"Yes, she's going to be in town for a speaking engagement. Brooke told her you might be interested in going out for coffee. Nothing stressful."

"Ah." Darren wiped a bit of mustard off his lip and took another bite of the sandwich.

"So, what about it? Saturday afternoon at four? That way she has plenty of time to get back to the hotel to prepare for her speaking gig. And look at it this way, if things don't work out, she won't be sticking around for any length of time."

"Right." It might be a safe plan. Not that he was hoping things would go wrong. He really didn't know what to think, to be quite honest. After another bite of sandwich and a few concerned thoughts, Darren shifted gears. He wanted to be polite. . .to stay focused on Andrea, but his thoughts kept shifting back to the beautiful woman he'd met a few nights before. Candy Carini.

"Can I ask you a few questions about Brooke's roommate?" he finally worked up the courage to ask.

"Which one?" Jason laughed. "Every other week there's a new one."

"The latest one." *The gorgeous brunette with those amazing eyes.* After a moment's pause, he added, "I'm so torn over this. You know my policy. I never date any of the flight attendants. Never."

"Flight attendants?" Jason sounded confused. "Wait. Who are we talking about here? Lilly or Shawneda?"

"Neither. I'm talking about Candy Carini."

"Darren, I—um—hate to be the one to tell you this, but Candy's not a flight attendant."

"Of course she is. I heard her say she just got hired on."

"Yes, she did. She's an Eastway employee, for sure. But she's not a flight attendant. She's a—"

Darren's stomach plummeted as he finished his friend's sentence. "She's a pilot?"

"Yes." Jason exhaled loudly. "Did you miss the part where she asked you where you got your wings? And that whole thing about the flight school in Tucson. She was telling you her own story, dude. You should've been reading between the lines."

Darren felt like slapping himself in the head. *How did I miss that?* "Did I say anything embarrassing about female pilots?" He squeezed his eyes shut. "Tell me I didn't."

"Nah. There was something about women making inroads in the industry, or something like that. But nothing negative. Why?" Jason appeared to hesitate before asking, "You got a problem with women pilots?"

"No. . .not really."

" 'Not really'?"

Darren sighed. "A couple of friends just lost their jobs, and I heard they were being replaced by new hires. Females." He went on to explain his mixed feelings. "Just seems pointless to let someone go because of their sex. Ya know?"

"Yeah," Jason agreed. "But I'd be willing to bet it has nothing to do with that. Brooke says this girl is really good. And she's thrilled to be flying for Eastway. So, go easy on her, okay?"

"Of course. Oh, and by the way. . ."

"Yeah?"

"You forgot to give me Andrea's number." Darren reached for a pen, ready to think of someone other than Candy Carini.

When he hung up from his call with Jason, Darren paced the room, a number of thoughts rolling through his head. *Candy is a pilot. A pilot.* That changed everything. Not that he had any intention of asking her out. Not at all. But, to even befriend a female pilot. . .in light of the current conditions? What would Gary say? Or the others, for that matter. No, he'd better tuck that idea right back into his flight bag and forget about it.

On the other hand, Candy was new to Eastway and would need friends. He couldn't very well avoid her just to save face, could he? And besides, she was a believer. God wouldn't think very highly of Darren if he deliberately opted out of a friendship because of the other guys.

Determined to shift his focus, Darren finally worked up the courage to call the politically perfect Andrea to confirm their coffee date. He felt like a traitor as he punched in her number. Hadn't he just told Candy over dinner that he didn't think much of dating? And here he was, calling up a stranger to ask her out.

I'm just doing this for Jason and Brooke. One date and I'll probably never see Andrea again.

She answered on the third ring. Andrea had a strong, confident voice. . . so strong that it took him by surprise. She jumped on the idea of the coffee date, adding that her schedule was tight. "I hope you're okay with a getting-to-know-you pre-date," she said. "Kind of gets the awkwardness out of the way."

Getting-to-know-you pre-date? He groaned internally. From the business-like sound in her voice, she'd probably record every detail of the evening on a spreadsheet. Or worse. Come with a prepared speech on men and politics. *Stop it, Darren. You don't know anything about her.*

By the time they ended the call, she'd won him over with her wit and her verbal speed. *Man, this girl can talk a mile a minute.* Not that he minded. No, having someone else do the talking saved him from having to do it.

Now, if only she could save him from having to actually meet her for coffee. . .that would be a trick.

Chapter 6

On Saturday afternoon Darren arrived at the coffee shop with his stomach in knots. What was it about first dates—especially blind dates—that made him feel like a kid all over again?

He looked around the room, thankful to see Andrea hadn't yet arrived. He knew what she'd be wearing—a navy blue jacket and slacks with a white blouse. She'd been very specific about that. For once, he was happy to be early. It would give him time to collect his thoughts while waiting.

Darren took a seat at a table and continued the silent prayer session he'd begun in the car. *Lord, You know my heart. And You know how awkward this is for me. Just please guide me. And, Lord, if the woman I'm supposed to marry comes walking through that door, then I give You permission to do whatever You like to let me know. It's gonna take something pretty big, though, 'cause I'm not convinced I'm supposed to be here at all.*

Minutes later, a petite redhead entered the store. Her hair, straight and squared off at the shoulders, gave her a professional appearance, sure. But the rest of her? Wow. Not what he'd been expecting at all. Her small physique caught him by surprise. Darren had imagined a political powerhouse to be tall and sturdy. Sort of a broad-shouldered woman. This one looked more like someone's kid sister. Dimples and all. Her shiny red hair looked just right against the pale complexion and splattering of freckles.

Okay, now what? He'd prepared himself to be disinterested. But so many things about this woman struck him as interesting.

"Darren Furst?" When he nodded, she extended her hand. "I'm Andrea. Great to meet you."

"You, too."

He rose and pulled out a chair. She sat and placed her briefcase on the table. He half expected her to open it and begin a business meeting. Her gaze followed his to the bag. "Oh, sorry about that. But it's leather, and I hate to put it on the ground."

"Oh, trust me, I understand," he said, once again taking his seat. "So, um. . ." He felt his nerves kick in and steadied his breathing. "Brooke tells me you're Paul Cromwell's campaign manager."

"That's right." Her face lit up. "Great man, and a great leader. Very well loved in Texas."

"How long has he been in office?"

"He came to D.C. in '96." She maintained her joyous expression as she talked about him. "And he's a well-respected senator. People on both sides of the fence love working with him."

"Wow."

"Yes. And I know we've just elected a new president, but it's not too soon to be thinking ahead. We're looking forward to the next presidential campaign," she explained. "And early polls have shown us that Senator Cromwell is a viable candidate to run for office. He's a great guy, and I know he'd be perfect for the job. He's truly one of the godliest men I've ever known, and his wife is amazing, as well. Perfect first couple. But we've got a long road ahead of us."

At this point, Darren had to wonder if Andrea had time for a relationship. Sounded like she was up to her eyeballs in work.

Still, there was something special about her. He sensed her passion, sure, but it was more than that. As she began to talk about the issues that affected their country, he saw her heart for the Lord shining through.

Eventually her conversation slowed, and Andrea pulled a slip of paper out of her briefcase. She showed him some things she'd jotted down. "I know this sounds crazy, but I've learned to just get this part over with. It's my getting-to-know-you list."

"What?" He glanced at it, intrigued. "Wow. I have to answer all of those questions?"

"Only if you want to." She laughed. "But trust me, it helps to get some of the big stuff out of the way first. So, if you're game, I'm game. I'll answer if you will."

"Sure. I guess so."

He spent the next few minutes answering her preliminary questions. "I grew up in California. I have never been married. My last relationship ended amicably. I've piloted for Eastway for four years. I'm hoping to find someone with an amazing work ethic who shares my love of God, church, contemporary worship music, and Christian concerts. And I like quiet walks on the beach."

I like walks on the beach? Where in the world did that come from?

Darren could've slapped himself. He'd only been to the beach three or four times since moving to New Jersey.

Andrea clicked off her answers to the same questions in short order: "I'm the oldest of four children. Raised in the D.C. area. Top of my graduating class, both in high school and at Stanford. Just out of college, I served as an aide to a prominent senator. Dated loosely but never had time for a serious relationship. No pets. Don't have time or energy. Love the Lord. Believe firmly in placing Him at the center of every relationship."

Darren gave the same one-word answer he'd used earlier: "Wow." For whatever reason, he couldn't think of anything else to say.

"C'mon, Candy. We won't stay long. Just come with us."

Candy looked up into Lilly's pouting eyes as she answered. "I have a flight tomorrow. My first. I can't stay out late."

"Late? It's not even five o'clock yet. And I'm just talking about coffee here, not dinner. You'll be back before the sun goes down. But come with us, please. We're bored."

As they made the drive, Shawneda carried on about a male flight attendant who'd caught her eye.

"You're thinking of dating a fellow employee?" Candy quirked a brow. "I thought most airlines advised against that."

Shawneda shrugged. "Not Eastway. As long as it doesn't interfere with my work in any way, I'm free to date who I like."

"Wow." Candy shook her head. "Well, you can count me out of that one."

"Listen to her." Lilly giggled. "She's probably got an old boyfriend back in Tucson that she's not telling us about. Someone other than that Russ guy, I mean. That's why she's got her antennae down. A handsome guy could walk right by her, and she wouldn't even notice."

"Oh, I'd notice." Candy forced herself not to think about Darren's gorgeous blue eyes. "But I'd look the other way. Right now God has given me a chance to have the job of my dreams, and I'm not going to do anything to blow it."

"So you're telling me. . .even if He brought Mr. Right and plopped him down right in front of you, you'd look the other way."

"Right now, yes." Candy nodded. "I wouldn't have any choice. And if he was truly God's man for me, he'd realize the timing wasn't right. Not yet, anyway. I've got to get through this transition I'm in before I could even think about a man." Should she tell them that she'd tried to balance work and relationships before, and it had never ended well? Maybe not.

Thankfully, Lilly dove into an animated story about a boy she used to date when she was in her teens. Shawneda countered with a harrowing tale of a relationship gone wrong when she worked at a pizza parlor during college. She'd just reached the crux of the story when they arrived at the coffee shop. They entered the crowded room, the scent of the coffee drawing them in.

Shawneda stopped her pizza story midstream just inside the door. "Whoa."

"What?" Candy followed her gaze. "Oh, wow." Darren Furst. With a woman. A really pretty woman. Polished and professional in appearance, the woman put her in mind of a talk-show host, or something along those lines. Was she a co-worker, perhaps? She sure didn't look like a pilot. Not that pilots had a particular look.

"Oh, man. I know that girl," Shawneda whispered after examining her from a distance. "High-powered political type. Andrea something-or-other. Brooke introduced me to her a couple months ago. She lives in DC."

"So, do we go over and say hello?" Lilly turned to head that way, but Candy grabbed her by the arm.

"No. It looks like they're on a date. Leave them alone." The last thing she wanted to do was interrupt someone's private time.

"A date?" Shawneda and Lilly practically squealed in unison.

Lowering her voice, Lilly echoed, "A date? From what I hear, he's too career focused."

Shawneda shook her head. "Personally, I think some woman must've broken his heart. Never made any sense to me that he didn't get out more and date. If I were five or six years older, I'd slip my arm through his and march him down the aisle." She giggled, but Candy could see a serious look in her eye.

"He told me he wasn't keen on dating, but it sure looks like he's getting out now." Candy grabbed a package of coffee to hide from Darren as he looked their way. *So much for all that stuff he said. Old-fashioned, huh?*

Lilly nudged her. "You're buying a bag of coffee to take back to the apartment?"

"Um, no. Yeah. Maybe." She peeked around the edge of the bag, trying to get a look at Andrea. She was pretty, no doubt. But was she Darren's type?

Darren's type? Where did that come from?

They inched their way up in line, the girls going on and on about Darren's sad dating life. . .or lack thereof, as Lilly put it. Candy refused to join in. He could date whomever he wanted. What business was it of hers?

"That Darren is a marshmallow," Shawneda said with a sigh. "I can't see him paired up with a dynamo like that."

"Oh?" Candy looked her way, curious.

"Yeah. She could steamroll right over him. Brooke told me she's a real powerhouse. She's been interviewed on nearly every major news station, and the *New York Times* ran a piece on her a few months ago. We're talking about a major player here. In political arenas, I mean."

"Not Darren's type at all." Lilly wrinkled her nose as they stepped forward in line. "I always pictured him with a schoolteacher. Or a librarian maybe."

"A librarian?" Shawneda snorted. "He needs someone with a lot of pizzazz to bring him out of his shell. Like, maybe a cruise ship singer or a Hollywood starlet."

Candy could hardly keep her thoughts to herself after such a ridiculous comment. Darren was an easygoing, friendly soul, someone who just needed a secure, steady woman at his side. "I see him with a businesswoman of some sort. Confident, but not outlandish."

"Why not a deep-sea diver or a brain surgeon?" A familiar male voice rang out from behind them. *Darren.* Candy felt her cheeks heat up. She didn't turn around. She didn't dare.

"Then again," he continued, "my aunt Lucy always said I'd be a pastor and would marry the church pianist. So I guess all of the females in my life have missed the mark when it comes to my dating life."

Shawneda and Lilly turned to face him, giggling like schoolgirls.

"Don't you know better than to sneak up on a girl when she's talking about a handsome man?" Shawneda crooned.

Candy cringed, thankful to suddenly be at the front of the line. She quickly ordered a cup of coffee, then paid for it, wishing she could somehow escape Darren's gaze. Still, she couldn't avoid him forever. She turned his way as Shawneda placed her order.

"I'm sorry about that. I'm usually not so free with my opinions. And I've never been accused of being a gossip before. Don't know what came over me." She tried to take a sip of her coffee, but it burned her lip. *Ouch.*

"Oh, I know what came over you." He gestured toward the other women. "I have it on good authority a lot of chatter about male-female relationships goes on in that apartment of yours."

"Hey now." Shawneda gave him a warning look. "We're not that bad."

"We're not that *good*, either," Lilly whispered, then laughed.

"Brooke says you're expert matchmakers," Darren added. "I think she credited Lilly for matching her up with Jason, even."

"That's right." Lilly grinned. "My doing. All my doing."

"Well, you and God." Shawneda jabbed her with an elbow. "But it's true, we're expert matchmakers. For everyone but ourselves."

"It's all harmless fun," Lilly said, as she stepped up to the counter to order her drink. "None of us has found the perfect man yet, anyway. Except Brooke, I mean."

Candy sighed. It might've been harmless fun, but Darren had overheard and possibly taken offense. Surely he didn't take well to being talked about behind his back. His dating life—or lack thereof—was none of their business.

The embarrassment that had taken hold of Candy just moments before was now replaced with shame. *Lord, I'm sorry. I try so hard to guard my tongue, and look what I've done this time.*

Darren reached the counter and ordered two coffees, then promptly returned to the cute little redhead. She talked a mile a minute, capturing his attention. Candy nudged the other girls toward the opposite side of the coffee shop. She'd suffered enough embarrassment for one night, thank you very much. No point in carrying things one bit further.

Still, as they took their seats, her gaze kept shifting back to Darren. She'd been right about one thing. He needed a confident woman at his side. Problem was, the woman in the seat next to his appeared almost too confident. More the steamroller sort. Darren was hardly getting a word in edgewise.

Then again, maybe he liked that. Some guys did.

Why am I even thinking about what Darren Furst likes and doesn't like? Candy shook her head and sighed, then shifted her focus back to Shawneda and Lilly. This quirky pair certainly gave her enough to think about, anyway.

❧

As his getting-to-know-you date with Andrea continued, Darren did his best to stay focused. She had no idea, of course, that his thoughts had shifted to the beautiful brunette who'd just entered the coffee shop. *Stop it, man. Be a gentleman.*

Thankfully, Candy and the other girls left after just a few minutes. Darren relaxed, finally able to be himself. Unfortunately, Andrea glanced at her watch and announced she had to leave.

"I've got a speaking engagement at seven, and I need to be a little early to set up my books."

"You're a writer. . .too?" He could hardly believe it. Was there anything the woman couldn't do?

"Yeah." She nodded and her cheeks turned pink. "Just a little book I wrote about allowing God back in the political arena. It's done pretty well on the New York Times bestseller list. I can't believe Brooke and Jason didn't mention it."

"I guess they wanted me to hear it from you. But, wow. A New York Times bestseller?"

"Aw, it's not a big deal." She rose to her feet and he joined her.

"No big deal?"

Andrea shrugged. "Trust me, in the circles I travel, having a book is nothing. The only thing that matters is making sure the right man—or woman—gets elected. And that's my real goal right now. Well, that and keeping my name before the public."

"Oh?"

"Might sound crazy. I'm not even all that interested in promoting myself or my book. But the more I can keep my name out there, the greater the chances I can help inner-city kids. That's my real passion."

"Right. Jason told me."

They headed toward the door of the coffee shop together. Andrea continued to share with enthusiasm in her voice. "I really am sorry that I have to leave. I was enjoying getting to know you."

"Same here."

Another glance at her watch caused her brow to wrinkle. "It's just that I'm speaking at a political fund-raiser tonight. Newark has plans for a wonderful new school of the arts for inner-city kids. They're planning to pattern it after a school in D.C. that I've worked with. Great things happening there. Wish I had the time to tell you all about it, but I've got to get going."

"Of course." He opened the door for her, and she extended her hand.

"Great to meet you, Darren." For a moment she looked directly into his eyes, and he thought he saw a glimmer of hope there.

"Great to meet you, too." He gave her hand a squeeze.

She disappeared in the direction of her rental car, and Darren stood in the open doorway, torn between returning inside for his half-filled cup of coffee and heading home to his empty house.

The coffee won out.

Chapter 7

The next morning Darren dressed for work, his thoughts shifting back and forth from Andrea to Candy. Sure, last night's date was supposed to be about one woman, but how could he think straight, once Candy Carini walked in the room? He couldn't. And he'd wrestled with the sheets through the night, half-guilty about the fact that Candy had consumed his thoughts while he was on a date with Andrea, and half-wondering when he might see Candy again.

As he drove to work, Darren's cell phone rang. He pulled his car into a nearby parking lot to take the call. Darren recognized his friend Gary's voice at once. "Hey, Darren, you got a few minutes to talk?"

"Sure." He shifted the phone to the other ear.

"Just wanted to update you, in case you hadn't heard. Some of the guys are talking about picketing, claiming discrimination. What do you think of that idea?"

"Picketing? Discrimination?" He sighed. "I don't know, Gary."

His friend's voice tightened. "Easy for you to say. You're not the one being scrutinized. But I'll bet you'd be thinking about it a lot harder if you were walking a mile in my shoes right now."

"Ouch."

"Sorry." Gary released a sigh. "That was completely out of line, and I really am sorry. I guess it's just my disappointment speaking. I know my record with the company isn't as clean as yours. Frankly, I don't know anyone whose is. Still, this is tough, man."

Darren thought about Gary. . .his quick temper, the write-up he'd received for the way he'd snapped at his crew. One incident, in particular, had raised hairs. Gary had chewed out his first officer—a woman—a few weeks back. And, from what Darren had heard, the incident was unwarranted. Likely that had been enough to put his job at risk. This wasn't the first time, after all.

So, was Eastway really applying pressure because of rising fuel costs, or was that just what Gary wanted people to think? Regardless, picketing wasn't the answer, at least not until Darren knew all the details. Even then, what would the new pilots think if he linked arms with the other men? Likely, the new female pilots had no idea what they were walking into.

Thankfully, Gary got another call. Darren slapped his cell phone shut and decided to spend the remainder of his trip to the airport in prayer.

He arrived at the parking lot with plenty of time to spare. Determined not to let the phone conversation get the better of him, he boarded the plane. Craig, a flight attendant in his early thirties, caught his attention right away. "Morning, Cap'n. We've got a new first officer onboard today."

"Oh?" Darren shifted his flight bag to the other shoulder. "Who is he?"

"He's a *she*." Craig's eyebrows elevated. "And a mighty pretty she, if I do say so myself. She's a new hire, by the way. Looks a little nervous."

"She?" Darren released a slow breath. He knew in his gut just who "she" would be.

"Name's Candy Carini. Brooke says we're supposed to call her Cotton Candy just to get her riled up."

"On her first flight? I don't think so."

Craig's expression changed. "Hey, what's up with you? You're usually the jokester."

"I'm just saying there will be plenty of time for the funny stuff later. This is her first flight, and I'm sure her nerves are going to be an issue. She doesn't need any distractions."

"O—okay. No problem."

"So. . ." Darren looked around. "Where is she, anyway?"

"Inspecting the aircraft."

With his nerves slightly jumbled, Darren said his hellos to rest of the crew, then settled into his seat to prepare for departure.

⊷

Though Candy had never flown for Eastway before today, she knew the drill. As copilot, she would carry out a visual inspection of the aircraft before entering the cockpit.

With some trepidation, she made her way around every square inch of the underbelly of the plane, checking for possible fuel leakage or hydraulic fluid dripping from pipelines. She scrutinized the landing gear and every tire, making sure they were in great condition, then inspected the engine turbine blades to make sure they were in tip-top shape. She continued on, going over everything with a fine-tooth comb. Thoroughly satisfied the aircraft was fit to fly, she made her way onboard.

Finally. The moment of truth. She approached the cockpit, surprised to find Darren Furst already seated. He turned to her with a brusque nod. She returned it, followed by a "Good morning, Captain."

"Morning."

Okay, we're a man of few words this morning. As she took her seat, Candy breathed a prayer for God's help. All the years of preparation, and yet here she sat, scared out of her mind. Not that she needed to be. She'd simply been called on to copilot with Darren, and he certainly knew his stuff.

She watched as Darren marked items off a pretakeoff checklist. While waiting for approval from the ground control to push back from the gate and start the engines, Candy tried to make small talk. She made a funny comment about their common love of coffee, and he smiled. *Ah. A connection. Finally.*

At last the moment came to start the engines. Candy pushed aside all distractions and focused on the job at hand. Though she'd flown hundreds of times before, Candy felt her heart in her throat as Darren released the brake and applied power to accelerate down the runway. She knew how important this part was. The engines were at maximum power to lift the aircraft. The roar of the engines, coupled with Darren's voice as he spoke with the air traffic controllers, made things all the more exciting.

At just the right moment, Darren pulled back the yoke, lifting the nose of the plane. She leaned back against her seat, marveling at his calm assuredness. Seconds after takeoff, he retracted the landing gear. Candy looked for the three green landing-gear lights on the instrument panel to go off. *There. Done.*

The aircraft began to climb to its cruising altitude. This process took several minutes, but Candy didn't breathe a word. She knew the drill. Other than radio calls and checklists, they needed to keep a sterile cockpit. This was all too exciting to interrupt with conversation, anyway. *Thank You, Lord. I'm here! In the cockpit of an Eastway plane, copiloting. I'm living my dream. How can I ever thank You?* There were no words to describe how she felt in this moment.

When Darren took the intercom in hand to speak to the passengers over the PA, she listened to his spiel. "Good afternoon, ladies and gentlemen. This is your captain, Darren Furst." He stopped short of saying the rest, glancing her way with a shrug. A feeling of pure shame washed over her. Her words about his comedic one-liner must've intimidated him. Now he didn't feel free to be himself. Candy swallowed hard. *Sorry about that, Lord. I'll make it up to him, I promise.*

Once they'd reached their cruising altitude, Candy felt relaxed enough for a little small talk.

"Great work, Captain." She gave Darren a smile, hoping to bring the tension in the cockpit down a little.

"Thanks." He nodded in her direction. "I appreciate your help."

"That's what they pay me to do." *That's what they pay me to do. Wow.* She marveled at the fact that God had truly answered her prayers and given her the job of her dreams. Before, it had all seemed such a lofty goal. Flying. Like some elusive thing a child would say: One day, I'm going to fly up above the clouds!

"Cotton Candy, you've got your head in the clouds again," she whispered.

"Pardon?" Darren looked at her, his brow wrinkled. "Did you say something?"

"Oh, I just. . ." She looked at him with a smile. "Just something my dad used to say. He always thought I had my head in the clouds when I was a kid."

"Looks like you still do." He flashed a winning smile as he gestured to the clouds outside.

"Mm-hmm." Candy forced her attention to the instrument panel, where she busied herself. Still, she had a hard time containing the smile that tried to creep up.

The rest of the flight went smoothly. In fact, the time seemed to pass too fast. Candy did well with her part. And she soon entered into easy conversation with Darren. He was all business on takeoff, but once the plane was safely in the air, his comfort level seemed to improve.

Less than an hour later, they approached Chicago's busy O'Hare airport. To date, Candy had only seen this airport from a passenger's point of view. She'd certainly never analyzed the runways with a pilot's eye before.

The control tower directed their aircraft to land into the wind to bring down the ground speed. In spite of some crosswinds, Darren managed to land with skill and precision. He pulled back on the throttles, raised the spoilers to disrupt airflow over the wings, and reversed the thrust of the engines while applying the brakes. *Wow. Nice job.*

Darren picked up the intercom to speak to the passengers. He gave the usual thank-you-for-flying-with-us spiel, then turned to Candy and quirked a brow before adding, "We'd like to ask that you remain seated until we reach the gate, ladies and gentlemen. To my knowledge, no Eastway passenger ever beat the plane to the gate."

She couldn't help but laugh. *Thank goodness. He's himself again.*

Within minutes they'd taxied into their parking bay. After shutting things down, Darren turned to her. "Let's go say good-bye to our passengers." He rose, then extended his hand to help her stand. Something about the feel of his hand in hers sent a feeling of warmth rushing through her. This was a man she could trust. . .not just with her emotions, but her very life.

She tagged along behind him as they joined Brooke and the rest of the crew to wave good-bye to their passengers.

"Great flight, Cap'n," Craig said, when the last of the passengers left.

"And great flight to you, too." Brooke gave Candy an admiring look. "How did it feel, being in the cockpit?"

"Wonderful." Should she add that being there with Darren gave her the security she needed to make it through her first Eastway flight?

"Now we get to turn around and do it all over again." Brooke glanced at her watch. "We'll depart for Newark in less than an hour. Should arrive just before six. Anyone up to dinner at DiMarco's after? Best Italian food in Newark."

"Italian food?" Candy shrugged. "My personal favorite."

Darren looked her way with a smile. "If you're in, I'm in."

Oh yeah, I'm in all right.

"Well then, when we get to Newark, we'll fly this coop." His eyes sparkled with excitement. . .an invitation, perhaps?

"Mm-hmm." With this man at the helm, she might just be willing to fly to the moon.

Chapter 8

At six forty-five that same evening, Candy found herself seated around a table at DiMarco's Italian restaurant with several fellow employees—Brooke, Shawneda, Darren, and a friend of Shawneda's named Teresa. The delicious smell of garlic hung in the air, and everywhere she looked, people dined on pizza, pasta, and other goodies.

Glancing at her new friends, she had to admit, there was a certain camaraderie here, one she loved already. These people were truly becoming family. . . and in such a short time. And now, as they sat with menus in hand, Candy marveled at the fact that she'd only known them weeks and not years.

"I'm so glad you like Italian food," Brooke said, leaning her way. "I can't live without it. It's in the Antonelli blood."

"Oh, I love it." Candy nodded, eyeing a plate of pasta as the waiter carried it by. "I'm a Carini, after all. Grew up in a fairly traditional Italian family."

"Really?" Darren looked her way. "So, what are you going to order? I think I'm going to have the spaghetti and meatballs."

"Just like a guy." Shawneda rolled her eyes. "You could eat spaghetti any night of the week, and you order it in a restaurant? C'mon. Live dangerously. Climb out of the box. Order something different for a change."

"Different?" He looked at her, perplexed. "But. . .I like spaghetti."

"Yeah, me, too." Candy shrugged. "But I'll bet the meatballs aren't as good as my mom's."

Darren gave her an inquisitive look. "So, your mom is a good cook?"

"Oh, the best." Candy smiled as she thought about the many ways her mother excelled above most other moms she knew. "You name it, she can make it. Main course, desserts, and you should see her ice cream cakes. She sells a lot of those at the store."

"Wow, she sounds great."

"Oh, she is. I truly think she's one of the biggest blessings in my life. And she's one of those women who's great at everything. Pop says she's got the Midas touch. But then again, he's always been the first one to sing her praises. I love it."

"Ah."

His expression shifted from interest to something. . .almost sad. Candy couldn't put her finger on it. Had she said something wrong? "So, tell me about your mom. Is she a good cook?"

"I guess so, but she never really enjoyed cooking, and I guess it showed in the food. It was good, don't get me wrong. Just not. . ." He paused and shook his head. Clearly, he did not want to be talking about this. "Anyway, our dinner table experiences weren't the best in town. But it didn't have a lot to do with the food."

Candy quickly changed the direction of the conversation. "Well, I'm not great in the kitchen, either. I don't mind admitting it. I've tried my hand at cooking, but I've burned half the stuff I attempted. Maybe I'll get better in time."

"You just need the right man to cook for." Brooke winked.

Candy did her best not to roll her eyes. *Please. Finding the right guy isn't going to make me want to cook.*

Then again, how did she know? Maybe finding the right guy would make her want to do all the things she hadn't enjoyed before.

Like now, for instance. She'd never been great at opening up and sharing in a group. As the middle child, sitting quietly while others talked around her had pretty much been the norm. But today, with Darren at her side, she was chattering about dozens of things. Maybe it was just the postflight nerves, but something gave her the added zeal to throw her two cents' worth in at nearly every turn.

"I'm glad to see this side of you," Brooke said, when Candy paused for breath. "I was starting to wonder if you'd ever come out of your shell."

Candy giggled. "I guess it took getting that first flight out of my system. But I think you're going to see a whole different side of me now."

Looking at Darren, she had to wonder if he would like the new and improved Candy Carini. Not that what he thought really mattered. Right? After all, he was just a fellow employee, nothing more.

Looking into his eyes she realized for the first time that she actually wanted it to be more.

&

As they waited on their food, the conversation shifted to the flight. Darren waited for just the right moment to share his thoughts with Candy. When the other girls entered into an exaggerated and somewhat annoying discussion about handbags, he turned to her and spoke quietly. "I just wanted to tell you that you did a great job today. I was impressed. And you looked at ease."

Candy's eyes sparkled as she responded. "Thanks. Don't know if I mentioned it to you or not, but I got in some of my flight hours working for a cargo carrier. I was with them a little over a year."

"Really?" He gave her an admiring look. "I got my hours in as a charter pilot in California."

"Same with a lot of my friends. But cargo jobs were easier to come by in Arizona." She shrugged. "Probably not as exciting, though."

"But it kept you in the air." He gave her a smile.

"Right. And anything that keeps you in the air is a good thing."

"Amen to that." He paused a moment. "You're a Christian, right?"

"Yes." She nodded, but quirked a brow, likely wondering where he was headed with this line of questioning.

"I haven't met a lot of other Christian pilots. A few, but not many. Just wondering. . ."

"What?" She gave him a curious look.

"Well, when I'm flying, I feel. . .closer to God. Does that make sense?"

The edges of her lips turned up as she responded. "Makes a lot of sense. It's one of the things I love most about flying. There's something about being up there in the clouds that makes Him seem so close. Like I could reach out and touch Him."

I couldn't have put it better myself. "There's a scripture I love. I think it's in Isaiah. It's the one about mounting up with eagle's wings."

"Sure. Of course." She gave him an inquisitive look.

"I waited a long time for the opportunity to fly," he said. "Dreamed about it when I was a kid. I was always the one jumping off the roof, pretending I could fly."

"Me, too." The dazzling smile that followed her words nearly caused him to forget the rest of his story.

Sounds like we have a lot in common. "Well, when I'm in the cockpit, I feel like everything I waited for was for a purpose. Like I'm that eagle, taking flight. Like nothing can stop me."

"Wow." Candy gave him a look of admiration, then paused for a moment, a thoughtful look on her face. "Whenever I'm flying, I think of that verse in Psalms about God mounting the cherubim and flying." She quoted the rest from memory: " 'He soared on the wings of the wind.' " Her eyes filled with tears. "Might sound crazy, but it's overwhelming to think that God is right there, flying alongside me. I sense His presence most when I'm in the air."

"Man. Me, too." Darren forgot just about everything he'd planned to say next. Looking into Candy's tear-filled eyes, he found himself completely over-whelmed—not just with her passion for flying, but her passion for the Lord.

Off to the side, something distracted him. Brooke looked back and forth between them, her eyes narrowed. Darren finally turned to her to ask, "What?"

"You two." She shook her head.

"What about us?" Candy took a sip from her glass of water.

"You're a match made in heaven. And this time, I mean that quite literally."

Thankfully, Darren didn't have time to comment. The waitress chose that moment to appear with their food. He caught Candy's eye as the steaming bowls of spaghetti and meatballs were placed before him. She gave him a little wink and his heart seemed to turn itself inside out.

After Darren prayed over the food, he turned his attention to Candy once again. "So, you were a cargo pilot."

"Yes. Got in a lot of hours. A little on the boring side, though. Hurry up and wait stuff. I also did a short stint as a skydiving pilot."

"Really. Ever witness any accidents?" He took a bite of the spaghetti, waiting for her response.

She shook her head. "No, but a couple of close calls. We had a guy who had to use his backup chute. And the worst was a woman who got tangled up in a tree. She was pretty scraped up, but no broken bones, thankfully."

Darren was just about to ask her if she'd ever jumped, but Brooke interrupted him. "I think you'd have to be nuts to jump out of a plane. I can't imagine doing it. . .on purpose, anyway."

"Well, how else would you do it?" Candy asked. Everyone laughed, including Darren. *See there. She's got a great sense of humor, too.*

Brooke put her hand up. "I'm just saying, in our line of work, it's better to keep all arms and legs inside the plane, not out."

"Yeah," Darren said, "but there's something about the idea of free-falling that's pretty amazing. Letting go of everything. Releasing every care, every anxiety. . ."

"Releasing anxiety?" Candy looked at him, her eyes wide. "Jumping out of a plane will help me release my anxieties?"

Okay. So there was his answer as to whether or not she'd ever jumped. Obviously not. "Well, you need to try it sometime. I think it's a blast. Very freeing."

"Darren's always coming up with kooky ideas." Brooke laughed. "But usually they're not life-threatening. One time he came up with this off-the-wall plan for our crew out of Chicago. He bought those goofy-looking fake teeth for all of the flight attendants. You know the ones I'm talking about? They look awful."

"Yes, I think so." Candy shrugged.

Darren groaned, realizing just how nutty this story would make him look.

Brooke continued, more animated than before. "Well, at the end of the flight, all the flight attendants turned toward the front of the plane to put the teeth in, then turned back to the passengers. When we opened our mouths. . ." Brooke started laughing so hard, she could barely continue. "When we opened our mouths, Darren came over the PA and told the passengers that Eastway had a crummy dental program. Told them to keep flying with us so the company could afford to get better coverage."

Candy chuckled as she looked at Darren. "That's hysterical."

At her words, his concerns vanished. *She thinks I'm funny.* That changed everything.

"And then he did this really horrible thing to his fabulous crew members once," Brooke continued. "This one really took the cake. We were on an evening flight, and the lights in the cabin were down. So, Darren comes on the PA and tells the passengers he's turned down the lights to enhance the appearance of the flight attendants."

"Ouch." Candy giggled.

"Hey, I thought it was funny," Darren said with a shrug. "And the passengers did, too. But. . .I ended up apologizing later. Should've stopped myself before poking fun at my own crew."

"Nah." Brooke laughed and dismissed it with the wave of a hand. "We all thought it was a hoot. In fact, we think all of Darren's jokes are funny, even the goofy ones. In fact, they're the funniest of all."

Darren took a bite of his spaghetti, finally starting to relax. Maybe Candy wouldn't think less of him, after all.

"So, let me ask you a question." She turned to face him. "Were you always the funny guy? Like, class clown? Where did all this humor come from, anyway?"

The conversation seemed to shift a bit as his gaze tipped downward. When he finally looked up, Darren said, "My parents didn't always get along. My mom. . .well, let's just say she wasn't easy to live with. And my dad pretty much checked out when she turned on him, which was a lot. So I tried to infuse humor whenever things got tense. And, um. . .they got tense pretty often."

"So you were the buffer?"

"I guess I've always believed God can use humor to lift people's spirits. I never know who's going to end up on one of my flights. But I pray before every one. And you never know. Someone might be having a terrible day, but then I give them something to laugh at and they feel better."

"And he does make them feel better." Brooke gave an emphatic nod, then turned Darren's way. "It's amazing how many passengers tell me how great they think you are."

He offered a quiet, "Thanks."

"And I hear Fred thinks you're pretty cool, too."

Darren groaned.

"Fred?" Candy gave him a funny look. "Who's Fred?"

"My new goldfish. Jason decided I was lonely, so he bought me a fish. Just brought it over a few days ago. Kind of a lonely little guy, swimming in that great big tank."

"Well, I'm just glad to finally hear there's a fish in the tank," Brooke said. "Never could figure out why you had an empty fish tank in your living room."

Same reason I have an empty house. I've got no one to put in it.

Darren cleared his throat. "Well, it's not empty anymore. Fred keeps me company now."

"I'd like to meet him someday." Candy gave him an unpretentious smile.

We will see to that. Darren took a bite of his pasta and tried to swallow down the remainder of his embarrassment with it.

The conversation quieted for a couple of minutes as everyone ate. Brooke finally broke the silence with an announcement.

"Before I forget. . .remember I promised to set up a trip to Atlantic City for the singles ministry?"

Candy looked across the table at her with a surprised look on her face. "You're going to my old stomping ground on a field trip? I don't remember hearing about it."

"Well, I'm doing it for Darren, really. He's never been to the boardwalk."

"Oh, wow." Candy looked at him with a stunned expression. "Well, you've missed out on a lot, then. The arcades, the shops, the hotels, the water. It's a pretty amazing place."

He shrugged. "I'm from the West Coast. I guess I've just had a hard time adjusting to the Atlantic. The Pacific is. . ." He sighed. "Well, where I lived in Southern California, it was pretty unbelievable."

"Trust me, we've got some pretty beaches on the East Coast, too," Candy said. As she began to describe the colors of the water against the white sand, Darren found himself hanging on every word. It had nothing to do with the description of the beaches. No, he could care less about beaches right now. All that mattered in this moment was the look of pure joy on the face of the prettiest pilot he'd ever met.

Chapter 9

Candy spent the rest of the meal laughing and talking with the others. The time passed far too quickly. By the time they finished their meal and the conversation, it was nine thirty.

Darren excused himself from the group. "I've got a long day ahead of me tomorrow."

"Me, too," Candy said. As the other girls murmured their agreement and began to get up from the table, Candy started to push her chair back, but he rose and helped her. *Wow. Okay, then. Either he's just incredibly friendly or he's paying me special attention.*

They said their good-byes and parted ways, but Candy couldn't stop thinking about Darren. All the way back to the apartment, her mind reeled. She replayed the whole day—the part on the plane and especially the part at dinner, where he gazed at her with such tenderness in his eyes.

After Brooke, Shawneda, and Candy arrived at their apartment, Candy slipped into her pj's, then knocked on Brooke's bedroom door.

"Come in."

She went inside, grateful that Shawneda was in the shower. Candy wanted to talk to Brooke alone, away from the crowd for a change. Brooke gestured for her to sit on the bed, so she did.

"So, tell me more about Darren." Candy hesitated. "He seems a little. . ."

"Soft?"

Candy nodded. "And funny." She paused, thinking through her words before speaking them. "It's so strange. When we're at church or in a restaurant or something, he's completely relaxed. But around some of the guys on the plane—like Craig, for instance—I noticed he was a little more guarded. The first few minutes of our flight today he was pretty cool toward me. He softened up, but it took a few minutes."

"Ah, well. . ." Brooke hesitated. "There's a reason for that."

"Really?"

Brooke sighed, and her gaze shifted for a moment. As she looked back in Candy's direction, she said, "I think it's a little complicated, actually."

"Tell me."

"Well, Darren talked to Jason about all of this just a few days ago. He's upset because a couple of pilots have lost their jobs at Eastway recently and others were hired on to take their place."

"Oh." Candy's heart felt like it hit her toes. "I had no idea they were letting people go. Do you know why?"

Brooke drew in a deep breath. "Jason said it has something to do with rising fuel costs, but I'm not so sure."

"Then why hire new pilots?" None of this made any sense.

"Well, they're hiring women, which has the guys worked up. They're speculating it has something to do with a quota, which is ridiculous. Eastway doesn't work like that. Their hiring practices have never come under question like this." Brooke's gaze shifted to the window, then back again. "But, look, don't take it personally. This is just scuttlebutt. The rumor mill at work. We don't know any of this for sure."

"Wow. So what should I do?"

"Just be yourself. And fly straight. Do your best." Brooke hesitated a moment. "But, Candy, be prepared for something, okay?"

"What?"

"Craig told me some of the men were thinking of making a bigger deal out of the incoming female pilots than they should. Involving the union. Picketing, even. They're all worked up and followed after Gary. He's the pied piper here, and a suspicious one, at best. He's had his share of problems with Eastway, but never admits when he's done something wrong."

Candy's heart suddenly felt like lead. "D–do you think Darren would join them?"

"I can't imagine it, but you never know. He's done his best to befriend Gary, mostly to witness to him. And like I said, Gary's the one who's the most worked up." Brooke sighed. "If you ask me, he had it coming. I've flown with him in the past and seen his true colors. He's pretty short with the crew and even with the tower. He was written up before, and his attitude doesn't seem to be improving."

"Ah." Candy relaxed a little bit at this news.

"Right. You get it. And I'm sure you've heard that runway incidents are up at Newark Liberty. Statistics aren't good. So, everyone's on guard. But Gary's got the guys in a frenzy, so be prepared. There's nothing worse than a band of angry men."

A shiver ran down Candy's spine. She'd run into her share of frustrated male pilots over the years, for sure. In flight school, and even on the job in Arizona. Still, she'd never seen them protest in a public way, like the kind of thing Brooke was talking about. Looked like she had plenty to pray about.

"Hey, you two look way too serious." Shawneda came out of the bathroom in some crazy-looking Pink Panther pajamas and her hair in a towel. "We need to lighten things up a little." She pulled the towel from her hair and began smacking them with it.

After a few minutes of laughter, Brooke spoke up. "Shawneda, I think you should've been born a boy."

"Hey now. Watch what you're saying. I'm a girlie girl." She smacked Brooke with the towel once again.

Still laughing, Candy excused herself and headed to her bedroom. Thankfully, Lilly was working a late-night shift, so she had the room to herself. As she climbed into bed, Candy pondered Brooke's words. *So, Darren is secretly upset with me for potentially taking a job away from one of the guys.*

That changed everything. Absolutely everything.

❧

Darren had just settled into bed when the phone rang. Looking at the caller ID, he noticed Jason's number.

He answered with the words, "You're up late."

"Yeah, I hear I missed a great time at dinner. Brooke filled me in. Wish I could've come."

"It was nice."

"So, how's Fred?" Jason's voice had a humorous edge to it.

"Lonely. But I think he's adjusting."

"Mm-hmm. Maybe you need to buy him a girlfriend. That way he's not alone in that tank of his. Oh, and speaking of females. . .Brooke told me that Candy copiloted today. How did that go?"

Darren leaned back against the pillows, noticing for the first time how bare his bedroom walls looked. *I really should hang a few pictures in here.* Snapping back to attention, he said, "Really well, actually. She knows her stuff. It's rare to find an incoming pilot this secure."

"Especially a woman?"

Darren groaned. "Look, I don't have a problem with female pilots. Just because Gary and the others are getting all worked up doesn't mean I have to."

"Ah. So getting to know her has changed your thinking, then."

"What do you mean?"

"I mean you were a little more adamant before. Tonight it seems like you're softening."

"According to your fiancée, I'm nothing but a marshmallow anyway."

"No, you've got a backbone. It's apparent to me. And there's nothing wrong with being nice. A lot of people I know are nice."

"Jason, *you're* the nice one." Darren laughed. "I guess I just didn't expect these incoming female pilots to be so. . .good at what they do. I was thinking they'd be a little sloppier. Some of the incoming pilots are, especially the nervous ones."

"But not Candy?"

"Nope. Not so far. And I guess I expected her to be really aggressive. More demanding. And Candy's nothing like that. She's. . ."

"Yeah, Brooke told me she's pretty great. So, are you thinking about—"

"No. You know my policy. No way."

"So, let me ask you a question. You're only interested in soft-spoken women? Don't want someone with chutzpah?"

"What are you talking about?"

"Well, give me a woman with spunk any day."

"Um, you've *got* a woman with spunk."

"Yeah, I do. No doubt about that." Jason laughed.

"And Candy has plenty of spunk, too," Darren added. "I also saw her business side in the cockpit today. She's really a well-balanced woman."

"Well, there you go. A well-balanced woman." Jason laughed. "Why does that surprise you so much?"

Darren sighed. "Look, Jason, we've known each other awhile, but you don't really know a lot about my background. It's kind of skewed my view of women."

"Then fill me in."

Darren paused a moment before explaining. "Look, here's the thing. My dad—I love him—but my mom's got him wrapped around her finger, and I don't mean that in a good way. She calls all the shots in that household. Always has." His mind reeled backward in time. He could see his father now in his mail carrier's uniform, walking in the door after a long day on his feet. Could hear his mother's voice, drilling him about this or that. She never asked him anything. Always told him. And never in a nice voice.

Jason's voice interrupted Darren's thoughts. "So you're looking for just the opposite? Is that why you're so relieved Candy's a softie like you?"

Darren sighed. He'd never come out and said it, but yes. Not that he wanted to tell anyone what to do, but it would be nice to have a woman's respect. And not because of anything he happened to do for a living. It wasn't about that.

"I'm just saying aggressive isn't terribly appealing to me, particularly from a woman." *And if you knew how aggressive my mother was—is—you'd understand.*

"Doesn't sound like that's what you're saying to me. I think you're really wishing your dad had been more aggressive."

Ouch.

"So, have you forgiven him?"

"Forgiven my dad?" Darren's jaw tightened as he contemplated Jason's words. "Why would I need to forgive my dad? He's a great guy. My mom is the one who—"

"Darren, listen. I don't know your parents and don't want to presume anything about them. But in a relationship that's completely out of balance—where one person clearly holds the reins—the guilt is on both sides. Men need to stand up and be men. Take responsibility. But that doesn't mean women have to roll over and play dead when a man walks into the room."

"Well, I never said—"

"No, but you're thinking it. You're okay as long as no one rocks the boat.

And maybe you thought Candy and these other incoming female pilots might do just that. But, so what if they had? Maybe the boat needs to be rocked."

Darren sighed. "Maybe. Never thought about that."

"Well, think about it. And Darren, it's not just your view on women that's skewed. You've spent too much time analyzing both sexes. I think you're secretly worried that you're not aggressive enough to handle a strong woman, but you are."

I hope so.

"So, your dad was too soft. And maybe you're worried you're a little soft, too. But I know you. I've watched you for years. Your strength is in God, not yourself. And that's a good thing. I think you're more balanced than you know. Soft on the outside, tough on the inside."

"Never thought about it that way."

"Just don't go too far out of your way to become something other than what you are, especially if these guys at Eastway get all riled up. You don't have to prove anything to anyone."

"Right."

"And don't worry about the female thing." Jason laughed. "God's going to bring you just the right person to balance you out. She won't be aggressive like your mother. You'll see to that. But she won't be a piece of fluff, either. She'll have a backbone. And you'll love that about her. So, get ready."

Oh, I'm ready all right. As he ended the call, Darren realized just how ready he was.

Chapter 10

The following Saturday morning, Darren paced his house, a nervous wreck. "Just call her, man. It's not rocket science. She's just a woman." He punched in Candy's number and, thankfully, she answered on the third ring.

"Candy? This is Darren," he managed. *Why are my palms sweating?*

"Darren, hi. Something happen I need to know about?" At once he picked up on a hint of anxiety in her voice.

"No, nothing happening at work, if that's what you mean. I, um. . .well, I have a friend who has a Cessna 400, and he's wondering if I want to take it out for a spin. I thought maybe you might like to come with me."

"Come fly with you?"

"Yes." There. He'd said it. Now, if she would just come back with an affirmative answer. . .

"Sounds like fun. Where? When?"

Whew. "This afternoon. Do you know where Essex County airport is?"

"Sort of. I know it's not far. Maybe northwest of here?"

"Yes. Won't take us long to get there, and I'll do the driving. I'll pick you up in an hour. . .unless that's too soon."

"An hour?" She paused and he almost cratered while waiting for her response. She finally came back with, "Um, sure. I've been out running errands this morning and look. . .well, not great."

As if that were possible. "Just come as you are," he said.

They ended the call and Darren flew into action. If things went as planned, Candy Carini would see a whole new side to him today. . .hopefully one she couldn't resist. He picked out a nice shirt to wear. Blue. Someone once told him it brought out the color of his eyes. He'd never forgotten that. And he spent a little extra time working on his hair today. No point in scaring her with unruly waves. He leaned in close to the mirror to examine every square inch of his face. *Ah. Missed a spot shaving. Better remedy that.*

As he prepared to leave the house, Darren stopped off at the fish tank to look at Fred. "Hey, little guy." The forlorn goldfish swam around the tank in solitude making *Ooo, Ooo, Ooo* faces. "I feel your pain. Should I get you a fish friend? Maybe a female? Someone in a great shade of orange?"

After no response from Fred, Darren hit the road. There would be plenty of time to worry about the fish's love life later. Right now he'd better focus on his own.

Candy touched up her makeup and double-checked her outfit in the mirror before Darren arrived. She could hardly wait to spend time with him one-on-one, away from the crowd. She marveled over how much her feelings for him seemed to be changing. Thinking of how she'd judged him that first day on the plane now brought nothing but shame. Any lingering questions she'd had about his flying abilities had been answered in the cockpit. And certainly, from their many times together in a group environment, his love for God had come shining through. Of course, there was that thing about the male pilots losing their jobs. . .

No, I'm not going to go there.

She pushed aside any troubling thoughts and prepared for her date with Darren. How wonderful it would be, to hit the skies in a small plane once again. Surely—after hearing her story the other night—he'd planned this day just for her. And she couldn't wait.

The doorbell rang promptly at 1:30 p.m., just as he'd said. Candy answered with a smile on her face. "You're right on time."

"Yes, I. . ." He looked at her, his eyes widening. "Wow."

His one word caused heat to rise to her cheeks. "Thanks. I wasn't sure what to wear."

"Anything but the uniform would be just fine." He laughed. "If you're like I am, you change the minute you get home. It's pretty confining."

She shrugged. "Oh, I don't know. I kind of like it. But I'm pretty new and all."

"Right. Well, that blouse is. . .wow. And I've never seen you in jeans before. They suit you."

"Thank you." His charming and somewhat embarrassing words made her feel like a high schooler all over again. And he didn't look half bad in that blue shirt, either. Really made his eyes pop. But, should she tell him? Did women say things like that to guys? Not on a first date, likely.

Thankfully, she never had time to carry through with the idea. He led the way out of the apartment and toward the parking lot. When they reached the car, he opened the front passenger door for her.

"Thank you, kind sir." She gave him a wink. *Where did that come from?*

"You're more than welcome." He returned the wink and closed the door.

Butterflies rose up in Candy's stomach, and they fluttered in greater anticipation as she glanced in the backseat and saw a large wicker picnic basket. *If he's got our lunch in there, I'm going to marry him today, whether he asks or not.*

Minutes later Darren pulled the car out onto the expressway, headed northwest.

"I haven't been to Essex County airport in ages," he said. "But my friend Jimmy works out there, and he's pretty proud of this new bird of his. It's a Cessna 400."

"I'll bet. I wouldn't mind owning a Cessna myself. But I like the Cessna 208. You can seat nine."

"Really?" Darren gave her a funny look. "That's funny. I was about to say the same thing."

"Well, I have a big family. My parents, two sisters, a brother-in-law, and a baby on the way."

"A baby on the way?"

"My sister. Taffie."

"Oh, right. The older sister."

"Yep. I've always thought it would be a blast to be able to fly my whole family away on a vacation someplace." She sighed as she contemplated the improbabilities of getting everyone in the family together at the same time in the same place. "Who knows. Maybe it'll happen someday."

"I hope so. Sounds like fun. I mean. . .if you're okay with me taking one of the leftover seats."

"Well, of course. We wouldn't dream of going without you." *Now, where did that come from?*

They lit into a conversation about small planes, chatting easily as he drove. Several times she caught him looking at her out of the corner of his eye. Unlike that day in the cockpit, he seemed more relaxed. More himself.

Candy wanted to ask about the situation with the men at Eastway, but decided this wouldn't be the time or the place. If he wanted to talk about all that, surely he would bring it up. But why ruin a perfectly wonderful afternoon?

They arrived at Essex County at two fifteen. As soon as Darren pulled his car into the parking lot, Candy's excitement grew.

"You ready for this?" he asked, as he turned to her with a boyish grin.

"I can't wait."

"So, you want to fly. . .or jump?"

"J–jump?" Her heart began to race. Jumping certainly wasn't in her plans.

"Hey, you told me you flew a skydiving plane. Right? I thought maybe you might like to—"

"Oh no!" She put her hands up, terrified at the idea. "It's one thing to fly the plane, another to jump out of it."

He chuckled as he got out of the car and came around to her side. Opening the door, he said, "Well, if you change your mind, let me know. I have it on good authority Jimmy will take over the flying if we decide to skydive. And I'm a consummate skydiver. Love it, in fact."

Candy shook off the idea right away. She'd never confessed this to a soul. . . didn't know if she ever would. . .but the idea of skydiving terrified her. Too many variables. No, she'd stick to piloting, thank you very much.

For the next half hour, Candy and Darren made the rounds from hangar to hangar to look at the various planes.

"Hey, check out this. . . ." She pointed to a single engine SkyCatcher. "What do you think of that?"

"Small." He shook his head. "After flying for Eastway, these planes look microscopic to me."

"Same here. But it's funny. That first flight with Eastway, the plane felt huge. Now it's just right."

"You sound like Goldilocks."

"What?"

"You know. This chair is too big. This one's too small. This one is just right." He started laughing and before long she joined in.

"I guess it's all a matter of perspective."

"Yep." He paused at a small jet. "Now we're talking. This is what I'd buy, if I could." He gave it a closer look. "I'd run a charter service back and forth from New York to DC. Can you imagine my clientele during an election year?"

"It would be crazy, but fun." She climbed inside the small aircraft and looked around. "This reminds me of being in Arizona. I flew a jet about this size once." She settled into the pilot's seat, feeling right at home. "Oh yeah." A couple of minutes later she emerged with a smile on her face. "So, where's this 400 we're supposed to fly?"

"Funny you should ask," a male voice rang out from behind them. "I'd just had to put her out of service. Engine trouble."

She turned to see a man, slightly older than Darren, approaching. Must be Jimmy.

"Oh no." Darren groaned. "So we drove out here for nothing."

"Oh, not for nothing." Candy drew near and gave him her best it-was-worth-it-anyway look. "It's been great, just seeing all of these planes and being at a small airport again. Reminds me of where I've come from. And I don't mind about the 400. Really."

Darren made introductions, but Candy could read the disappointment in his eyes.

"I can still take you up in the SkyCatcher," Jimmy said. "She's a beauty."

"No, don't worry about it. We can still look around, and I brought lunch. . . ."

Candy gave him a reassuring look. "I think that sounds great. Really. We can fly anytime."

"Well, tell me if you change your mind," Jimmy said. "In the meantime, if you're interested in climbing aboard the Chariot for a view of the cockpit, feel free."

"The Chariot?" Candy's confusion grew.

"Oh, that's what I call my 400. She's my Chariot. Only, not today. She's just outside the hangar, drinking up some sunshine." He led them around the side of the building.

Candy gasped as she saw the beautiful plane with THE CHARIOT emblazoned in gold letters on the side. "Oh, she's gorgeous. Look at those colors."

"And great lettering. Jimmy did all of the detailing himself."

"Flattery will get you everywhere." Jimmy winked. "You kids go on and climb aboard. I've got to get back up to the office. Stop by after you've had your lunch and we'll chat awhile."

"Thanks, Jimmy." Darren reached to shake his hand.

"No problem." Jimmy headed off toward the terminal, and Darren gazed at Candy with renewed hope in his eyes. "Want to climb aboard?"

"Do I ever!"

"Well, madame. . .your chariot awaits." After a quick glance at the words on the side of the plane, he added, "Literally."

Chapter 11

D arren's frustrations over the grounded plane lifted the minute he saw the joy in Candy's expression. Clearly she didn't mind if they only saw the view from the ground. She was content to do just that.

He helped her onboard, then joined her. Once inside, they sat together in silence for a moment, looking things over. Candy finally spoke up. "If I closed my eyes, I could see myself back in Arizona. What about you?"

"Hmm. Well, I guess I could see myself back in California. I haven't flown many small planes since then."

"Okay, let's do it." She gave him a playful smile.

"Do what?"

"Close our eyes and pretend."

"Um. . .okay." He shrugged, then squeezed his eyes shut.

"What do you see?" she asked after a minute.

"The inside of my eyelids?"

Candy laughed. "No, where do you see yourself flying? Use your imagination. If you could fly anywhere in the world. . .if money and time were no object, where would you go?"

"Oh, that's easy." He relaxed a bit, his eyes still shut. "I've always wanted to fly over the countryside in England. In a plane just like this one."

"We're there right now." The enthusiasm in Candy's voice prompted him to play along. "Just use your imagination. What do you see?"

"Hmm." He paused a moment to think about it, never opening his eyes. "I see the tops of country houses with smoke coming from the chimneys."

"Sounds amazing. What else?"

Darren opened one eye long enough to sneak a peek of her beautiful face. Sure enough, her eyes were still closed. She was taking this game very seriously. "Well, I see green. Everywhere. Green rolling hills. And a river. It's beautiful. Oh, and look. . .there's a castle. With a moat."

"It's a shame I left my ball gown and tiara at home." She sighed. "We'll have to miss the fun. But what else do you see?"

"Well. . ." He stretched his imagination. "I think we're coming into a city. Oh, it's London. Look there. It's Big Ben. Want a closer look?"

"Sure!"

He let out a whooshing sound. "Whew. Barely missed it. But it's seven forty-five London time, in case you missed that."

"No, I saw it." She laughed. "You're really good at this."

I wouldn't be caught dead doing it in front of any of the guys I know, but thanks.

Deciding to play along, Darren turned the question on her. "So, your turn. Where do you want to go?"

"Hmm. Well, I've always wanted to fly way out over the ocean," she said. "We didn't see a lot of water in Arizona."

"So, where are you taking me?" He smiled as soon as the words were spoken. Darren knew where Candy Carini was taking him, of course. Right over the edge. Into the vast unknown. Into uncharted territory, places his heart had never visited. Not that he minded. He'd play along, if it meant being with her. And besides, he was rather enjoying this.

"I think I'll fly us over the Hawaiian Islands," she said, her voice taking on a dreamy sound. "We'll start with the big island, okay?"

"Sure."

"Oh, do you see that?"

"See what?" He opened one eye again, half expecting to really see something.

"That volcano. It's erupting off in the distance. Made the plane shake. Oh, man. I've got to get us out of here. Look at that ash." Her tone grew more soothing. "But don't worry about that now. We're back out over the water. It's gorgeous. Have you ever in your life seen water like that before? I've never seen that color. Would you call that teal or cerulean?"

"Cerulean?" His eyes opened instinctively. "What in the world is cerulean?"

"A shade of blue. How can anyone *not* believe in God when they see a color like that? Close your eyes, now. No peeking."

Her eyes were closed tight. *How in the world could she. . . ?*

"Oh, hold on!" she called out. "We're about to fly over a really nice hotel with a beautiful white sand beach. I want to see if I recognize any movie stars. Oh, look right there. I'm pretty sure that's. . .aw, never mind. It's not her. Tell the paparazzi to put their cameras away. They're always such a nuisance, don't you think? Popping up behind trees and bushes just to snag a photograph."

Darren opened his eyes and sat straight up in his seat. "Candy, can I ask you a question?"

Her eyes popped open and she looked at him, seemingly confused. "What?"

"Did you play games like this when you were a kid?"

She gave him a sheepish look. "M—maybe."

"Mm-hmm." He paused a moment. "So, all that stuff about you having your head in the clouds came from games like this."

"I suppose." She shrugged. "How come?"

"Oh, I don't know." An uneasy feeling came over him as a new revelation surfaced. "You're a daydreamer, but in a really nice sort of way. Me. . ." He paused, wondering if she would be bothered by his next words. "When I was a kid, there wasn't a lot of time for daydreams. My mom was a taskmaster. Always after me to get things done. I hardly remember any free time. Certainly no time to allow my mind to wander like this."

"Ah." She gave him a sympathetic look. "My parents were. . .*are* both hard workers. But they certainly gave us kids room to dream. My mom always said I was like Joseph from the Old Testament. . .dreaming the day away. Talking about things that seemed improbable. Oh, but you should meet my dad. He's the biggest dreamer of them all."

"I wish I could say the same." Darren exhaled. . .a little too loud. "But anyway, I stopped dreaming a long time ago. Maybe that's what wrong with me."

"What's wrong with you?" She gave him a curious look. "Who says there's anything wrong with you?"

He pondered that a moment. Yeah. Who said there was anything wrong with him?

Candy gave him a look so sweet he felt the grip around his heart give way at once. "Darren, you can't let whatever happened to you as a child keep you from being all God wants you to be. And it's not too late to dream. There's still plenty of time. . .for both of us."

Yes, there is. Staring into her eyes, he truly believed it.

"C'mon, there's one more place I want to take you. Close your eyes."

Darren suppressed a laugh as he jumped into the game once again.

"I've always wanted to see Tuscany." Candy sighed. "Oh, but Darren, look. It's so much prettier than I thought it would be. Do you see those colors? This is the most amazing landscape I've ever seen. Would you like to go to Rome next, or Venice?"

"Venice. I've always wanted to see the canals."

"Me, too. My grandfather was from Italy, you know."

"Really?" He opened his eyes and stared at her, surprised. "I didn't realize that."

"Yes. He came to America in the '30s, just before the Second World War. His family was originally from a small village in central Italy. So when I say I want to go there someday, I really mean it. It's where my people are from. Only, I've never seen it. Kind of sad, really."

Well, I'll see that you do see it. Someday. Somehow.

After a bit more daydreaming, Darren suggested they eat their lunch. He climbed out of the plane first, then reached up to take Candy's hand as she stepped down. Her foot slipped on the top step, and she let out a small holler as she tumbled forward. . .directly into his arms. Talk about a happy disaster. They ended up face-to-face, just inches apart.

Who's dreaming now?

As he loosened her hold enough to let her feet touch down, she gasped.

"I. . .I'm so sorry."

"I'm not." He kept his arms around her, enjoying the moment.

She looked up into his eyes. "I'm fine now, I promise. Thanks for catching me."

"My pleasure." He eventually released his hold completely but, after just a second apart, took her hands in his.

"Scared to let me go?" Candy gave him a sheepish look. "Afraid I'll fall again?"

"Something like that." Darren drew near. . .so near he could feel her breath on his cheek. He took a fingertip and traced her cheekbone. He could read the startled expression in her eyes at first, but it was soon replaced with a look of anticipation.

As he pulled her close, his heart rate seemed to pick up. He gave her a gentle kiss, first on one cheek, then the other. He paused to gaze into those gorgeous brown eyes.

Ironically, they now glistened with tears. "Are you all right?" he whispered.

"Yes, I. . ." She leaned her head against his chest. "Embarrassed, but. . .I'm very all right, actually." After a moment, she lifted her head and looked up at him, providing the perfect opportunity to kiss her. Never mind the fact that Jimmy's voice now rang out from behind him. Never mind that they stood in open view of half the airport. No, the only thing that mattered right now was the woman in his arms, the one he'd go on dreaming about for the rest of his life.

&

Candy closed her eyes and enjoyed the unexpected kiss. It had come from out of the blue. She certainly hadn't planned to fall, let alone into Darren's arms. But being in his arms felt so right, so safe, she had to wonder why she hadn't fallen sooner.

Or maybe she had. Maybe she'd fallen some time ago and just not admitted it to herself. Surely he'd fallen, too, or his lips wouldn't be firmly locked onto hers. *Hmm.* In spite of her silliness in the plane, he obviously still found her grown-up enough to kiss.

And kiss again.

Her thoughts shifted in a dozen different directions at once, but she stopped them immediately. No point in thinking when one was kissing, right? And who cared that they were standing in a public place with people looking on?

After the second sweet kiss, Darren released her and the tips of his ears turned red. *I hear ya, mister.* Her cheeks felt like they were on fire.

"I don't know if I should apologize or throw a party." Darren gave her a sheepish look. "Did I. . .did I embarrass you?"

"Embarrass me?" She laughed. "I'm pretty good at doing that on my own, thank you very much."

He gave her an admiring look. Oh, how she wished she could read between the lines, to get into his head and figure out what he was thinking right now.

"You're good at a lot of things," Darren said.

"Like. . .?"

"Like, bringing me out of my shell, for instance. And flying planes. And taking me places I've never been before. Places I didn't even know I wanted to see."

"It's just a little game I like to play."

She closed her eyes again and he whispered, "Tell me what you see now, Candy."

"I see. . ." She couldn't help but smile. "I see you."

He responded with a kiss that sent her heart soaring to the clouds.

Chapter 12

The next few weeks raced by. Before long, Candy found herself completely comfortable in the cockpit. She also found herself comfortable in Darren's arms. Their date in the Cessna 400 had been the perfect catalyst. Tumbling into his embrace might've been an accident, but it was the happiest one of her life. And talk about a great story! Who else could say their first kiss had happened while falling out of a plane? She couldn't have dreamed up such a happy tale.

Thankfully, Candy and Darren had plenty of time to explore their new relationship. Attending the same church helped. . .a lot. It gave them the perfect place to meet in a group setting. And, of course, they spent several off-duty hours hanging out with her roomies and Jason, too. Neither Candy nor Darren knew much about the Newark area, so they went from place to place, acting like silly tourists.

Before long, they settled into a comfortable routine. In fact, she could scarcely remember what life was like before Darren. Did she have a life before Darren? Funny, she couldn't picture it now.

More than anything, she looked forward to introducing him to her family. That dream would become a reality on August 19. . .the Saturday Jason and Brooke had chosen for the singles group outing to the boardwalk in Atlantic City. Till then, she would just have to be content sending pictures of Darren by e-mail and singing his praises to her sisters, who took the news with great zeal.

Unfortunately, not everything in Candy's life seemed to be moving in the same positive direction. As the days ticked by, tensions at Eastway grew, especially when another female pilot—Anna—was hired just three days after Darren's friend Gary received a second written warning.

By the second week in August, talks of union involvement had become more than a rumor. Even Darren, who rarely got worked up about anything, looked nervous. He occasionally shared his thoughts with Candy, but more often than not just shook his head whenever she asked him what the men were thinking of doing. Surely this would blow over in time.

In the midst of this turmoil, an idea occurred to Candy, one she couldn't seem to shake. She approached several of Eastway's female employees, hoping for their support. After a bit of corralling, a group of them met at DiMarco's on a Tuesday evening to implement a plan, one she'd dreamed up after some serious prayer on the matter.

After they had ordered their food, Candy broached the subject at hand. "So, here's what I'm thinking. Women have worked for the airlines for decades. Females in the industry. . .that's not a new thing. Not even close to new."

"Yeah, but our roles have sure changed," Shawneda said. She placed her glass back down on the table and gave Candy a pensive look. "It's not the coffee, tea, and me thing anymore. Flight attendants are taken more seriously. And most of the stereotypes are gone."

"Praise God for that." Brooke nibbled on a piece of garlic bread.

"A lot has changed. . .for sure," Candy said. "But the more I thought about this, the more I realized just how blessed we are that so many women walked this road ahead of us. They paved the way. You know?"

"I know I wouldn't be flying today if other women hadn't opened the doors for me." Anna nodded. "It's hard for us, but can you imagine how difficult it was for most of them? Back in the '30s and the '40s, when the industry was completely run by men?" She gestured for Brooke to hand over the loaf of garlic bread, which she did with a look of mock protest.

"We've come a long way," Candy agreed. "Especially in the last twenty years. And we have a lot to be thankful for." She took a sip of her diet soda and leaned back in her chair.

"Go on." Lilly gave her a curious look. "I have a feeling you're up to something."

"I am." Candy exhaled, working up the courage to continue. "This is what I'm thinking. What if we hosted a banquet honoring women who've made a real difference in aviation history? We could ask one of the women from the Ninety-Nines to come and speak. An older woman. Someone who's flown for years and has gained some notoriety for her achievements."

"Whoa." Brooke gave her an admiring look. "Do you really think we could pull that off? Get someone famous to come?"

"I guess we'll never know unless we ask. Right? And there are so many other women who were true pioneers in this industry. Some of the established members of Women in Aviation, for instance. What if we invited them to attend and honored them in some way? Then the men would see that women have a long-standing history in the aviation industry. And we could turn this whole thing into a fundraiser for scholarships."

"You don't think this would worsen the problems with the guys?" Lilly's wrinkled brow let Candy know how she felt about the idea. "I mean, they could just take this banquet as a sign we're trying to prove a point."

"Well, in some ways we are. But we're not trying to prove that women are better than men. Not at all." Candy grew more passionate about her subject matter as she continued. "I think we would be wrong to even attempt that. We're simply trying to prove that nothing has changed. We've been around in the industry for years. We're part of the past. . .and part of the future."

"So, how do we sell the guys on this idea?" Shawneda looked her way with a doubtful look in her eye.

"Why don't we enlist Darren?" Brooke suggested. "He's the perfect one to win over the other guys. He's more open-minded than most and he's a great communicator. Everyone respects him, too, and that's so important."

"I think that's a great idea." Lilly nodded. "He's so great at keeping people calm, and you're right. . .he's won the respect of both the men and the women."

"He's the perfect candidate, then." Brooke nodded. "And I'm pretty sure he's at the Eastway offices right now. Something about a meeting, I think. This would be just the right time to catch him and get his opinion."

"So, am I elected?" Candy looked at her friends.

"You're the best one to ask," Brooke assured her.

The food arrived and over steaming plates of lasagna and fettuccine, along with chilled Caesar salad, the women discussed ideas for the best possible banquet. By the time they finished, Candy had filled three tablet pages with notes. She could hardly wait to track down Darren to get his thoughts.

As soon as she ended her meal, Candy went up to the Eastway offices to find him. She ran into Marcella, one of the flight attendants, in the hallway. "Hey, I heard Darren was here in a meeting of some sort."

"Yeah, he's in a meeting of some sort." Marcella rolled her eyes. "With all the guys. But they wouldn't dare meet here. They're over in the small conference room at the Marriott."

"Oh?" Candy shrugged. "What kind of meeting?"

A strange look came over Marcella's face. "Candy, look. . .you're a great pilot and a wonderful girl. I don't like to be the one to tell you this, but the guys are all putting their heads together in preparation for Gary's meeting with union leaders tomorrow. Darren's right there with the other guys. . .in the thick of it."

"Oh, but he wouldn't—"

Marcella put her hands up in the air. "I can't read his mind, that's for sure. But he's in that meeting—not that you could call it a meeting, really. It's just a bunch of hot-headed guys blowing off steam. But if you don't believe me, go on over there and see for yourself."

"Okay." Candy wrestled with her thoughts, determined to give Darren the benefit of the doubt. "I'll go. But I know you're wrong. There's no way he would do that to me."

With determination settling in, she turned on her heels and headed for the Marriott.

❧

Darren sat in on the meeting in the familiar conference room, doing his best not to get involved. He'd come—not to link arms with Gary and the others, who'd simmered to the boiling point over the past few weeks—but to be a calming force. Unfortunately, he hadn't had a chance to get a word in edgewise, at least not yet.

Gary's face grew red as he spoke. "Eastway needs to be hiring based on skill and time in the air, not how pretty a pilot looks in her uniform."

Darren had to respond to that one. "Look, Gary, I think you're taking this a bit far. It's not a matter of getting more pretty faces onboard. These women are skilled pilots. I've flown with them and—"

"That's not all you've done with them." A snicker went up from the crowd after Gary's shocking statement. Darren felt his blood begin to boil. How dare they insinuate such a thing?

"For your information, my personal relationships are just that. . .personal. And I would never. . ." He wanted to finish the statement. Wanted to tell them he'd never cross lines of propriety with Candy in the way they had suggested. Wanted to tell them that a man of God guarded himself and the woman he cared for. Wanted to give them a piece of his mind. Instead, he drew in a deep breath and counted to ten, which opened the floor to one of the other disgruntled employees.

"Look," one of the pilots said. "This isn't about Darren or any other individual. It's simply about Eastway doing the right thing."

Darren struggled to keep from responding. Eastway didn't discriminate against men or women. Never had. From his point of view, the hirings and firings over the past few months had been based on performance. . .or the lack thereof. But how could he say so without hurting Gary and a couple of the others? If Eastway let them go, maybe they needed to go.

As he listened to the raised voices, Darren prayed. *Lord, I need Your perspective on this. If You want me involved, then You're going to have to really make it clear.*

Though he didn't agree with the arguments of the others, he couldn't help but feel he should play some role in calming the waters.

๏

Candy paced the hallway outside the conference room and prayed. She'd cracked the door and peeked inside but only saw the backs of the men's heads. Darren's voice hadn't been distinguishable from the others in the crowd, so she felt sure he wasn't in there. On the other hand, he wasn't answering his phone. Maybe he was home. . .sleeping. Catching a few z's before his next flight. Yes, that was surely it.

She turned to leave, but a rush from behind caused her to turn back. The conference room door flung open, and men began to flood toward her. *Yikes.* She'd never seen so many male Eastway employees in one place before. And talk about catching them at their worst. Several were using language she'd just as soon forget, and a couple were even spouting not-so-nice things about female pilots.

Until they saw her. One of them—Craig, the male flight attendant who'd always treated her kindly, at least to her face—took one look at her and turned the other way.

Coward.

A couple of the other men passed by with cold, hard looks on their faces. . . cold enough to cause a shiver to run down her spine. Candy couldn't control whatever they were thinking or feeling. Only the Lord could do that.

She stood to the side of the hallway, waiting for the crowd to clear. Just one last peek in the room would do it. She would prove Marcella wrong. Darren couldn't possibly have supported these guys in their endeavors, particularly not with them so worked up.

The last of the men passed, and she breathed a sigh of relief. *See. I knew he wasn't here.*

Then she heard his voice. "Gary, you're my friend. You can count on me. You know I'd do anything for you." Darren slapped him on the back.

" 'Count on me'?" she whispered the words. "He's getting caught up in this now?" She ducked behind a large silk tree as Darren and Gary stepped out of the room, side by side. Thankfully, he never turned to look her way. And after today, she didn't know if she would ever turn his way again.

Chapter 13

Candy managed to avoid a couple of calls from Darren in the days following his meeting with the men. She replayed his words in her mind several times over, trying to make sense of them: *"Gary, you're my friend. You can count on me. You know I'd do anything for you."*

How did this happen? Darren, of all people, knew Gary's record with the airline. Why not let the union officials take it from here? Why did he feel compelled to get involved. . .and on the men's side, no less?

Candy stewed over his sudden participation, but decided not to say anything about it, wondering if, instead, he would bring it up. Ironically, the two phone messages he'd left were completely unrelated to work. One had to do with an air show he was hoping they could attend together in a few weeks. The other had to do with the singles group trip to Atlantic City on Saturday. Candy didn't respond to either, unsure of what to say. Or do.

On Thursday morning, with plenty of free time ahead of her, she decided to take a walk to clear her mind. Maybe she could get some prayer time in along the way. She'd already poured her heart out to the Lord about all of this, but He seemed distant and quiet on the matter.

Though she and Darren had seen some of the sights in Newark, there were still so many places she had yet to discover. She'd heard the girls talk about Washington Park but had never seen it, except in passing. Today would be the perfect day to see things for herself. And to straighten out the troubling thoughts rolling through her mind.

Minutes later, Candy strolled the streets of the historic district, taking in the sights. By the time she arrived at Washington Park, she'd already hashed out several of her more troubling questions with the Lord, questions like, "Whatever happened to all of that discernment I used to have?" and "When am I ever going to feel like an equal in this industry?"

Before long, she took a seat on a park bench, staring up at a statue of George Washington, mesmerized. Now, there was a man who'd stood up for what he believed in. A man who stuck to his guns, even when everything. . .and everyone. . .opposed him.

"Hmm." Things hadn't really changed all that much in the past two hundred years, had they?

Looking at the other statues, Candy's mind wandered. This whole place was filled with the memories of people who'd stood up for what they believed.

Heroes who'd won the right. . .to live where they wanted, worship where they wanted, and work in occupations they loved. They'd sacrificed. . .and come out winners in the end.

"Lord, have You brought me here for a reason?"

Goose bumps covered her arms as she recognized the similarities to her situation. She began to pray. *Lord, I know You've called me to fly. I've known it since I was little. And I'm not ashamed of the fact that I'm doing what You called me to do. Help me overcome the fear of not being good enough. Take my insecurities and my worry about what people think. This isn't about what they think anyway, Father. It's about what You think. As long as I'm doing what You called me to do. . .*

Peace settled over her heart as she contemplated that fact. What was it Pop always said? *"The safest place to be is at the very center of God's will."* Storms could swirl around her, but in that safe place, she could move forward with confidence.

Still, there was that issue with Darren and the other men to iron out. Whenever she replayed the scene in her head, Candy could hardly believe it. Had Darren—the same man who'd kissed her that day at Essex County airfield— turned on her? Or was she just imagining it?

Every time his name flitted through her imagination, she saw those beautiful blue eyes. That dark wavy hair. She heard his voice. . .kind and yet authoritative. She saw his broad shoulders and the captain's bars on his sleeve. Every thought, every memory was a good one.

Still, all the good things she knew of him faded away with the memory of his words: *"Gary, you're my friend. You can count on me. You know I'd do anything for you."*

Ugh. So much for trusting him. Now she couldn't even imagine spending time with him. How would she make it through the upcoming trip to Atlantic City with the singles group?

Candy cringed, thinking about going anywhere with him right now. Not with so many unspoken words between them. Still, how could she avoid the trip, especially when Jason and Brooke had gone out of their way to plan it with her in mind?

She rose from the bench and began to walk through the park, finally settling on a plan, one she felt sure everyone could live with. One that would give her the perfect opportunity to spend some time alone—to think and to pray.

Candy made the trek back to the apartment, then gathered her roomies together in the living room for an announcement.

"I, um. . .I've got several days off, so I think I'm going to head back home this evening."

"Home?" Lilly gave her a funny look. "You mean Atlantic City?"

"Yeah. I miss my family. And my younger sister, Tangie, is coming in from New York for her birthday. I really want to be there for that."

"But what about our trip to the boardwalk on Saturday?" Brooke's brow wrinkled. "You're not canceling, are you? I know Darren is really looking forward to meeting your family and seeing your old stomping ground. You're not going to let him down, are you?"

Let him *down?* Candy sighed. Maybe she should just come out and tell Brooke and the others what she'd overheard. Then they'd understand why she couldn't possibly spend a casual weekend with him. And they'd also see that he was the one letting her down, not the other way around.

On the other hand, why stir up a hornet's nest? The men were already worked up enough. Why get the women more involved than they already were?

"Candy, I haven't known you long, but I feel like we've been sisters forever." Brooke gave her a pensive look. "If you're going through some sort of problem with Darren—or anyone else, for that matter—don't run from it. You of all people have sticking power. Hang on and deal with it. That's what you'd tell me."

"I'm not running." She frowned. "It really is my sister's birthday. And I'm really going to Atlantic City to see my family." She paused, then added, "And I'm sure they'd be thrilled if you guys stopped by the candy shop for the party. It's going to be on Saturday night at eight, just after the store closes."

"Okay. Well, we'll be there. It'll be fun to see Ryan and Taffie again. And I wish I could talk you into joining us on the boardwalk for a couple of hours before that, but I understand if you want to be with your family."

"Yeah." Candy sighed. "I need to be around my sisters right now. Does that sound silly?"

"No." Lilly bit her lip before continuing. "But are you saying you might be thinking of quitting your job? 'Cause if you are. . ." Her voice trailed off.

"I don't know." Candy shrugged. "I don't like to see everyone so worked up. And based on the reactions of some of the guys, things aren't going to get any better for the female pilots. I sure don't enjoy working under this kind of stress."

"Well, forget about all that." Brooke gave her a sympathetic look. "Spend time with your sisters, and then we'll join you Saturday night. We'll put all of this other stuff out of our minds for now. How does that sound?"

"Amazing."

"I can't wait to meet your sisters." Shawneda grinned. "I have a feeling we're all going to be friends. If they're anything like you, I mean."

"Hmm." Candy couldn't help but smile as she thought about them. "To be honest, we're as different as night and day. Taffie's a homebody, always staying put. And Tangie. . ."

"What?" Lilly gave her a curious look.

"Well, she's going to be the next Broadway star. At least that's what she believes. And I don't doubt it. She's very at home on the stage. Performing."

"Wow. You are different, then," Shawneda said.

"Not so different, really." Brooke shrugged. "You just have a different stage to perform on. Yours is in the cockpit. But you're still the star of the show."

"I don't know about that."

"Well, you know what they say, 'The show must go on!' So, whatever you're struggling with, work through it with God, then get right back to the stage, okay?"

Candy sighed. "Okay. But in the meantime, just be praying for me, all right? I have a lot on my mind. A lot to work out."

"Will do."

Candy ventured off to her bedroom to pack. Surely a few days at home would do the trick. She hit the road by late afternoon, fighting traffic as she headed south on the Garden State Parkway. As she drove, she did her best to collect her thoughts and to focus on her family. Surely these next few days would help her put everything in perspective.

&

Late Thursday afternoon Darren tried one last time to call Candy. She'd avoided him for two days, but why? Had he done something—said something—to offend her? Had he somehow overlooked a birthday or forgotten a date? Not to his knowledge.

When she didn't answer the phone, he decided to give Jason a call. His best friend answered on the third ring with a jovial, "Hey, Darren. How are—"

"I blew it."

"Blew it? Blew what?"

"This thing with Candy." Darren paced the room. "I think I kind of. . .sort of. . ."

"What are you talking about? What have you done?"

"I have absolutely no idea."

Jason laughed. "Welcome to the world of male-female relationships. I'm not kidding when I say that half of the arguments Brooke and I have make no sense to me at all. Usually by the end of them I can't even remember how they got started."

"Well, we're not arguing. It's not like that."

"You're not? That's so strange, because Brooke just told me Candy had asked you to act as mediator in the Eastway dispute."

"Wait. . .really? 'Cause she never talked to me about that. In fact, she hasn't talked to me in days. And she won't answer my calls. Not a one. So, I've been thinking—"

"Well, that's your problem. You spend too much time doing that. Cut it out."

"Please. I might like to analyze things, but I don't usually overthink them." Darren exhaled, frustrated with the direction this conversation seemed to be going.

"Go ahead and believe that, if you like." Jason paused. "But maybe she just needs some space. Sometimes women are like that."

"Well, I've given her plenty of it. And actually, that's what I'm calling about. Trying to decide if I should give her even more."

"Oh?"

"I have a flight tomorrow," Darren explained, "but I'm still free on Saturday. Should I still go to Atlantic City with you guys, even if she doesn't go?"

"I think she's already there, actually."

"What?" *In Atlantic City? How come I'm the last to know this?*

"Brooke mentioned something about Candy driving down there tonight to see her family. I think she's staying till we get there."

"Really?" Darren brightened immediately. "So, maybe she's not avoiding me at all? Maybe she's just preoccupied with her family."

"That's likely." Jason laughed. "But don't worry. Remember, if this relationship with Candy is God's will, then any obstacles will be overcome in time. Even a deep thinker like yourself can't thwart God's plan. So, rest easy, okay?"

"I guess."

Darren ended the call and stared at the aquarium once more. No matter how many circles Fred made, he never actually went anywhere. Oh, he seemed content enough, but was it really enough, to get so settled in your ways you couldn't break free?

Darren approached the fish tank and dropped in a pinch of food. Fred swam up to the surface to grab it, then eventually went back to swimming around and around.

"Don't you ever just want to bust out of there?" Darren asked. "Swim in bigger ponds?"

Fred made the *Ooo* face again, then swam back down to his castle. Somehow the little guy had learned to be content with his circumstances, even without female companionship.

"I don't know, man." Darren sat on the sofa and stared at the fish tank. He watched as Fred swam in endless circles, going round and round the colorful castle in the center of the aquarium.

Fred, I know just how you feel.

Chapter 14

Darren walked the boardwalk with Jason and Brooke, breathing in the salty air. The others in their group had stepped out ahead of them. A few headed over to the pier and a couple wanted to see a feature at the IMAX theater. Darren was content to stroll with no agenda in mind. It felt good to relax, to just be himself. To unwind. Leave the cares of the world—and Eastway—behind.

Of course, the crowd along the busy Atlantic City boardwalk proved problematic. And every few minutes another one of those rolling chairs came by, startling him. Interesting idea, folks being pushed around in wicker, canopied chairs-on-wheels. Still, he couldn't help but find the whole place. . .what was the word the women would use? Quaint? Yes, quaint.

"So, this is where Candy grew up." All his talk about how much prettier the Pacific was than the Atlantic might have to be taken back. This was a great spot. And talk about attracting tourists. Umbrellas dotted the sand, and beachgoers toted their gear back and forth from the boardwalk to the water's edge.

Yes, this had a familiar feel to it. And with the scent of hot dogs and roasted peanuts in the air, he found himself drawn in.

"I'm getting hungry."

"Yeah, there's a great seafood place Ryan and Taffie told us about," Jason said. "Let's grab a bite to eat."

"Sounds good."

Minutes later they entered an eclectic fishy-smelling place with the words High Seas above the door. The decor was traditional coastal stuff, though Brooke was quick to warn him to use the word *shore* and not *coast*.

"What's the difference?" he asked with a shrug.

Brooke slapped herself in the head. "You're a California kid through and through, aren't you?"

"Well, yeah." No point in denying it.

Brooke rolled her eyes. "I don't expect you to understand. Just trust me on this. I grew up in Jersey, and around here, it's the shore."

As the waiter arrived at the table with their glasses of water, Darren turned to Brooke. "So, tell me what Candy said. She won't return my calls. And I don't have a clue what I've done."

"I don't know." Brooke shrugged, then took a sip of her water. "If she's upset

197

with you, she's keeping it to herself. I just know she's been here in Atlantic City since Thursday, seeing her sister. And we're all invited to the party at the candy shop tonight."

"Why don't we head over there now when we're done eating? I want to see her." He glanced at his watch. Three fifteen. Hmm. A little early.

"Darren, just give her some space. She obviously wants it. I'm sure it's all going to be clearer before long, but not if you push too hard."

"Sounds just like what I told him." Jason looked up from his menu. "One thing I've learned about women. When they need their space, they need their space. There's no crowding them. And you'll do more damage than good if you push things."

"I guess." He shrugged. "And it's not that I feel like pushing. I just need to know that she's okay, that I haven't upset her in some way." He turned to Brooke. "Surely she would tell you if she was upset with me, right?"

"Darren, I've only known Candy a couple of months. She's different from most of the others in our apartment. And even though she's opened up to me about a lot of things, she hasn't mentioned anything specific about her relationship with you. Not lately, anyway."

"Not lately?"

"Well, I heard every detail of how she fell out of the plane into your arms, and how you kissed her on the fly." A grin slowly spread across Brooke's face as she repeated, "On the fly. Hey, that's pretty good. But anyway, that's old news."

"But you two are definitely an item, right?" Jason gave him an inquisitive look. "Sure seems that way."

"I thought so."

"And whatever happened with Andrea?" Brooke asked.

"I got another call from her a few days ago." He sighed. "She's coming back in town this weekend and wants to get together. I don't want to hurt her feelings, but I just don't feel right about it. Even though Candy and I aren't officially a couple, my heart is certainly. . .involved."

"Just tell Andrea you're seeing someone else." Jason shrugged. "She'll get it."

"Yeah." He paused a moment. "I'm just worried because I'm not actually 'seeing' someone else at the moment. I can't even get Candy to respond to me."

"Time and space." Jason repeated the words, then glanced at his watch. "Let's get your mind off of women after we eat. Want to play some Skee-Ball?"

"Waste of money." Darren leaned back in his chair, defeated. No point in playing games without Candy around.

"What's the problem with spending a few bucks on a little harmless fun? I'm not asking you to gamble it away, after all. What've you got to lose?"

Yeah. What've I got to lose? After all, the only thing he'd lost so far. . .was his heart.

COTTON CANDY CLOUDS

Candy spent her afternoon at her parents' house, chatting with Tangie. She felt a little guilty letting Taffie and Ryan handle things at the shop without her, but they'd insisted. When the clock in the living room struck six, their mother called out from the kitchen.

"Okay, you two. We're leaving in fifteen minutes for the shop to set up for the party."

"How many people are coming, Mom?" Candy asked as she rose from the sofa.

Her mother rounded the corner into the living room to join them. "I'm thinking probably forty or more." She paused to dry her hands on the dishcloth she was holding. "All of Tangie's closest friends from high school will be there, and half the kids who were in the youth group with you girls. 'Course I guess they're not kids anymore. They're all twenty-somethings."

"Yes, but it'll make us feel like kids again." Tangie's eyes sparkled with delight.

"You *are* a kid." Candy sighed as she looked at her very eclectic-looking younger sister. The shocking red orange hair always took people by surprise. So did the pierced nose. But underneath that colorful exterior lay a heart of gold, one that was often overlooked by folks who refused to dig deeper than the physical.

"So, do you think Corey Lutton's going to be there tonight?" Tangie waggled her brows. "He always had such a crush on you when we were kids. And I hear his fiancée just broke his heart a few months ago, so he's available. Might help you through the heartbreak over you-know-who."

" 'You-know-who'?" Their mother put her hands up in mock despair. "Is there something you need to tell me?"

"Well, I. . ."

"Did you meet someone while Pop and I were off RVing? Why am I always the last to know?"

Candy shrugged, feeling conflicted. "I don't know. I mean, I was seeing someone, but now he's. . ."

"He's what?" Tangie's eyes widened, showing off her heavy eyeliner. "Married to someone else? In a coma? Incapacitated in some way? C'mon, Candy. Why don't you just tell us what happened between you and Darren?"

"Darren?" Their mother looked back and forth between them. "His name is Darren? The one who broke your heart?"

Could this get any worse? "Well, he didn't really break my heart. He doesn't even know that I know. . .oh, never mind." Candy groaned.

"I'm so out of the loop," Candy's mother said with a look of exaggerated despair. "I guess that's what happens when your kids grow up. The mother is replaced by sisters and friends. No one ever calls. No one ever writes. . . ." Her voice drifted off and she sighed. Loudly.

"No, Mom." Candy laughed. "I could never replace you. And Darren didn't really break my heart. We've just. . .well, something's happened and I had to step back."

"Oh. . ." Tangie's mouth stayed in the perfect *O* position for a moment before she whispered, "Were you two getting too close, too fast?"

Their mother paled and excused herself to the kitchen.

"No. Nothing like that." Candy gave her sister a friendly punch in the arm. "You know me better than that. I have every intention of staying pure until I'm married."

"Right. But sometimes people slip up, especially when they're in love."

In love? Am I in love with Darren?

"So, what happened?" Tangie asked. "Why did you back off?"

"You're just going to have to trust me when I say it's for the best. I have a few things to figure out. And I think Darren does, too."

"Darren. I still can't get over that name." Tangie wrinkled her nose. "Not very romantic."

"Don't even get me started on names." *Not when I've been "Cotton Candy" all my life.* She took a couple of steps toward the hallway. "I've got to get dressed so we can leave. What about you?"

"What's wrong with what I'm wearing?" Tangie gestured at her mismatched shorts and T-shirt, then added, "Kidding. Kidding." She padded along behind Candy, whispering, "Hey, while you're figuring this out, take another look at Corey Lutton, okay? 'Cause if you don't, I just might."

Candy laughed. "You go right ahead. Won't bother me a bit."

Tangie shrugged. "His mother never liked my tattoos or my hair. I think she's looking for a different kind of girl for her son."

"And I'm that girl?"

Tangie grinned. "Well, I have it on good authority you're pretty high on the list."

A groan escaped Candy's lips. "Stop it, Tangie. No matchmaking. Not tonight."

"Who, me? This time it's Mom and Mrs. Lutton conspiring against you. Or for you. Or, whatever you call it."

"I call it unnecessary."

"Well, to Mom's credit, she didn't know about Darren. I can't believe you never told her, by the way."

"I was actually going to tell her tonight. He's coming to the party with Jason and Brooke and a few others from our singles group, so I'm going to have to explain. And besides, he doesn't know I'm—"

"Wait. He doesn't know you're upset with him?" Tangie's eyes widened. "Man, this is going to be great. Better than a soap opera. Corey and Darren in the same room. Darren not knowing you're dumping him because of. . .why are you dumping him again? Anyway, I'm getting dressed in a hurry. Don't want to miss a thing."

Candy sighed, then walked into her room and closed the door. As she changed for the party, she thought about Darren. *Why? Why is he pretending to be interested in me, then going behind my back to help the men? Is he using me? Have they put him up to this?*

The more she thought about it, the more her skin began to crawl. It did make sense. All of that getting-to-know-you stuff at Essex County airport could just as easily have been a ruse. . .a way to get her to open up and talk. Thank goodness she'd kept her thoughts about Eastway to herself that day.

On the other hand, she'd acted like a silly kid in the cockpit of the Cessna 400, hadn't she? And her childishness had surely given Darren and the other men plenty of fodder. By now they probably all thought her to be immature, at best.

Fully dressed, she paused to check her reflection in the mirror above her childhood dresser—the same mirror that she'd stared into hundreds, if not thousands, of times as a teen. "Mirror, mirror on the wall. . ." She mouthed the words, "Who's the most naive of all?"

Only one name came to mind.

Candy exhaled loudly. Perhaps she'd been naive up till now, but no more. Staring into her reflection, she made up her mind, once and for all. Pop had been right. All of that head-in-the-clouds stuff. And look where it had gotten her. Her daydream mentality had landed her squarely in the middle of a controversy at Eastway.

Well, no more. From this point on, she'd guard her every move. No more being taken advantage of. She would put away childish things once and for all.

Chapter 15

Darren's anticipation grew as the hours ticked by. He'd seen enough of the boardwalk, already. Played enough games. Nearly been run over by those goofy chairs half a dozen times at least. Listened to kids screaming and parents scolding. Eaten fried fish. Couldn't they just get on with it?

Finally, around 7:40 p.m., he managed to convince Brooke and Jason they should go to the candy shop. Who cared if they were a little early for the party? He wanted to see Candy. And surely she wanted to see him. . .in spite of the unanswered calls.

At exactly 7:43, Darren, Brooke, Jason, and the others from the singles group stood in front of the colorful candy shop.

"Wow." So this is where she grew up. The playfulness of the place fit right in with her girlish charm. He looked up at the sign above the door. Beneath the words CARINI'S CONFECTIONS they'd placed a scripture from Psalm 119:103: HOW SWEET ARE YOUR WORDS TO MY TASTE, SWEETER THAN HONEY TO MY MOUTH! Clever.

"You ready?" Jason slapped him on the back.

"Like we could stop him." Brooke rolled her eyes, then turned to the others in the group. "He's been begging us for hours to bring him here."

Darren's heartbeat escalated as he looked back at the sign. Looked like he was about to meet Candy's family face-to-face. And the idea of seeing her again. . .especially on her own turf. . .put knots in his stomach. *Why can't things just be easy?*

He followed along behind Jason as they entered the crowded shop. Darren looked around in awe. "Wow. I've never seen anything like this." The right side of the shop was dedicated to candies. And talk about color! He stared in awe at the rows and rows of sweets. Everything from large glass jars of saltwater taffy to caramel apples to rock candy. And the smell! A distinct sugary sweetness hung in the air, one that put him in mind of his childhood.

He looked to his left, taking in the trendy coffee bar. Looked—and smelled—very tempting. And the old-fashioned ice cream area put him in mind of something from the turn of the century. The whole place amazed him. People of any and every age would feel at home here.

Others in the group scattered to various places in the store. . .most of the women heading over to purchase taffy and other candy products. Darren worked his way through the crowd, almost losing sight of Jason and Brooke.

They finally arrived at the coffee counter where Brooke squealed with delight.

"Ryan!" She quickly made introductions. "Guys, this is my cousin, Ryan Antonelli. Ryan, you know Jason." When the dark-haired stranger nodded, Brooke added, "And this is our friend, Darren."

"Darren, good to meet you." He extended his hand. "Let me see if I can find my wife. She's going to be so glad you're here."

Minutes later, Darren stood in front of an unfamiliar woman, slightly older than Candy, yet resembling her in every conceivable way. "Wow. You must be Taffie."

"My fame precedes me." She laughed. "How did you know that?"

"Oh, your sister Candy. She and I are. . ." He wasn't sure how to finish the sentence. If someone had asked him a couple of weeks before, he would've said "dating." No problem. But, now? When she wouldn't even answer his calls. . .

"Oh, I remember now." Taffie's face lit up. "You're the guy in the pictures."

"Pictures?"

Taffie nodded. "Candy sent pictures of you a couple of weeks ago. There was one of you standing next to a small plane. I think the caption said something about Big Ben. Or the English countryside. Maybe both."

Okay, well, that's embarrassing. Still, it gave him hope. If Candy had told her sister about their date, maybe her silence of late was simply a coincidence.

"Candy just got here," Taffie said. "She's with my mom and Tangie back in the office. They're dealing with decorations. We're about to close the shop to the public and set things up for the party. You're just in time to help."

"Help decorate?" *Is she kidding?*

"Why not?" Brooke nudged him, then whispered, "You want to make a good impression on the family, right? Well, here's your chance."

Taffie put him to work filling balloons at the helium tank. With his attention more on the back of the room than the task at hand, he sent a couple of balloons sailing off across the room.

"He can fly a plane *and* a balloon," Brooke teased.

"Here, let me do that." Ryan took over. "You're a guest, after all."

Darren nodded and muttered an apology, all the while keeping his gaze on the back of the room. His heart could hardly stand the wait.

Thankfully, a couple of minutes later, Candy emerged with an older woman on one side and a younger woman on the other. *Okay, that's her mom. Typical Italian mama with salt and pepper hair—more salt than pepper. And that's got to be Tangie. The piercings and tattoos are a dead giveaway. And the orange hair. Couldn't miss that if I wanted to.*

Darren's attention shifted at once to Candy. The moment their eyes locked, her expression changed—from joy to one of concern, then. . .something else. He couldn't quite place it, but she didn't exactly look happy to see him.

"Candy!" Brooke grabbed her and gave her a hug. "Darren could hardly wait to get here. Hope you don't mind that we're early."

Tangie's brow wrinkled. She appeared to be sizing him up. "So, you're Darren."

"I'm Darren."

"Mm-hmm." She stared a bit longer, then turned to her sister. "He's handsome, Candy. A lot more handsome in person than in the pictures you sent."

Darren felt the heat rise to his cheeks at her words. On the other hand, this might just work to his advantage. If he could win over the sisters, surely any fences could be mended.

"I'm not sure Corey's going to stand a chance next to this guy." Tangie nudged Candy with her elbow.

Corey? Okay, that changed everything.

Candy's cheeks reddened, and she mumbled something about decorating the cake.

"So, you're Darren." Her mother gave him a suspicious look as if to ask, *"What have you done to hurt my daughter?"*

"I. . .I'm Darren." He extended his hand in her father's direction.

The older man appeared to be oblivious to any problems. He shook Darren's hand and offered a warm smile. "Nice to meet you. We're glad you could come." He gestured around the room. "All of you."

"It's great to finally meet you, too. I've looked forward to this day for ages." Darren stumbled his way into a rehearsed speech about how much he'd enjoyed getting to know Candy, and how he'd wanted to meet her parents ever since their first date. "As a Christian, it's just so important to me to have a good relationship with the whole family, not just the girl I'm dating."

" 'The girl I'm dating.' " Mrs. Carini drew in a deep breath and shook her head. "Strange. Just so strange." She turned back toward the ice cream counter, and Candy followed on her heels. Darren watched it all in a state of confusion. What in the world had he done to upset everyone. . .and how could he possibly undo it?

★

Candy's heart raced as she followed on her mother's heels. When they reached the area behind the ice cream counter, her mom opened the freezer door and hid behind it.

"Tell me again why I'm not supposed to like this guy?" she whispered. "He's great. Sounds like he's a strong Christian. . .handsome, too. And he's clearly head over heels for you."

"I know, but. . ." Candy couldn't think of anything else to say. Not now. Why ruin her sister's big night? Besides, her mother didn't need to know that Darren's kindness was possibly just an act. That he'd gone behind her back to. . .

Hmm. To do what? She still hadn't really figured all of that out yet.

Her mother handed her the ice cream cake. With a shaky hand, Candy wrote, HAPPY 21ST, TANGIE! on top. Her hand trembled so much the words were barely distinguishable.

Taffie approached. She glanced down at the cake and said, "Wow. Hmm." They both continued to stare at the sloppy script for a moment.

"I know." Candy sighed. "I don't know what's wrong with me."

"No problem. I'll just scrape that off and rewrite it. Won't hurt your feelings, will it?"

"No. Won't hurt my feelings."

Funny. At the words "hurt my feelings," her gaze shifted to Darren. Standing there, chatting with her parents and Ryan, he looked to fit right in. She could see him merging into the Carini clan with little effort, especially after his impassioned speech about falling in love with the whole family.

If only they didn't have that one obstacle to overcome. . .the one where he had turned on her behind her back.

Determined to focus on other things, she went to work helping Ryan fill helium balloons, then place them around the shop. She sighed with relief as the bell jangled. Good. Party guests. That would provide a nice distraction.

Or not.

She looked over into the anxious eyes of Corey Lutton and his parents. *Oh no.* Corey looked at her with a hopeful expression, then walked her way for a hug. Every eye in the place looked their way as Corey's strong arms wrapped her in a slightly-too-long embrace. In that moment, she contemplated taking ten or twelve of the helium balloons. . .tying them together. . .and soaring off over the Atlantic.

Instead, she returned Corey's hug, welcomed his family, then went to work. . . pretending everything was all right.

Chapter 16

Darren managed to make it through the party, but not in the best frame of mind. Candy had avoided him all night, even going so far as to sit with that Corey fellow and his parents during the party, but no more. He would get to the bottom of this if it killed him. And it just might.

He approached her just as the others were beginning to leave. "Candy?"

She turned his way with a cautious look on her face. "Yes?"

"We need to talk." Darren didn't mean for his words to come across sounding gruff, but they did.

Candy sighed before answering. "Yes, I know. We do." Without so much as a word, she set off toward the door.

Darren followed along behind her until they stood outside the shop on the boardwalk. She then took several rapid steps, moving them farther away from the store. *Where are you going?*

"Candy, slow down."

When she turned to him, he noticed tears in her eyes. "Wait. Why are you crying? What in the world is happening here? Has someone done something to hurt you?"

Pain registered in her eyes immediately. "Darren. . ." She seemed to be grasping for words. "I told you that day at Essex County that I've always been a dreamer. Always had big ideas."

"Right." He shrugged. *What does this have to do with anything?*

"I need you to know that I've worked really hard to get to the place I'm at."

"Well, I can certainly appreciate that. I've done the same."

A tear spilled over her lashes, and she brushed it away. "I've spent nearly two years away from my family. . .getting my wings. Building time. Taking the job in Newark. It's been a huge sacrifice."

"I know. I never said—"

A large group passed by them, laughing and talking loudly.

Candy put her hand up to stop him from continuing. "I'm just saying that I didn't just decide one day I wanted to fly. I've poured every ounce of strength into making this dream a reality, and I've prayed about it every step of the way. Every door that's opened has been opened by God. Yes, my dreams are big, but they're mine. And I'm not going to let anyone shoot them down."

"Shoot them down?" He paused, completely dumbfounded. What did this have to do with him? "Are you talking about the guys? 'Cause if you are, you need to know that—"

"I'm talking about you." She faced him dead-on and looked him squarely in the eye.

"W–what?"

"I'm talking about you going behind my back to meet with the men. Making promises to help them try to bring me down. Supporting them behind my back."

"Bring you down?" He shook his head, confused. "Wait a minute, Candy. There's been some kind of misunderstanding here."

"So, you can honestly stand there and tell me you're not working with the guys?"

"Working with them?" He stared at her, completely stunned. "What makes you think that? I'm certainly not in favor of what they're doing, if that's what you think." Could she really think that of him? If so, how could he possibly convince her otherwise?

❧

Shame washed over Candy as she stared into Darren's pain-filled eyes. "So, that day at the Marriott. . ."

"Day at the Marriott?" Wrinkles formed between his eyes for a second, then his eyes widened. "Candy. . .you were at the Marriott on the day the men met?"

She nodded, feeling the lump rise in her throat. "I was."

"I never saw you."

"I was, um, hiding behind a tree."

Darren laughed. "Well, why didn't you make your presence known?" Just as quickly he caught himself. "No, never mind. I get it. The men weren't in the best frame of mind. But when you saw me, why didn't you say something? Jump out from behind the tree? Give me a piece of your mind? If you thought I was—"

"I don't know." She groaned. "I saw you patting Gary on the back and telling him that you would support him. . . ."

"Ah, I get it. You thought I meant support him in the cause?" Darren shook his head. "No, I was talking about something else entirely. He'd just told me about a possible job offer with a charter service in Philly. I'd told him I'd support him in prayer. Told him I was onboard to pray for favor for the new job."

"Oh no." She groaned again, more than a little ashamed for her assumptions.

"He's my friend. And even though he's had some problems, I still care about him. He's got an attitude, but he's a good pilot. A little time working for less money will do him some good. But did you really think. . .?" Darren's voice trailed off.

Candy sighed and shook her head. "How did I do this? How did I mess this up so royally?"

"You didn't. It's just a misunderstanding."

"But that's just it. I'm tired of misunderstandings. I'm tired of the junior-high problems in a grown-up world. I've always been accused of being flighty. And I can't act like a grown woman, even when I try."

"Oh, you're wrong about that." He drew near, and her arms instinctively wrapped around his waist as he pulled her close. Anticipation washed over Candy, along with pure joy. "You're a very grown-up woman, Candy Carini. Plenty grown-up for me." He kissed the end of her nose, and she felt every anxiety lift. Funny how just one kiss could do that. It spoke a thousand words. No, a hundred thousand.

His lips met hers for a gentle kiss. Well, gentle at first. After a moment, the intensity of the moment seemed to sweep over them both. Darren backed up and smiled at her. "I think we've just proven you're not a little girl. But I think we'd better stop while we're ahead. You might be a little *too* much woman for me."

Candy felt her cheeks warm. "Somehow I doubt that. But you're right. I'm just so. . .so happy right now."

"Me, too." He pulled her close and kissed her forehead. "Now, we've got to promise we'll always talk things through. No more avoiding, okay?"

"Okay." She sighed, but inwardly rejoiced. Something about his use of the word *always* gave her such hope.

Though the crowd of people pressed in around him, Darren felt like he and Candy had slipped off into their own private world. Had she really thought he would turn on her? He could never do that. Still, with the little she'd over-heard at the Marriott, her reactions now made sense.

"Candy, I have to tell you something."

She looked up at him with a hopeful expression.

"These past few days have been awful. Just being away from you for that length of time almost did me in. My heart is. . . ." He pushed beyond the lump in his throat to continue. "My heart is completely. . ."

"What?"

"It's not mine anymore." He smiled as the words settled into his spirit. "Ugh. I'm not saying this right."

"No, you're doing fine," she said.

"What I'm trying to say. . .what I need to say. . .is, I love you."

Her eyes filled with tears. "Do you mean that?"

"Of course." He planted kisses in her hair. "And don't ever doubt it."

"I won't." She rested comfortably in his embrace as the reality of her feelings became clear, then whispered, "You know I love you, too, right?"

"Mm-hmm."

Nothing else needed to be said for a few moments. Darren finally broke the silence. "I'm going to do my best to keep the lines of communication wide open from now on. And as far as the men at Eastway go, well, I'm going to do my best to put them in their place. You're too good a pilot to take the kind of flack they've dished out. And you're too good a woman. . ." Here he stumbled over the words, "to ever have to deal with unnecessary pain."

"Thank you." Her eyes brimmed over.

"Sorry. I didn't mean to make you cry."

"Oh, I'm not sad." A girlish giggle escaped. "Sometimes I just get emotional when I'm happy. And right now, I'm very, very happy."

"Me, too."

He wrapped her in his arms for a final embrace. Funny, standing here on the boardwalk with people passing by, there were no problems left for the two of them to solve. And if life did happen to toss them any unexpected challenges. . . with God's help, they would soar above them.

Chapter 17

In the days following his trip to Atlantic City, Darren found himself on a proverbial roller-coaster ride. Every time he thought about Candy...about their conversation and the kiss that followed, he wanted to shout for joy. Then, just about the time he started to do so, something at Eastway would come along to bring him down, if only for a moment.

One major complication had arisen. In spite of Gary's meetings with union officials, Eastway carried through with its threats and fired him. No issues of sexism from the airline could be proven, nor should they, at least to Darren's way of thinking. Gary had made his mistakes when he demeaned his crew and now paid a hefty price. This had nothing to do with the hiring or firing of anyone else. Still, there remained an undercurrent of discontentment among the men, and Darren made it a priority to pray about the situation every day.

He prayed about something else, too, something hidden deep in his heart that he hadn't shared with anyone—an idea that had been formulating for some time now. One that could very well change the course of his life, if he made the right move at the right time. If the Lord would give him the go-ahead, Darren just might find himself soaring in a completely new and different direction.

But first, he would have to get a rock-solid answer from on high. No point in flying off on a tangent without asking the Lord His opinion first.

Oh, but if only the heavens would open up and rain down his answer. Then Darren Furst would be the happiest of men.

Not that he wasn't happy already. These days, he found himself cracking more jokes than ever, and waiting for every opportunity to make people smile. Joy flooded his heart, particularly when he spent time with Candy. And he finally found himself free to dream again...really dream. She had that effect on him, to be sure.

There were other changes, as well. With Jason's help, Darren spent some time talking through the problems he'd faced because of the poor interaction between his parents. Maybe, with time, he could develop a better relationship with them. Of course, it might require a trip to San Diego, but he could manage that.

In the meantime, there was plenty to take care of in Newark. Candy and her friends were all abuzz about an upcoming banquet they were hosting. Hopefully it would be just the ticket...just the thing to bring the men and women of Eastway together.

෨

Candy returned to Newark with renewed joy and peace in her heart. Despite Gary's firing, she knew it had nothing to do with her hiring. . .or anyone else's for that matter. So, in spite of any communication issues with the men—or lack thereof—she decided to move forward with the banquet featuring prominent women in aviation.

With Brooke, Anna, and Shawneda in tow, she selected the perfect spot— the Dorothy Ball House at Lincoln Park. All around the park stood brownstone mansions, built in the mid-nineteenth century. . .homes of the elite of the day. In that place, so rich with history, they would celebrate the achievements of women from the past, the present, and the future.

Candy had managed to secure two speakers for the evening, an elderly woman named Margaret Franklin, aged seventy-nine. She'd flown a medic plane during the Vietnam War and agreed to speak on the topic, "The Changing Role of Women in Aviation." And then there was Norah Bonner, the youngest woman working for a commercial airline. Funny, how close Candy came to winning that prize herself. Norah agreed to share her story of how she came to fly.

On the first Saturday in September, Candy met with the other women from Eastway at the banquet site to finalize plans. They walked through the various rooms of the facility, finally stopping in the banquet room. Once there, they paused and looked around.

"How many people are we expecting again?" Shawneda asked with a dubious look on her face.

"At last count, one hundred twenty. Maybe a few more." Candy reached for her clipboard, flipping pages until she found the one she was looking for. "Yes. One-twenty. More or less."

"Hope it's less." Shawneda pursed her lips as she reexamined the room.

"I've got a couple of RSVPs still to come." Candy shrugged. "But I'm sure this will all work out."

"Hope you're right. I don't know how we're going to fit that many people in here." Brooke looked doubtful.

Candy sighed. "We have no choice. But how did I know so many of the women would respond? We've got ladies coming from five different states. I couldn't fathom there would be such an amazing turnout. But it's such a great thing. The money we raise will go for scholarships for incoming female pilots."

"I don't know if I ever told you, but I got a scholarship when I first started flight school," Anna said. "It helped a lot. I could never have paid for it on my own, and I know my parents couldn't have, either."

Shawneda sighed and dropped into a nearby chair.

"What's wrong?" Candy looked her way, puzzled by her friend's reaction.

"You're just bringing up old memories. I wanted to. . ."

"What?" All of the women gathered around her.

Shawneda's eyes brimmed over with tears. "You all see me as this happy-go-lucky flight attendant, and for the most part I am. But you don't know that I really wanted to go to flight school. My parents got divorced when I was in high school, so just about the time I really started thinking about it, well. . ."

"Oh, I never knew." Brooke knelt down next to her. "Why didn't you tell me?"

Shawneda shrugged. "I don't know. I guess I didn't want to get into the whole story about my family's lack of finances. And trust me, just the idea of taking out loans to go to flight school was out of the question. So, I went the other route. And don't get me wrong, being a flight attendant is great, but. . ."

"It's not too late." Anna pulled up a chair next to her. "Maybe some of the scholarship money could be used for you."

"Oh, no. I wasn't implying anything like that." Shawneda looked stunned at first, and then embarrassed. "Just hearing about it made me a little. . .reminiscent. Besides, it's all water under the bridge now. The past is in the past. You know?"

"Well, yes," Candy agreed. "But the purpose of this banquet is to celebrate where we are today. . .and where we're heading. So, if I were you, I'd be praying about this, Shawneda. Seriously. Because God just might open a door. I happen to know of a great flight school on Long Island. You could get your training there." She put her clipboard down, sat down, and went into a lengthy explanation of what it would take for Shawneda to get her license.

By the time their conversation ended, nearly twenty minutes had passed. Candy and the others prayed with Shawneda—right there in the Dorothy House—about her secret desire to fly. Candy knew from her own experience that the desire usually didn't go away on its own. No, most of the people who had the bug ended up flying. . .sooner or later. The more Candy thought about it, the more excited she got. Perhaps, with some of the event's incoming scholarship money, she could play a role in helping her roomie fulfill a lifelong dream.

They wrapped up their prayer time just as a familiar voice rang out. "Are we having church?"

"Darren!" She rose and rushed his direction. "What are you doing here?"

"Well, a little bird told me you'd be here. I thought maybe you might let me take you to dinner. Are you hungry?"

"Am I ever! But can you give us a few more minutes to wrap up? We were just about to shift gears and talk about decorations."

"Woo-hoo. It's my lucky night. One lone man in a banquet room with four women talking about decorations."

"Hey now." She gave him a pouting look. "We want this night to be a rousing success and half the fun is the decorating." She turned to the others, excitement growing. Reaching for her clipboard once again, she read some things she'd written down. "We're going with a fairly simple theme with great fall colors. I've come up with a fun idea for centerpieces for the table, but I need someone to make them." Her gaze shifted to Darren, who'd taken to cleaning his nails.

After a moment's pause, he looked up. "What? Who, me?"

"Yes, you and Jason and maybe some of the other guys. We need model airplanes."

"Oh, that's easy. I've got at least five or six at my place."

"I know. But we're going to have fifteen tables at least," she explained. "And then the head table for the speakers and their husbands. So, we're probably talking at least twenty model airplanes. Planes from all different eras, I mean. And wouldn't it be cool to have several hanging up, too?"

"Twenty?" Darren shook his head. "Do you have any idea how long it takes to put together even one? It's tedious work."

Candy sighed. "Well, maybe if we check around we'll find a few more already made. But let's go to the hobby shop this afternoon, Darren. Okay? Before we eat?"

He shrugged. "Sure. Why not. When is this shindig again?" He raked his fingertips through his now-messy hair. "I might have to hire outside help."

"It's the last Saturday of this month, so you have three weeks."

"Three weeks." He whistled. "Man. You don't know what you're asking."

"Oh, and tell me what you think about this." Candy turned back to her friends. "I'm thinking we can elevate the model planes in the center of each table. . .maybe on a small box. And we'll cover each box with polyfill to look like clouds."

"Too cool." Brooke nodded.

Anna added an affirmative, "I like it."

They wrapped up the rest of their plans, focusing primarily on the menu, then Candy turned to Darren. "Ready to go shopping?"

"My favorite question." He grinned. "I'm fine with it. Just don't take me to the mall or make me watch you pick out shoes for this big event, okay? I have my limits." He winked at her and she laughed in response.

"Oh, you just reminded me, I do need to get some new shoes. And a new dress, too."

The women dove into an animated conversation about their attire for the banquet, and Darren sighed. Candy knew he wasn't really frustrated. He was used to hanging around the women, after all. He knew how they were. And he never seemed to mind.

Still, as they went on and on about evening gowns versus party dresses, she did notice when he began making his way to the door. He mouthed, "I'll be waiting outside," and she nodded. Hopefully she wouldn't keep him waiting long.

Darren heard his cell phone ring and reached to answer it. He glanced down at the phone, stunned to see a familiar number with a 619 area code displayed.

"Mom?" He spoke the word hesitantly.

"Darren, it's Dad. I'm using your mother's cell phone. She's. . ."

"What, Dad?"

"We're at the hospital. She's having a little procedure done."

"Procedure? What kind?"

"Well. . ." He paused long enough for fear to kick in. "Some sort of thing where they put dye into your arteries so they show up on an x-ray. I think they called it a. . ." He paused again. "Hang on, son. Let me look at this paper they gave me. Oh, okay. It's called a cardiac catheterization."

"Wait." Darren allowed the words to register. "Are you saying that Mom has a heart problem?"

"Well, they're not sure yet. But she had a little spell a few days ago. Wasn't the first one."

"Dad, you should've called me."

"She didn't want me to. You know how stubborn your mom can be."

"Yes, but I still need to know these things so I can be praying."

"Well, she's been through a lot of stress at work over the past few weeks, so I was hoping they'd come back and say she was just having an anxiety attack or something like that, but the cardiologist said it might be something else. So they're doing this procedure."

Darren shuffled the phone to his other ear. "Is this some sort of surgery?"

"Not really. And she's wide awake. They're putting a catheter through an artery in her leg and somehow leading it up to her heart. Then they put the dye in."

"She's awake? Why aren't you in there with her?"

Another sigh from his father let him know exactly why. "She wouldn't let me. You know how she is."

"Stubborn." They repeated the word in unison.

"Your mother's got a mind of her own." His dad sounded weary. "And heaven knows I've tried to get her to slow down. She works too hard. And she's always anxious or upset about something. Her blood pressure's been running on the high side, but the doctor said that's probably a result of stress. The lawyer she works for is representing some guy in a high-profile case, and she's been up to her ears in paperwork as they prepare for trial."

Darren shook his head, unable to figure out what to say next. His mother had always been high-stress. Always in command. Always demanding and bossing others around, even at the law firm where she worked. No doubt her body had finally started to react. No one could keep up that kind of pressure without eventual problems.

"Dad, I know you don't want to hear this," he finally worked up the courage to say, "but you're going to have to get Mom to listen to you. She's got to follow the doctor's orders and slow down. Stay calm."

"Humph."

"I know. But..." Darren sighed. "Let's just pray about this. And in the meantime, I'll be praying for the results of this test. Keep me posted, okay?"

"I will." Another hesitation followed, then, "Son?"

"Yes, Dad?"

"I love you. And we miss you. Wish you'd come for a visit."

"I will, Dad. Especially if you need me."

They ended the call, and Darren gripped the phone in his hands. At that moment, Candy and the others emerged from the building, still chirping like baby birds as they talked about the banquet. His father's news still gripped his heart.

Candy looked over at Darren, her brow wrinkled in concern. "Darren? What's happened?"

"My mom." He shook his head. "She's been having some heart problems. That was my dad on the phone."

"Oh no."

The other ladies quickly said their good-byes, leaving Darren and Candy to themselves. She drew near and wrapped her arms around his neck. "I'm sure she's going to be fine. This isn't major, right?"

"I don't know. And even if it is, I doubt she'll crack the veneer to let us in to help. She's pretty self-sufficient."

"Oh, you might be surprised." A look of compassion came over Candy as she spoke. "I don't know if I've ever told you this, but my mom had cancer several years ago. Now, she's always been a real softie—a lot different from the way you've described your mom—but the illness really changed her. For the better, I mean. Yes, she went through a lot physically, but she came out of it a lot stronger, and more dependent on God. So, that's how I'm going to pray for your mom. That the Lord will use this situation to draw her to Him."

Darren nodded. "Thank you. I needed to hear that."

"He can do it. And your mom's in the perfect place to hear right now. He's got her full, undivided attention."

"True." Darren shook his head. "I feel so. . .conflicted. She's my mom, you know?"

"Of course."

"I love her, but she doesn't always make it easy. And now I'm scared something will happen to her before I've had a chance to really work on restoring our relationship. Not that I haven't tried in the past. I have. . ."

"Well, just think about what I've said. This illness is likely going to change her. She's facing her own mortality. And I'd be willing to bet God will use it as a catalyst to mend not just her relationship with you, but her relationship with your dad, as well."

"I hope you're right."

"Time will tell." She gave him a light peck on the cheek. "So, do you want to pray about it?"

He knew what she meant, of course. Right here. Right now.

"Sure. You already prayed inside. No reason to think we can't do the same out here." Darren took Candy's hands in his and began to pray. Then, after a time, she took over, praying for his mother's healing. . .both physical and emotional.

As Candy prayed, Darren realized just how different his relationship with Candy was from his parents' relationship. *Lord, thank You for sending her to me. I'm going to seal the deal, Lord, just as soon as You give me the go-ahead. Gonna wrap up this Candy and take her home. . .for good.*

Chapter 18

The day of the banquet arrived at last. Candy worked with the other women to prepare the ballroom at the Dorothy House. She brought in easels and large photos of Amelia Earhart, along with several other women who'd made such a huge difference in the industry over the years.

Once everything was in place, Candy, Anna, Brooke, and Shawneda stared at the room in silence.

"I'm so proud of you." Anna gave her hand a squeeze. "You're doing a great thing here."

"You think?" When they all nodded, she said, "I'm so excited. And I'm so grateful. None of this would have been possible without you. Have I told you how much I appreciate all of you?"

"Only twenty or thirty times," Brooke said with a crooked smile.

They all laughed and shared a group hug. Candy enjoyed the moment. It felt so good to have the support of her friends. And how good of Brooke to give so much of her time, especially in light of her wedding plans.

By six o'clock, both the guest speakers had arrived, along with their spouses. Candy showed them to their seats and gave them the program schedule. She paused for a few minutes to talk to Margaret Franklin, the older of their two speakers. She paused a moment as she took in the woman's beautiful face. The wrinkles around her eyes were clearly laugh lines, judging from her joyous expression.

"I just want you to know how much it means to me that you've come." Candy couldn't hide her smile. "We're just so blessed to have you here."

"I'm the one who's blessed." Margaret gave her a motherly look. "I've asked the Lord to open any doors I'm to walk through, and He opened this one. I'm here because He's led me here. And I hope the stories I share will bring hope to all of you younger women. That's my plan, anyway."

"Oh, I'm sure it will."

Less than an hour later, the room filled with beautifully dressed people. Most were women, naturally, but a few had brought their spouses or boyfriends along. Lilly came with a handsome fellow she'd met at the library. . . an elementary school teacher. She buzzed with excitement as she introduced him to the group.

"Everyone, this is Phil. Phil, this is everyone."

They welcomed him in style, then Candy turned to Darren and whispered,

"Will you hang out with him while we're working? Make him feel welcome?" Darren readily agreed.

Candy barely had time to blink before she was whisked away to deal with a technical issue. The PowerPoint presentation she'd prepared had a glitch. No problem. She'd get it straightened out.

At ten minutes till seven, her family arrived. She could hardly believe it when she saw a very pregnant Taffie heading in her direction. "No way. You're huge!"

"Well, thanks a lot." Taffie laughed, then pretended to pout.

"Oh, you know what I mean. You look radiant. You're glowing."

"Aw, thanks. I'm enjoying this part of the pregnancy. But that third trimester's sneaking up on me. . .and soon. Hope you plan to come home for the big event."

"I wouldn't miss it for the world." Candy gave her sister a hug, then turned her attention to her parents. "I'm so glad you came. This means the world to me. And if it weren't for the two of you. . ." She couldn't finish the sentence.

"Oh, don't make me cry." Her mother reached for a tissue and dabbed her eyes. "I'm already menopausal. And I'm about to be a grandmother. I cry at the drop of a hat now."

Something about that got Candy tickled. She laughed.

Until she looked at the clock. Five till seven. Better stay on top of things.

At seven ten, with everyone seated at their tables, Candy took the podium and welcomed their guests. She could hardly believe the crowd. And the room! It looked amazing. Her nerves almost got the better of her as she delivered her opening welcome. She fought her way past the tremor in her voice as she spoke.

"Good evening, everyone. I'm thrilled to welcome you to this, the first annual Newark Liberty International Airport banquet for women in aviation. We're about to be served our meal, but before we do, I'd like to specifically thank those who've worked so hard to make this evening possible." She began to reel off the names of the many people who'd come to her aid over the past few weeks, then paused to pray for the meal. Afterward, she told the guests to hang on to their hats, that an awesome presentation would follow dinner.

But first things first. She'd made arrangements with the caterer to have a fabulous meal—prime rib, au gratin potatoes, and a vegetable medley, along with bread and yummy slices of cheesecake for dessert.

Candy took her place at the head table alongside the speakers. Their conversation was so lively that she almost let the time get away from her. At 7:40, just as dessert was being served, she made her way to the podium once again. With great joy, she introduced their first speaker.

Margaret Franklin rose and came to the microphone. She wrapped Candy in a tight embrace and whispered, "You go, girl! I'm so proud of you for putting together this fabulous event," in her ear. Then, with the assurance of a skilled public speaker, she stood before the crowd and told the story of her adventures as a young pilot in the '60s, focusing on some rather harrowing flights during the Vietnam War. The room was still and silent. People hung on her every word.

"I want to give a word of encouragement to the young women in the room tonight," Margaret said. "Those of you who might be thinking you've got it hard. Life is full of challenges. The question is not whether you will face challenges. We all do. The question is. . .will you triumph over them?"

Candy caught a glimpse of Darren, who sat at a nearby table. He had certainly faced his share of challenges of late. He'd shared many phone calls with his father in recent days. She knew he was concerned about his mother's health.

Tonight, however, he seemed more like the old Darren, the one with the ever-present smile and twinkling blue eyes. He gave her a wink and mouthed, "I love you." She grinned, felt her cheeks warm, then turned her attention back to the podium.

A hearty round of applause followed Margaret's heartfelt speech.

Next came the part Candy had been waiting for. She'd prepared a fabulous PowerPoint presentation, focusing on the history of women in aviation. The first photos had been harder to come by. . .female pilots from the 1920s. A few rare photos of the women who'd started the Ninety-Nines. Then the slide show traveled the decades. Everyone laughed at some of the uniforms worn by the women, especially in the thirties and forties, but Candy also heard several positive vocal responses from the crowd as the show progressed.

Finally, the photos transitioned to modern women. Women like Brooke, Anna, Lilly, Shawneda, and herself. Women like Norah, their next speaker.

When the presentation ended, Candy proudly introduced the petite young pilot, who came to the podium, her face awash with joy.

"How do I follow that?" Norah laughed. "Margaret was flying planes before I was even born. And she's flown to places I can only dream of flying." After a chuckle from the crowd, Norah spent the next ten minutes telling her story. How her parents had listened to her dreams of flying from early childhood on. How they'd supported her and helped her fulfill her dream.

At this point, Candy turned her attention to her parents and her siblings, who sat with Darren. She could barely restrain the tears as Norah talked. If not for the loving support of her family, her dream would never have become a reality.

Cotton Candy, you've got your head in the clouds again.

She could almost hear her father's teasing words. They'd bothered her as a child, but no longer. Now she loved the fact that her dreams. . .her childish, grandiose dreams. . .had finally become a reality.

And, oh! What a reality.

&

As the evening wound down, Darren found himself distracted. While he enjoyed the presentation immensely, and while he felt overwhelmed with pride at the amazing job Candy had done, he had something else on his mind. Something else altogether.

After weeks of praying, he'd finally come to a conclusion, one he felt sure the Lord had confirmed. Two conclusions, actually. As soon as the crowd cleared, he needed to talk to Candy. If she responded well to the first matter of business, he would make his move toward securing the second.

He reached into his pocket for the umpteenth time to make sure the tiny box was still there. Then again, where else would it be? His heart raced in anticipation. *First things first, Darren. Tell her what you're planning before you pop the question. And wait for the perfect moment. No point in jumping the gun.*

He watched as the crowd began to clear. Several people approached Candy, telling her what a great job she'd done. He couldn't help but agree. After several rounds of good-byes, Candy kicked off her shoes and proclaimed it was time to get to work.

"We've got a lot to load up," she said, looking around the room. "The model planes and all of the other decorations need to be boxed up. And anything you see that belongs to us."

She and the other women went to work, loading up her car with the planes Darren and Jason had worked so hard to build. Even from here, every move she made drew him in. Did she have any idea how beautiful she was, especially in that blue gown? Did she know it made her upswept hair look like something out of a magazine? Could she even fathom that the sound of her laughter caused his heart rate to jump and his head to swim?

Soon. She would know it all very soon.

"Here, let me help you with that." Darren woke himself up from his daydreaming and went to work, grabbing one of the heavier boxes she had filled.

Finally, once the car was loaded and the room completely cleared, Darren and Candy said their good-byes to her family, promising to come down to Atlantic City for the birth of Taffie's baby.

When they were the last two remaining, Darren finally found the perfect opportunity to talk to Candy. . .alone.

"Sit a minute." He gestured at the bench outside the banquet hall.

"I'm tired, Darren. Can't we just—"

"It won't take long. But there's something I need to tell you."

"But I'm so worn out. Can't it wait until—"

"I've had something on my mind for ages." He put his hand in his pocket once more. *Yep. Still there. I'll get to that in a moment. But something else to deal with first. . .*

"What is it?" She yawned, then leaned back against the bench, her eyes half-closed.

"Something about my career, actually."

"Oh?" Her eyes popped open at that. "What about it? Has something else happened at Eastway that I need to know about?"

"No. This isn't about Eastway."

"It's not?"

He sat next to her on the bench. "No. And before I tell you any of this, I want you to know that I've prayed it through. I've got a real peace about this. It's going to rock my world. . .our world. . .a little, but I know it will be worth it in the end." *And once you're onboard with this plan, I have an even bigger one.*

"I think you'd better spit it out. I'm getting nervous."

"Okay." He stood and began to pace, ready to deliver the speech he'd rehearsed in his head all evening.

She gave him a pensive look. "Darren, you're scaring me."

"Don't be scared." He turned to face her. "Okay, this is it. All of my life, I've wanted to fly."

"Right." She shrugged, then stifled another yawn.

"And flying for Eastway has been great. Most of the time. But in my heart, I want something more. Something different."

"What? Are you serious?" She began to wind her hair around her index finger, something she only did when nervous. "Like what?"

"Candy, I want to start my own charter service." He spoke the words as fast as possible, just wanting to get them out. Candy's mouth rounded in an *Ooo* that reminded him of Fred, his goldfish. He plowed ahead, hoping to get the hardest part over first. "I know. It doesn't make a lot of sense. I have a great job. But every time I think about flying, I think about doing it in a plane that I own."

"You're buying a plane?"

"Well, not today. And probably not tomorrow, either. But I've had my eyes on a Cessna 208. And Jimmy's been talking to me about this King Air a friend of his is selling. It's in tip-top shape. And we could grow from there."

"Wait. We? Are you talking about. . .you and me?"

Yikes. "Well, yes. And no. I'm actually talking about Jimmy. He and I would do this together. Between us, we could get the financial backing. I know we could. And if we start out small, then add jets later on, we'll have a huge range of aircraft and pricing to meet the needs of individuals at all income levels. And who knows. . .maybe at that point, you could come and fly with us, too. I mean, if you want to."

"I. . .I don't know." She stared at him, clearly confused. "I've only been at Eastway a couple months and I love it. I'm not saying I wouldn't ever want to do that, but right now it just doesn't make sense. And I'm not sure that you're thinking clearly, Darren. What you're talking about. . .it's going to cost a fortune. And it's risky. You've got great job security at Eastway. Why would you give all of that up?"

"I'm not saying I'd give up anything." He felt his patience wearing thin. "And this is something I've really prayed about. Jimmy's been checking into the licenses we'll need. And he's been researching to see what the competition is charging for their services, so we'll know what to charge."

"Okay. . ." She leaned back against the bench, a look of exhaustion on her face.

"Candy, think about it. I could do away with a lot of the stresses related to flying for someone else. And best of all, I could be living my dream."

"Living your dream." She paused a moment, then sighed.

"You, of all people, know about dreams. So, I thought you'd. . ." He didn't finish. Suddenly he felt completely deflated.

"Darren, I want you to be happy." Her smiled seemed a bit forced. "I'm just. . .surprised. And I'm so tired that none of this is really registering right now. Would you mind if we talked about this tomorrow night, after I get back from my flight to Minneapolis? I'm sure it'll all make more sense then."

"I guess." He tried not to let his disappointment show. Still, he had to wonder how she could get so excited about women in aviation. . .and couldn't even muster up the tiniest bit of enthusiasm for his project.

Besides, if he didn't get past this first question, he'd never get to the second one. The one where he would pull the ring from his pocket and slip it on her finger.

Determined not to give much away with his expression, he walked with her to her car. All the while, he tried to formulate a new plan regarding the intended proposal.

As they walked, she grumbled about how much her feet ached after wearing heels all night. Then she transitioned into a lengthy dissertation about Margaret Hamilton's magnificent speech. Darren tried to get a word in edgewise, but couldn't.

Lord, help me out here. Please. Everything is unraveling. I need some direction.

Just as they reached the car, she paused for breath. *Perfect opportunity. I'm going to do this. . .right now. Even if the timing isn't what I thought it would be.*

In that very moment, his cell phone rang. Darren groaned and pushed the volume key to mute, not even looking at the number.

"Someone's calling pretty late. Must be important."

He glanced down at the number and his heartbeat skipped to double time. "It's my dad." He answered right away. "Dad?"

"Son?" His father's voice was barely recognizable. "Did I wake you?"

"No, it's fine. I'm still up. What's happened?"

"Your mother. . .well, she's had a heart attack. It's a bad one."

A lump rose in Darren's throat, and he felt the sting of tears. "I–I'll be on the next flight out, Dad."

"Thank you. I really need you here. I'm so. . .I don't know what to do. She's always the one who handles things. . .like this."

"Tell me where you're at."

"UCSD. Fourth floor. ICU."

"I'm coming. I'll call when I have a plan of action. And Dad. . ."

"Yes?"

"Please tell Mom I love her." It felt like a rock lodged in Darren's throat as the words were spoken.

"I'll do that," his father whispered.

Darren ended the call, then turned to Candy, not even trying to stop the overflow of emotions. In one instant, everything had changed. The news about his business ideas would have to wait. The proposal would have to wait. Right now, there was someone in California he needed to see. . .and the sooner, the better.

Chapter 19

Candy entered the apartment at a quarter till one, fighting the mixture of emotions that threatened to overtake her. After stopping by Darren's house to help him pack, she'd driven him to the airport, where he'd managed to catch a flight to San Diego with a brief layover in Phoenix. For now, all they could do was pray. And wait.

Her heart twisted in several different directions at once. In spite of the news about Darren's mom, she still longed to celebrate the evening's events. Together the women had pulled off a smashing night, after all. Everyone said so.

Just as quickly, realization set in. *Lord, You did it. We could never have put this together on our own, and we certainly couldn't have raised forty thousand dollars in scholarships for women who want to fly.* She still marveled at the fact that so many people had been willing to make donations above and beyond the cost of their ticket to the event. And a couple of corporations had come onboard, as well, promising support both now and in the future. This news thrilled her.

She opened the door to her bedroom to find that Lilly was already fast asleep. Doing her best to remain quiet, Candy tiptoed to her dresser and opened a drawer to pull out her pj's.

As she dressed for bed, Candy replayed the night in her mind. Over and over again she thought about Margaret Franklin and the words she'd spoken from the podium. Her stories had held everyone captivated. What a difference one woman had made in the industry.

Lord, I want to be like that. I want You to use me.

After brushing her teeth, she crawled under the covers and rested her head against the pillow. As weariness set in, everything from the banquet began to run together. The women. The stories. The decorations. The pretty dresses. The speeches.

Darren.

He'd been there all evening, right in the thick of things. And he'd obviously had a wonderful time, judging from his reactions during the event. Before the phone call from his dad, of course. But all that stuff about starting a charter service. . .was he really serious? Would he give up a steady job to set off on his own in a risky business? How in the world could he fund such a venture?

Nah. He's just dreaming out loud.

Maybe.

Who was she to question his dreams? Wasn't she the queen of dreams? *I should have offered more support.*

And now. . .the situation with his mother.

Candy's breath caught in her throat as she realized all that Darren was facing at once. And alone, no less. If only she could've gone with him. That would have changed everything. Maybe, through the haze of emotions, they could have made sense of things. She hadn't exactly been a bastion of support when he'd told her his ideas, had she? But exhaustion had set in. Surely he understood that.

Exhaustion. Hmm.

She glanced at the clock and groaned. One fifteen? Her flight to Minneapolis left at nine. If she could get her thoughts to stop fast-forwarding through her brain like a sepia tone movie, she might just get some sleep.

❧

Darren flew through the night, this time in a first-class seat. He spent much of the time in prayer for his mother. He wasn't sure about her walk with God. Maybe he'd have an opportunity to talk with her about that when he arrived. He hoped.

With nothing else to do—and with so much on his mind—Darren spent the two and a half hours between Newark and Phoenix interceding for the one person he'd always had the hardest time praying for.

Lord, it feels like the rug's been pulled out from under me. I've lost my bearings. Everything is in turmoil. My job. My mom's health. My relationship with Candy. He swallowed hard at that one. One thing he hadn't counted on was the lack of enthusiasm from Candy at his news about the business venture.

Lord, show me what to do. I need Your guidance. Show me what to say to my mom and what not to say. And help me figure out where to go from here. . .with my career. With my personal life. With my future.

He leaned back against the seat and plugged in the earphones to his MP3 player. A worship song played in the background. He listened to the words, finally able to calm down. They reminded him that God was bigger than any problems he might face. . .now or in the future. Now, if he could only go on believing that after the song ended.

Darren finally managed to doze off. He knew he'd need his sleep. Likely he wouldn't get much once he arrived in San Diego.

When he reached Phoenix for the layover, Darren called his father. "Any change?"

"No. She's. . ." His father choked back tears. "She's pretty heavily medicated right now, Darren. And I don't know what to expect. They're not really telling me much, and I don't want to speculate."

"I'll be there in an hour and a half, Dad. You sound exhausted."

"I am."

"Well, try to get some sleep. And when I get there, we can take turns watching over her."

"Okay. I'm glad you're coming." After a moment's hesitation, his father added, "Want me to pick you up at the airport?"

"No. I'll catch a cab. You just stay with Mom."

They ended the call, and Darren prepared to board his next flight. For once, he wanted to be free from airplanes. . .to have his feet on solid ground. On the other hand, as the nose of the plane tipped upward. . .as they took to the skies, he was reminded once again of the Lord's earlier admonition to soar above his circumstances.

Only one way to do that.

He'd have to completely let go of the controls and leave the piloting to God.

❧

Candy awoke a couple of times in the night. Each time she prayed for Darren and his mom. She couldn't shake the nagging feeling that something was wrong. Very wrong.

On the other hand, she knew better than to let fear get the better of her. So, every time fear rose up, she prayed all the harder.

Lord, I don't know what's going on here, but You do. I just ask that You take control, Father. Take my emotions and my fears. And be with Darren as he travels.

Darren.

Her heart grew heavy at the mention of his name. How would she manage these next few days without him? Determined to sleep, she rolled over and gave the pillow a firm whack.

She must've made more noise than she knew because Lilly sat up in her bed and began to stammer. "W–what happened?"

"Nothing. Sorry. Go back to sleep."

"Okay." Lilly lay back down and mumbled, "You, too, Candy. We've got a long day ahead of us tomorrow."

"Yes, I know."

After a few minutes, Candy's eyes grew heavy, and she found herself drifting off. . .at last.

Chapter 20

On Sunday morning Candy awoke just in time to catch a quick shower and head to the airport. Thankfully, Lilly would be on the same flight, so they shared a ride.

Though Lilly chattered at will as she drove, Candy couldn't stop thinking about Darren. And though she'd tried a couple of times to call him, he wasn't picking up. Likely he'd turned his cell phone off in the hospital. Still, she didn't feel right about taking off without talking to him. They hadn't ended things on the best of notes last night.

And there was something else, too. Just before the call from his father, he'd looked as if he wanted to say something to her. He'd pulled back at the last minute with a sad look on his face. But, why?

I deflated his ego. I didn't support him when he told me about his dream. I'm a sorry excuse for a girlfriend.

Before boarding the 747 to Minneapolis, she made one last attempt to call him. Again, he didn't pick up. She shut off her phone and headed to the plane, ready to put this day behind her. As always, she prayed as she settled into the cockpit. And, in spite of the ups and downs of the last twenty-four hours, felt comfortable behind the wheel.

Adam Landers, her captain, looked at her with a smile. "Minneapolis, here we come."

"Yep." She gave him a confident smile. "Then it's back home to Newark. All in a day's work."

"All in a day's work," he repeated.

She offered him a smile. . .and then they took to flight.

❧

Darren paced the halls of the hospital, talking to his father. His mother's condition appeared to be stabilizing. And a recent visit with the cardiologist confirmed that her medically induced coma would soon be behind them.

"I want you to be prepared for a long haul," the doctor admonished. "She's got quite a journey ahead of her. It's going to take patience and a firm hand. Her best chance will be a serious change in diet and a low-stress environment."

Darren had cringed at that last part. He couldn't imagine the words *low stress* used in the same sentence as his mother. And how would his dad cope? She'd be a tough case, no doubt. Did his father have it in him to make her line up and walk straight? Only time would tell.

He made his way back into his mother's room, standing at her bedside in quiet reflection. Sometime later, the craziness of the past several hours caught up with him, and his eyes grew heavy. Darren took a seat in the chair to his mother's right. His father—who looked equally as exhausted—sat opposite him on the left side of the bed.

Just after noon California time, Darren received a call from Jason. It jarred him from his slumber. He answered right away.

"Hey, thanks for calling." He lowered his voice, so as not to wake his father, who slept in a nearby chair. "I guess you heard about my mom."

"Yes." Jason's voice trembled as he spoke. "And I'm praying. But, Darren. . . are you watching the news?"

"The news?" He glanced up at the television, which hadn't been turned on all day. "No. Should I be? What's happening?"

"There's a. . .well, you'd just better look and see. I'm watching CNN, but I'm sure this is on every major news station."

Darren reached for the remote and clicked on the television. Immediately his heart went to his throat as he saw the news flash. EASTWAY PILOT ATTEMPTS EMERGENCY LANDING IN NEWARK.

"Darren, what's happening?" His father came awake with a start.

"It's. . ." He couldn't finish the sentence. Darren watched, gripped with fear, as the 747 pointed itself at the runway, nose gear still up.

The news reporter's voice jarred him. "The control tower has confirmed that the front landing gear of Eastway flight 4582 is not down. But it looks like the pilot is trying to bring the plane down without the landing gear. He's got the aircraft under control for the moment but. . .ah, I've just been told the first officer—a female—is actually flying the plane while the captain works to rectify the problem. She's doing an admirable job of—"

Oh, Lord. . .no. Please, no.

The reporter's voice paused for a few seconds. Just when the plane looked as if it would come in for an attempted landing, the nose lifted once again and it disappeared from view.

"Not sure what just happened there," the reporter picked back up again. "Must've had a change of heart." The camera zoomed in on the plane as it continued to ascend. "This has got to be frightening for the passengers and the crew. And for the family members watching."

"Darren?" Jason's voice came over the phone line, startling him back to attention. "Are you there?"

"I'm here. Jason, that's. . ."

"I know. And I'm praying. I'm going to hang up now so we can focus on doing that."

"No, wait. The Bible says if two or more agree in prayer. . ." Darren didn't take time to finish the scripture. Instead, he began to pray aloud from the depths of his soul. . .for Candy and the other crew members on the 747 and for the passengers and people on the ground as well.

Just as he finished, the reporter came back on. "It looks as if that's foam they're applying to the runway, to reduce the risk of fire when the plane makes its final attempt."

"Could you not say *final* in that tone?" Darren directed his words to the television.

"We've just confirmed there are seventy-three passengers onboard the Eastway flight, including one infant and one wheelchair-bound passenger." The reporter went off on a tangent about the various passengers, but Darren barely heard a word. Everything seemed to be moving in slow motion, including the reporter's voice.

"Darren, God is in control." Jason's voice again. Calm. Controlled. "We can trust Him."

"Yes. I know."

"Darren, do you know someone on that plane?" His father's concerned voice brought him back to reality.

"I do."

The camera flashed to the aircraft, which had made a wide circle and now pointed itself at the runway once again.

"C'mon, Candy. You can do this."

"Candy?" His father whispered the word. "Your Candy?"

He nodded.

"It looks as if the pilot is going to make another attempt." The reporter's voice rose with anticipation as the plane began to descend.

Darren began to pray, silently at first, and then aloud as he watched. "You can do it, Candy," he whispered, when he'd finished praying. "You've been trained. You know what to do. Just listen to your gut. Do what you've been taught."

"You can do it, girl," his father joined in.

Then, as if she'd planned for this moment her entire life, Candy brought the aircraft down to the ground. It skidded off to the left of the runway, wreaking havoc with the foam. Darren wanted to scream. To jump for joy. Instead, he looked at his father with tears in his eyes, overcome with relief.

The reporter's voice kicked in. "Folks, she's done it. That's some first officer. She pulled off a textbook landing."

Darren's hands began to tremble. He heard Jason's voice on the other end of the phone. "Thank You, Jesus," and added a tearful, "Amen."

He watched in awe as the aircraft came to a complete stop. After a moment's pause, the reporter jumped back in with his comments. "Looks like they'll be implementing an emergency evacuation."

"Wow. I've only seen this in the movies." Darren's father stood close to the television, watching in rapt awe.

"Yes, they've just deployed the chutes," the reporter continued. He went on to describe in detail the layout of a 747, honing in on where the emergency exits were located.

"I don't believe this." Darren shook his head. His father was right. It really was like watching a movie. . .only, the woman he loved was playing the lead role.

The reporter's inflection changed. "Folks, we've just been joined by Marcus Blackwell, a spokesman with the Newark Airport Authority. Mr. Blackwell, what can you tell us about what we've just seen? And when will we know the condition of the passengers and crew?"

Another voice, this one a bit calmer, took over. "The pilot of Eastway flight 4582 reported the faulty landing gear at 2:52 p.m. Newark time."

"And when something like this happens, the pilot has been trained to respond accordingly?" the reporter asked.

"Every pilot is taught to prepare for the worst, and is trained accordingly. The pilots aboard the Eastway flight today worked with the tower to bring the aircraft down in the safest possible manner."

Darren continued to watch as people began to descend the emergency ramps. He'd had nightmares about flights like this. Likely every pilot had.

"As you can see, we've got fire and rescue personnel on the ground to receive any people who might need to be evaluated or transported to hospitals," Mr. Blackwell continued. "At this time we have no word as to the condition of the passengers or crew, but we are very relieved, as you might imagine."

Relieved? Relieved hardly described the feeling that swept over Darren as he watched the passengers exit the plane. *Why am I in California instead of Newark? I need to be there for her. I've got to leave. Got to—*

His heart nearly leaped into his throat as a weak voice interrupted the moment. "D–darren? Darren, is that you?"

He turned toward the bed to face his mother, whose eyes were half-opened.

"I'm here, Mama." He rushed to her side and gripped her hand. "You rest easy now. Rest easy. Everything's going to be all right."

"Thank you for coming," she whispered, then squeezed his hand. "We need you right now."

"I–I'm here."

Yes, he was here. Oh, but how he wished he could be in two places at once.

≈

Candy sat in the cockpit, shaking like a leaf. For a moment she felt dizzy, then a wave of nausea swept over her. "I'm going to be sick." The captain reached for a bag and pressed it into her hand. Candy sat, breathing deeply, until the feeling passed. Even so, she still felt woozy.

Adam—the captain who'd kept his cool throughout the ordeal—reached out to touch her arm. "Candy, I have something to say. You did an amazing job. Thanks to you, our passengers and crew are safely home."

"No, not thanks to me." She shook her head, unable to take the credit. "I had nothing to do with it, trust me. Only the Lord could have accomplished that."

"Well, He apparently used you to help." Adam nodded. "And I couldn't have taken on the job of troubleshooter without you actually flying the plane. But just prepare yourself. I'd say there's going to be an outpouring from the community. And you're about to get swarmed by the media. Are you up for it?"

"The media?"

Man. After weeks of trying to stay out of the limelight at Eastway, suddenly I'm thrust into the spotlight in front of the entire nation?

"That landing was textbook. I can't imagine doing a better job myself. And I don't think you'd be giving yourself too much credit if you admitted you did a fine job."

"T–thank you."

Adam rose to his feet and looked her way. "Ready to get off of this bird?"

"Mm-hmm." She nodded. "Am I ever."

"Well, just be prepared. I have a feeling we're about to be inundated."

One look outside convinced her he was right. With so many ambulances and fire trucks about, they were sure to be swamped with people. And where there was a story, there were sure to be journalists.

A shiver went down her spine as she thought about that. *Journalists. News. Man.* Talk about throwing a kink in her plans to keep a low profile.

She and Adam reached the door where the emergency chutes were in place. With all their passengers safely on the ground, they could take their final ride toward freedom.

Funny. All she could think of as she slid down the chute was what she'd told Darren that day on the Cessna 400. "I've never jumped out of a plane before."

And though this probably wasn't the kind of jump he had in mind, she had to admit. . .it looked like there was a first time for everything.

When she reached the ground, people swarmed her. Medics, police. . .she could scarcely breathe for all of the people. And they all talked on top of one another. "Are you hurt?"

"Great job!"

"You should win an Emmy for that performance."

"We're so proud of you."

She and Adam were taken by patrol car to the Eastway offices, where she was met with the craziest mob of media folks she'd ever seen.

I didn't even know we had this many newspapers and television stations in Newark.

Turned out folks from the New York media had already arrived and were ready for a story. A national story.

More than an hour of craziness slipped by before she was finally able to reach for her cell phone to call Darren. She stared transfixed at the phone, noticing for the first time how many times he'd called her. She'd missed every one, thanks to the chaos.

"Better put his mind at ease."

She punched in his number, tears welling. Only one thing could make her feel better. Scratch that. Only one *person* could make her feel better. And he was on the other side of the country, handling a crisis of his own.

Chapter 21

Darren paced the halls of the hospital, nearly frantic. He finally managed to reach Brooke. "Have you heard from her?"

"She's up at the Eastway offices, Darren. They've got her secluded. I'm sure she's going to call you."

"Who was on that flight with her?"

"Adam Landers. And Lilly."

"Lilly. Really?" His heart twisted. "And Adam." Both friends. And both very much alive, thanks to the Lord's intervention and Candy's skillful landing.

"I'm still trying to reach Candy, but if you hear from her—"

"I'll have her call you, I promise." After a moment's pause, Brooke asked, "How's your mom, Darren?"

"Awake. Ornery. The doctors are going to perform some sort of procedure on her in a couple of days to see about clearing up the blockage. And then she's going to have a major change in lifestyle. Just pray she'll go along with it, and pray for my dad, too, okay? He's going to have to step up to the plate and. . .well, he's got his work cut out for him."

"Of course. Would you like me to pray right now?"

A wave of peace washed over him. Darren slumped in a chair. "W–would you? I feel like the biggest wimp on planet Earth. It'll be good to have someone agree with me in prayer."

"Of course. And hey, I head up the prayer chain for the singles group, so I'm used to praying over the phone." She began to pray, starting with a joyous praise for God's hand of protection, which He'd placed on both Darren's mother and on Candy and the crew aboard flight 4582. Then she shifted gears, praying for healing for his mom and provision for his father. By the time she ended, Darren had tears in his eyes.

"Thanks, Brooke."

"You're welcome."

She'd no sooner said the words than a *beep* interrupted their call. He looked at the number and practically dropped the phone. "Gotta go. It's Candy."

Without so much as a good-bye, he clicked over, speaking her name undergirded by emotion.

"Darren?" Her trembling voice showed her feelings immediately.

"Candy, I'm here," he managed. "I'm so glad to hear your voice. I've been worried sick."

233

"I knew you would be. I wanted to call right away, but they wouldn't let me. You should have seen it. There were so many people, and they had so many questions. I felt like I was on trial."

"I'll bet. But you're okay?"

"Physically. My insides are mush. And I don't know if I'll ever be able to get back in the cockpit again. I. . ." She began to cry.

"You will. I know you. You're great at this, Candy. And you're called to it. You can't give up. You've got to get right back in there and get to work."

"Well, not today. I think I'm going to go home and take a hot bath. Maybe eat some Chinese food. Then I'm going to pull the covers up over my head and pretend none of this ever happened."

"I'd probably do exactly the same thing. Only I'd eat a cheeseburger, not Chinese."

She offered up a nervous laugh, then added, "I wish you were here."

"Me, too." He paused, and tried not to let his emotions get the better of him. She needed him to be strong. "Do you want to talk about what happened, or wait till after you've had some food?"

"I can talk about it, I guess. But first tell me about your mom. I've been so concerned about her. And when I saw that you'd called so many times, I was afraid. . ."

"She's better." Darren quickly filled her in on his mother's condition, honing in on the part of the story where his mother had asked him to pray.

"She was barely awake, but she knew who I was. And she had tears in her eyes. I think God is working on her, Candy. Just like you predicted."

"She's a captive audience. Kind of like I was in that cockpit today."

"So, you want to talk about it?"

"Yeah." She paused a moment, then began to tell her story, her voice shaking every step of the way. "We'd had the smoothest flight ever. Nothing suspicious. And I had no reason to think the landing gear would stick. Our landing in Minneapolis was great. No indications of any problems." She paused a moment. "A lot of things went through my mind in that cockpit once I realized we were in trouble. Of course, I thought about all the things I would miss if I. . ."

"Don't even say it." A shiver ran down his spine just thinking of the what-ifs.

"Well, I know where I'm going when the time comes," she reminded him, "so it wasn't really a fear about that part. It was more about the responsibility I had to protect the passengers. And Lilly. And Adam. The responsibility was overwhelming, really."

"I have to admit, my faith just flew right out the window when I got the call." He pursed his lips. "And I went into a panic when I watched the news footage. I told Brooke, I'm a spiritual wimp in a crisis. I never knew that till now."

"No you're not." The tenderness in her voice brought him comfort.

"Well, just the thought of losing you. . ." His eyes filled with tears. "I couldn't stand it."

"That's what I was about to say. I am ready to go, if the Lord calls me home. I'm confident of that because I've put my trust in Jesus. But on the other hand, the idea of all the things you and I would miss. . ." She paused. "I don't want to miss a day with you."

"Me, either."

"And I want you to be happy, Darren."

"Happy?" He could hardly stand the joy that flooded over him. "I am happy. You make me the happiest man on earth."

"I'm talking about something other than our relationship. You're content working for Eastway, but I don't think you're really happy. It doesn't put a sparkle in your eye."

"Ah."

"You tried to tell me last night, and I was too tired to listen. Or maybe I didn't want to listen because I don't handle change well. But God really dealt with me in the night. Reminded me of what a dreamer I've always been. It only makes sense that I'd fall in love with a dreamer, too."

"Ah." He smiled. "I've got my head in the clouds. Is that what you're trying to say?"

"Something like that." She laughed, but grew serious very quickly afterward. "Remember that day on the Cessna 400? You flew me over the English countryside. And a castle. And Big Ben."

"Right."

"You were free to dream that day. To see the impossibilities as possibilities. That's one of the things I love most about flying. It's something that, when we're children, seems impossible. And yet, we're doing it. We're spreading our wings and flying. So, go ahead and dream. I'll dream right alongside you. You tried to share your heart last night. . .to talk about your plans for the future, but I was too tired to listen. And it haunted me today in that cockpit. I should have taken the time to really hear everything you wanted to say."

"Wait. Are you saying you're okay with the idea of the charter service?"

"I'm okay with it."

"Candy, I've really been praying about this."

"I know. Me, too. Well, today mostly. But you know what? I totally think you should do it."

"You do? What changed your mind?"

"Well, my near-death experience, for one thing."

He grimaced.

"I had a thousand things flash through my mind when I was circling the airport that second time. And, strange as it may sound, one of those things was your charter plane service." She laughed. "I was thinking, actually, how much easier it would be to attempt a landing with a smaller plane with the landing gear up."

"Hope I never have to find out personally."

"I hope you don't, either. It was scary." She paused a moment. "But when I thought about you running your own company, one thing stood out. You're so good with people. You are funny and sweet and—"

"Wait." He grinned. "Not that I don't appreciate the endorsement. Flattery will get you everywhere, after all. But what does this have to do with flying small planes?"

"Oh, everything." Her words were filled with encouragement. "When you're flying for Eastway, you really don't have much opportunity to connect with the passengers. Your whole job—well, except for the part where you greet them as they come onboard or when they're leaving—is in that cockpit."

"Right."

"Well, that works well for me. I'm fine with that. But you"—her voice grew more animated—"you've got an evangelist's heart. I can see you really interacting with your passengers if you have your own service."

"Yes. Me, too." He nodded. "And these days so many executives in the corporate world are chartering private planes. I really think this could be a profitable business. And you're right. . .it's a great way to get to know people. Establish relationships, not just with individuals, but with the kinds of people who hire private planes. . .political people who need the added security, and even sports teams." His excitement grew as he continued. "And I really meant what I said the other night. I'll start with a couple of smaller planes, and maybe—say in a year or so—add a Boeing Business Jet. Or two."

"Or three." She giggled. "Sounds like you're talking about adding children to our brood."

Both of them stopped talking at once. Darren grinned as he pondered her words. They gave him such hope.

Candy finally interrupted the awkward silence. "I, um, I have no idea why I just said that. I wasn't implying—"

He laughed, mostly out of relief. "Well, I do. I plan to add children to our brood." He grinned. "Not that we'll use the word *brood* on a regular basis, but you know what I mean."

"So. . ."

"You know me. I'm the funny guy. But you've just opened the door for me to ask this question that's been burning a hole in my heart and my pocket for the past twenty-four hours."

"W–what?"

"This is the goofiest way in the world to do this, but I. . .I'm asking you to be my—"

"Wait. A–are you proposing. . .over the phone?"

"I know, I know." He shook his head, thinking about how ridiculous this was. "It's dumb. I want to hold you and tell you how much I love you. I want to show you the ring that I had in my pocket last night, the first time I planned to ask this question."

"Y–you had a ring?" She groaned. "Oh, man. I totally blew it, didn't I?"

"Well, I think we both did. I picked the wrong time to start the conversation. You were exhausted and. . ." He paused, thinking things through. "Actually you've had a pretty rough day today, too, so my timing is probably even worse now."

"Oh no it's not. Keep going, you. You're not stopping now."

He stood up and began to pace. "I've thought about this a hundred times. Jason tried to help me come up with something funny to say to pop the question."

"Like?" Her voice now had that dreamy childlike quality he'd grown to love.

He tried to match it with his enthusiasm. "Well, like 'Come fly with me' or 'Love is in the air.' I told him he was crazy. And I stopped cold every time I rehearsed the line, 'I'd like you to be Mrs. Candy Furst.'"

She laughed. "Oh, no! I can't believe I never thought about that before. Candy Furst. What a name."

"Trust me, I thought about it. In fact, I wondered if it would be enough to keep you from saying yes."

"Oh, I'm saying yes, all right."

His heart kicked into overdrive. "R–really? Even without a ring?"

"Oh, I'm holding you to the ring. But I think I can wait till you get back to let you slip it on my finger."

"I'm going to find the most romantic way to do that, I promise." Ideas began to click. "What do you think? A walk in the park? Maybe somewhere along the boardwalk? The beach at sunset?"

"Darren?"

"Yes?"

"The bride-to-be isn't supposed to plan her own proposal."

"Right, right." He sat down once again. "I know. I'm just so excited. I don't want to blow this again."

"Um, I've already said yes. How could you blow it?"

She actually said yes!

Candy began to giggle. "So, I go from being Cotton Candy to Candy Furst. Trading up, I guess."

"I hope you really feel that way."

"Oh, yeah. I'm trading up all right."

A thousand thoughts rolled around in Darren's head. There was so much to do. He had to get home. . .and soon. Funny, the minute he thought about home, another thought occurred to him. "One more thing."

"What's that?"

"When I get back to Newark, I'm buying Fred a girlfriend."

"Excuse me?" She laughed. "Say that again."

"Fred. My goldfish. He's been swimming around in that tank of his completely alone for far too long. He needs a wife. And a brood of baby goldfish."

"You mean a school, don't you?"

"Whatever."

Candy laughed. "We'll go to the pet store and pick out the perfect bride for Fred. But in the meantime, you take care of your mama. And give her my love. Tell her she's got to get well. We need her to come to a wedding."

"Will do. And Candy. . .I love you."

꙳

"I love you, too." As Candy spoke the words, a rush of emotion overtook her. Everything she'd been through—last night's banquet, today's near-disaster, Darren's mother, the proposal—all hit her at once. She began to cry. No, not cry. Sob. Deep, gut-wrenching sobs.

Darren responded immediately. "Are you okay?"

"Y–yes." She spoke through the tears. "This has just been such an amazing, crazy, wonderful, terrible day." She paused to dab her eyes, then took a couple of deep breaths to get things under control. "We're going to have quite a story to tell our brood of children someday."

"Which story?" he asked. "The one where I messed up the proposal or the one where you made the national news?"

"Both." She laughed. "We're a fine pair, aren't we?"

"We are." He grew silent for a moment. "But seriously, we are a fine pair, Candy. You're strong in the areas where I'm weak. My perfect helpmate."

"And vice versa," she whispered.

"And I love you more than. . .than flying. More than dreaming. More than anything. . .except the One who brought us together."

"Me, too."

After a couple more "I love you's," Candy ended the call, her mind reeling.

Darren had been carrying a ring in his pocket last night at the banquet? He'd planned to propose on the steps of the Dorothy House. And she'd botched it! Botched it! But God, in His own humorous way, had redeemed the moment.

Who else ever received a proposal by phone?

Not that she minded. Not one little bit.

But never mind all that! Candy had phone calls to make. Likely her parents were still worried sick about the news story. She'd fill them in. Tell them the story of how, in one lone day, she'd nearly lost her life. . .then gained it all over again.

Chapter 22

Exactly one year to the day after Candy's fated flight, she prepared to don her wedding dress for a trip down the aisle.

Well, not exactly an aisle. Getting married in the middle of a runway at Essex County Airport made the whole aisle thing a bit problematic. Still, with the white rental chairs set up à la church-style, they'd concocted something that looked and felt like a center aisle.

Not that anyone expected anything traditional or normal from Candy and Darren. Hardly. These days folks had figured out that the happy couple could be a little on the flighty side. And flighty they would remain.

Now, as she stood in Darren's office at the airport with her bridesmaids soon to arrive, a thousand things went through her mind. *Did I bring everything I needed from home? When are my sisters going to get here? Where in the world is Darren taking me on our honeymoon? Why is he being so secretive?*

A rap on the door caught her attention. Her mother popped her head inside. "We're here!"

"Mama!" She ushered her mother into the room and started talking a mile a minute.

"Wait." Her mother backed up with a stunned expression. "Why are you still dressed in jeans? Shouldn't you be getting ready?"

"I need help with my dress so I was waiting on the girls. Brooke was here a while ago, but had to, um. . ."

"What?"

"Take a potty break. She's six months pregnant, you know."

"Ah. That's right. I'd forgotten about their little surprise package."

Candy smiled, remembering the day she'd gotten the news. Brooke and Jason had only been married three months at the time, and they'd hardly planned for a baby. But God had other ideas.

"Hey, speaking of babies. . ." Candy gave her mother an imploring look. "Where are—"

"Taffie's here with Maddy. She's in the bathroom, changing her diaper. You'll see them in a minute."

Another rap on the door caught their attention. Her father stuck his head in. "Wow. Great dress."

"Very funny, Pop." She laughed and pointed to the dress, which hung on a hook above the door. "This is it. Your hard-earned dollars at work."

"Very pretty." He entered the room, closing the door behind him. "So, we bought this one with taffy money. Oh, speaking of taffy."

"Yes?"

"We brought a couple of big bags of our latest best seller—wedding cake flavor. Thought it would be a nice addition."

"Of course."

Her father settled into the chair behind the desk. "So, where are you two going on your honeymoon?"

"I have no idea." She turned toward the mirror to continue putting on makeup.

"Seriously? I thought Darren was just messing with me when he wouldn't tell me."

She looked up with mascara wand in hand. "He won't tell me either. But he instructed me to pack for moderate weather, whatever that means."

"So, no place tropical."

"Guess not." She turned back to the mirror. "I do know we're taking the 208 to La Guardia and flying out commercial from there. But he won't tell me our destination."

"That's kind of what it's like walking with God, too." Her mother smiled. "You can only see so far out over the horizon. But you really don't know what's beyond that." She paused and smiled. "I think it's better that way. Makes the journey ahead more of an adventure."

"True." Candy's eyes filled with tears, thinking of all the Lord had already done in her life. Could she possibly handle more of His goodness?

Their conversation was interrupted by the sound of a baby's cry. Taffie entered holding baby Maddy, now eight months old. Candy *ooh*ed and *aah*ed over her gorgeous niece. "Taffie, she's prettier than ever. And look at this dress! It's darling."

"Yes, she's a little doll, isn't she? Looks just like Ryan."

"No, she looks like her mama." Candy ran her fingertip along baby Maddy's soft cheek. "She's a Carini, for sure."

"That she is." Pop grinned. "Not that either of you girls are Carinis anymore. Taffie's an Antonelli. And now you're about to be. . ." He grinned, not saying it.

"Pop, don't."

"Well, I just have one question. Now that you're the 'Furst lady,' does that mean you get to live in the White House?" He slapped his knee. "C'mon, that was a good one, you have to admit."

"Funny. But with all the politicians Darren is flying back and forth, you never know. The possibilities are endless."

Another rap sounded at the door and Tangie stuck her head inside. "Howdy, y'all. Just moseyed into town from my rehearsal."

"Oh?" Candy looked her way with a smile.

"It's a melodrama," Tangie explained. "I got the role of sweet Nell. Snidley Whiplash is going to tie me to the tracks, but Dudley Do-Right will rescue me just in the nick of time."

"Ah. Now here's a girl who's destined to carry the Carini name for a while longer," Pop said, rising to meet her.

"Thanks a lot." She rolled her eyes as she stepped into the room.

"Tangie." Candy gasped as she got a close look at her younger sister. She could hardly believe it. Tangie had dyed her hair back to its original brown. And the gorgeous blue bridesmaid dress covered up her tattoos. She looked downright beautiful. "You look. . . gorgeous."

Tangie's cheeks turned pink. "Aw, stop. You're embarrassing me."

"Like that would be possible." Candy laughed. She glanced at the clock on the wall, then turned to her father. "Um, Pop? It's a quarter to two. Taffie and I really need to get dressed."

"I can take a hint."

"Will you take the baby to Ryan?" Taffie asked. "His mom is going to watch her during the ceremony."

"Well, of course."

Candy watched as her father took his granddaughter in his arms and then backed out of the room, leaving the women to their own devices.

Brooke joined them moments later and the girls went to work, first getting Taffie ready, then getting Candy into her gown. Her mother zipped it up, then they all stood back and stared.

"Wow," Brooke said. "You look amazing."

"Doesn't she?" Candy's mother agreed. Then the tears started. "I'm sorry. I didn't mean to get to emotional. It's just. . .my girls are growing up. And all these weddings. . ."

"This is certainly going to be one no one will forget," Brooke added.

"You know, I thought my wedding was different." Taffie drew near and the two sisters stood side by side, looking at their reflections in the full-length mirror that leaned against the wall. "Getting married on the beach was pretty amazing. But I have to admit, getting married in the middle of a runway. . . that's pretty adventurous."

"You know what a dreamer I've always been," Candy said. "I love an adventure."

"Me, too." Taffie slipped an arm around her waist and gave her a squeeze.

Tangie stood apart from the others, quieter than usual. When she turned around, Candy saw the shimmer of tears in her younger sister's eyes.

"What's wrong?" She walked over to her and grabbed her hand.

"Oh, nothing." Tangie shrugged. "It's just. . .both of you are married now. And I'm. . ."

"You're the next big Broadway sensation," Taffie said with a smile.

"No, I'm not." Tangie sat, her sky blue dress billowing around her in a fluffy cloudlike circle. "I'm going to go on doing goofy shows in small theaters for the rest of my life. Who's going to want to marry sweet Nell?"

"I said the same thing two years ago," Taffie said. "I couldn't imagine who would want to marry me. Then God brought Ryan."

"And you know me," Candy added. "I was convinced I'd be single forever. And now Darren and I. . ." A lump formed in her throat. "Anyway, I was wrong, and I'm happy to admit it. And you're wrong, too."

Their mother drew near and wrapped Tangie in her arms. "Honey, don't you fret about who you'll marry. . .or when. I've been praying for all of you since you were children, that God would bring just the right mate. Now that my prayers have been answered for both of your sisters, I have more time to focus on you. And you know what a prayer warrior I am. Why, I'll pray in your real Dudley Do-Right in no time. Watch and see."

Tangie laughed. "Okay. Well, just make sure he likes girls who are. . . different."

"You're not different, honey. You're just you. And you're the very best you, you can possibly be. When the fellow I've been praying for lays eyes on my darling baby girl, he's going to see you for who you are. . .inside and out."

"Thanks, Mama." She sniffled. "I feel better."

Brooke reached for a tissue and dabbed at her eyes. "You Carinis are so. . . emotional. You're not making this easy on me. I'm pregnant, you know."

"Yes, we know," they all echoed in chorus.

A knock on the door startled them back to attention. Candy looked up at the clock once more. Yikes. One fifty-eight p.m.

"Candy?" her father called out.

"Come in, Pop. We're ready for you."

He entered the room, a smile lighting his face the moment he laid eyes on her. She glanced at him and smiled. "Yes?"

"Cotton Candy." He gave her a wink.

"You're not going to say I have my head in the clouds are you, Pop? 'Cause if you are—"

"No." His eyes misted over. "You've definitely got your feet on the ground. Well, at least in matters of the heart. I was going to say. . ." His eyes misted over. "I was going to say you're the prettiest bride I've ever seen."

"Dad, I distinctly remember hearing you say that to me on my wedding day," Taffie said.

"Well, yes." He shrugged.

"And you're going to say it to me on my wedding day, too, right?" Tangie added.

He shrugged. "Of course." He turned his attention back to Candy. "But honey. . .today, standing here, you're the prettiest bride that ever walked the aisle. And I mean that from the bottom of my heart." He leaned over and whispered, "Just don't tell your mama I said that. She looked mighty good on our big day, too."

"I heard that, Carl." Their mother leaned over and gave him a peck on the cheek. "But I forgive you. And besides, I think you're right. We've got the prettiest—and the sweetest—girls who ever walked an aisle. Er, *runway*."

Candy chuckled, then gasped as she looked at the clock. Two o'clock? Better get this show on the road!

ꝫ

Darren paced the lobby of the small airport, staring at the clock on the wall. Two o'clock. Yikes. Better get going. Guests were waiting. Over one hundred and fifty of them, from what he'd been told.

As Darren, Jimmy, Jason, and Ryan made their way toward the runway, he stared at the setup, amazed. "I still can't believe this. It's. . .perfect."

"Yeah, I wasn't sure what to expect when the event planners showed up with the chairs and decorations," Jimmy said. "Never threw a wedding on a runway before. But I think the gazebo area looks great up at the front. And that runner gives the impression of an aisle. You've got to admit. . .it's different."

"It's different all right. But so are we." Darren smiled, then turned to Jimmy. "I can't thank you enough for shutting things down long enough for the wedding. You, um, *did* shut things down, right? No traffic on our runway during the ceremony?"

"No traffic on *any* runway during the wedding," Jimmy assured him.

"Thank you. I owe you big time." Darren took his place at the front next to Pastor Richardson, from their church. The other guys headed to the area in the back to meet up with their bridesmaids.

As he settled into place at the front of the crowd, Darren looked to the front row where his parents sat together holding hands. Wow. Talk about progress. His mother flashed a smile, and he responded by mouthing, "I love you." He then watched as she reached for a tissue. My, how things had changed. He could hardly wait to see what God had planned for the next phase of their journey.

As the piped-in music began to play, Darren thought about all the changes the past few months had brought. He'd officially proposed to Candy onboard a flight to Chicago in front of ninety-seven passengers. Thankfully, she had agreed. Again. He'd also purchased the Cessna 208 from a friend of Jimmy's and routinely flew back and forth between D.C. and New York, carrying some pretty well-known political types. . .thanks to Andrea Jackson and her new fiancé, a great guy named Marcus who worked for FOX News. And she promised him even more business in the future, particularly if Paul Cromwell made his run for the presidency. Maybe, before long, Darren would own a whole

fleet of planes, hire pilots to fly for him. Perhaps the best news of all. . .a sub-
dued, repentant Gary had recently approached him, asking for a job. Darren
had promised to pray about it.

But right now he had other things to pray about.

He watched as the bridesmaids made their way up the makeshift aisle in
their blue dresses with groomsmen at their side.

Brooke came first on her husband's arm. Darren had to laugh every time he
remembered their announcement about the baby. Jason was about to become
a father, whether he'd planned for it or not. And he'd be a great one.

Next came Taffie on Ryan's arm. They had a lot to celebrate these days,
now that little Maddy was in the picture. And they beamed with joy on this
special day.

Tangie entered last on Jimmy's arm. He could hardly believe the transformation. She looked. . .normal. No piercings. No orange hair. No tattoos. At
least not any visible ones. And Jimmy grinned like a Cheshire cat.

Finally the long-awaited moment came. As Candy, on her father's arm,
stepped out from behind the makeshift wall at the rear of the aisle, Darren gasped. Her white dress was perfect. She looked like something out of a
magazine.

*Oh, Candy, just wait. I'm going to fly you to places you've never seen before. Like
Italy, for instance. Tomorrow.*

Another glance her way and his hands started trembling. She took steps in
his direction, a confident smile on her face. As she drew near, he was better
able to see the details of her dress. With the brilliant blue sky in the background, her billowing white gown looked as pretty as a cloud. . .a cotton candy
cloud.

Chapter 23

Candy watched as her sisters walked out onto the runway ahead of her. Off in the distance, she saw the Cessna 208, Darren's new charter plane. Once the ceremony ended, the two of them would climb aboard and fly off into the sunset. Just like a scene from a movie, only with a real, God-created backdrop. No more flight of fancy. No more pretending. This was the real deal.

She glanced up at the sky. It was a brilliant blue with white cumulus clouds hanging like fluffs of cotton candy. "Just for me, Lord. Thanks for the reminder."

The sound of the bridal march brought her attention back to the wedding.

"You ready, Cotton Candy?" Her pop gazed down at her with tenderness in his eyes.

"Yep. Let's get this plane off the ground."

The next twenty minutes passed like a whirlwind. She vaguely remembered Pastor Richardson's introduction. Heard the beautiful song that her sisters sang. Saw the tears in Darren's eyes as they took their vows. Felt the presence of the Lord as they shared their first kiss as a married couple. Heard the cheers from the crowd as the pastor introduced them as man and wife.

What stood out the most, however, was the feeling of pure joy that wrapped her like a blanket throughout the ceremony. . .a God-breathed joy. And by the time the pictures were taken and the guests convened in the hangar for the reception, she truly felt as if she were walking on a cloud. The whole thing had been simply breathtaking. Fast, but breathtaking.

As things began to slow down, she finally managed to get a good look at the hangar, completely overwhelmed at the transformation. She wouldn't have believed it if she hadn't seen it with her own eyes, but the wedding coordinator was right. . .the tent they'd erected inside the large space did the trick. It gave the room a cozy, elegant feel. Ribbons of blue satin hung in strips above the room, giving a sky-like effect. And the decorations! How fun to see Darren's model planes in use once again.

It's perfect! I couldn't have dreamed up anything better.

While she and Darren shared their first dance, she finally had a few minutes to whisper words of love into his ear. He responded with misty eyes and a promise to love her, whatever circumstance life brought their way. With God at the helm, they certainly had the promise of wonderful, adventurous days ahead.

After a great meal, the time came to cut the cake. Ice cream cake, of course.

Candy had her mother to thank for that. And the wedding taffy! The guests ate it up and asked for more. Looked like the Carinis had outdone themselves this time around. Nothing new there.

When the reception ended, the moment arrived. The one she'd been longing for and dreading all at the same time. Instead of driving off in a car, she and Darren had—naturally—opted to fly off in his new 208. It wasn't the fear of flying that made her breath catch in her throat. No, it was something else entirely.

Candy and Darren changed into their going-away clothes, said their goodbyes, then headed hand in hand to the plane.

He looked up at the plane, a look of pure contentment on his face. "I can't believe she's ours."

"The first in our brood." Candy gave him a wink.

They climbed aboard the plane, and Darren turned to her, a look of surprise on his face when he noticed Jimmy in the pilot's seat.

"Wait." Darren turned to Candy, confused. "I definitely don't think we need three pilots here. What's going on?"

Her hands shook with excitement as she explained. "Well, um, there's something I need to tell you. Sort of a wedding surprise." *Help me, Lord!*

"O–okay." He looked at her, clearly confused.

She tried to keep her voice steady as she spoke. "I think it's time I made the jump."

"We just did." The confusion on his face remained for a moment, then morphed into understanding. "Oh, do you mean. . .are you saying what I think you're saying?"

She nodded, though she could feel the color draining from her face as Jimmy handed them their chutes. Her knees started knocking and her hands shaking. "But we'd better do this now, or I'm going to change my mind."

"Oh no you're not!" He helped her into her chute, then prepared his own, offering up a celebratory prayer all the while.

With Jimmy at the helm, the small plane made its ascent into the beautiful blue skies. Cotton candy clouds beckoned, and at just the right moment, with friends and family looking on, Candy and Darren made their first leap together. . .into the vast unknown.

SWEET HARMONY

Dedication

In loving memory of one of my dearest drama buddies of all time, Robin Tompkins, currently performing on the greatest stage of all.

Chapter 1

L ife is better in Harmony. If you don't believe me, come on up here and
see for yourself."

Tangie laughed as she heard her grandmother's cheerful words. Leaning back against the pillows, she shifted the cell phone to her other ear and tried to imagine what her life would be like if she actually lived in her grandparents' tiny hometown of Harmony, New Jersey. "Thanks, Gran-Gran, but I'm no small-town girl," she said, finally. "I've spent the last four years in New York, remember?"

"How could I forget?" Her grandmother's girlish laugh rippled across the telephone line. "I've told every person I know that my granddaughter is a Broadway star. . .that she knows all of the big names in the Big Apple."

Tangie groaned. "I might know a few people, but I'm no star, trust me." In fact, these days she couldn't even seem to find a long-term acting gig, no matter how far off-Broadway she auditioned. So, on Christmas Eve she'd packed her bags and headed home to Atlantic City. Tangie had spent much of the drive praying, asking God what she should do. His silence had been deafening.

Now Christmas had passed and a new year approached. Still, Tangie felt no desire to return to the Big Apple. Safely tucked into the same bed she'd slept in every night as a little girl, she just wanted to stay put. Possibly forever. And maybe that was for the best. She'd felt for some time that things were winding down, career-wise. Besides, she'd seen more than enough drama over the past four years. . .and not just on the stage. So what if her acting days were behind her? Maybe—in spite of her best efforts—she wasn't destined to perform on Broadway.

"I'm telling you, Harmony is the perfect place for you." Gran-Gran's words interrupted her thoughts. "You need a break from big-city life. It's peaceful here, and the scenery is breathtaking, especially during the holidays. It'll do you good. And it'll do my heart good to have you. I'm sure Gramps would agree."

"Oh, you don't have to win me over on the beauty of upstate New Jersey," Tangie assured her. She'd visited her mom's parents enough to know that Harmony was one of the prettiest places on planet Earth, especially in the wintertime when the snows left everything a shimmering white. Pausing a moment, she thought about her options. "Might sound silly, but my first reaction is to just stay here."

"In Atlantic City?" her grandmother asked, the surprise in her voice evident.

"Would you work at the candy shop? I thought you'd given up on that idea years ago when you headed to New York."

"Yeah." Tangie sighed as she shifted her position in the bed to get more comfortable. "But Mom and Dad are about to head out in their RV again, so Taffie's bound to need my help, especially with a toddler to take care of."

Tangie couldn't help but smile as she reflected on her older sister's mothering skills. Little Muddy had lovely brown tufts of hair and kissable apple dumpling cheeks. And her big brown eyes melted Tangie's heart every time.

Yes, it might be nice to stay home for a change. Settle in. Hang out at the candy shop with people who loved her. People who would offer encouragement and help her forget about the thousand ways she'd failed over the past few years, not just professionally, but personally, as well. All the parts she'd auditioned for but hadn't received. All the plays she'd been in that had closed unexpectedly. All the would-be relationships that had ended badly.

Tangie sighed.

"Let me tell you the real reason for my call." The determination in her grandmother's voice grew by the minute. "No point in beating around the bush. Our church is looking for a drama director for the kids' ministry. I suggested you and the pastor jumped on the idea."

"W—what?"

"There's nothing wrong with your hearing, honey. Harmony might be small, but the church certainly isn't. It's grown by leaps and bounds since you were here last, and the children's ministry is splitting at the seams. Our music pastor has been trying to involve the kids in his productions, but he doesn't know the first thing about putting on a show. Not the acting part, anyway. We need a real drama director. Someone skilled at her craft. . .who knows what she's doing."

"Why hire one?" Tangie asked. "Why not just find someone inside the church with those talents and abilities?"

"No one has your qualifications," Gran-Gran stated. "You know everything about set design, staging, costumes, and acting. You're a wealth of knowledge. And you've worked on Broadway, for heaven's sake. Gregg doesn't mind admitting he knows very little about putting on shows. He attempted one with the kids last week. A Christmas production. But it was, well—"

"Wait. Who's Gregg?" Tangie interrupted.

"Gregg. Our music pastor. The one I was just talking about. You remember him, right?"

"Hmm." Tangie paused to think about it. "Yeah, I think I remember him. Sort of a geeky looking guy? Short hair. Looks like his mother dressed him?"

Gran-Gran clucked her tongue. "Tangie, shame on you. He's a wonderful, godly man. Very well-groomed. And tidy."

Tangie looked at the mess in her bedroom and chuckled. "Sounds like my dream guy."

"Well, don't laugh. There are reams of young women trying to catch his eye. Good thing they don't all see things the way you do. Besides, half the women in our Prime Timers class are praying for a wife for Gregg, so it's just a matter of time before God parts the Red Sea and brings the perfect woman his way."

"Mm-hmm. But let's go back to talking about that show he put on. What happened?"

"It was terrible." Gran-Gran sighed. "And I don't just mean terrible. It was awful. Embarrassing, actually. The kids didn't memorize any of their lines, and their costumes—if you could call them that—looked more like bathrobes. And don't even get me started on the set. He built it out of cardboard boxes he found behind our local hardware store. You could still see the Home Depot logo through the paint."

"Ugh. Give me a break." Sounded pretty amateurish. Then again, she'd been in some productions over the years that weren't exactly stellar. . .in any sense of the word, so who was she to pass judgment?

"The music part was great," Gran-Gran said. "That's Gregg's real gift. He knows music. But the acting part was painful to watch. If my best friend's grandkids hadn't been in it, Gramps and I probably would've left during the intermission."

"I've seen a few shows like that," Tangie said. She chuckled, and then added, "I've *been* in a few shows like that."

Her grandmother laughed. "Honey, with you *everything's* a show. And that's exactly why I think you'd be perfect for this. Ever since you graduated from acting school last spring, you've been trying to find out where you belong. Right?"

"Right." Tangie sighed.

"And didn't you tell me you worked with a children's group at the theater school?"

"Yes. I directed a couple of shows with them. They were great." In fact, if she admitted the truth to herself, working with the kids had been one of the few things she'd really felt good about.

"Think of all the fun you'll have working with the children at church, then," Gran-Gran said. "You'll be able to share both your love of acting and the love of the Lord."

"True. I was really limited at the school." The idea of working in a Christian environment sounded good. Really good, in fact.

"They need someone with your experience and your zeal. I've never known anyone with as much God-given talent and ability, and so creative, too. Gregg is pretty much 'in the box.' And you, well. . ." Her grandmother's voice trailed off.

"Say no more." Tangie laughed. She'd busted out of the box years ago when she dyed her spiky hair bright orange and got that first tattoo. Glancing down at her Tweety Bird pajamas and fuzzy slippers, she had to wonder what the fine folks of Harmony, New Jersey, would think of such an "out of the box" kind of girl.

Only one way to know for sure. Maybe it would be best to start the new year in a new place, after all.

Tangie drew in a deep breath, then spurted her impromptu answer. "Gran-Gran, tell them I accept. Look for me tomorrow afternoon. Tangie Carini is coming to Harmony!"

❧

Gregg Burke left the staff meeting at Harmony Community Church, his thoughts tumbling around in his head. He climbed into his car and pointed it toward home—the tiny wood-framed house on the outskirts of town. With the flip of a switch, the CD player kicked on. Gregg continued to press the FORWARD button until he located the perfect song—a worship tune he'd grown to love.

Ah. Perfect.

He leaned back against the seat and shifted his SUV into DRIVE. As he pulled out onto the winding country road, Gregg reflected on the meeting he'd just attended. The church was growing like wildfire; that was a fact. And while he understood the need to keep up with the times, he didn't want to jump onboard every trend that came along. He'd seen other churches pull out the stops to become hip and trendy, and some of them had lost their original passion for the Word and for prayer. No way would he go along with that.

On the other hand, some folks had accused him of being set in his ways. Unwilling to bend. What was it the pastor had just said at the meeting? "Gregg, you're the oldest twenty-six-year-old I've ever known." Dave's words had pricked Gregg's heart. He didn't want others to see him as stiff or un-bending.

Lord, am I? I don't want to get in the way of whatever You want to do, but I think we need to be careful here. I know we need to do everything we can to reach out to people. I'm all about that. I just pray we move carefully. Thoughtfully.

As Gregg maneuvered a sharp turn, a bank of snow on the side of the road caught his eye. Late December was always such a beautiful time of year in Harmony, but this year he looked forward to the change of seasons more than ever. The countless piles of snow would melt away into oblivion. Gregg could hardly wait for the warmth of spring. Gramps—his adopted grandfather—had already informed him there were at least ten or twenty trout in the lake with his name on them. He could hardly wait to reel them in.

On the other hand, the eventual change in seasons forced Gregg to think about something he'd rather *not* think about—the Easter production he'd just agreed to do with the children.

At once, his attitude shifted. While Gregg wanted to go along with Dave's idea of reaching out to the community, the suggestion of putting on three to four musical performances a year with the children concerned him. First, he didn't want to take that much time away from the adult choir. Those singers needed him. Second, he didn't work as well with kids as some people thought he did. In fact, he wasn't great with kids. . .at all.

"It's not that I don't like children," he said to himself. "They're just. . . different."

The ones he'd worked with in the Christmas play were rowdy, and they didn't always pay attention. And, unlike his adult choir members, the kids didn't harmonize very well, no matter how hard he worked with them. In fact, one or two of the boys couldn't carry a tune in a bucket. Why their parents had insisted they participate in the musical. . .

Stop it, Gregg.

He shook his head, frustrated with himself for thinking like that. Every child should have the opportunity to learn, to grow. How many chances had he been given as a kid? He'd struggled through softball, hockey, and a host of other sports before finally realizing singing was more his bag.

The more he thought about it, the worse he felt. How many of those boys, like himself, were without a father? He knew of at least one or two who needed a strong, positive male influence. Had the Lord orchestrated this whole plan to put him in that position, maybe? If so, did he have it in him?

"Father, help me. I don't want to blow this. But I guess it's obvious I'm going to need Your help more than ever. Remind me of what it was like to be a kid." He shivered, just thinking about it.

Gregg pulled the car onto the tiny side street, then crawled along the uneven road until he reached his driveway. His house sat back nearly a quarter mile, tucked away in the trees. At the end of the driveway, he stopped at the mailbox and snagged today's offering from the local mail carrier. Then he pulled his car into the garage, reached for his belongings, and headed inside.

Entering his home, Gregg hung his keys on the hook he'd placed strategically near the door and put his jacket away in the closet, being careful to fasten every snap. He placed the pile of mail on the kitchen counter, glanced through it, then organized it into appropriate categories: To be paid. To be tossed. To be pondered.

Oh, if only he could organize the kids with such ease. Then, perhaps, he wouldn't dread the days ahead.

Chapter 2

Tangie made the drive from Atlantic City to Harmony in a little less than three hours. Though the back roads were slick—the winter in full swing—she managed to make it to her grandparents' house with little problem. In fact, the closer she got to Harmony, the prettier everything looked, especially with Christmas decorations still in place. Against the backdrop of white, the trees showcased their bare branches. Oh, but one day. . .one day the snows would melt and spring would burst through in all its colorful radiance. Tangie lived for the springtime.

"Color, Lord," she whispered. "That's what gets me through the winter. The promise of color when the snows melt!"

As she pulled her car into the drive, a smile tugged at the edges of her lips. Little had changed at the Henderson homestead in the twenty-two years she'd been coming here. Oh, her grandfather had painted the exterior of the tiny wood-framed house a few years ago, shifting from a light tan to a darker tan. It had created quite a stir. But other than that, everything remained the same.

"Lord, I'm going to need Your strength. You know how I am. I'm used to the hustle and bustle of Times Square. Eating in crowded delis and listening to taxi cabs honk as they go tearing by. Racing from department store to theater. I'm not used to a quiet, slow-paced, solitary life. I—"

She didn't have time to finish her prayer. Gran-Gran stood at the front door, waving a dish towel and hollering. Tangie climbed out of the car, and her grandmother sprinted her way across the snowy yard like a track star in the making. *Okay, so maybe not everything moves slowly here.*

"Oh, you beautiful thing!" Her grandmother giggled as she reached to touch Tangie's hair. "What have you done now?"

"Don't you like it? I thought red was a nice color with my skin tone."

"That's *red*?" Gran-Gran laughed. "If you say so. In the sunlight, I think I see a little purple in there."

"Probably. But that's okay, too. You know me, Gran-Gran. All things bright. . ."

"And beautiful," her grandmother finished. "I know, I know."

Tangie grabbed her laptop and overnight bag, leaving the other larger suitcases in the trunk.

Gran-Gran chattered all the way into the house. Once inside, she hollered,

"Herbert, we've got a guest!"

"Oh, I'm no guest. Don't make a fuss over me." Tangie set her stuff on the nearest chair and looked around the familiar living room. The place still smelled the same—like a combination of cinnamon sticks and old books. But something else had changed. "Hey, you've moved the furniture."

"Yes." Gran-Gran practically beamed. "Do you like it?"

Tangie shrugged. "Sure. I guess so." To be honest, she felt a little odd with the room all turned around. It had always been the other way. *Whoa, girl. You've never cared about things staying the same before. Snap out of it! Let your grandmother live a little! Walk on the wild side!*

Seconds later, her grandfather entered the room. His gray hair had thinned even more since her last visit, and his stooped shoulders threw her a little. When had this happened?

"Get over here, Tangerine, and give your old Gramps a hug!" He opened his arms wide as he'd done so many times when she was a little girl.

Tangie groaned at the nickname, but flew into his arms nonetheless. Sure enough, he still smelled like peppermint and Old Spice. Nothing new there.

"How are your sisters?" he asked with a twinkle in his eye.

"Taffie's great. Motherhood suits her. And Candy. . ." Tangie smiled, thinking of her middle sister. "Candy's still flying high."

"Loving her life as a pilot for Eastway, from what I hear." Gramps nodded. "That's my girl. A high-flying angel."

"And you!" Gran-Gran drew near and placed another kiss on her cheek. "You're straight off the stages of Broadway."

"More like off-off-Broadway." Tangie shrugged, determined to change the direction of the conversation. "I come bearing gifts!" She reached for the bag she and Taffie had carefully packed with candies from the family's shop on the boardwalk.

Gramps' eyes lit up as he saw the CARINI'S CONFECTIONS logo on the bag. "Oh, I hope you've got some licorice in there."

"I do. Three different flavors."

"And some banana taffy?" Gran-Gran asked.

"Naturally. You didn't think I'd forget, did you? I know it's your favorite."

Gramps tore into the licorice and popped a piece in his mouth. As he did, a look of pure satisfaction seemed to settle over him. "Mmm. I'm sure glad that daughter of mine married into the candy business. It's made for a pretty sweet life for the rest of us."

Tangie nodded. "Yeah, Mom was born for the sweet stuff. Only now she seems happier touring the country in that new RV she and dad bought last month."

"I heard they had a new one," Gran-Gran said. "Top of the line model."

"Yes, and they're going to travel the southern states to stay warm during the winter." Tangie couldn't help but smile as she reflected on the pictures Mom had sent from Florida a while back. In one of them, her father was dressed in Bermuda shorts on bottom and a Santa costume on top. The caption read CONFUSED IN MIAMI.

"I've never understood the fascination with going from place to place in an RV," Gramps said, as he settled into his recliner and reached for another piece of licorice. "Who wants to live in a house on wheels when you've got a perfectly good house that sits still?" He gestured to his living room, and Tangie grinned.

"You've got a good point," she said as she reached for a piece of taffy. "But I think Mom was born with a case of wanderlust."

"Oh yes," Gran-Gran agreed. "That girl never could stay put when she was a little thing. Always flitting off here or there."

"I'm kind of the same way, I guess." Tangie shrugged. "An adventurer. And I do tend to flit from one thing to another." She sighed.

"Well, we hope you'll stay put in Harmony awhile," Gramps said, giving her a wink. "Settle in. Make some friends."

A mixture of emotions rushed over Tangie at her grandfather's words. While there was some appeal to long-lasting friendships, she wasn't the type to settle in. No, the past four years had proven that. Jumping from one thing to another—one show to another—seemed more her mode of operation. Was the Lord doing something different this time? Calling her to stay put for a while?

"Let's get you settled in your new room." Gran-Gran gestured toward the hallway. "Do you need Gramps to get your things?"

"Oh, I don't mind getting them myself."

"Not while I'm living and breathing!" Her grandfather, rising from the recliner, gave her a stern look. She tossed him her keys, then watched with a smile as he headed outdoors to fetch her bags.

Tangie traipsed along on her grandmother's heels until they reached the spare bedroom—the second room on the right past the living room. She'd slept in the large four-poster bed dozens of times over the years, of course, but never for more than a couple of nights at a stretch. Was this really her new room?

She smiled as she saw the porcelain dolls on the dresser and the hand-embroidered wall hangings. Not exactly her taste in decor, but she wouldn't complain. Unless she decided to stay long-term, of course. Then she would likely replace some of the wall hangings with the framed playbills from all the shows she'd been in. Now that would really change the look of the room, wouldn't it!

Tangie spent the next several minutes putting away her clothes. The folded items went in the dresser. Gran-Gran had been good enough to empty the top three drawers. The rest of Tangie's things were hung in the already-crowded closet. Oh well. She'd make do. Likely this trek to the small town of Harmony wouldn't last long, anyway. Besides, she knew what it was like to live in small spaces. She and her roommate Marti had barely enough room to turn around in the five-hundred-square-foot apartment they'd shared in Manhattan. This place was huge in comparison.

As she wrapped up, Gran-Gran turned her way with a smile. "Let's get this show on the road, honey. Pastor Hampton is waiting for us at the church. He wants to meet you and give you your marching orders."

"A–already?" Tangie shook her head. "But I look awful. I'm still wearing my sweats, and my hair needs a good washing before I meet anyone." She pulled a compact out of her purse, groaning as she took a good look at herself. Her usually spiky hair looked more like a normal "do" today. And without a fresh washing, even the color of her hair looked less vibrant. . .more ordinary. Maybe freshening up her lipstick would help. She scrambled for the tube of Ever-Berry lip gloss.

"Oh, pooh." Gran-Gran waved her hand. "Don't worry about any of that. We've got to be at the church at three and it's a quarter till. If you're a good girl, I'll make some of that homemade hot chocolate you love so much when we get back."

"You've got it!" Tangie pressed the compact and lip gloss back into her purse—a beaded forties number she'd purchased at a resale shop on a whim.

Minutes later she found herself in the backseat of her grandparents' 1998 Crown Victoria, puttering and sputtering down the road.

"This thing's got over two hundred thousand miles on it," Gramps bragged, taking a sharp turn to the right. "Hope to put another hundred on it before one of us gives out."

"One of us?" Tangie's grandmother looked at him, stunned. "You mean you or me?"

"Well, technically, I meant me or the car." He grinned. "But I'm placing my bets on the car. She's gonna outlive us all."

"I wouldn't doubt it."

Gramps went off on a tangent about the car, but Gran-Gran seemed distracted. She turned to wave at an elderly neighbor shuffling through the snow, dressed in a heavy coat and hat. "Oh, look. There's Clarence, checking his mail. I need to ask him how Elizabeth's doing." She rolled down her window and hollered out, "Clarence!" The older man paused, mail in hand, and turned their way.

As the others chatted about hernias, rheumatism, and the need for warmer weather, Tangie pondered her choice to move here. *Lord, what have I done? If I've made an impulsive decision, help me unmake it. But if I'm supposed to be here. . .*

She never got any further in her prayer. Though it didn't make a lick of sense, somehow she just knew. . .she was supposed to be here.

❧

Gregg worked against the clock in his office, transcribing music for the Sunday morning service. The musicians would be counting on him, as would the choir. As he wrapped up, he glanced at his watch and sighed. Three forty-five? Man. He still had to call Darla, the church's part-time pianist, full-time self-appointed matchmaker, to talk about that one tricky key change. She'd struggled with it at their last rehearsal.

Leaning back in his chair, Gregg reflected on a conversation he'd had with Dave earlier this morning. Looked like the church had decided to hire a drama director. Interesting. In some ways, he felt a little put off by the idea. Was he really so bad at directing shows that they needed to actually hire someone?

On the other hand, the notion of someone else helping out did offer some sense of relief. That way, he could focus on his own work. Work he actually enjoyed. Music was his respite. His sanctuary. He ran to it as others might run to sports or TV shows. Music energized him and gave him a sense of purpose. Daily, Gregg thanked the Lord for the sheer pleasure of earning a living doing the thing he loved most.

Now, if only he could figure out how to get around that whole "productions" thing, he'd be a happy, happy man.

At four thirty, he finished up his tasks and prepared to leave. His thoughts shifted to Ashley, the children's ministry leader. At Darla's prompting, Gregg had worked up the courage to ask Ashley out and she'd agreed. Wonder of wonders! Would tonight's dinner date at Gratzi's win her over? From what he'd been told, she loved Italian food. For that matter, he did, too. Still, a plate of fettuccine Alfredo didn't automatically guarantee true love. No, for that he'd have to think bigger. Maybe chicken parmesan.

Deep in thought, Gregg left his office. He walked down the narrow hallway, arms loaded with sheets of music. Just as he reached Dave's office, the door swung open and Gramps Henderson stepped out. The two men nearly collided. Gregg came to such an abrupt stop that his sheets of music went flying. He immediately dropped to his knees and began the task of organizing his papers.

"Let me help with that."

Gregg looked up into the eyes of a woman—maybe in her early twenties—with the oddest color hair he'd ever seen. He tried not to stare, but it was tough. He went back to the task at hand, snatching the papers. She worked alongside him, finally handing him the last page.

"Ooo, is that the contemporary version of the 'Hallelujah Chorus'?" she asked, gazing at him with soul-piercing intensity. For a second he found himself captivated by her dark brown eyes.

"Yes." He gave her an inquisitive look. How would she know that?

She flashed a warm smile, but he was distracted by all the earrings. Well, that and the tiny sparkler in her nose. Was that a diamond? Very bizarre. He had to wonder if it ever bothered her. . .say, when she got a cold.

Gregg rose to his feet, then reached a hand to help the young woman up. By the time they were both standing, Mrs. Henderson's happy-go-lucky voice rang out. "Gregg, we want you to meet our granddaughter, Tangie Carini. She's from Atlantic City."

"Nice to meet you." As he extended his hand, Gregg realized who this must be. Earlier this morning, Dave had said something about counseling a troubled young woman who'd recently joined the church's college and career class. How could Gregg have known she'd turn out to be the granddaughter of a good friend like Herb Henderson?

His heart broke immediately as he pondered these things. Poor Gramps. How long had he quietly agonized over this granddaughter gone astray? Surely they still had some work ahead of them, based on her bright red hair—were those purple streaks?—and piercings that dazzled.

Not that you could judge a person based on external appearance. He chided himself immediately. He wouldn't want people to make any decisions based on how he looked.

Tangie shook his hand, and then nodded at the papers he'd shoved under his arm. "Great rendition of the 'Hallelujah Chorus.' We performed that my senior year in high school. I'll never forget it."

"Oh? You sing?" When she nodded, he realized at once how he might help the Hendersons get their granddaughter walking the straight and narrow. If she could carry a tune, he'd offer her a position in the choir. Yes, that's exactly what he would do. And if he had to guess, based on her speaking voice, he'd peg her for an alto. Maybe a second soprano.

"We'll see you Sunday, Gregg," Gramps said, patting him on the back. "In fact, it looks like we'll be seeing a lot more of you from now on."

A lot more of me? What's that all about?

Oh yes, Gregg reasoned, it must have something to do with the snows melting. Gramps was anxious to go fishing. Still, the older fellow sure had a strange way of phrasing things.

As Tangie and her grandparents disappeared from view, Gregg made his way to his car. Tonight's date with Ashley would start a whole new chapter of his life. Suddenly, he could hardly wait to turn the page.

Chapter 3

On Sunday morning, Tangie and her grandparents left for church plenty early. With the roads still covered in snow and ice and Gramps' plan to stop for donuts along the way, they could use the extra time. Besides, she wanted to get to the church in time to acclimate herself to her new surroundings.

Tangie had given herself a quick glance in the mirror just before they left. She'd deliberately chosen her most conservative outfit—a flowing black skirt with a seventies hippie feel to it, and a gray cashmere sweater. Wrapping a black scarf around her neck, she leaned forward to have a look at her makeup. Not too much, not too little. . .just right. She chuckled, realizing how much she sounded like Goldilocks. If only she had the blond hair to make the picture complete. Nah, on second thought, she definitely looked better as a redhead. Or purple, depending on the angle and the lighting.

As they drove to the church, Tangie thought about the events about to transpire. A sense of excitement took hold. The more she thought about it, the more her anticipation grew. This wasn't about shaking people up, as Gran-Gran had said. No, Tangie had come to Harmony to help the kids develop their God-given talents so they could further the kingdom. She wanted to reach people for the Lord, and could clearly see the role the arts played in that. Oh, if only everyone could catch hold of that!

They stopped at the local bakery on the way and Gramps went inside. Tangie and her grandmother chatted while they waited in the Ford.

"I still can't wait to see the looks on everyone's faces when they find out you've been hired as drama director," Gran-Gran said, and then snickered. "Ella Mae Peterson is going to have a fit. She thinks the church spends too much money on their arts programs, as it is."

Tangie sighed. How many times had she heard this argument over the years? "Mrs. Peterson needs to realize the arts are an awesome way to reach people. When you present the gospel message through drama, music, or other artistic venues, people's lives are touched in a way unlike any other. Performing for the Lord isn't about the accolades or even about ability. It's about using the gifts God has given you to captivate the heart and emotions of the audience member. You can't put a price tag on that."

"Exactly." Gran-Gran nodded. "Which is exactly what some of these set-in-their-ways folks need to realize. You're going to shake them up, honey. Give 'em a run for their money."

"Not sure I want to!" she admitted. In fact, this was one time she'd rather just fit in.

"Well, trust me. . .some people could use a little shaking. You'd be surprised how stiff people can be. And I'm not talking arthritis here." Gran-Gran winked.

Stiff? Oh, great. And it's my job to unstiffen them? Just as quickly she chided herself. *No, it's the Lord's job to unstiffen them. . .if He so chooses.*

Gramps returned to the car with a large box of donuts. He reached inside and snagged one, taking a big bite. Gran-Gran scolded him, but he didn't let that stop him. Finishing it, he licked his fingers, then set the car in motion once again.

They arrived at the church in short order. Tangie could hardly believe the mob of cars in the parking lot. "When did this happen, Gran-Gran? It wasn't like this last time I was here."

"Told you! This church is in revival, honey. We're bursting at the seams. Before long, we'll have to build a new sanctuary. In the meantime, we're already holding two Sunday services and one on Saturday evenings, too. Even at that, parking is a mess."

"Wow." Tangie could hardly believe it. Her church in New York City wasn't this full on Sunday mornings, not even on Christmas or Easter.

Once they got inside the foyer, she found herself surrounded on every side by people. "Man, this place has grown."

Gran-Gran flew into action and, over a fifteen-minute period, introduced Tangie to dozens of church members, young and old alike. She met so many people, her head was swimming. Tangie fervently hoped they wouldn't quiz her on the names afterward. She'd fail miserably.

As the word *fail* flitted through her mind, Tangie sighed. *Lord, I don't want to fail at this like I've done so many times.* How many times had she fallen short of the mark in her acting career? How wonderful it would have been to land a lead role just once. She'd dreamed of it all her life, but never quite succeeded. Oh, there had been callbacks. Wonderful, glorious callbacks that got her hopes up. But each time she'd been disappointed, relegated to a smaller role.

On the other hand, Tangie didn't really mind the secondary roles. . .if only they had lasted more than a week or two. So many of the shows she'd been in had closed early, due to poor reviews. Was she destined to remain the underdog forever? Almost good enough. . .but not quite?

And what about her personal life? Would any of her relationships stand the test of time, or would she always bounce from one relationship to the next, never knowing what true love felt like? *I'm asking You to help me succeed this time. Not for my glory, but for Yours. Help me see this thing through from start to finish. I don't want to be a quitter.*

JERSEY SWEETS

Through the sanctuary doors, she heard the beginning strains of a familiar praise song. As they entered the auditorium, she looked around in amazement. The place was alive with excitement. People clapped their hands along with the music, many singing with abandon. She followed behind Gran-Gran and Gramps to the third row, where they scooted past a couple of people and settled into seats.

Glancing up to the stage, Tangie watched Gregg standing front and center with a guitar in hand. His fingers moved with skill across the strings, and his voice—pure and melodic—immediately ushered her into the presence of God. *See, Lord? That's what I was trying to tell Gran-Gran. It is possible to stand center stage, not for the applause of men, but to bring people closer to You.*

She closed her eyes, thankful for the opportunity to worship. The music continued, each song better than the one before. Tangie watched as the choir geared up for a special number—the contemporary version of the "Hallelujah Chorus." The soloist—a beautiful young woman in her mid-twenties—floored Tangie with her vocal ability.

"That's our children's minister, Ashley Conway," Gran-Gran whispered. "Isn't she something?"

"To say the least," Tangie responded in a hoarse whisper. "I think she rivals anyone I've ever seen or heard on a Broadway stage."

"Yep. We've got some talent here in Harmony, that's for sure." Her grandmother winked before turning to face the stage once again.

Tangie reached for an offering envelope and scribbled the words, "Why doesn't Ashley just help Gregg with the kids' production?" on it. She gave the girl another glance, then penciled in a few more words: "She's got the goods."

Gran-Gran frowned as Tangie handed her the envelope. After reading it, she scribbled down, "Too busy. Ashley works five days a week at the elementary school and Sunday mornings and Wednesday nights at church. No time."

"Ah." Tangie looked up, focusing on the choir. With Gregg at the helm, Ashley and the other choir members performed flawlessly. They were every bit as good as the choir at her home church. Maybe better. And Gregg's heart for God was evident, no doubt about that. Tangie felt shame wash over her as she thought about the way she'd described him to Gran-Gran over the phone.

Lord, forgive me for calling him geeky. This is a great guy. And he's doing a wonderful work here.

In fact, she could hardly wait to work alongside him.

After the choir wrapped up its number, the singers exited the stage. Tangie watched as Gregg trailed off behind them. He reached to pat Ashley on the back, giving a smile and a nod.

"See? He has the gift of encouragement, too," Gran-Gran whispered. "That's a plus."

Finally the moment arrived. Pastor Hampton took the stage. Though she didn't usually struggle with stage fright, Tangie's nerves got the better of her as she listened for his prompting to come to the front of the church for an official introduction to the congregation. As she waited, she narrowed her gaze and focused on Gregg Burke, who now sat in the front row of the next section. He turned back to look at her—or was he looking at Gramps?—with a confused expression on his face. What was up with that?

She found herself staring at him for a moment. Maybe he wasn't as geeky looking as she'd once thought. In fact, that blue shirt really showed off his eyes. . .his best feature.

She'd almost lost her train of thought when Pastor Hampton flashed a smile and said, "I'd like to introduce our new drama director, Tangie Carini." With her knees knocking, she rose from her seat and headed to the stage.

From his spot in the front row, Gregg turned, then stared at the young woman rising from her seat. Wait. *This* was their new drama director? Surely there must be some mistake. The woman Dave had told him about was polished, professional. He would never have described this girl in such a way.

Slow down, Gregg. Don't judge a book by its cover. People did that with your mom, and look what happened.

He forced his thoughts away from that particular subject and watched as Tangie made her way from the pew to the stage. Oh, if only he could stay focused. Her bright red hair—if one could call it red—was far too distracting. Underneath the sanctuary lights, it had a strange purple glow to it. And then there was the row of earrings lining her right ear. Interesting. Different.

She looked his way and offered a shy smile, as if she somehow expected him to know exactly who she was and what she was doing here. He hoped the smile he offered in response was convincing enough.

As she brushed a loose hair from her face, he noticed the tattoo on the inside of her wrist. He strained to make it out, but could not.

"Dave, what have you done?" he whispered. "You've slipped over the edge, man." Tangie Carini was the last person on planet Earth Gregg would've imagined the church hiring. She was the polar opposite of everything. . .well, of everything he was.

On the other hand. . .

As she opened her mouth, thanking the congregation for welcoming her to Harmony Community Church, nothing but pure goodness oozed out. He found himself spellbound by the soothing sound of her voice—very controlled and just the right tone. She'd done this before. . .spoken in front of a crowd.

Then again, if what Dave had said about her was true, she'd performed in front of thousands, and on Broadway, no less. Suddenly Gregg felt like crawling under his pew. Just wait till she got a look at the video of the Christmas play. She'd eat him for lunch.

૨◆

Tangie shared her heart with the congregation, keenly aware of the fact that Gregg Burke watched her every move. What was he staring at? Surely the pastor had filled him in. . .right?

Oh well. Plenty of time to worry about that later. With a full heart, Tangie began explaining her vision for the drama program.

"I'm a firm believer in stirring up the gifts. And each of these children is gifted in his or her own way. I plan to spend time developing whatever abilities I see in each child so that he or she can walk in the fullness of God's call."

She paused a moment as members of the congregation responded with a couple of "Amens." Looked like they were cool with her ideas thus far.

After that, she went into a passionate speech about the role of the arts in ministry. "God has gifted us for a reason, not for the sake of entertainment—though we all love to entertain and be entertained. However, He has gifted us so that we can share the gospel message in a way that's fresh. Creative. Life-changing."

As she spoke, Tangie noticed the smiles from most in the congregation. Sure, Ella Mae Peterson, Gran-Gran's friend, sat with her arms crossed at her chest. Well, no problem there. She and the Lord would win Mrs. Peterson over.

As she wrapped up her speech, Tangie turned to nod in Gregg's direction. The music pastor flashed a smile, but she noticed it looked a little rehearsed. She knew acting when she saw it. He wasn't happy she was there.

Hmm. Maybe Ella Mae wasn't her only adversary. Well, no problem. Tangie made up her mind to win over Gregg Burke, too. . .no matter what it took.

Chapter 4

On New Year's Eve, Tangie went with her grandparents to a party at the church. It sure wouldn't be the same as celebrating the New Year in Times Square, but she'd make the best of it. She decided to let her hair down—figuratively speaking—so that the people of Harmony could see the real Tangie. The one with the eclectic wardrobe. She settled on black pants, a 1990s zebra-print top, and a lime green scarf, just for fun. For kicks, she added a hot pink necklace and earring ensemble. Standing back, she took a look at the mirror. "Hmm. Not bad. Nothing like a little color to liven things up."

They'd no sooner arrived at the church than the chaos began. Kids, food, games, activities. . .the whole place was a madhouse. In a happy sort of way.

"Told you we know how to have fun," Gran-Gran said with a twinkle in her eye. "Now, just let me drop off this food in the fellowship hall, and I'll introduce you to a few people your own age."

Minutes later, Tangie found herself surrounded by elementary-age kids. They weren't exactly her age, but they'd gravitated to her nonetheless.

A pretty little thing with blond hair tugged at Tangie's sleeve. "I'm Margaret Sanderson and I'm an actress, just like you," the girl said, puffing up her shoulders and tossing her hair. "My mama says I was the best one in the Christmas play. They should've given me the lead part. Then the whole play would've been better."

"Oh? Is that so?" Tangie tried to hold her composure.

"Yes, and I can sing, too." The little girl's confidence increased more with each word. "Want to hear me?"

Before she could respond, the little girl began to belt "The Lullaby of Broadway." To her credit, Margaret could, indeed, sing. And what she lacked in decorum, she made up for in volume. Still, there was something a little over the top about the vivacious youngster.

I know what it is. She reminds me of myself at that age. Only, she's got a lot more nerve.

Tangie released a breath, wanting to say just the right thing. "We'll be holding auditions for an Easter production soon, and I certainly look forward to seeing you there."

"Oh, I know. I've been practicing all week," Margaret explained with a knowing look in her eye. "I'm going to be the best one there. And Mama says that if they don't give me the main part, I can't do it at all."

We'll see about that.

Tangie turned as a little boy grabbed her other sleeve. "Hey, do I have to do that stupid Easter play?" he grumbled. "I don't want to."

"Well, I suppose that's up to your mom and dad," she said with a shrug. "It's not my decision."

"I don't have a dad." His gaze shifted downward. "And my mom always makes me try out for these dumb plays. But I stink at acting and singing."

Tangie quirked a brow, wondering where he got such an idea. "Who told you that?"

He stared at her like she'd grown two heads. "Nobody has to tell me. I just stink. Wait till you see the video. Then you'll know."

"Ah. Well, I suppose I'll just have to see for myself, then."

From across the room, Tangie caught a glimpse of Gregg standing next to the young woman who'd sung the solo on Sunday. What did Gran-Gran say her name was again?

Determined to connect with people, Tangie headed their way. As she approached the couple, she could see the look in Gregg's eyes as he talked to the beautiful brunette. Ah. A spark. He must really like her.

Gregg turned Tangie's way and nodded. "Tangie Carini."

"Gregg Burke." She offered a welcoming smile. "We meet officially. . .at last."

"Yes. Sorry about the other day in the hallway. I didn't know who you were, or I would have said something then. I'm glad you're here."

"Thanks." Maybe this wouldn't be as tough as she'd feared. Looked like he was a pretty easygoing guy.

Gregg nodded as he gestured to the brunette at his side. "Tangie, this is Ashley Conway, our children's director."

Ashley. That's it.

Ashley looked her way with curiosity etched on her face. "Tangie?" she said. "I don't think I've ever heard that one before. You'll have to tell me more about your name."

Tangie groaned. Oh, how she hated telling people that she was named after the flavor of the month when she was born. Having parents in the taffy business didn't always work to a girl's advantage.

Thankfully, Pastor Hampton made an announcement, giving her a reprieve.

"I know the kids are anxious to see the video of the Christmas performance," he said. "So why don't we go ahead and gather everyone in the sanctuary to watch it together."

Gregg groaned and Ashley slugged him in the arm. "Oh, c'mon. It's not so bad."

"Whatever." He shook his head, and then looked at Tangie with pursed lips. "Just don't hold this against me, okay? I'm a musician, not a drama director."

"Of course." With anticipation mounting, Tangie tagged along behind Gran-Gran and Gramps to the sanctuary to watch the video. Finally! Something she could really relate to.

"Now, don't expect too much," Gran-Gran whispered as they took their seats. "Remember what I told you on the phone the other day."

"Right." Tangie nodded. Surely her grandmother had exaggerated, though. With Gregg being such an accomplished musician, the production couldn't have been too bad, right?

The lights in the auditorium went down, and she leaned back against her pew, ready for the show to begin. Up on the screen the recorded Christmas production began. Someone had taped the children backstage before the show, going from child to child, asking what he or she thought about the upcoming performance.

"How sweet."

Tangie was particularly struck with the boy who'd approached her in the fellowship hall, the one without a father. Watching him on the screen, she couldn't help but notice how rambunctious he was.

"That's Cody," Gran-Gran said, elbowing her. "One of the rowdy ones that comes with a warning label."

"He's as cute as he can be," Tangie said. She wanted to ruffle his already-messy hair. "I wonder if he can sing."

At that, Gramps snorted. "Wait and see."

"Yikes." Didn't sound promising.

Tangie continued watching the video as the opening music began. The children appeared on the stage and sang a Christmas song together. "Not bad, not bad." Tangie looked at her grandmother and shrugged, then whispered, "What's wrong with that?"

"Keep watching."

At this point, the drama portion of the show began. Tangie almost fell out of her seat when the first child delivered his lines.

"Oh no." He stumbled all over himself. And what was up with that costume? Looked like someone had started it, but not quite finished. At least his was better than the next child's. This precious little girl was definitely wearing something that looked like her mother's bathrobe. It was several inches too long in the arms. In fact, you couldn't see the girl's hands at all. As she tried to deliver her lines—albeit too dramatically—her sleeves flailed about, a constant distraction.

"Ugh." Tangie shook her head. Only five minutes into the show and she wanted to fix. . .pretty much everything.

At about that time, a little girl dressed as an angel appeared to the shepherds and delivered a line that was actually pretty good. "Oh wait. . .that's the girl I just met," she whispered to her grandmother. "Margaret Sanderson."

"A star in the making," Gran-Gran whispered. "And if you don't believe it, just ask her mother."

Tangie's laugh turned into a honking sound, which she tried to disguise with a cough. Unfortunately, the cough wasn't very convincing, so she resorted to a sneeze. Then hiccups. Before long, several people were looking her way, including Gregg.

Focus, Tangie. Focus.

Turned out, Margaret was the best one in the show. Many of the really good ones came with some degree of attitude. Pride. Oh well. They would work on that. Maybe that's one reason Tangie had come, to help Margaret through this.

Tangie watched once again as Cody took the stage, dressed as a shepherd. Poor kid. He stumbled all over himself, in every conceivable way.

Maybe that's another reason I'm here. He needs a confidence boost.

Funny. One kiddo needed a boost. . .the other needed to be taken down a notch or two.

Oh well, she had it in her. Nothing a little time and TLC couldn't take care of. Determined to make the best of things, Tangie settled in to watch the rest of the show.

&

Gregg cringed as the video continued. On the night of the performance there had been excitement in the air. It had given him false hope that the show was really not so bad. But tonight, watching the video, he had to admit the truth.

It stunk.

No, it didn't just stink. It was an embarrassment.

He glanced across the aisle at Tangie and her grandparents, wanting to slink from the room. Oh, if only he could read her thoughts right now. Then again, maybe he didn't want to. Maybe it would be best just to pretend she thought it was great.

He watched as Tangie slumped down in her chair. Was she. . .sleeping? Surely not. He tried to focus on the screen, but found it difficult when a couple of people got up and slipped out of the sanctuary, whispering to each other. Great.

Lord, I don't mind admitting this isn't my bag. But I'm feeling pretty humiliated right now. Could we just fast-forward through this part and get right to the next?

Gregg was pretty sure he heard the Lord answer with a very firm, *"No."*

&

Tangie continued to watch the video, but found the whole thing painful. Gran-Gran had been right. It wasn't just poorly acted; the entire show was lacking in every conceivable way. And talk about dull. How did people stay awake throughout the performance? Looked like half the folks in this place had fallen asleep tonight. Not a good sign.

She glanced across the aisle at Gregg Burke, saddened by the look of pain on his face.

Poor guy. He had to know this wasn't good. Right?

Surely a man with his artistic abilities could see the difference between a good performance and a bad one. And, without a doubt, Gregg Burke was a guy with great artistic skill. By the end of Sunday's service, both his voice and his heart for God had won her over. The way he led the congregation in worship truly captivated her. And though she'd performed on many a stage over the years, Tangie couldn't help but think that leading others into the throne room of God would far surpass any experience she'd ever had in a theater setting.

She snapped back to attention, focusing on the video. For a moment. As a child on the screen struggled to remember his lines, Tangie's thoughts drifted once again. She pondered her first impression of Gregg—as a stodgy, geeky guy. Tonight, in his jeans and button-up shirt, he was actually quite handsome. Still, he looked a little stiff. Nervous. But why? Did he ever just relax? Enjoy himself?

At that moment, a loud snore to her right distracted her. She looked as Gran-Gran elbowed Gramps in the ribs. Tangie tried not to giggle, but found it difficult. She didn't blame her grandfather for falling asleep. In fact—she yawned as she thought about it—her eyes were growing a little heavy, too.

Before long, she drifted off to sleep, dreaming of badly dressed wise men and Christmas angels who couldn't carry a tune in a bucket.

Chapter 5

It didn't take Tangie long to settle into a routine at Gran-Gran and Gramps' house. Her creative juices skittered into overtime as she contemplated the task of putting on a show with the children. Oh, what fun it would be. She could practically see it all now! The sets. The costumes. The smiles on the faces of everyone in attendance. With the Lord's help, she would pull off a toe-tapping, hand-clapping musical extravaganza that everyone—kids and church staff, alike—could be proud of.

Tangie received a call from the pastor on Monday morning, asking if they could meet later that afternoon. She stopped off at Sweet Harmony—Gramps' favorite bakery—to pick up some cookies to take to the meeting. Unable to make up her mind, Tangie purchased a dozen chocolate chip, a half dozen oatmeal raisin, and a half dozen peanut butter. Just for good measure, she added a half dozen of iced sugar cookies to her order.

"I can't live without my sweets," she explained to the woman behind the counter. "My family's in the sugar business, and I've been in withdrawal since moving away from home."

The clerk—an older woman whose name tag read PENNY—gave her a funny look as she rang up the order. "Sugar business?"

"Yes, we run a candy shop on the boardwalk in Atlantic City, specializing in taffy." Tangie pulled a cookie from the plain white bag and took a big bite. "Mmm. Great peanut butter. They're my favorite."

"You really do have a sweet tooth." Penny laughed as she wiped her hands on her apron. "Well, just so you know, I'm hiring. Sarah, the girl who usually helps me in the afternoons, has gone back to college. So, if you're interested. . ."

"Hmm." Tangie shrugged. "I'll have to see how it works with my schedule. In the meantime, these cookies are great. If you're interested in adding any candies, I'd be happy to talk with you about that. I'd love to bring some of our family favorites to Harmony. I think you'd like them."

"Let me think about it," Penny said. "And you let me know when you've made up your mind about the job. Otherwise, I might put a 'help wanted' sign in the window."

"Give me a couple days to pray about it." Tangie took another bite of the cookie, then headed to her car.

By four o'clock, she and Gregg Burke sat side by side in Dave's spacious office, all three of them nibbling on cookies.

"I'm so excited about what God is doing, I can hardly stand it," Dave said between bites. "We've already got the best music pastor in the world, and now we've just added a Broadway-trained actress to our staff to head up the drama department. Between the two of you, the Easter production is going to be the best thing this community has ever seen."

Tangie felt a little flustered at the pastor's glowing description of her. If he had any idea of the tiny bit parts she'd taken over the past four years, he'd probably rethink his decision. On the other hand. . .

God brought you here, Tangie, she reminded herself. *So don't get in the way of what He's doing.*

"What are you looking for, exactly?" Gregg asked Dave as he reached into the bag for another cookie. "What kind of production, I mean? More of a variety show or an all-out musical?"

"Doesn't really matter. I just want a production that will work hand in hand with the outreach we'll be doing for the community," Dave explained. "I'd like to see something that's different than anything we've done before."

"Different?" Gregg's eyebrows arched as he took another bite. "How different?"

"That's for you two to decide," the pastor said. "We're going to be hosting an Easter egg hunt for the neighborhood kids, as always. But this year we're looking at this as an outreach—the biggest of the year, in fact."

"Easter eggs? Outreach?" Gregg shook his head. "Not sure those two things really go together in one sentence."

"Oh, I think it's a wonderful idea," Tangie said, her excitement mounting. "The Easter egg hunt will be a great draw. And people are always more willing to hear about the Lord during the holidays, so we'll have a captive audience."

Dave nodded. "My thoughts, exactly. We'll advertise the Easter egg hunt in the paper and draw a large crowd. Then, just after the hunt is over, we'll open up the auditorium for everyone to come inside for the production. It will be free, of course."

"I think that's a wonderful idea," Tangie said. "That way all of the kids can watch the show, even the ones who wouldn't be able to afford it otherwise."

"You've got it!" Dave looked at her and beamed.

Clearly, they were on the same page.

She looked at Gregg, hoping for a similar response. He sat with a confused expression on his face. What was up with that?

"I don't really have anything specific in mind, as far as what kind of production it should be," the pastor continued, "just something that appeals to kids and shares the real meaning of Easter in a tangible way. But different, as I said. Something kid-friendly and contemporary."

Gregg looked a little dubious. "How will we get the kids and their families to stay for the musical? I can see them coming for the Easter egg hunt, maybe, but how do we get them inside the building once it's over?"

"I've been thinking about that." Dave rolled a pen around in his fingers. "Haven't exactly come up with anything yet, though."

"Oh, I know," Tangie said. "Maybe we could do some sort of a drawing for a grand prize. A giant Easter egg, maybe? The winner to be announced after the production. That might entice them to stay."

"Giant Easter egg?" Gregg asked.

"Made of chocolate, of course." Tangie turned to him, more excited than ever. "At my family's candy shop, we have these amazing eggs. . .oh, you have to see one to believe it! They're as big as a football. No, bigger. And they're solid chocolate, hand decorated by my sister. I know Taffie will help. She loves things like this."

"Taffy will help?" Gregg looked at Tangie curiously. "What does that mean?"

"Oh, sorry." She giggled and her cheeks warmed. "Taffie is my older sister. There are three of us—Taffie, Candy, and me."

"Tangie." Dave said with a smile. "Your grandmother told me they sometimes call you Tangerine, just to be funny."

"Terrific." Tangie groaned. "As you might imagine, Tangie wouldn't have been my first choice for a name. How would you feel if you were named after the flavor of the month when you were born?"

Gregg chuckled, offering Tangie her first glimmer of hope from the beginning of the meeting till now. His eyes sparkled and a hint of color rose to his cheeks. "So, we're giving away an egg, then?" he asked.

"If that's okay with both of you." Tangie looked back and forth between them "They sell for a fortune, but I'm sure Taffie would send one for free, especially if I tell her what it's for. My sister and her husband love the Lord and would be thrilled to see one of their candy eggs used for ministry."

"Eggs for ministry." Gregg groaned and shook his head. "What's next?"

"Oh, that's easy." Tangie nodded. "Sheep, bunnies, and chicks, of course. And anything else that might appeal to little kids. Oh"—her heart swelled with joy as the words tumbled out—"this is going to be the best Easter ever!"

☙

Gregg watched with some degree of curiosity as Tangie and Dave talked back and forth about the production. Talk about feeling like a third wheel. Why was he here, anyway? He did his best not to struggle with any offense. He'd been through enough of that as a kid. No, in fact, he looked forward to Tangie's help with the production, though he still had a hard time admitting it to anyone other than himself.

Still, that bunnies and chicks line had to be a joke. Right?

Listening to her talk, her voice as animated as her facial expression, he had the strangest feeling. . .she was dead serious.

He glanced at his watch and gasped. "Oh, sorry to cut this short, but I've got a date with my mom. I'm taking her to the movies this afternoon."

"A date with your mom?" Tangie flashed a smile. He couldn't tell if she was making fun of him or found the idea thoughtful. Not that it really mattered. No, where his mom was concerned, only one thing mattered. . .convincing her that the Lord loved her. And there was only one way to accomplish that really. . .by spending quality time with her and loving her, himself. Not an easy task sometimes, what with her brusque exterior. But Gregg was really working on not judging people by outward appearance, especially his own mom.

"When can we meet to talk about the production?" Tangie asked. "One day this week?"

"Mornings are better for me," he said as he rose from his chair. "What about Thursday?"

"Thursday it is. Where?"

"Hmm." He reached for his coat. "The diner on Main? They've got a great breakfast menu. Very inspirational. I'm going to need it if we're talking about putting on a show, trust me."

Tangie grinned. "Okay. I'll see you there. Will seven thirty work?"

"Yep." He nodded. "Sorry I have to bolt, but my mom is expecting me." After a quick good-bye, he headed toward the car, his thoughts whirling in a thousand different directions.

Chapter 6

Tangie pulled herself out of bed early on Thursday morning and dressed in one of her favorite outfits—a pair of faded bell-bottoms and a great vintage sweater she'd picked up at a resale shop—a throwback from the 1960s in varying shades of hot pink, orange, and brown. Why anyone would've parted with it was beyond her. Sure, the colors were a little faded, but that just gave it a more authentic look. And coupled with the shiny white vinyl go-go style boots, which she'd purchased for a song, the whole ensemble just came together. Once you added in the hat. She especially loved the ivory pillbox-style hat with its mesh trim. Marti said it reminded her of something she'd once seen on *I Love Lucy*. What higher compliment was there, really?

Tangie made her way into the living room, laptop in hand.

Gramps took one look at her and let out a whistle. "I haven't seen a getup like that since Woodstock. Not that I went to Woodstock, mind you."

"I believe I wore a little hat just like that on our wedding day," her grandmother added. "Wherever did you find that?"

"Oh, I get the best bargains at resale shops," Tangie said with a nod. "Who wants to shop at the mall? The clothes are so. . ."

"Normal?" her grandfather threw in.

Tangie laughed. "Maybe to you, but I think I'll stick with what makes me feel good."

"And all of that color makes you feel good?"

"Yep." In fact, on days like today—dressed in the colorful ensemble—she felt like she had the world on a string.

After saying good-bye to her grandparents, she eased her car out of the slick driveway. As she drove through town, Tangie passed Sweet Harmony and smiled as she remembered meeting Penny. What a great lady.

"Lord, what do You think about that job offer? Should I take it?" Hmm. She'd have to pray about that a bit longer. In the meantime, she had one very handsome music pastor to meet with.

Handsome? Tangie, watch yourself.

She sighed, thinking of how many leading men she'd fallen in love with over the past four years. Taffie and Candy had always accused her of being fickle, but. . .was she? After less than a second's pause, she had to admit the truth. She *had* been pretty flighty where talented guys were concerned. And the more talented, the harder she seemed to fall. All the more reason *not* to

274

fall for Gregg Burke.

Not that he was her type, anyway. No, he seemed a little too "in the box" for her liking.

She arrived at the diner a few minutes early, but noticed Gregg's SUV in the parking lot. "He's very prompt," she said to herself. Pulling down the visor, she checked her appearance in the tiny mirror. Hmm. The eyeliner might be a bit much. She'd gone for a forties look. But she'd better touch up the lipstick to match in intensity. Tangie pulled it from her purse and gave her lips a quick swipe, then rubbed them together as she gazed back in the mirror. "Better."

Then, slip-sliding her way along, Tangie made the walk across the icy parking lot, cradling her laptop and praying all the way. She arrived inside the diner, stunned to find it so full. Gregg waved at her from the third booth on the right, and she headed his way. As she drew near, his eyes widened.

"What?" she asked, as she put her laptop down, then shrugged off her jacket.

"N–nothing." He paused, his gaze shifting to her hat. "I, um, just don't think I've ever seen a hat like that in person. In the movies, maybe. . ."

"I'll take that as a compliment." She laughed, then took her seat. Glancing around, she said, "You were right. This place is hopping."

"Oh, this is nothing. Most of the breakfast crowd has already passed through. You should see it around six thirty or seven." He continued to stare at her hat, and she grew uncomfortable. Should she take it off? Maybe it was distracting him.

"The food must be good," Tangie managed. She reached to unpin her hat just as a young waitress appeared at the table and smiled at her.

"Oh, please don't take off that hat! It's amazing!"

Tangie grinned and left it in place.

The girl's face lit up. "You're Tangie Carini."

Tangie nodded.

"I knew it had to be you. That's the coolest outfit I've ever seen, by the way. Seriously. . .where did you get it? Is that what they're wearing on the runway this season?"

"Thanks. And, no. This is just vintage stuff. I love to shop in out-of-the-way places."

"I have a feeling I'm really going to like you," the waitress said. "I've been wanting to meet you ever since I heard you speak in church on Sunday morning."

"Oh?" Tangie took the menu the girl offered and glanced up at her with a smile. "Why is that?"

"Brittany is one of the leaders of the youth group," Gregg explained. "She was a big help to me with the Christmas production."

"I've always been interested in theater," Brittany said. "Our high school did

The Sound of Music my sophomore year."

"She played Maria," Gregg said. "And she was pretty amazing."

Brittany's cheeks turned red. "My favorite role was Milly in *Seven Brides for Seven Brothers*. We did that show my senior year, and I loved every minute of it."

"Oh, that's one of my favorites," Tangie said. "I played the role of Milly at our local community theater back in Atlantic City."

"Oh, I can't believe you just said that!" Brittany clasped her hands together and grinned. "This is a sign from above. A community theater is exactly what I wanted to talk to you about." Brittany's eyes lit up and her tone of voice changed. She grew more animated by the second. "Several of us have been wanting to start a community theater group here in Harmony. There's an old movie theater that would be perfect. It's not in use any more, but would be great. Just needs a stage."

"Do you have funding?"

Brittany shrugged. "Never really thought about that part. I guess we could hold a fund-raiser or something like that. But I'd love to talk to you more about it. Maybe. . ." The teenager flashed a crooked grin. "Maybe you could even direct some of our shows."

"Ah ha." *I see.* So, that's what this was about. First she was directing at the church, now a community theater? *Lord, what are You up to, here? Trying to keep me in Harmony forever?*

Just then, the manager passed by and Brittany snapped to attention. "Are you ready to order?" she asked, grabbing her notepad and pen.

"I'll have two eggs over easy, bacon, toast, and hot tea," Tangie said.

"I'll have the same." Gregg closed his menu. "But make mine coffee. I'm not into the tea thing."

Brittany took their menus and headed to the kitchen.

"She's a great kid," Gregg said. "Very passionate about the theater. Hoping to go to New York one day."

"She's really talented, then?"

"She's pretty good, but I don't think she realizes what she'd be up against in the Big Apple."

"I could fill her in, but it might be discouraging," Tangie said with a shrug.

"So, you didn't just jump into lead roles right away?" he asked, peering into her eyes.

Tangie couldn't help but laugh. "I didn't jump into lead roles, period. Trust me, I was fortunate to land paying gigs at all, large or small. And they didn't last very long, sometimes. A couple of the shows I was in folded after just a few performances. Life in the theater can be very discouraging."

He shrugged, and his gaze shifted down to the table. "I guess it's the same in the music industry. I tried recording a CD a few years ago, but couldn't get any radio stations to play my tunes. Pretty sobering, actually."

"Man, they don't know what they're missing." Tangie shook her head, trying to imagine why anyone would turn Gregg's music away. "You've got one of the most anointed voices I've ever heard."

"Really? Thanks." He seemed stupefied by her words, but she couldn't figure out why. Surely others had told him how powerful those Sunday morning services were, right?

Brittany returned with a coffeepot in hand. She filled Gregg's mug. Then she started to pour some in Tangie's cup, but stopped just as a dribble of the hot stuff tumbled into the cup. "Oops, sorry. You said you wanted tea."

"Yes, please." When Brittany left, Tangie smiled at Gregg. "It's funny. I love the smell of coffee, but I don't really like the way it tastes. My roommate back in New York used to drink three or four cups a day."

"It's great early in the morning." He took a sip, then leaned back in his seat, a contented look on his face. "I've been addicted since I was in my late teens. My mom. . ." He hesitated. "Well, my mom sometimes let me do a few of the grown-up things a little earlier than most."

"Speaking of your mom, how did your date go?"

He laughed. "Good. She's a hoot. You'll have to meet her someday."

"Does she go to the church? Maybe I've met her already."

"The church?" Gregg's brow wrinkled. "No. I wish. But I'm working on that."

"So, she let you have coffee as a kid?" Tangie asked, going back to the original conversation.

"Yes." He grinned. "First thing in the morning, we'd each have two cups. Then she'd leave for work, and I'd get on the bus to go to school. Wide awake, I might add."

"Well, maybe that was the problem. I was never up early in the morning when I lived in New York. I rarely got to bed before three or four and usually slept till ten or eleven in the morning. By the time I got up and running, it was practically lunchtime."

"Are you a night owl?" Gregg asked.

"Always have been." She smiled, remembering the trouble she'd gotten in as a kid. "So, life in the theater just works for me. . .at least on some levels. Shows never end till really late, and there's always something going on after."

"Like what?"

"Oh, dinner at midnight with other cast members." Tangie allowed her thoughts to ramble for a moment. She missed her roomie, Marti, and their midnight meetings at Hanson's twenty-four-hour deli after each show.

"I've always been a morning person," Gregg said. "Sounds crazy, but evenings are tough on me. When nine o'clock rolls around, I'm ready to hit the hay."

"That's so funny." Tangie tried not to laugh, but the image of someone dozing off at nine was humorous, after the life she'd led in the big city. She paused and then opened her laptop. "I guess we should get busy, huh?"

Gregg's expression changed right away. Gone were the laugh lines around his eyes. In their place, a wrinkled brow and down-turned lips.

Tangie studied his expression, sensing his shift in attitude. "You're not looking forward to this?"

He shrugged and offered a loud sigh in response. "In case you didn't notice from that video you watched, I'm not exactly a pro at putting on shows with kids. If we could sing our way through the whole performance, fine, but anything with lines and costumes sends me right over the edge."

"Well, that's why I'm here." She grinned, feeling the excitement well up inside her. "I want you to know I'm so hyped up about all of this, I could just. . .throw a party or something."

"Really?" He looked at her as if he didn't quite believe it.

"Yes, I don't know how to explain it, but there's something about putting on a show that makes my heart sing. I love every minute of it—the auditions, reading the script for the first time, building the set, memorizing lines. . ." She paused, deep in thought, then said, "Of course, I'm usually the one on the stage, not the one directing, but I have worked with kids before, and I just know this will be a ton of fun."

"Humph." He crossed his arms at his chest and leaned back against his seat. "If you say so. I'd rather eat a plateful of artichokes—my least favorite food on planet Earth, by the way—than put on another show. But we'll get through this." He reached for his cup of coffee and took a swig, then shrugged.

"Oh, we'll more than get through it," she promised him. Reaching to rest her hand on his, she gave him a knowing look. "By the end of this, you're going to be a theater buff, I promise."

Gregg laughed. "If you can pull *that* off, I'll eat a whole plate of artichokes. In front of every kid in the play."

"I'm not going to let you forget you said that." Tangie nodded, already planning for the event in her head. "I'm going to hold you to it." She glanced at her laptop screen, and then looked back up at him. "In the meantime, we should probably talk about the production. I had the most wonderful idea for the Easter play. I hope you like it."

"Wait." He shook his head. "You mean, you actually wrote something? Already?"

"Well, of course. You didn't expect me to get one of those canned musicals from the Bible bookstore, did you?"

He shrugged. "I didn't know there was any other way."

Tangie laughed. "Oh, you really don't know me. I don't do anything by the book. And while there are some great productions out there, I really felt like Pastor Dave wanted us to cater specifically to the community, using the Easter egg hunt as our theme. Didn't you?"

Another shrug from Gregg convinced her he hadn't given the idea much thought.

"Well, I don't know about all that," he said. "And I definitely think a traditional Easter pageant is the safest bet. People expect to see certain things when they come for an Easter production, don't you think?" He began to list some of the elements he hoped to see in the show, and Tangie leaned back, realizing her dilemma at once.

She eventually closed her laptop and focused on the animation in Gregg's voice as he spoke. He hadn't been completely honest with her earlier, had he? All that stuff about how he didn't like doing performances wasn't true at all. Right now, listening to him talk about his version of an Easter pageant—which, to her way of thinking, sounded incredibly dull—she could see the sparkle in his eye. The tone of his voice changed.

In that moment, she realized the truth. It wasn't that he didn't like putting on shows. He just hadn't done one he could be proud of. That's all. But if they moved forward with the pageant he had in mind, things were liable to fall apart again. She didn't see—or hear—anything in his plan that sounded like what Pastor Dave asked for.

Tangie swallowed hard, working up the courage to speak. *Lord, show me what to say. I don't want to burst his bubble, but we're supposed to be doing something different. Something original.*

When he finally paused, Tangie exhaled and then looked into his eyes, noticing for the first time just how beautiful they were.

He gazed back, a boyish smile on his face. His cheeks flushed red and he whispered, "Sorry. Didn't mean to get carried away."

"Oh, don't be sorry." She hated to burst his bubble, but decided to add her thoughts. "I, um, was thinking of something completely different than what you described, though."

"Oh? Like what?"

"Well, hear me out. What I've written is really unique, something people have never seen before."

He gave her a dubious look.

"Just don't laugh, okay?" She proceeded to tell him about her plan to use talking animals—sheep, bunnies, baby chicks, and so forth—to convey the message of Easter.

"I've been thinking about this whole egg theme," she explained. "And I think we need to start the show with a giant Easter egg—maybe four or five feet high—in the center of the stage. We'll get some really cute kid-themed music that fits the scene, and the egg can crack open and a baby chick will come out. Of course, it'll be one of the kids, dressed as a chick. He—or she—can be the narrator, telling the rest of the story. There's going to be a shepherd, of course. He'll represent God. We'll need an adult for that. And then the little sheep—and we'll need lots of them—will be us, His kids. Make sense?"

Gregg stared at her like she'd lost her mind. Still, Tangie forged ahead, emphasizing the takeaway at the end of the play.

"See? It's an allegory," she explained. "A story inside a story. The baby chick hatching from its egg represents us, when we're born again. We enter a whole new life. Our story begins, in essence. The same is true with rabbits. Did you realize that bunnies are symbols for fertility and rebirth?"

"Well, no, but I guess I can see the parallel," he said. "Rabbits rapidly reproduce."

"Say *that* three times in a row." Tangie laughed.

He tried it and by the end, they were both chuckling.

Once she caught her breath, Tangie summed up her thoughts about the play. "So, the chicks and the bunnies are symbols of the rebirth experience. And the bunnies—because they rapidly reproduce—will be our little evangelists. Get it? They'll hop from place to place, sharing the love of Jesus."

"Um, okay."

"And the little sheep represent us, too. One of them wanders away from the fold and Jesus—the shepherd—goes after him. Or her. I haven't decided if it should be a boy or girl. But there's that hidden message of God's love for us. . . that He would leave the ninety-nine to go after the one. I think the audience will get it if they're paying attention."

"Maybe." He shook his head. "But I don't know about all that. I still think it's better to do something tried and true."

"Like your Christmas play?" Tangie could've slapped herself the minute the words came out. "I–I'm sorry."

He shook his head. "I've already admitted that I'm no director."

"I'm sure that's not true," she said. "You just haven't found the right show yet. But I think this Easter production has the capability of turning things around for both the kids who are in it and the ones who come to see it." She offered what she hoped would be taken as a winning smile. "And you'll see. By the end of this, you're going to fall in love with theater. It won't just be a means to an end anymore. It's going to get into your blood. You'll be hooked."

"Somehow I really doubt it." Gregg took a swig of his coffee and gave her a pensive look. "But, for lack of a better plan, I'll go along with this little chicks and bunnies play you're talking about. Just don't credit me with writing any of it, okay?"

He dove into a lengthy discussion about how he'd already been embarrassed enough with the last play and how he had no intention of being the subject of ridicule again. Tangie listened in stunned silence, realizing just how strongly he felt about her ideas, in spite of her persuasive argument, seconds earlier. But, why? Was it just her ideas he didn't like. . .or her?

Tangie's heart plummeted to her toes. Not only did he not like her ideas, he acted like he thought she was crazy. Well, she'd show him a thing or two about crazy over the next few weeks. And then, if she ended up failing at this gig in Harmony. . .she might just give some thought to heading back home. . . to the Big Apple.

ᴈ▲

Gregg could've slapped himself for making fun of Tangie in such a pointed way. From the look in her eyes, he knew he'd injured her pride. He knew just what that felt like. Still, he wasn't sure how to redeem the situation now. *Lord, I'm going to need Your help with this one. It's beyond me.*

Yes, everything about this was beyond him—the production, the outreach. . . and the beautiful woman in the nutty outfit seated across from him with the look of pain in her eyes.

Chapter 7

"Gran-Gran, you know I love you, right?" Tangie paced her grandparents' living room as she spoke with great passion.

"Of course!" Her grandmother looked up from the TV and nodded. "But you're blocking the TV, honey. We're trying to watch *Jeopardy*."

Tangie sighed and took a giant step to the left. Nothing ever got between Gran-Gran and her TV when the game shows were on. Still, this was important. Tangie attempted to interject her thoughts. "Gran-Gran, you know I would never do anything to hurt you."

"Never."

"What is *the Sears Tower!*" Gramps hollered at the TV. Tangie looked his way and he shrugged. "Sorry, honey. The question was, 'What is the tallest building in America?' and I happened to know the answer."

He and Gran-Gran turned back to the TV, and Tangie knew she'd lost them. She took a seat on the sofa and sighed. Gran-Gran looked her way.

"You're really upset, aren't you?"

Tangie nodded. "Sort of." She worked up the courage to say the rest. "Now, don't be mad, but I'm giving some thought to only staying in Harmony till after the production, then going back to New York."

"What?" Her grandmother turned and looked at her with a stunned expression on her face, then reached for the remote and flipped off the TV. "But why?"

How could she begin to explain it in a way that a non-theater person could understand? "I. . .I need artistic freedom." There. That should do it.

"Artistic freedom?" Gramps rose from his well-worn recliner and snagged a cookie from the cookie jar. "What did someone do, kidnap your creativity or something?"

"Very nicely put," she said. "That's exactly what someone did. He stole it and put it behind bars. And as long as I stay in Harmony, I'm never getting it back. I'm destined to be dull and boring."

Her grandmother's brows elevated slightly. "You? Dull and boring? Impossible." Gran-Gran stood up and approached Tangie.

"I can see how it would happen here," Tangie said. "I feel like my voice has been squelched."

"Impossible. You've got too much chutzpah for that. Besides, folks can only take what you give, nothing more."

"Maybe I just don't know enough about how to compromise with someone like Gregg Burke. But one thing is for sure, this gig in Harmony doesn't feel like a long-term plan for me."

Gran-Gran's eyes misted over right away. "Are you serious?"

"Yes." Tangie sighed when she saw the hurt look on her grandmother's face. "I'll stay till the Easter production is over at the beginning of April. But then I'm pretty sure I'd like to go back to New York."

"Really? But I thought you were done with New York," Gramps said, a confused look on his face.

"Well, see, I got an e-mail from my friend Marti last night. She just found out about auditions for a new show. They're going to be held a few days after the production, and the director, Vincent, is an old friend of mine. He directed a couple of plays I was in year before last. I'll stand a better shot with this one, since I know someone."

"Honey, I know you enjoy being in those shows. You're a great little actress."

Tangie cringed at the words *little actress*. How many times had her father said the same thing? And her directors? She didn't want to be a *little* actress. She wanted to have a career. A real career.

Gran-Gran continued, clearly oblivious to Tangie's inner turmoil. "But, as good as you are, that's not your ministry. You're a teacher. You said it yourself when you stood up in front of the church to talk to the congregation. You're a gift stirrer. Your real ability is in motivating and teaching those kids. And if you go away. . ." Gran-Gran's eyes filled with tears. "Well, if you go away, nothing will be the same around here. There's no one to take your place."

Tangie shrugged. "Gregg will do fine. And Ashley. . .she's great with the kids."

"Yes, but she's too busy. That's what I was saying before. She has a full-time job at the school, teaching second grade."

"Right." Tangie sighed.

"That's why she couldn't help with the Christmas production. She was doing a show of her own. I know her pretty well, honey. She would probably agree to help, just to appease Gregg, but she's just too overwhelmed to take on anything else right now."

"I'm sorry, Gran-Gran. I just don't think I'm up for the job long-term. It's going to be hard enough to make it through one show." Tangie tried not to let the defeat show on her face but couldn't seem to help herself.

Gran-Gran plopped down in a chair, a somber look on her face. "Well, I'm sorry to hear that. Very sorry."

As she left the room, Tangie reached for an oatmeal raisin cookie—her third. She took a big bite, pondering everything her grandmother had said. Looked like Tangie was right all along. She wasn't meant for small-town life.

What did it matter, really? Apparently she was destined to fail at everything she put her hand to—whether it was in the big city or in a tiny place like Harmony, New Jersey.

☙

Gregg picked up the phone and called Gramps for a much-needed chat. The elderly man answered on the third ring, his opening words packing quite a punch. "What took you so long, son?"

"H–hello?"

"I know it's you, Gregg. Saw your number on the caller ID. I've been sitting by the phone for the past hour, ever since Tangie talked to us about that meeting you two had at the diner this morning. She was plenty worked up."

"Oh, I'm sorry," Gregg started. "I—"

"Ruined a perfectly good round of *Jeopardy*," Gramps interrupted. "I figured you would've called me before this."

Gregg groaned. "I guess I should have. Things didn't go very well."

"So I hear. There's actually talk of her leaving. Going back to New York City. I'd hate to see that happen. Why, the very idea of it is breaking my heart."

"No way." She was giving up. . .that quickly? Why? "Can you put her on the phone, please?" Gregg asked.

He heard Gramps' voice ring out, "Tangie, you've got a call."

Seconds later, she answered. "Taffie, what happened? Everything okay with the baby?"

"Taffy?" Gregg repeated. "What does taffy have to do with anything?"

"O–oh, I'm sorry. I thought for sure Gramps said my sister was on the phone. Who is this?"

"Gregg Burke."

"Oh." The tone of her voice changed right away. In fact, her initial excitement fizzled out like air from a flat tire.

"I'm calling to apologize," he said, his words coming a mile a minute. "I've really messed this one up. Please don't go anywhere. I need you too much for that."

"You do?"

"Yes." He sighed. Might as well just speak his mind. "To be honest, I think I'm just insecure. I don't know the first thing about drama, but it's still hard to admit that I'm a failure at anything. Does that make sense?"

"More than you know."

"I think my pride was a little hurt, is all. I'll be the first to admit it." He paused a moment. "Your ideas about the Easter play are. . .different. Very different from anything I would've come up with. But maybe that's why they hired you. They want different. And this is for kids. Kids need kid stuff, and I'll be honest, I don't know the first thing about kid stuff. I think I proved that with the Christmas play."

"Well, I'm different, all right," Tangie responded. "But I don't want you to

284

think I'm so off the wall that I'm going to end up embarrassing you or the kids in any way. That's not my intention. I can see this production being really cute, but if you'd rather do something more traditional. . ." Her words faded away.

"No, it's fine. I just think we need to meet to get this settled, one way or the other. Can you send me a copy of what you've written by e-mail attachment? I'll take a look at it and see what I can do with it from a music standpoint. Then we can talk again before next week's auditions. How does that sound?"

She hesitated, but finally came back with, "Good. Thanks for giving me a second chance."

"No." He sighed. "I shouldn't have been so quick to shut you down the first time. I'm just used to being the creative one, and you. . ."

She laughed. "I know, I know. When God handed out creativity, He gave me a double portion. I've never understood why."

"Oh, I think I do," Gregg said. "He knew He could trust you with it."

She paused for a moment and then a much quieter Tangie came back with, "Thank you. That's the nicest thing anyone's said to me in a long time. I needed to hear that."

By the time they ended the call, Gregg felt a hundred pounds lighter. Until he thought about the giant Easter egg she'd proposed for the opening scene. Then his stomach began to tighten once again. *Lord, this is going to be. . .different. Give me patience. Please.*

❧

Tangie sighed as she hung up the phone. Gregg's plea for help had surprised her, especially after his reaction this morning. Who put him up to this?

"Gramps?" She called out for her grandfather, but he didn't answer. Tangie looked around the living room, but couldn't find him anywhere, so she bundled up in her coat and headed out to his workshop behind the house. There she found him, carving a piece of wood.

"Oh, wow." She looked around the tiny room, amazed by all the things she found there. "You're very crafty, Gramps."

"That's what they tell me." He held out a wood-carved replica of a bear and smiled. "What do you think of this guy?"

"I think he's great. I also think. . ." The idea hit her all at once. "I also think I'm going to use your services for the kids' production."

"So, you're sticking around? Gregg did the right thing?"

"I'm sticking around." She shrugged. "I would've stayed till after the play anyway, remember?"

"Now you'll stay longer?"

She sighed and rested against his workbench, thankful for the tiny space heater at her feet. "I can't make any promises. Who knows where things will be in a few months? There's this really great show. . ."

"I know, I know." He sighed, then reached to give her a peck on the cheek.

"In New York. A chance of a lifetime. Something you've been waiting for...forever." He stressed the word *forever*, making it seem like a mighty long time.

"I know you want me to stay here," Tangie said. "And I promise to pray about it."

"That's all I ask, honey." He nodded and smiled. "But let me say one more thing." Gramps peered into her eyes, his gaze penetrating to her very soul. "Your mother isn't the only one with a case of wanderlust."

"What?"

"I mean, you have a hard time staying put in one place for long. And with one job for long." He paused. "Now, I don't mean anything negative by that; it's just an observation. Maybe your trip to Harmony is a lesson in staying put awhile."

"Hmm." She shrugged. "I don't know, Gramps. I just know that I always get this jittery feeling. And bolting is. . ."

"Easier?"

"Sometimes." She sighed. "I'm sure you're right. It's a learned behavior. I wasn't always this way. But when one show after another shut down, I just got in the habit of shifting gears. Now I've turned so many corners, I can hardly remember where I've been and where I'm going. And bolting just comes naturally. I'm not proud of it. I'm just saying it's become second nature, that's all."

"Well, pray before you bolt. That's all I ask this time." He wrapped her in his arms and placed a whiskery kiss in her hair. " 'Cause when you leave this time, it's gonna break some poor fella's heart." He dabbed his eyes, then whispered, "And I'm not just talking about Gregg Burke's."

Chapter 8

On Friday morning, Tangie stopped off at Sweet Harmony, the bakery where she'd purchased the cookies. Penny greeted her with a welcoming smile.

"Great coat. Love the shoulder pads. Very 1980s."

"Thanks." Tangie chuckled. "That's the idea. I love wearing clothes from every era."

"Kind of reminds me of something Joan Collins would've worn in *Dynasty*." Penny paused, then gave Tangie a pensive look. "Been thinking about that proposition I made?"

"I have." Tangie smiled. "I think I'd like to work here, but I might only be staying in town till the first week in April. Would that be a problem?"

"Hmm." Penny shrugged and wiped her hands on her apron. "Well, I can really use the help, even if it's temporary. I'll take what I can get."

"We'll need to come to some agreement about my schedule. I'm working part-time at a local church."

"Church?" Penny rolled her eyes. "I used to go to a church. . .back in the day."

"Whatever happened with that?" Tangie asked.

Penny shrugged. "Gave it up for Lent." She slapped herself on the knee and let out a raucous laugh. "Oh, that's a good one. Gave up church for Lent." After a few more chuckles, she finally calmed down. "Let's just say God and I aren't exactly on speaking terms and leave it at that."

"Ah."

"And I guess I could also add that the church hasn't exactly laid out the welcome mat for me. But, mind you, I haven't been to one since I was in my thirties, so I'm not talking about any church in particular here. I just know that churches, in general, don't take too kindly to unmarried women with kids."

"Whoa. Really?" Tangie thought about that for a moment. Most of the churches she'd attended—both at home in Atlantic City and in New York—had always reached out to single moms. But it looked like Penny had a different story. Then again, Penny was—what?—in her late fifties, maybe? So, anything that happened to her had to have happened twenty or thirty years ago, right?

"Back to the bakery. . ." Penny gave her a scrutinizing glance. "How are your cake decorating skills?"

Tangie shrugged. "We didn't do much pastry work at the candy shop, but I've decorated cookies and other sweets, and I've got a steady hand."

"You're hired."

"Just like that?" Tangie laughed. "You don't need references or anything?"

"Your grandfather is Herbert Henderson?" Penny stared at her thoughtfully.

"Yes. How did you know that?"

"He's my best customer, and he's been telling me all about this granddaughter of his from the candy shop in Atlantic City. He described you to a tee, right down to the tattoo on your wrist. What is that, anyway? A star?"

"Yeah." Tangie shrugged. "A theater friend of mine talked me into it years ago. She said I was going to be a big star someday, and that looking at my wrist would be a good reminder not to give up."

"Have you?"

"W—what?"

"Given up?" Penny gave her a pensive look.

"Oh, no. Not really. I, um, well, I'm just on hiatus from acting right now."

"Okay." Penny pursed her lips, then spoke in a motherly voice. "Just don't let me hear that you've given up on your dreams. You need to go after them. . . wholeheartedly. I let mine die for a while." She looked around the bakery, then grinned. "But eventually got around to it. Just wasted a lot of time in between."

"I understand. And part of the reason I'm in Harmony is to figure all of that out."

"Well, if Herbert Henderson is really your grandfather, I'd say you'll have a lot of wise counsel. He's a crackerjack, that one."

"You know him well?" Tangie asked, taking a seat at one of the barstools in front of the counter.

"He buys kolaches and donuts for his Sunday school class every Sunday morning. He's got quite a sweet tooth. My boys were always partial to sweets, too."

"Tell me about your boys." Tangie leaned against the countertop, ready to learn more about her new friend.

"What's to tell? They're boys. And besides, if you go to your grandpa's church, you probably know at least one of them."

"Wait. Who?"

"My oldest, Gregg. He plays the guitar and sings."

Tangie stared at Penny, stunned. "Gregg Burke. . .is your son?"

"Well, sure. I thought you knew that. Figured your grandfather told you."

"Grandpa didn't say anything." Tangie would have to remember to throttle him later. How interesting, that she would end up working with Gregg at the church and with his mother at the bakery.

She startled back to attention. Turning to her new boss, she asked, "When would you like me to start?"

Penny reached behind the counter and came up with an apron with the words SWEET HARMONY emblazoned on the front. "How about right now? I've got to make a run to the doctor in Trenton."

"Trenton?"

"Yep. Planned to close the place down for the rest of the day, but I'd rather leave it open, if you're up to it. Can you handle the register until I get back?"

"Mmm, sure." Tangie slipped the apron over her head. "I operated the cash register at our candy store for years as a teen. Anything else?"

"Yes, let me run over a few things with you." Penny quickly went over the price list, focusing on the special of the day—two cream-filled donuts and hot cocoa for three dollars. Then she gave Tangie a quick tour of the building. When they finished, the older woman turned to her with a smile. "Do you think you'll be okay?"

"Should be."

"Great. Oh, one more thing. When the timer goes off, pull those cookies out of the oven and set them on the rack to cool." Penny pointed to the tall chrome double oven and then reached for her purse. "Wish I didn't have to go at all, but I won't be long." She took a few steps toward the door, but then turned back. "Oh, and if you see an older fellow—about my age—with white hair and a thick moustache, don't sell him a thing."

"W–what? Why?" Tangie asked.

"That's Bob Jennings. He's a diabetic. Comes in nearly every afternoon around this time, begging for sweets. His wife would kill me if I actually sold him anything."

"Why don't you offer sugar-free options?" Tangie asked. "We sell a whole line of sugar-free candies at our store."

Penny put her hands on her hips. "See! That's why I need you. Now that you're here. . ." Her voice faded as the door slammed closed behind her. Tangie watched through the plate-glass window as Penny scurried down the sidewalk toward the parking lot, talking to herself.

"Lord, how am I going to give her all of the help she needs in only three months?" Three years might be more workable. Still, all that stuff about not giving up on your dreams. . .was the Lord speaking through Penny, perhaps? Stranger things had happened. Maybe God's plan for Tangie included at least one more shot at Broadway.

"April." She whispered the word. Auditions for *A Woman in Love* were going to be held just after the Easter production, according to Marti. And Vincent Cason, the director, had specifically asked about Tangie for the lead. Though flattered, the idea of going back home to the Big Apple scared her senseless. On the other hand, she didn't want to miss God. Was He wooing her back to finish what He'd started four years ago, perhaps?

Minutes later, a customer arrived—a woman ordering a wedding cake. Thankfully, Tangie had some experience with cakes. Her mom made ice cream cakes for brides all the time. How different could a baked cake be? She located Penny's sample book and walked the young woman—who introduced herself as Brenna—through the process.

"I've already talked to Penny about the size and style," Brenna explained. "We settled on a four-tier with cream cheese frosting. But I wasn't sure about my wedding colors until this week."

"Sounds like I'll need some specifics about the wedding, then," Tangie said, reaching for a tablet.

"The wedding is on April 14," Brenna responded with a smile. "I've waited for years for Mr. Right, and now that I've found him, I can't stand waiting three months. Is that silly?"

"Doesn't sound silly at all. What's the point in a long engagement when you've done nothing but wait up till then?" She scribbled the date on the notepad and then looked up at Brenna. "Where is the wedding taking place?"

"Harmony Community Church."

"Oh, that's my church," Tangie said.

"Really? I don't recognize you. But then again, that church is growing like wildfire, so it's getting harder to recognize everyone."

"I'm new. They just hired me to direct the children's plays."

"Oh, wait. . ." Brenna looked at her with renewed interest. "Is your name Tangie or something like that?"

"Yes."

Brenna nodded. "I was working in the nursery the week you were introduced, but my son Cody told me all about you. He's scared to death I'm going to make him be in the next play. He, um. . .well, he didn't have the best time in the last one."

"Ah." So this was Cody's mom. "Well, I think I can safely say this one will be more fun." She hoped.

"It's hard, being a single mom and trying to keep your son interested in things going on at church." Brenna's words were followed by a dramatic sigh. "I have to practically wrestle with him just to get him through the kids' church door on Sunday mornings. I'll be so glad when Phil and I get married. He's going to be a great dad for Cody."

Tangie paused to think about the little boy. Gran-Gran had mentioned he came from a single-parent home, but didn't say anything about an upcoming wedding. Then again, maybe she didn't know.

Nah. Scratch that. In Harmony, pretty much everyone knew everyone else's business. And then some.

"Let's talk more about the cake," Tangie said, offering Brenna a seat. "What are your wedding colors and what type of flowers will you carry?"

"The bridesmaids' dresses are blue and the flowers are coral and white. Lilies. I know Penny can make the lilies because I've seen her sugar-work in the past."

"Wonderful. I'll just write this down and give it to her when she gets back," Tangie explained. "If she has any questions, I'm sure she'll call. And I'll let her take care of getting your deposit."

"Oh, no bother." Brenna reached into her purse for her checkbook. "We've already talked through this part. I'm leaving a hundred dollar deposit today and will pay the rest the week before the wedding."

They wrapped up their meeting and Brenna rose to leave. Afterward, Tangie went to work in the back room, tidying things up. Looked like Penny hadn't stayed on top of that. Likely her workload was too great.

About three hours later Penny returned, looking a bit winded. "Sorry, hon. But it's gonna be like this till my treatments end."

"Your treatments?"

"Forgot to mention that part, didn't I? I drive over to Trenton for chemo two days a week. Breast cancer. I was just diagnosed about two months ago."

"Oh, Penny. I'm so sorry." Tangie shook her head. "You should have told me."

With the wave of a hand, Penny went back to work. "I'm trying not to let it consume me. But I must warn you"—she began to look a little pale—"that sometimes my stomach doesn't handle the chemo very well."

At that, she sprinted to the back room. Tangie followed along behind her, stopping at the restroom door. "You okay in there?" she called out.

"Mm-hmm." Penny groaned. "Nothing I haven't been through before." After a pause, she hollered, "Would you mind putting another batch of sugar cookies in the oven? The after-school crowd will be here in less than an hour, and I'm not ready for them. The cookie dough is already rolled into balls in the walk-in refrigerator. Just put a dozen on each tray. Bake them for ten minutes."

"Of course." Tangie carried on with her work, silently ushering up a prayer for Penny. Looked like she needed all the prayers she could get.

❧

Gregg sat at his desk, reading over the script Tangie had e-mailed. Though different from anything he would have ever chosen, he had to admit the story line was clever, and probably something the kids would really get into. He would play along, for the sake of time—and in the spirit of cooperation. But as for whether or not he would enjoy it? That was another thing altogether.

He exhaled, releasing some of the tension of the day. In some ways, it felt like things were spinning out of control. Not that he ever had any control, really. But the illusion of having any was quickly fading. Gregg couldn't control the things his mother was going through. He couldn't control things with Ashley, who'd just informed him she might give her relationship with her old boyfriend another try. And he certainly couldn't control the madness surrounding Tangie Carini and the kids' musical.

"Lord, what are you trying to show me here?"

As if in response, Gregg's gaze shifted up to the plaque on the wall, one the choir members had given him for his last birthday. He smiled as he read the familiar scripture: FINALLY, ALL OF YOU, LIVE IN HARMONY WITH ONE ANOTHER. 1 PET. 3:8. He smiled as he thought about the irony. *Live in harmony.*

Sometimes it was easier living in the *town* than living in the sort of harmonious state the scripture referred to. Still, he'd give it his best shot. God was calling him to no less.

With a renewed sense of purpose, Gregg turned back to his work.

Chapter 9

On the following Sunday afternoon, Tangie stood in the fellowship hall, preparing herself for the auditions. She placed tidy stacks of audition forms on the table, alongside freshly sharpened pencils and bottles of water for the directors. Brittany had agreed to help, thank goodness. And Gregg would take care of the vocal auditions. Yes, everything was coming together quite nicely. Now, if only they could find the right kids for each role, then all would be well.

"Ready for the big day?"

She turned as she heard Gregg's voice. "Hey. Glad you're here. I want to run this form by you before the kids arrive."

"What form?" Gregg drew close and glanced at the papers in her hand. "What have you got there?"

"Oh, it's an audition form, designed especially for today. Look." She held one up for his inspection. "See this section at the top? Brittany and I will use this section for the drama auditions. There's a column for characterization— does the child really look and act the part? Then there's another for inflection, another for expression, and another for volume. It's pretty straightforward. You'll see a spot at the top where the child fills out his or her name, age, and prior experience on the stage."

"Ah ha." He seemed to be scrutinizing the page.

"I've created a separate section at the bottom for the vocal auditions," Tangie added, pointing. "It gives you a place to comment on things like pitch, projection, harmonization skills, tone, and so forth."

He pursed his lips, then said, "Good idea. We could've used something like that when we auditioned the kids at Christmastime."

His words of affirmation warmed Tangie's heart. "Did you use some sort of form for the Christmas play?"

"Nope. The whole thing was organized chaos. We were all in the room at the same time."

"That's your first problem." Tangie laughed. "It's always better to hold auditions in a private setting, one at a time. Helps the child relax and that way they can't copy from one another." Tangie spoke from experience. She'd been through too many open auditions where candidates tripped all over themselves to one-up the people who'd gone before them. But none of that here. No sir.

"I never thought of doing it this way." Gregg shook his head. "But I'm always open to ideas. When we did the last auditions, it literally took all day. Each child wanted to audition for half a dozen parts. And then there were the would-be soloists." He groaned. "You wouldn't believe how many times I had to listen to 'Silent Night.' Trust me, it wasn't a silent night. Chaotic, yes. Silent, no." He offered up a winsome smile and for the first time, she saw a glimmer of hope.

"Well, here's something I've learned from other shows I've been in," Tangie said. "It's best to get the music auditions over with first. That way, you can mark on the form if you think the child can handle a lead role before I ever let him or her read for a part. Then I'll know which roles they can and can't be considered for."

"Sounds like a good plan. I'll have your grandmother bring the child's form to you after the vocal audition. That way the kids can't see what we're doing."

Tangie nodded. "Oh, one more thing. . ." She handed him a stack of the papers. "Some of the kids probably won't be interested in auditioning for vocal solos, so they can come straight to the drama audition. I've got plenty of roles to go around, and many of them aren't singing roles."

"I'd still like all of the children to be in the choir, though," he added. "We need as many voices as we can get."

"Well, let's talk about that afterward, okay?" She gave him a pensive look. "Not every child is an actor, but not every child is a vocalist, either. Some aren't crazy about singing in a group. So, why don't we pray about that?"

For a moment, he looked as if he might refute her. Then, just as quickly, he nodded. "I'm sure the sanctuary is about to burst at the seams with kids by now. Let's get in there and give our instructions. Then we'll start."

"Before we do, would you mind if we prayed about this?"

"Of course not."

As a matter of habit, Tangie reached to take his hand. She bowed her head and ushered up a passionate prayer that the Lord's will would be done in these auditions—that exactly the right child would get each part.

"And, Lord," she continued, "if there's a child here who hasn't come to know You, may this be the production that leads him or her to You. And for those who do know You, Father, please use these next few weeks to stir up the gifts You've placed in each boy and girl. Help develop them into the person they will one day be."

"And, Lord," Gregg threw in, "we ask for Your will regarding the ones who don't fit in. Show us what to do with the ones who are, well, difficult."

They closed out the prayer with a quick "Amen," and Gregg's smile warmed Tangie's heart. "Thanks for suggesting that. I always pray with the kids before every practice, but I never thought about actually praying for the audition process before the fact."

"It always helps." She shrugged. "And besides, if we ask God to be at the center of it, then—when we're in the throes of rehearsing and things are getting rough—we can be sure that we've really chosen the right people for the job. We won't be tempted to toss the baby out with the bath water."

He quirked a brow and she laughed.

"I just mean we won't be tempted to take the part away from him—or her—and give it to someone else. If we pray about this ahead of time, then we're confident that God has special plans for that particular child in that role. See what I mean?"

"Yes." He nodded. "But I never really thought about it like that before. I guess I never saw this whole process as being terribly spiritual. It's just a kids' play."

"Oh no." She shook her head. "It's not just a kids' play. It's so much more than that." Tangie was tempted to dive into a lengthy discussion, but one glance at her watch served as a reminder that dozens of kids waited in the sanctuary.

"After you," she said, pointing.

He turned her way one last time, a curious expression on his face. "Before we start, I just have one question."

"Sure. What's up?"

"I just need to know. . .what *are* you wearing?" He pointed to her beret, which she pulled off and gripped with a smile.

"Ah. My cap. I always wear it on audition day. It puts me in a theatrical frame of mind."

"Mm-hmm." He chuckled, and they headed off together to face the energetic mob.

❧

Gregg looked up as Margaret Sanderson entered the choir room, a confident smile lighting her cherub-like face. She wore her hair in tight ringlets, and her dress—an over-the-top frills number—convinced him she was here to do business.

"Good to see you, Margaret. Are you ready to audition for us?" Gregg asked, trying to remain positive.

Margaret nodded. "Oh, I am. And my mother says I should tell you that I'm interested in trying out for the leading role."

"Yes, but would you be willing to take any role if you don't get a lead?" It was a fair question, one Gregg planned to ask every child who auditioned.

Margaret paused and bit her lip. After a second, she said, "I, well, I guess. But my mom says I have the best voice in the whole church."

"Ah." Gregg stifled a laugh and looked down at his papers. "You do have a nice singing voice," he said. "But, of course, we have to listen to everyone before making our decision."

He took a seat at his piano and began to play the introduction to "Amazing

Grace," the song he'd instructed all of the children to prepare in advance.

Margaret interrupted him, setting a piece of music down in front of him. "I've brought my own audition music. I would prefer to sing *it*—if you don't mind. My mother says it showcases my voice." She belted out "The Lullaby of Broadway," which to her credit, did sound pretty good.

Gregg covered her form with high marks, then handed it to Tangie's grandmother, who had agreed to run interference between the music department and the drama department.

Next Cody arrived. His mother practically pushed him in the door. "Go on in, son. You can do this."

"But I don't want to!" He groaned, then eased his way toward the piano.

"Lord, give me strength," Gregg whispered. "This one tries my patience." He turned to the youngster with a smile. "Cody, let's hear a couple lines of 'Amazing Grace.'"

The boy groaned. "Remember we did this last time? I stink. Why do I have to do it again?"

Gregg began to play. "Well, you've had some musical experience since then. Maybe there's been some improvement."

Cody began to sing, just not exactly in the key Gregg happened to be playing at the moment. Looked like nothing had changed, after all. After just a few notes, Cody stopped and crossed his arms at his chest. "See what I mean? I stink."

"Well, I understand Miss Tangie has some drama roles that don't require singing this time around," Gregg said. "So why don't you head on over to the fellowship hall and audition for her?"

"Really? I don't have to sing?"

"That's right."

When Gregg nodded, the youngster looked at him as if he'd just been offered an eleventh hour stay. He sprinted out the door with more exaggerated energy.

The next child in the room was Annabelle Lawrence. She was a sweet thing—probably eight or so—but a little on the shy side. Understandable, since her family was new to the church. As Gregg listened to her sing, he was pleasantly surprised. Nice voice. Very nice. "Have you done any performing, Annabelle?"

She shook her head and spoke in a soft voice. "No, but I think I would like it."

He filled out her form, smiling. Over the two and a half hours, the kids came and went from the room. Gregg heard those who could sing, and those who couldn't. A couple of them insisted upon rapping their audition and one sang "Amazing Grace" in Spanish. In all, the variety was pretty interesting. His favorite was a little boy named Joey who proclaimed, "I want to sing. . .real bad!"

Unfortunately his audition proved that he could. Sing bad, that was.

By the time the afternoon ended, Gregg had a much clearer picture of where they stood. Thankfully, there were some great singers in the bunch. Looked like the Easter production might just turn out okay, after all.

❧

Tangie scribbled note after note as the children came and went from her room. Some were better than others, naturally, but a few were absolutely darling. And, as they read the lines from the play she'd written, the words absolutely sprang to life. There was something so satisfying about hearing her words acted out.

Not that all of the kids were actors. No, a few would be better served in smaller roles, to be sure. And a couple of the ones who could act—though good—struggled with a little too much confidence. There would be plenty of time to work on that.

By the time the last child left, things were looking a little clearer. Yes, Tangie could almost see which child would fit which part. Now all she had to do was convince Gregg. Then. . .let the show begin!

Chapter 10

After the auditions ended, Tangie sat with papers in hand, going over every note. Looked like this was going to be easier than she'd first thought. Some of the kids were obvious; others, not so much.

She laughed as she read some of the forms. Under PRIOR EXPERIENCE, one little boy had written *I sing in the shower*. One of the girls had scribbled the words, *Broadway, Here I Come!*

Ah, yes. Margaret Sanderson. Tangie sighed as she looked at the youngster's rèsumè, complete with head shot. "She really wants the lead role something awful."

Awful being the key word. The little darling had pretty much insisted she get the part. That didn't sit well with Tangie.

She flipped through the forms until she found one for a little girl named Annabelle. Though Annabelle had no prior experience, there was something about her that had captivated Tangie right away. Her sweet expression as she read the lines. Her genuine emotion as she took on the character of the littlest sheep. Sure, she needed a bit of work. Maybe more than a bit. But Tangie always rooted for the underdog. Nothing new there. And from Gregg's notes, she could tell the child had a wonderful singing voice.

Tangie yawned and looked at Brittany, who laughed.

"Had enough fun for one day?" the teen asked.

"Mm-hmm. Don't think I could do this for a living." Tangie paused a moment, then added, "Oh, yeah. I already do." A grin followed.

"I'm still hoping you'll think about that community theater idea," Brittany said, her brow wrinkling as she spoke.

Tangie sighed, not wanting to burst the teen's bubble. How could she tell her she was thinking of leaving Harmony in April? Today wasn't the day.

Tangie turned her attention back to the audition forms, placing them in three stacks: To be considered for a lead. To be considered for a smaller role. To be dealt with. Thankfully, the "To be dealt with" pile was the smallest of the three. Still, it contained Cody's form. Poor guy couldn't sing or act, at least from what she could tell. "Lord," she whispered, "show us where to place him. I don't want to put him—or us—through any more agony than necessary."

As she pondered the possibilities, Gregg entered the room, a look of exhaustion on his face.

"How did the vocal auditions go?" she asked. "Or is that a silly question?"

He shrugged. "Not too bad, actually. Things were a lot smoother with the forms you created. Still, if I have to hear 'Amazing Grace' one more time. . ." He laughed. "I just don't know if I can take it."

"Any ideas about lead roles?" Tangie asked, preparing herself to show Gregg the completed audition forms. "Because I have so many thoughts rolling through my head right now." She picked up the first stack of papers, ready to dive in.

He looked at the papers and grinned. "I have a few ideas, but let me ask you a question first."

"Sure."

"Did you really stack those forms like that, or did someone else do it?"

"I did it." She shrugged. "I'm usually right-brained, but not when it comes to something like this. When it comes to the important stuff, I have all my ducks in a row." She paused a moment, then added, "Why do you ask?"

He shrugged. "It's just that I'm like that. . .pretty much all the time. You should see the stacks of mail at my place." A boyish grin lit his face. He paused a moment, then asked, "Are you hungry?"

"Starved." Tangie nodded, hoping her grumbling stomach wouldn't show him just how hungry she was.

"Want to go to the diner for some food? It's open late and we can eat while we talk. I'll drive, if it's okay with you."

"Sounds amazing."

"As in 'Amazing Grace'?"

Tangie laughed.

Brittany spoke up, interrupting their conversation. "Tangie, I told my mom I'd be home right after auditions. I've got school tomorrow."

"Thank you so much for your help." Tangie smiled at the exuberant teen. "Don't think I could've done it without you."

"Sure you could've." Brittany grinned. "But I'm glad you didn't choose to."

Ten minutes later, amid steaming cups of coffee and tea, Tangie spread the audition forms across the table. "Let's start with the ones who can sing."

"Sure. We have quite a few in that category." Gregg took a drink of his coffee, thumbing through the forms. "Now, Margaret Sanderson will play the lead, right? She's by far our best singer."

Tangie bit her tongue, willing herself not to knee-jerk. This was bound to be a source of contention.

"She's our strongest vocalist *and* has a lot of experience." Gregg looked over her form, nodding as he read the comments. "And she's tiny enough to play the role of the little sheep, don't you think?"

"Yes, she's the right size, but. . .well, experience isn't always the only thing to consider."

"What do you mean?" He looked up from the form, a puzzled expression on his face.

Tangie leaned her elbows onto the table and stared at Gregg. "Don't you think she's a little. . .well. . .stuck-up?"

"Hmm." He shrugged. "*Stuck-up* might not be the words I would've come up with. When you're really good at something, sometimes you come across as overly confident."

"She's overly confident, all right. She pretty much told me I was giving her the lead in the show. And you should hear what her mother's been saying to people."

Gregg laughed. "She's used to getting her way. I've seen that side of her before."

Tangie opted to change gears. "What about Annabelle? How did she do in the vocal audition?"

"Annabelle Lawrence? The new girl?" He shuffled through his papers until he found the right one. "Oh, right. She had a nice voice for someone with no experience. Pitch was pretty good. Nice tone. But she's not a strong performer."

"What do you mean?" Tangie felt more than a little rankled at that comment. "She did a great job in the drama auditions."

"Really? Hmm." Gregg shrugged. "Well, maybe you can give her a small part or something. And she can always sing in the choir."

"I don't think you're hearing me," Tangie said, feeling her temper mount. "If Annabelle can sing, I'd like to consider her for the lead role."

Gregg paled, then took another swig of his coffee. "Lead role? Are. . .are you serious?"

"Of course." Tangie stood her ground. "Why not?"

He shook his head and placed his cup back on the table. "Look, I already botched up the Christmas play. I have a lot to prove with this one. My best shot at pulling this off is using kids who are seasoned. Talented."

"So, this is about making you look good?" Tangie quirked a brow. Looked like he was trying to prove something here, but at whose expense? The kids?

He groaned and shook his head. "Maybe I put too much emphasis on that part. But I feel like I need to redeem myself after what happened before."

"But at whose expense?" She stared him down, curious how he would respond.

"Whose expense?" Gregg looked flustered. "What do you mean?"

"I mean, Margaret Sanderson is at a crossroads. She's a little diva and she needs to understand that she won't always be the one in the lead role. Sometimes the underdog needs a chance."

At once, Tangie's hands began to tremble. Something about the word *underdog* sent a shiver down her spine. How often had she been in that position over the years? Too many to count. Take that last play, for example. The one where she'd been promised the lead, but had had to settle for a bit part in the chorus. She'd handled it as well as could be expected, but when would she get her turn? When would she take center stage?

Tangie sighed, then turned her attention back to the forms. This time she could actually control who landed in which spot. And she would make sure she didn't botch it up.

❧

Gregg stared across the table at Tangie, confused by her words. "Tell me what you're really thinking here, Tangie. How many grown-up Margaret Sandersons have you had to work with?"

"W–what do you mean?"

"I mean, maybe you're sympathetic toward Annabelle because you can relate to her. That's my guess, anyway. How many times did you try for the lead role and someone like Margaret got it instead?"

Ouch. "A million?" Tangie responded, after absorbing the sting of his question. "But I got over it."

"I'm not so sure you did. I think maybe you're still holding a grudge against leading ladies and want to prove a point. So, you're going to use Margaret to do it. If you prevent her from getting the lead, it will be payback to all of those leading ladies who got the parts you felt you deserved over the years."

Tangie's face paled. "Nothing could be further from the truth," she argued. "It's just that the character of the baby ewe is a really sweet personality and Annabelle can pull that off. Margaret couldn't pull off sweet without a significant amount of work."

"But I want her in the lead because she's the strongest vocalist." Gregg stood his ground on this one. If they put anyone other than Margaret in the role, it would double his workload.

"I have to disagree." The creases between Tangie's brows deepened and she leaned back against her seat, arms tightly crossed.

Gregg stared at her, unsure of what to say next. Why was she going to such lengths to challenge him on this? Margaret was the better singer. Who cared if she had a little attitude problem? They could work with her and she would get over it. Right? Yes, this production would surely give them the platform they needed to further develop her talents while giving her some gentle life lessons along the way.

Tangie began to argue for Annabelle, but Gregg had a hard time staying focused. Thankfully, the waitress showed up to take their order. That gave him a two-minute reprieve. After she left, Tangie dove right back in. They were able to cast everyone in the show—except Margaret and Annabelle. This was an easy one, to his way of thinking. Give Annabelle a smaller part and let Margaret take the lead.

Unfortunately, Tangie refused to bend.

They finished the meal in strained silence. Afterward, Gregg led the way to his car. He'd never had someone get him quite as riled up as he felt right now. As he opened the car door for Tangie, he paused to tell her one more thing. "It's obvious we're two very different people with two very different ways of looking at things."

"What are you saying? That I'm too different for this church? For this town?"

He paused, not knowing how to respond. "I just think we need to pick our battles, Tangie. Some mountains aren't worth dying on."

She stared at him, her big brown eyes screaming out her frustration. "We both need to go home and sleep on this," she suggested. "I'm too tired to make much sense out of things tonight. And besides, we're meeting tomorrow afternoon at the church to finalize things, right? Let's just drop it for now."

"But I don't want to leave it hanging in midair till then." Gregg shook his head. "I want to understand why you're being so stubborn about this. What are you thinking, anyway?"

"I'm thinking this will be a good time to teach Margaret a couple of life lessons. The top dog doesn't always get the bone, Gregg."

"She's a kid, not a golden retriever," he responded.

Back and forth they went, arguing about who should—or shouldn't—play the various roles in the play. All the while, Gregg felt more and more foolish about the words coming out of his mouth. In fact, at one point, he found himself unable to focus on anything other than the pain on her beautiful face and guilt over the fact that he'd put it there.

Tangie's hands began to tremble—likely from the anger—and he reached to take them, suddenly very ashamed of himself for getting her so worked up.

With hands clasped, she stared at him, silence rising up between them. Except for the sound of Gregg's heartbeat, which he imagined she must be able to hear as clearly as he did, everything grew silent.

Then, like a man possessed, Gregg did the unthinkable.

He kissed her.

Chapter 11

On the morning after auditions, Tangie wandered the house in a daze. *He kissed me. He. Kissed. Me.*

"But, why?" She'd done nothing to encourage it, right?

Okay, there had been that one moment when she'd paused from her righteous tirade, captivated by his bright blue eyes. . .eyes that had held her attention a microsecond longer than they should have, perhaps. But had that been enough to cause such a reaction from him? Clearly not. And wasn't he interested in Ashley, anyway? Why would he be so fickle as to kiss the wrong woman?

Hmm. She couldn't exactly accuse others of being fickle when she had flitted from relationship to relationship, could she?

"Still. . ." Tangie paced the living room, her thoughts reeling. "What in the world is wrong with him?"

"Wrong with who?" Gramps asked. "Or would it be whom? I never could get that straight."

"Oh, I. . ." Tangie shook her head, unable to respond. She raked her fingers through her hair. "Never mind."

"What has Gregg done now?" Gramps asked, putting up his fists in mock preparation for a boxing match. "If he's hurt your feelings or gotten you worked up over something, I'll take him down. Just watch and see. I'm not too old to do it."

Tangie chuckled and then released an exaggerated sigh. "Gramps, there are some things about men I will never understand. Not if I live to be a hundred."

"I feel the same way about women, to be honest," he said, and then laughed. "And I'm three-quarters of my way to a hundred, so I don't have a lot of time left to figure it all out. So I guess that makes us even. We're both equally confused."

Yes, confused. That was the word, all right. Everything about the past couple of weeks confused her. Driving in the dead of winter to a town she hardly knew. Taking a job at a church where she didn't fit in. Working with a man who. . .

Whose eyes were the color of a Monet sky. Whose voice sounded like a heavenly choir. When he wasn't chewing her out or accusing her of being too outlandish.

She turned to Gramps with a strained smile, determined not to let him see any more of her frustration or her sudden interest in the music pastor. He'd seen enough already. "Are you hungry? We could go to the bakery." Tangie reached for her keys and then grabbed her coat from the hook in the front hall. "My treat."

"Sweet Harmony? I'd love to!" His eyes lit up. "I'm always up for an éclair or one of those bear claw things. Or both. Just don't tell your grandmother when she gets back from her nibble and dribble group."

"Nibble and dribble?" Tangie turned to him, confused.

He shrugged. "You know. That ladies' tea she goes to every month. It's just an excuse for a bunch of women to sit around and sip tea and nibble on microscopic cookies and cakes and dribble chatter all over one another. Never could figure out the appeal. I'd rather have the real thing from Sweet Harmony. Now there's some sugar you can sink your teeth into."

Tangie laughed. "Ah, I see. Well, I'm in the mood for something over the top, too. But you'll have to hide all of the evidence if you don't want Gran-Gran to know."

"Good idea. I'll bring some chewing gum with me. That'll get rid of the sugar breath and throw your grandmother off track."

"You sound like you've done this before."

He gave her a wink. "Let's hit the road, girlie."

"I'm ready when you are."

All the way, she forced the conversation away from Gregg Burke and toward anything and everything that might cause distraction.

Her thoughts kept drifting back to the auditions. The kids expected the cast list to be posted on Wednesday evening before service. How could they post it if she and Gregg couldn't even come to an agreement? When they met together this afternoon, they would come up with a logical plan. Surely the man could be reasoned with. Right?

Every time she thought about spending time with him, Tangie's thoughts reeled back to that tempestuous kiss. Sure, she'd been kissed before, but never by a man so upset. Gregg had been downright mad at her just seconds before he planted that kiss on her unsuspecting lips. She hadn't seen either coming— the anger or the startling smooch. And both had left her reeling, though for completely different reasons. She didn't know if she wanted to punch his lights out or melt in his arms.

The former certainly held more appeal than the latter, at least at the moment.

Tangie did her best to focus on the road, happy to finally arrive at the bakery. With Gramps leading the way, she entered the shop.

"Hey, Penny," Gramps called out.

"Well, Herbert, it's not Sunday," Penny responded, her brows rising in surprise. "What brings you to the shop today?"

"This granddaughter of mine. She talked me into it. Tangie's got sugar in her veins. It's from all those years working at the candy shop in Atlantic City."

"She's working for me now, you know," Penny said. "And we're talking about adding candies to Sweet Harmony."

"Ya don't say." His eyes lit up.

"Yes. And by the way, Tangie can take home leftovers any afternoon when we close. So, between you and me, you don't have to pay for your sweets anymore. Except on Sundays."

"Are you serious?" From the look on Gramps's face, he might as well have won the lottery. He turned in Tangie's direction. "Well, why didn't you tell me?"

She shrugged. "I didn't know. But we'd better take it easy with the sweets. Don't want your blood sugars to peak."

"My blood sugars are perfect," he explained. Turning to Penny, he said, "So I'll have a bear claw, an éclair, and a half dozen donut holes for good measure."

"Sure you don't want a kolache to go along with that?" Penny asked.

"Why not?" He shrugged.

"Penny might have to mortgage the business to cover that order," Tangie said with a laugh. When his eyes narrowed in concern, she added, "But that's okay. You're worth it, Gramps. You're worth it."

On Monday around noon, Gregg slipped away from the office to grab a bite to eat at home. After taking a few bites of his sandwich, he paced his living room, thinking back over the events of the past twenty-four hours.

He still couldn't get over the fact that Tangie didn't want to cast Margaret Sanderson in the lead role. Didn't make a lick of sense to him. Then again, women didn't make a lick of sense to him.

On the other hand, his *own* actions didn't make sense, either.

Had he really kissed Tangie? Right there, in the diner parking lot for the whole town of Harmony to see? Why? What had prompted such irrational behavior on his part? Something about her had reeled him in. *What is my problem lately? Why is everything upside down in my life all of a sudden?*

Something about that crazy, unpredictable girl had gotten to him. And it frustrated him to no end. Gregg took a seat at the piano. . .the place where he always worked out his troubles. Somehow, pounding the black and white keys brought a sense of release. And there was something about turning his troubles into beautiful melodies that lifted his spirits. No, he certainly couldn't stay upset for long with music pouring from his fingertips, could he?

Gregg was halfway into a worship medley when the doorbell rang. He answered the door, stunned to see his younger brother.

"Josh?" Gregg swung the door back and grinned. "You should tell a person when you're coming for a visit."

"Why?" Josh shook off the snow and shivered in an exaggerated sort of way. "It's always so much more fun when I just show up. Besides, you know I don't stay in one place very long. I always end up back here, in Harmony."

"Yes, but you're back sooner than usual this time. What happened in New York?"

Josh shrugged as he eased his way through the front door. "Oh, you know. A little of this, a little of that. More this than that."

"Mm-hmm. What's her name?"

After a moment's pause, Josh offered up a dramatic sigh. "Julia."

"She broke your heart?"

"No, but her boyfriend almost broke my nose." Josh grinned, then rubbed his nose, making a funny face.

"You've got to get past this thing where you jump from girl to girl," Gregg said. "It's not healthy—for you or the girls."

"Might work for you to dedicate yourself to one at a time, but I'm not wired that way." Josh shrugged. "Got anything to eat in that refrigerator of yours?"

"Sure. Help yourself." Gregg sat back down at the piano and continued to play. A few minutes later, Josh showed up in the living room with a sandwich in hand. "That's a great piece you're playing. What do you call that?"

Gregg looked up from the piano and shook his head. "Not sure yet. I'm just making it up as I go along."

"No way." Josh smiled. "I thought it was a real song."

"It will be." Gregg allowed a few more notes to trip from his fingertips, then turned around on the piano bench to face his younger brother. They hadn't seen each other in months. And knowing Josh, he wouldn't be here for long.

Gregg spent the next hour talking to his brother—catching up on the time they'd been apart.

"I've been talking to Mom at least once a week," Josh said. "So, I know everything that's going on. She's doing better than I thought she would."

"Yes. Does she know you're back?"

"Yeah. I stopped by the shop just now. She seems to be doing okay. I hear she's hired someone to help."

"Yes. Someone I know pretty well, actually. A girl from church."

Josh's brows elevated. "Oh?"

"She's not someone you would be interested in. She's a little on the wacky side."

"I like wacky. You're the one who picks the straight arrows. Not me."

Gregg changed the direction of the conversation right away, realizing he and Josh were now talking about two completely different things. "I'm glad you're back. Mom really needs us right now."

"I know." Josh nodded. "I might be a wanderer, but even I know when it's time to head home for a while."

"Good." Gregg released a sigh, feeling some of his anxieties lift. "Well, I'm glad you're home. He glanced at the clock on the wall, rising to his feet as he realized the time. "I hate to cut this short, but I've got a meeting at the church in twenty minutes."

"Oh? Should I tag along?"

Gregg shrugged. "A couple of us are meeting in the choir room to talk about the Easter production. Pretty boring stuff, unless you're involved."

"Any beautiful females in the mix?"

Gregg hesitated to answer, knowing his brother's penchant for pretty women. "Oh, you know. Just church ladies." That was only a slight exaggeration. Tangie did go to the church after all, and she was a lady.

"Church ladies." Josh laughed. "Sounds intriguing. Thanks for the invitation. I'd be happy to."

Chapter 12

Tangie looked up from her notes as Gregg and the handsome stranger entered the choir room.

Her heart began to flutter as she turned her attention to Gregg. *Lord, help me through this. I don't know if I'm ever going to be able to look him in the eye again after what happened last night.* If she closed her eyes, she could relive the moment over and over again. Why, oh why, hadn't she pulled away when he leaned in to kiss her? Why had she lingered in his arms, enjoying the unexpected surprise of the moment?

Because she was a fickle girl who fell in love more often than she changed her hair color. And that was pretty often.

As Gregg made introductions, her gaze lingered on Josh. So, this was Gregg's brother. They resembled each other in many ways, but there was something different about Josh. He was younger, sure. And trendier. He certainly wore the name-brand clothes with confidence. The look of assurance—or was that cockiness?—set him apart from Gregg in many ways.

"So, where do you hail from?" she asked Josh as he took the seat across from her.

"Manhattan."

That certainly got Tangie's attention. She turned to him, stunned. "You're kidding. Where do you live in Manhattan?"

"East end. I love the city life. Always seems strange, coming back to Harmony."

"Oh, I know. Tell me about it."

Within seconds the two of them were engaged in a full-on conversation. Tangie could hardly believe it. Finally! Someone who shared her enthusiasm for big city life.

"What do you do for a living?" she asked.

"I'm a reporter. Did some work for the *Times*, but that's a tough gig. A couple of the local papers bought my pieces, but the competition in the city is fierce. So, I'm back in Harmony."

"As always." Gregg walked over to the coffeemaker and switched it on.

"Yeah." Josh shrugged. "I usually come back home when things slow down. The editor at the *Gazette* always gives me my old job back."

"Oh? They let you come and go like that?"

"He's a great guy." Josh sighed and leaned back against the seat. "Not that there's ever much news in this town. But I can always write stories on Mr. Clark's rheumatism and Mrs. Miller's liver condition." He laughed. "Not quite the same buzz as New York City, but it pays the light bill."

"Oh, I understand. I love the city. And you're right. . .it's filled with stories." Tangie dove into a passionate speech about her favorite places to go in Manhattan and before long, she and Josh were in a heated debate over their favorite—and least favorite—restaurants.

"What did you do in New York, anyway?" he asked.

"Tangie's a Broadway star," Gregg interjected.

That certainly caught Tangie's attention. She'd never heard him describe her in such a way. Glancing at Gregg, she tried to figure out if his words were meant to be flattering or sarcastic. The expression on his face wasn't clear.

"Really?" Josh looked at her with an admiring smile. "You're an actress?"

"Well, technically, I only did a couple of bit parts on Broadway. Most of my work was in theaters a few blocks away. But I did have a few secondary roles that got written up in the paper."

"Which paper?"

"The *Times*. It was a review of *Happily Never After*. I played the role of Nadine, the embittered ex-girlfriend."

"Wait, I saw that show. It shut down after just a couple of weeks, right?"

Tangie felt her cheeks warm. She looked at Gregg, wondering what he would make of this news.

"Yes. But that's okay. It wasn't one of my favorites. We never found our audience."

"Lost 'em, eh?" He laughed. "Happens to shows all the time. I just hate it for the sake of those involved. And I especially hated writing some of those reviews. It's always tough to crush people."

"Wait. . ." She paused, looking at him intently. "You said you wrote for the paper, but you didn't mention you were a reviewer."

"I'm not. . .technically." He laughed. "But whenever the other reviewers were too busy, I'd fill in. I got stuck with a lot of off-off-Broadway shows and some of them were, well, pretty rank."

"Mm-hmm." A shiver ran down Tangie's spine. Before long, he might start naming some of those not-so-great shows.

"How does a reviewer receive his training, anyway?" she asked. "On the stage or off?"

"Both." Josh shrugged. "In my case, anyway."

"Oh, he's got a lot of experience." Gregg approached the table with a cup of coffee in his hands. "Josh here is quite the actor. He's been in plays since we were kids."

"Really." Tangie scrutinized him. "We need someone to play the role of the shepherd in our Easter production. Would you be interested in auditioning?"

Josh turned her way with a smile. "Now that's a proposition I just might have to consider."

❧

Gregg could have kicked himself the minute he heard Tangie's question. Putting on this Easter production was going to be tough enough. Factoring Josh into the equation would only complicate things further.

"Josh is too—" He was going to say *busy*, when his brother interrupted him. "I'd love to."

"It's for the church," Gregg explained. "And I'm not sure you're the best person for the job."

"Why not?" Josh gave him a pensive look. "You said you needed an actor. I'm here. What else is there to know?"

Gregg bit his tongue. Literally. Josh's walk with the Lord wasn't as strong as it once was. In fact, Gregg couldn't be sure where his brother was in his spiritual journey. In order to play the lead—the character of the Good Shepherd—the actor should, at the very least, understand God's heart toward His children. Right?

Gregg sighed, unsure of where to take this conversation. He'd have to get Tangie alone and explain all this to her. However, from the enthusiastic look on her face, persuading her might not be as easy as he hoped.

Lord, show me what to do here. If You're trying to nudge my brother back home— to You—I don't want to get in the way.

"Okay, everyone." Tangie's words interrupted his thoughts. "Aren't we here to cast a show? Let's get to it."

With a sigh, Gregg turned his attention to the matter at hand.

❧

Tangie arrived home from the meeting, her thoughts going a hundred different directions. Gregg had finally agreed that Annabelle could play the lead, but he wasn't happy about it. Tangie couldn't help but think Gregg was put off by her ideas, across the board. Of course, he just seemed "off" today, anyway. That much was obvious when he knocked over her cup of tea, spilling it all over the table. She could also tell the stuff about his brother being in the play bothered him. . .but why? Sure, Josh was a schmoozer. She knew his type. But Gregg was acting almost. . .jealous. Surely he didn't think Tangie would be interested in Josh.

No, guys like Josh were too familiar. They came and went through your life. Besides, she and Josh had far too much in common. What would be the fun in that?

As she entered the house, Tangie made her way into the kitchen to grab a soda and a snack. With all the goodies from the bakery on hand, she felt sure she'd end up packing on the pounds before long. Especially if she couldn't get her emotions under control. Still, she couldn't stop thinking about Gregg.

About that kiss. Was it keeping him preoccupied today, as well? She hadn't been able to tell while they were together. Maybe he was a better actor than she thought. Or maybe. . . She sighed. Maybe he regretted what he'd done.

As Tangie left the kitchen, a soda in one hand and two peanut butter cookies in the other, she ran into Gran-Gran in the hallway.

"Well, there you are. That meeting went longer than you expected." Her grandmother gave her an odd look. "Everything okay?"

"Yeah." She shrugged. "It took us a while to figure out which child should play which part, and we didn't all agree, even in the end. I guess you could say not everything is as harmonious in Harmony, New Jersey, as it could be," she admitted with a shrug. "Let's just leave it at that."

"Well, don't get too carried away thinking about that," Gran-Gran said. "While you were out on your date with Gregg last night—"

"Date?" Tangie gasped. Did Gran-Gran really think that? "We were having dinner after auditions to discuss casting the play. That's all."

"Okay, well while you were having dinner with Gregg—for two and a half hours—Pastor Dave called, looking for you. He wants you to sing a solo at the Valentine's banquet next week. He said to pick out a love song and e-mail the title to him so Darla can find the piano music."

"W–what? But he's never even heard me sing. How does he know that I can. . ." Tangie pursed her lips and stared at her grandmother.

"What?" Gran-Gran played innocent. "So, I told him you could sing. So what? And I happened to mention that you'd done that great Gershwin review a few years ago off-Broadway. What can I say? The man likes his Gershwin."

"Mm-hmm." Tangie sighed. "So, what am I singing?"

"Oh, that's up to you. Just something sweet and romantic. It is Valentine's, you know." Gran-Gran disappeared into the kitchen, chattering all the way about her favorite tunes from the forties and fifties.

Oh, Gran-Gran, you're the queen of setting people up, aren't you? You planned this whole thing.

Tangie sighed as she thought about Valentine's Day. Last year Tony had taken her to La Mirata, one of her favorite Italian restaurants in the heart of the city. It had been a magical night. This year would be a far cry from that romantic evening.

Not that romance with Tony was ever genuine. No, ever the actor, he'd managed to convince her she was his leading lady. But, in reality. . .

Well, to say there were others waiting in the wings would be an understatement.

Tangie put the cookies and soda down and went to the piano. Once there, she pulled back the lid, exposing the keys. She let her fingers run across them, surprised to hear the piano was in tune.

"We had it tuned the day you said you were coming," Gran-Gran hollered from the kitchen. "That way you wouldn't have any excuses."

Tangie shook her head and continued to play. Before long, she picked out th chords for one of her favorite Gershwin songs, "Someone to Watch over Me. After a couple times of running through it, she felt a bit more confident.

The words held her in their grip, as always. A good song always did that— grabbed the listener and wouldn't let go. Just like a good book. Or a great pla Yes, anything artistic in nature had the capability of grabbing the onlooker b the throat and holding him or her captive for just a few moments.

Isn't that what the arts were all about? They lifted you from the everyday. . .th mundane. . .and took you to a place where you didn't have to think. Or worry. A you had to do was to let your imagination kick in, and the everyday woes simpl faded away.

❧

Gregg fixed a peanut butter and jelly sandwich, carried it to the small break fast table, and took a seat. He went back over every minute of today's meetin in his mind. Tangie had been awfully impressed with his brother, hadn't she For some reason, a twinge of jealousy shot through Gregg as he thought abou that.

Josh came across as a suave, debonair kind of guy, no doubt. But his motive weren't always pure, especially where women were concerned. And he seeme to have his eye on Tangie. Should Gregg say something to warn her?

No. Not yet, anyway. Right now, he just needed to finish up his sandwich and head over to Sweet Harmony. His mom needed him. And, unlike hi brother, when Mom called. . .Gregg answered.

Chapter 13

As the evening of the Valentine's banquet approached, Tangie faced a mixture of emotions. She found herself torn between being drawn to Gregg and being frustrated with him. Clearly, they were as different as two people could possibly be. And while he seemed attracted to her—at least on the surface—Gregg had never actually voiced anything to confirm that. Other than that one impulsive kiss. The one he never mentioned, even in passing.

Maybe he had multiple personality disorder. Maybe the man who kissed her wasn't Gregg Burke. Maybe it was his romantic counterpart. Tangie laughed, thinking of what a funny stage play that would make. *Slow down, girl. Not everything is a story. Some things are very real.*

The fact that her heart was getting involved after only a few weeks scared Tangie a little. She didn't want to make the same mistake she'd made so many times before. . .falling for a guy just because they were working on a show together. She'd had enough of that, thank you very much. Still, Gregg was different in every conceivable way from the other men she'd known. And his heart for the Lord was evident in everything he did.

Tangie smiled, thinking about the night they'd posted the cast list. The children—well, most of them, anyway—had been ecstatic. Margaret had sulked, naturally, but even she seemed content by the time Tangie explained her role as narrator. Excited, even. Of course, they hadn't faced her mother yet. And then there was the issue of Josh. He'd shown more than a little interest in her, something which ruffled her feathers. She'd finally put him in his place, but would he behave himself during the rehearsals? Had she made a mistake by putting him in such a pivotal role?

With the casting of the show behind her, Tangie could focus on the Valentine's banquet. On the evening of the event, she looked through her clothing items for something appropriate to wear. Thanks to her many theater parties in New York City, she had plenty of evening wear. She settled on a beautiful red and black dress with a bit of an Asian influence. Tony—her one-time Mr. Right—had said she looked like a million bucks in it. But then, he was prone to flattery, wasn't he?

At a quarter till seven, a knock sounded at the door.

"Come in." Tangie sat at the small vanity table, finishing up her makeup but paused to look up as Gran-Gran whistled.

"Tangie." Her grandmother's eyes filled with tears. "I don't believe it."

"Believe what?" She slipped her earrings on and gave herself one last glance.

Gran-Gran drew close. "You look so much like your mother did at this age. And I just had the strangest flashback."

"Oh?" Tangie looked at her with a smile. "What was it?"

Her grandmother's eyes filled with tears. "This was her bedroom, you know. And I remember the day she got married, watching her put on her makeup and fix her hair in that very spot." She pointed to the vanity table, then dabbed at her eyes. "Look at me. I'm a silly old woman."

Tangie rose from her seat and moved in her grandmother's direction. "There's nothing silly about what you just said. I think it's sweet. And it's fun to think that Mom used to get ready in this same room. I guess I never thought about it before." She pointed at her dress. "What do you think? Do I look okay?"

"Oh, honey." Gran-Gran brushed a loose hair from Tangie's face, "I've never seen you look prettier. In fact, I want to get some pictures of you to send to your parents. They're never going to believe you're so dolled up."

"Sure they will. Remember the bridesmaid's dress I wore at Taffie's wedding on the beach? And don't you remember those dresses we wore at Candy's wedding last year?"

"Yes." Gran-Gran nodded. "But I think tonight surpasses them all."

Gramps stuck his head in the door and whistled. "I'm gonna have the prettiest two women at the banquet. How lucky can one guy be?" After a chuckle, he headed off to start the car, hollering, "Don't take too long, ladies. The roads are bad and we'll need a little extra time."

Tangie donned her heavy winter coat and reached for a scarf. After one last glance in the mirror, she grabbed her purse and followed along on her grandmother's heels to the garage, where Gramps was waiting in the now-heated Ford.

"Are you ready for the program tonight?" Gran-Gran asked as they settled into the car.

"I guess so. I found the perfect song."

"Oh?"

"Gershwin, of course. 'Someone to Watch over Me.'"

"I heard you playing it. Of course, I've heard you play a great many things over the past few days. It's good to have music in the house again. But I'm tickled you chose that particular song. It's one of my favorites from when I was a girl."

"Really?"

"Oh yes. I used to be quite the performer. I'd stand in front of that vanity— the same one you used to put on your makeup—and hold a hairbrush in my hand, pretending it was a microphone. Then I'd sing at the top of my lungs.

And I was always putting on little shows and such in the neighborhood."

"Yes, she's always been quite the performer," Gramps added. "She even had a starring role in a community theater show about twenty years ago. Back when we had a community theater, I mean. It's long since been torn down."

"So, what happened?" Tangie asked. "Why did you stop?"

Gran-Gran sighed. "I don't know. Just fizzled out, I guess."

"I can understand that."

"Dreams are like flowers, honey," her grandmother said. "They need watering and tending to. If you neglect them, well, they just die off."

Sad. But true. And hadn't Penny pretty much said the same thing? Dreams needed to be chased after. Tangie wondered if the Lord might be nudging her back to New York to pursue some of those dreams she'd given up on. Perhaps the answer would be clearer in time.

In the meantime, Tangie focused on her grandmother's words as they made the short drive to the church. When they arrived, Tangie searched for Darla, the pianist. Hopefully she would have time to run over her song one last time.

As she rounded the corner near the choir room, Tangie paused. The most beautiful tenor voice rang out. The voice drew her, much like one of the Pied Piper's tunes that captivated children.

She peeked inside the room and caught a glimpse of Gregg, dressed in a dark suit. He stood with his back to her, singing another one of her favorite Gershwin songs, "But Not for Me." She listened intently as he sang the bittersweet words about a man who feared he would never find love. Tangie heard genuine sadness in Gregg's voice. Either that, or his acting skills really were better than he'd let on.

She slipped into the room and sat in a chair at the back. When he finished, she applauded and he turned her way, his cheeks flashing red. "Tangie. I didn't know you were here."

She slowly rose and walked to the piano. "Dave asked me to sing tonight, too. Hope that's okay."

"Of course. He told me. Your grandmother thinks very highly of your singing abilities."

"Hmm." Tangie shrugged. "Well, we'll see if anyone else agrees, or if her opinion of me is highly overrated."

She handed her music to Darla, and the introduction for "Someone to Watch over Me" began. With Gregg standing at her side, Tangie started to sing.

❧

Gregg could hardly believe what he was hearing. Tangie's singing voice blew him away. And as she sang the familiar words, he almost felt they were directed at him. *She's looking for someone to watch over her.*

Just as quickly, he chided himself. They were here to work together. Nothing more. Still, as the music flowed from page to page, Gregg found himself captivated by this chameleon who stood before him. She was both actress and singer. And amazing at both, from what he could tell. Not to mention beautiful. In this red and black number, she looked like something straight off the stages of Broadway.

When she ended the song, Gregg shook his head, but didn't speak. He couldn't, really. Not yet, anyway.

Thankfully, he didn't have to. Darla clapped her hands together and turned to him. "I have the most amazing idea," she said, turning pages in the Gershwin book. She dog-eared a couple of pages, then kept flipping, clearly not content as of yet with her choices. "You two need to sing a song together."

"W—what?" Tangie shook her head. "But the banquet starts in ten minutes and we haven't rehearsed anything."

"You won't need to." Darla began to play, her fingers practically dancing across the keys. "You two can pull off a last minute performance, no problem. Trust me. You don't need rehearsal time. You each have the most beautiful voices. And I'm sure the blend will be amazing." She turned to face Tangie. "Now, you sing alto, Tangie. And, Gregg, you sing lead."

"B—but. . ." He gave up on the argument after just one word because the first verse kicked in. He began to warble out the first words to "Embraceable You," fully aware of the fact that he was singing directly to—and with—one of the most beautiful women he'd ever laid eyes on. Within seconds, Tangie added a perfect harmony to his now-solid melody line and they were off and running.

Lord, what are You doing here? First I kiss her, now I'm singing her a love song?

After just one verse, Darla stopped playing and looked back and forth between them, shaking her head. Her gaze landed on Tangie. "You know, for an actress, you're not giving this much effort."

"E—excuse me?" Tangie's eyes widened.

"You're not very believable, I mean. This is a love song. You two act like you're terrified of each other. Can't you hold hands and look each other in the eye while you sing? Something like that? Isn't that what they teach you to do on Broadway? To play the part?"

"Well, yes, but. . ."

Drawing in a deep breath, Gregg took hold of her hands. "We don't want to get Darla mad, trust me. I did that once in a vocal team practice, and she knuckled me in the upper arm."

"Did not," Darla muttered.

"Did, too," he countered. Gregg turned to look at Tangie, unable to hide the smile that wanted to betray his heart. "We might as well go along with this. Besides, tonight is all about romance, and half the people in the room are huge Gershwin fans. So, why not?"

"O—okay."

Darla began the piece again, and this time Gregg held tight to Tangie's ands, singing like a man in love from start to finish. Tangie responded with passion in her eyes—and her voice. If he didn't know her acting skills were so good, Gregg would have to think she really meant the words of the song.

He could barely breathe as the music continued. The voice flowing out of her tonight was pure velvet. And the way they harmonized. . .he could hardly believe it. While he'd sung with hundreds of people over the years, none had blended with his voice like this. Never.

As they wrapped up the last line, Dave stuck his head in the door. "Gregg, are you ready?" He took one look at the two of them holding hands and stared in silence. "Whoa."

Tangie pulled her hands loose and started fidgeting with her hair. She reached to grab her purse and scooted past him. "I'll see you in the fellowship hall. Just holler when you're ready for me."

Darla rose from the piano bench and gave him a knowing look. She, too, left the room. Dave took a couple of steps inside. "Someone having a change of heart?"

"I. . ." Gregg shook his head. "I don't have a clue what's happening."

"That's half the fun of falling in love," Dave said, slapping him on the back. "What fun would it be if you knew what was coming? Let it be a surprise. Besides, you could use a few surprises in your life. You're a little. . .predictable."

"Not always," Gregg countered.

"Oh yeah?" Dave laughed. "Do you realize you always order the same meal at the diner?"

"Well, yeah, but. . ."

"And what about your clothes? Did you realize you always wear a blue button-up shirt on Fridays?"

"Well, that's because Friday was our school color day when I was a kid."

"This isn't grade school, my friend." Dave chuckled. "And what's up with your hair? You've combed it exactly the same way ever since I met you."

"I have?"

"You have. And I'd be willing to bet you're still listening to that same CD I gave you for Christmas last year."

"Well, it's a great CD. I love those songs."

"Mm-hmm." Dave paused, his eyes narrowing. "You eat the same foods, you keep the same routine, you wear the same clothes. And your office is meticulous. Can't you mess it up, even just a little? Do something different for a change! Live on the edge, bro."

Gregg sighed. "Okay, okay. . .so I'm predictable. But I'm working on it. Wait till you see that new song we're doing in choir on Sunday. I'm trying to stretch myself."

Dave grinned. "That's great. But don't jump *too* far out of the box. Might scare people."

"There's little chance of that." Gregg chuckled as he thought about it. N[e]
where music was concerned, he was liable to stick with what he knew. But i[n]
matters of the heart? Well, that was something altogether different.

❧

Tangie somehow made her way through the meal portion of the banque[t]
nervous about the music, which was scheduled to begin during dessert. Some
thing rather magical had happened in that choir room, something undeniable
She and Gregg sang together as if they'd been born to do so, but there wa[s]
more to it than that. Chemistry. That was really the only word to describe it
And not the kind in a science lab.

As she nibbled on her baked potato, Tangie caught a glimpse of Gregg
who was seated across the table and down a few feet. In his dark suit and tie
he looked really good. She watched as a couple of the young women from
the church vied for his attention. Though polite, he didn't seem particularl[y]
interested in any of them.

"Where's Ashley tonight?" Tangie asked, turning to her grandmother.

"Ah. She's out with an old beau." Gran-Gran's eyebrows elevated. "A gu[y]
from college."

"Oh, I'm sorry she's not going to be here. I was looking forward to hanging
out with her."

"Well, get to know some of the other people your age," her grandmothe[r]
suggested. She nodded in Gregg's direction. "I see someone about your sam[e]
age sitting right there."

"Gran-Gran. No matchmaking."

"Matchmaking? Me?" Her grandmother shook her head. "Heavens, no. [I]
wouldn't think of it."

"Sure you wouldn't. And I'm pretty sure you didn't put Darla up to any
tricks, either."

"Darla? Hmm? What did you say, honey? I'm having a little trouble hearing
you tonight with all of the people talking."

"Sure you are."

The meal wrapped up in short order, and the lights in the room went dow[n]
as the small stage area at the front was lit. Tangie smiled at the decorations
Cupids, hearts, and candles. . .as far as the eye could see.

As Gregg sang his song, Tangie closed her eyes and listened. With her eye[s]
shut, she could almost picture him singing on a huge stage at one of the bigger theaters in New York. He had that kind of voice—the kind that lande[d]
lead roles. Why hadn't he gone that direction? He could've made a lot o[f]
money with a voice like that.

Just as quickly, she knew the answer. His love was the Lord. . .and th[e]
church. She saw it on Sunday mornings as he led worship. She'd witnessed i[t]
on Thursday nights as she walked past the choir room and heard him leading
the choir.

Still, as he crooned the familiar love song, she couldn't help but think of all the possibilities he'd missed out on.

When his song came to an end, Gregg introduced her to the dinner guests. "Ladies and gentlemen, one of our newest members—straight from the stages of New York City—Tangie Carini."

Gran-Gran nudged her. "Your turn, sweetie. Show 'em what you've got."

"I–I'll do my best," she whispered. "But remember, I'm an actress, not really much of a vocalist."

"Humph. That's for us to decide."

As she made her way to the stage, Tangie whispered a prayer. She somehow made it through her song, but found herself facing Gregg, who'd taken a seat at the table nearest the stage. The words poured forth, and she allowed them to emanate with real emotion. How wonderful would it be, to have someone to watch over her? To love her and care for her? Someone with sticking power.

As the song came to a conclusion, the audience erupted in applause. Tangie's cheeks felt warm as she gave a little bow. Then, with her nerves climbing the charts, she nodded in Gregg's direction and he joined her on stage.

"We've decided to try our hand at a duet," he said, after taking the microphone in hand. "Though we haven't had a lot of practice." He turned to Tangie and whispered, "You ready for this?"

She nodded, realizing she was, indeed, ready...for anything life might throw her way.

Chapter 14

The Valentine's banquet ended on a high note, pun intended. Everyone in the place gathered around Tangie and Gregg after they sang, gushing with glowing comments. She heard everything from, "You two are a match made in heaven," to "Best harmony in Harmony!"

Oh, but it *had* felt good to sing with him, hadn't it? And gazing into his eyes, their hands tightly clasped, she could almost picture the two of them doing that. . .forever.

Of course, she might be leaving in April. That would certainly put a damper on forever. Still, she could imagine it all, if even for a moment.

After the crowd dissipated, Tangie helped her grandmother and some of the other women clean the fellowship hall. She noticed that Gregg disappeared and wondered about it, but didn't ask.

Gran-Gran's voice rang out, interrupting her thoughts. "Honey, they need your help in the choir room."

"They? Who are *they*?"

"Oh, I'm pretty sure Darla and Dave are in there with Gregg. Seems like someone said something about putting music away. Or maybe they said something about music for the Easter production. I can't remember." Gran-Gran yawned. "I just know I'm tired."

"Oh, I'm sure this can wait till later. I'm ready to go."

"No." With the wave of a hand, her grandmother shooed her out of the room. "You go on, now. Do whatever you have to do."

Tangie headed off to the choir room, where she found Gregg alone, seated at the piano. With his back turned to her, he didn't see—or hear—her enter. She found herself intrigued by the piece of music pouring out of him. It was truly one of the most beautiful melodies she'd ever heard. Truly anointed.

He continued to play and she drew near, pulling up a chair next to him. Not that he noticed. No, as the music poured forth, his eyes remained closed. For a moment, Tangie wondered if she might be invading his privacy. *Lord, is this how he worships?*

There wasn't time for a response. The music stopped abruptly and Gregg turned her way, a startled look on his face.

"I–I'm sorry." She stood. "I didn't mean to interrupt."

"No, it's fine." His eyes flashed with embarrassment. "I just needed a little alone time after that banquet. Might sound weird, but I usually don't leave the

320

church until I've spent a little time on the piano. It helps me wind down."

"Makes perfect sense to me." After pausing a moment, she asked the question on her heart. "Did you write that piece?"

He nodded. "I have quite a few worship melodies like that. If you listen on Sunday mornings, sometimes I play them during the quiet times in worship, when people are at the altar praying. There's something about worship music that's so. . ."

"Anointed." They spoke the word together.

"Yes." Gregg nodded. "And to be honest, I like to close out the day with worship because it helps me put things in perspective."

"Me, too," she said. "But I usually just listen to CDs or songs on my MP3 player. Can you play something else?"

He looked her way, their eyes meeting for one magical moment. Then, just as quickly, he turned his attention to the keys. The music that poured forth was truly angelic. She'd never heard anything quite like it. Tangie closed her eyes, lifting her thoughts to the Lord.

As the song ended, she sighed. "Thank you for that. It's good to just slow down and spend some time focusing on the Lord, especially after such a hectic day."

"It was hectic, wasn't it?"

"Yes." She smiled. "But it was wonderful, too. I had such a great time."

He gazed into her eyes, a hint of a smile gracing his lips. "I don't mind saying, you've got one of the best voices I've ever heard."

"I was just going to say the same thing to you." A nervous laugh erupted. Then Tangie glanced up at the clock on the wall and gasped. "Oh no. Gran-Gran and Gramps are waiting for me. I have to go."

"Kind of like Cinderella at the ball?"

She looked at Gregg, curious. "What do you mean?"

He shrugged. "Just when things were getting exciting, Cinderella took off. . . left the prince standing there, holding a shoe in his hand."

"Well, my feet are aching in these shoes, but I promise not to leave them with you." Tangie rose and grinned. *Though you definitely look like prince material in that suit.* "But I do have to go. Thanks again for the great evening."

"Hang on and I'll walk with you. I just need to turn out the lights in here." He led the way to the light switch by the door. As he flipped it, the room went dark. Standing there, so close she could almost feel his breath against her cheek, Tangie's heart began to race. Seconds later, she felt Gregg's fingertip tracing her cheekbone.

"Life is full of surprises, isn't it?" he whispered.

"Mm-hmm." She reached up with her hand to take his, then gave it a gentle squeeze.

He responded by drawing her into his arms and holding her. Just holding her. No kiss. No drama. Just a warm, embraceable moment, like they'd sung about.

Gregg finally released his hold and stepped back. "They're going to come looking for us if we don't get out there."

"R–right." Tangie smiled at him, wishing the moment could have lasted longer. Still, she didn't want to keep her grandparents waiting.

She walked back into the fellowship hall, stunned to see Gran-Gran missing. "That's so weird. Well, I know Gramps was tired. They're probably waiting in the car." Gregg helped her with her coat, and she wrapped her scarf around her neck.

"I'll walk you out." Gregg turned out the lights and locked the door and they headed to the parking lot, chatting all the way.

She wanted to reach for his hand. In fact, she felt so comfortable around him that she almost did it without thinking. But Tangie stopped herself, realizing that others might see. She didn't want to get the rumor mill started.

When they reached the parking lot, she gasped. "What in the world?"

"Did they leave?" Gregg looked around.

"Surely not. Maybe they just took a spin around the block to warm up the engine or something like that."

She picked up her cell phone and punched in Gran-Gran's number. When her grandmother's sleepy voice came on the line, Tangie realized she must be in bed.

"Gran-Gran?"

"What, honey?"

"Did you forget something?"

"I don't think so." She gave an exaggerated yawn. "What do you mean?"

Tangie shivered against the cold, and Gregg pulled off his coat and draped it over her shoulders. She turned to him with a comforting nod as she responded to her grandmother. "I mean, you left me here."

"Oh, that." A slight giggle from the other end clued her in immediately.

"Gran-Gran, what are you up to?"

"Up to? We were just tired, honey. We're not spring chickens, you know. Gramps has to be home to take his blood pressure medication at a certain time every night."

"He took it before we left. I saw him with my own eyes. And besides, I was only in the choir room fifteen minutes," Tangie argued. "I thought you were waiting on me."

"We started to, but then I noticed Gregg's car was still there, and he lives so close and all. . ."

"Gran-Gran." Tangie shook her head. "You're up to tricks again."

"Me? Tricks?" Another yawn. "What do you mean?"

"Nothing. Just leave your granddaughter stranded in the cold on a winter's night. No problem."

Gran-Gran laughed aloud. "I daresay that handsome choir director will bring you home. And I'm sure there's a heater in his car. So, don't you worry, honey. Just enjoy your time together."

Enjoy our time together? Yep, we've been set up, all right.

As Tangie ended the call, she turned to Gregg, trying to decide how to tell him. Thankfully, she didn't have to.

"They left you?" he asked, his brow wrinkled in concern.

"Yep." She turned to face him with a sigh. "I don't believe it, but. . .they ditched me."

ð

Gregg couldn't help but laugh at the look on Tangie's face. "So, we've been set up."

"Looks that way."

"Someone's doing a little matchmaking."

"Gran-Gran, of course. But I didn't think she'd go this far."

Gregg reached to take Tangie's hand. "Oh, I'm not complaining, trust me. This is probably the first time in my life I'm actually thrilled to be set up."

"R—really?" Tangie's teeth chattered and he laughed.

"Let's get you out of the cold." He walked over to his car and opened the passenger side door. She scooted into the seat and smiled at him as he closed the door in the most gentlemanly fashion he could muster. Then, he came around to the driver's side and settled into his own seat. Turning the key in the ignition, a blast of cold air shot from the vents. "Sorry about that. Takes a while for the air to warm up."

"Good things are worth waiting for," Tangie said, giving another shiver.

He looked her way and smiled. "Yes, they are."

Their eyes met for another one of those magical moments, one that set a hundred butterflies loose in his stomach.

Gregg finally managed to get a few words out. "I. . .I guess I'd better get you home."

They made the drive to Tangie's grandparents' house, and Gregg pulled the car into the driveway, his nerves a jumbled mess.

Tangie smiled at him as he put the car into PARK. "Thanks for the ride. Sorry about all of this."

"Oh, I'm not, trust me." Gregg watched as she opened her door, but then stopped her before she stepped out. "Hey, can you wait just a minute?"

"Oh, sure." She looked at him with that piercing gaze, the one that made him a bumbling schoolboy once again. She pulled the door shut, then turned back to him. "What's up?"

"I, um. . .I just wanted to say something about the other night when I, um. . ."

"Ah." She smiled, suddenly looking like a shy kid. *"That."*

"Yeah, that." He looked down to hide the smile that threatened to betray his heart. "First, I was out of line."

"Oh?" She sounded a little disappointed.

"Yes. I feel like I took advantage of the situation. But"—he looked at her—"I'm not sorry I did it."

In that moment, the tension in the car lifted. Tangie's voice had a childlike quality to it as she whispered, "I'm not sorry, either."

At once, Gregg felt as if his heart might burst into song. Maybe even another Gershwin tune. She wasn't sorry he'd kissed her. That answered every question.

"I'm usually the most predictable guy on planet Earth," he said. "But that kiss. . ."

She grinned. "Was unpredictable?"

"To say the least." He paused a moment. "It was downright impulsive. And it totally threw me." He couldn't stop the smile from creeping up. "In a good way, I mean."

"It feels good to be unpredictable every now and again, doesn't it?" She giggled, and he thought he might very well go sailing off into space.

Yes, it felt good. Mighty good. In fact, he could go on feeling this good for the rest of his life. "I want to say one more thing. I had a great time singing with you tonight. I felt like our harmony was. . ."

"Amazing?"

"Yes." He smiled. "Sometimes life does surprise you, doesn't it? And how interesting that two very different people could sound so totally perfect together."

"Mm-hmm." Tangie sighed. "Just goes to show you. . . We have to give things a chance."

"Yes, we do." He smiled, thankful she'd given him the prompt for what he wanted to say. "And that's really what I wanted to ask you. . .if you'd be willing. . .to give a boring, predictable guy like me a chance."

"You mean *un*boring and *un*predictable, right?" Tangie grinned, her eyebrows elevating mischievously. "I think you've crossed the line into a new life, my friend."

"You—you do?" Gregg never really had time to add anything more than that. Tangie's lips got in the way.

Chapter 15

Rehearsals for the children's production began the last Saturday in February. The children gathered in the sanctuary and, after a quick prayer, were immediately divided into two groups—singing and non-singing. Gregg took the vocalists into the choir room to practice, and Tangie worked with the actors and actresses. For weeks, she'd planned how the rehearsals would go, had even mapped them out on paper, accounting for every minute of time. But now that the moment had arrived, things didn't go exactly as planned.

For one thing, several kids were missing.

"Where's Margaret Sanderson?" she asked, looking around.

"Margaret's not going to be in the play," a little girl named Abigail said. "She's really mad."

"Oh?" Tangie forced herself not to knee-jerk in front of the kids, though everything inside her threatened to do so.

"She wanted to get the main part." Abigail shrugged. "But she didn't."

"All parts are equal in this play," Tangie explained to the group. "There's a saying in theater: 'There are no small parts, only small actors.' In other words, whether your part is little or big isn't the point. It's how much effort you put into it that counts."

"Well, she's not going to put any effort into it, 'cause she's not coming," Abigail said.

Tangie's mind reeled. She'd specifically asked Margaret if she would be willing to accept any role she received, and the little girl had agreed. And now this? *We're not off to a very good start, Lord.*

Out of the corner of her eye, she caught a glimpse of Gregg's brother, Josh, as he swaggered up the center aisle of the church. Tangie glanced at the clock. Yep, just as she thought. He was ten minutes late. Looked like he wasn't taking his role very seriously, at least not yet.

He drew near and whispered, "Sorry I'm late," in her ear, then muttered something about his mom not feeling well. Tangie softened immediately. "Ah. Okay."

After a few seconds of glancing over her notes, she began to call the children to the stage. "Missy, you stand over here. Kevin, stand over there. Cody, take your place upstage right."

"Upstage right?" He gave her a funny look, and she pointed to the spot where he needed to go.

JERSEY SWEETS

Once all the players were in place, Tangie clapped her hands. "Now, let's do a quick read-through of the first scene. Starting with the narrator."

She looked center stage, remembering Margaret—the narrator—was missing. "Hmm. I guess I'll read the narrator's lines." She began to read, but off in the corner one of the boys distracted her. Tangie stopped and looked at Cody, who'd just punched Kevin in the arm. "Cody! What are you doing?"

"He called me a chicken."

"Well, you *are* a chicken," Kevin said with a shrug. "Aren't you playing the part of a chicken in the play?"

"Yeah, but that doesn't mean I want to." Cody groaned, his hands still knotted into tight fists. "My mom is making me do this dumb play just like she made me do the last one. I'm going to be a lousy chicken."

Kevin began to squawk like a chicken and before long, everyone was laughing.

"Hey, at least you're not one of the singing rabbits like me," one of the other boys said. "Can you imagine telling your friends at school you have to wear rabbit ears in a play?"

"Yeah? Well what about me? I'm a sheep," one of the little girls said with a sour look on her face. Everyone began to *baa* and before long, the stage was filled with squawking, bleating, squealing noises representing the entire animal kingdom.

Finally, Tangie had had enough. She felt like throwing her hands up in the air and walking away. If she felt this way on the first day, what was the week of performance going to be like?

A shiver ran down her spine as she thought about it. *One mountain at a time, Tangie. One mountain at a time.*

❧

Gregg sat at the piano, playing a warm-up for the children in the choir. As they "la-la-la'd," he listened closely. They sounded pretty good, for a first rehearsal. One or two of the kiddos were a little off-pitch, but this was certainly better than the Christmas production. Tangie was right—it worked out best for the nonsingers to take acting roles. That way, everyone was happy. Well, mostly. Some of the boys still balked at the various roles they'd been given, but they'd get over it. In time. With therapy. Perhaps before they went off to college.

Out of the corner of his eye, Gregg saw someone come in the back of the room. Margaret Sanderson. According to his schedule, Margaret wasn't supposed to come to the vocal room for another half hour. Perhaps she'd missed the memo. He paused as she approached the piano.

"My mom said I should talk to you." She pushed a loose blond hair behind her ear.

"Oh?"

Margaret crossed her arms at her chest and glared at him. "She's mad."

"Ah ha."

"Really mad." Margaret began to tap her foot on the floor.

"Margaret, I'm sorry she feels that way." Gregg lowered his voice. "But this

326

isn't the time to talk about it. Perhaps you could tell your mom that I'll be happy to meet with her after we're done with the rehearsal."

Margaret sighed. "I don't think she'll come." She shuffled off to the side of the room and took a seat, a scowl on her face.

Wow. Tangie was right about that one. The child did have some major attitude problems. Even more so when she didn't get her way.

The rehearsal continued with few mishaps. Afterward, Margaret's mother met with Gregg in the hallway, voicing her complaints, one after the other.

Gregg did his best to stay cool. "Mrs. Sanderson, I'm sure you can see that we have a lot of talented children in this congregation."

"Humph."

"And we did our best to put the children in the roles where they could grow and develop."

"How is playing the narrator going to help Margaret develop? There's no vocal solo. We're talking about a child with an extraordinary gift here, one who's going to go far. . .if she's given the right opportunities."

"Actually, she does have a solo in the midst of the group numbers. And the narrator threads the show together, after all. Margaret is onstage more than any other character, in fact. So, in that sense, I guess you could say that she's got the lead role."

Mrs. Sanderson's face tightened even further—if that were possible. "Mr. Burke, you and I both know that Margaret should have been given the role of the littlest lamb, the one with the beautiful solo. Instead, you gave it to an unknown."

An unknown? Was she serious? These were children.

For a moment, Gregg had the funniest feeling he'd slipped off into another galaxy, one where determined stage mothers ruled the day and lowly music directors became their subjects. Only, he didn't want to subject himself to this madness—not now, not ever. He immediately prayed that the Lord would guard his tongue.

"Mrs. Sanderson, I'm sorry you and Margaret are disappointed, and I will understand if you withdraw her from the play. However, I want you to know that we've prayed over these decisions. At length. And we feel sure we've placed the children into the roles they have for a reason."

The woman's countenance changed immediately. "So, this is God's doing? Highly unlikely. The God I serve doesn't like to see church folks embarrassed. And this play is going to be an embarrassment to our congregation, just like the last one."

Hang on a minute while I pull the knife from my heart, and then I'll respond. Gregg exhaled slowly. *One. Two. Three. Four. Five.* Then he turned to her, determined to maintain his cool.

"I'm not saying we're perfect, and I certainly can't guarantee this show will be any better than the last one. I can only assure you that we prayed and placed the children accordingly. Again, if you want to pull Margaret from the play, we will miss her. But we will certainly understand."

At this point, he caught a glimpse of Tangie coming up the hallway. She looked as exhausted as he felt. Mrs. Sanderson turned to her, an accusing look in her eye. "We all know who's to blame for this, anyway."

"W–what?" Tangie looked back and forth between them, a shocked look on her face. "What am I being blamed for?"

"You know very well. You waltz in here in those crazy clothes and with that ridiculous spiked-up hair and stir up all kinds of trouble. Obviously, you need glasses."

"G–glasses?"

"Yes. Otherwise you would have already seen that Margaret is the most talented child in this church." Mrs. Sanderson grabbed a teary Margaret by the hand and pulled her down the hallway, muttering all the way.

Tangie looked at Gregg, her eyes wide. "Do I even want to know what that was about?"

"No." He gestured for her to follow him into the choir room, where they both dropped into chairs. "Let's just say she was out of line and leave it at that. And I also need to say that you were right all along about Margaret. Though, to be fair, I can't really blame the child when it's a learned behavior."

"Right." Tangie nodded. "I've met so many drama divas through the years. . . they're getting easier to recognize. Still, I can't help but think Margaret is supposed to be in this play. The Lord wants to soften her heart."

"Sounds like He needs to start with her mom."

Tangie gave Gregg a look of pure sweetness and reached out to touch his arm. "Let's pray about that part, too, okay? I honestly think God has several plans we're unaware of here. Putting on a show is always about so much more than just putting on a show. You know? God is always at work behind the scenes, doing things we can't see or understand. We see the outside. He sees the inside."

Gregg took her hands in his and sighed. "Tangie, you've managed to sum up so many things in that one statement."

"What do you mean?" She looked puzzled.

"I mean, man looks at the outward appearance. God looks at the heart. He's not interested in the clothes we wear—colorful, outlandish, or otherwise."

"Hey, now."

Gregg chuckled. "You get what I'm saying. He's too busy looking at our hearts. And you're right. He's working behind the scenes. I know He has been in my life. . .ever since you arrived. And now you've made me look for the deeper meaning, not just in a kids' play, but in my own life. That's one of the things I love most about you. You *always* look for deeper meaning in everything."

Almost immediately, he realized what he'd said: *One of the things I love most about you.* Wow. A slip of the tongue, perhaps, or was Gregg really starting to fall in love? Gazing into Tangie's eyes, he couldn't help but think it was the latter.

Chapter 16

On the Monday after the first rehearsal, Tangie went to work at the bakery. The place was buzzing with customers from early morning till around eleven. Then things began to slow down.

"People like their sweets early in the morning," Tangie observed, pulling an empty bear claw tray from the glass case.

"And late in the afternoon. The after-school crowd can be quite a handful." Penny wiped her hands on her apron, then leaned against the counter and took a drink from a bottle of water.

"How are you feeling, Penny?"

Penny shrugged as she went to work putting icing on some éclairs. "Chemo's making me pretty squeamish. I've lost ten pounds in the last three weeks alone. And I want to pull this wig off and toss it across the room. Makes my head hot. And it itches."

Tangie offered up a woeful smile. Penny's last statement confirmed a suspicion she'd had all along. So, she did wear a wig. The hair seemed a little too perfect. But if anyone deserved to look extra-special, Penny did. Especially now.

Tangie paused to whisper a little prayer for her new friend. Penny had made it clear how she felt about the Lord, but that didn't stop Tangie. She'd started praying daily about how to reach out to her. What to say. What not to say. She didn't want to get in the way of what God might be doing in Penny's life. *Use me in whatever way You choose, but help me not to overstep my bounds.*

Though she'd worked several days at the bakery now, Tangie still felt a sense of disconnect between herself and Penny. Seemed like the older woman kept her at arm's length. Not that Tangie blamed her. Penny had plenty of other things on her mind right now.

In the meantime, Tangie had a couple of questions, from one female to another. "Penny, can I ask you something?"

"Sure, kid." She continued icing the éclairs, never looking up. Still, Tangie knew she was paying attention.

"Have you ever been in love?"

Penny snorted, nearly dropping her icing bag. "Only ten or twenty times."

"Really?" Tangie looked at her, stunned. "Are you serious?"

"Yes." Penny nodded, then went right back to work. "Remember, I told you those church folks didn't know what to make of me. I was a single mom with two boys and no husband in sight. I guess I was so desperate to find a father

329

for them that I checked under every bush."

"Including the church."

Penny shrugged. "Maybe my motives for attending weren't exactly pure. But, hey, I thought a good Christian man would be just the ticket for my kids, ya know? Most of the ones I knew were pretty nice."

"But, you never found one?"

"Oh, I found a few." She winked. "Problem was, a couple were already involved with other women. And I, um. . .well, I broke up a couple of relationships."

"Ah." Tangie pondered those words. "But you never married any of the men you fell for?"

"No." Penny's expression changed. "Never found one that really suited me or my boys."

"How did Gregg end up working in a church, then?" Tangie began to stack fresh bear claws on the empty tray, more than a little curious about the answer to this question.

Penny closed the glass case and shrugged. "There was one man, a youth pastor, who took an interest in the boys when they were in their teens. Offered to drive them to church. Even paid for Gregg to have voice lessons. He was a great guy. And I seem to recall a female choir teacher at school who spent a little extra time with him. She was a churchgoer. So, I guess he got sucked in that way."

"Ah." So not everyone had rejected them, then. After a moment's pause, Tangie couldn't hold back one particular question. "Has, um. . .has Gregg mentioned anything to you about the play we're doing with the kids?"

"Heavens, yes." Penny laughed as she began to roll out dough for cinnamon rolls. "I've heard all about it. He says you wrote it, too. Is that right?"

"Yeah."

"He told me about the singing rabbits and the little sheep. That part sounded cute. And then there was something about a chicken hatching out of an egg. Did he get that part right?"

"He did." Tangie realized just how silly the whole thing sounded, when described in only a sentence or two. Still, the idea worked for the kids, even if the grown-ups couldn't quite figure it out.

"Well, all I know is, it's a kids' play and I'm no kid." Penny went off on a tangent, going on and on about singing rabbits and dancing chickens. Tangie couldn't tell if she was being made fun of, or if Penny really found the whole thing entertaining.

"I want you to make me a promise." Tangie stopped her work for a moment. She took Penny's hand and squeezed it. "Don't let anyone else's opinions sway you. Promise me you'll come see the play for yourself. The performance is in a couple of weeks. You decide if it's too much fluff or if it's something the kids can relate to."

"You're asking me to take sides?"

"No. I really want to know what you think. Besides, Gregg is working hard at this, and I know he'd love it if you came."

Penny shook her head. "He knows me better than that. I haven't graced the doors of a church in years."

"Well, this Easter might just be a good time to give it a try. What have you got to lose, anyway?"

Penny snorted, then turned back to her work, muttering under her breath. Still, Tangie would not be swayed. Somehow, knowing that this woman—this wonderful, witty woman—was Gregg's mom, made her want to pray all the harder. . .not just for her healing, but for her very soul.

ૐ

On Monday afternoon, just as Gregg closed the door to his office, his cell phone rang. He looked down at the caller ID and smiled. "Hey, Mom," he answered. "What's up?"

"Pull out your rabbit ears, son. Mama's coming to church."

"W–what?" Maybe he was hearing things. "What did you say?"

"Said I'm coming to church. Oh, don't get all worked up. I'm not coming this Sunday or even next. But you give me the date for that rabbit and chicken show you and Tangie are directing, and I'll be there for that."

"Mom, I really wish you'd come on a regular Sunday first. I think your opinion of me will be much higher."

"Are you saying the play's going to be awful?" she asked.

"Well, I can't imagine it will be awful," he said. "Not with Tangie behind the wheel. But let's just say we're off to an interesting start."

"Interesting is good." She let out a yelp, followed by, "Oops! Gotta go. Burned the oatmeal raisin cookies."

As she disappeared from the line, Gregg pondered his mother's words: *"Pull out your rabbit ears, son. Mama's coming to church."*

He couldn't help but laugh. After all these years, the Lord had finally figured out a way to get his mom back in church. And to think. . .she was coming because of a goofy play about singing rabbits. Gregg shook his head, and then laughed. In fact, he laughed so loud—and so long—that the door to Dave's office opened.

"Everything okay out here?" Dave gave him a curious look.

"Yes, sorry." Gregg chuckled. "It's just. . .the strangest thing has happened. I think God has cracked open my mom's shell." Images of the four-foot Easter egg floated through his mind, and Gregg laughed again.

"Oh?" Dave gave him a curious look.

"Let's just say God is using Tangie in more ways than we thought. She's somehow managed to convince my mom to come to church to see the play."

"Oh, really?" Dave's face lit into a smile and he whacked Gregg on the back.

"Well, why didn't you say so? That's awesome news, man."

"Yes, awesome." Just as quickly, the laughter stopped.

"You okay?"

"Yeah." He nodded toward Dave's office. "Is it okay if I come in?"

"Of course. I'm done with my work for the day."

Gregg's emotions took a bit of a turn.

"Why don't you tell me what's going on?" Dave took a seat behind his desk.

"Ever since my mom was diagnosed, I've been so worried that she might. . ." He didn't say the word for fear it might somehow make it true.

"You're afraid she might not make it." Dave leaned his elbows on the desk and gazed at Gregg. "Is that it?"

"Yes. And I think Josh must be worried about that, too. That's why he came back to Harmony, I think. But neither of us has said it out loud. Till now."

"It's good to get it off your chest," Dave said. "Helps you see what you're really dealing with."

"I've been trying to figure out a way to witness to her for weeks now," Gregg admitted. "And every attempt has failed. I couldn't get that woman through the doors of a church if my life depended on it. And now Tangie's done it with a goofy kids' musical."

"First of all, you've been living your life in front of your mom. That's the best witness of all. Second, we can never predict what might—or might not—be a good avenue to get someone in church. That's why we try so many different things. Different things appeal to different people."

"Right." Gregg sighed.

Dave paused a moment, rolling a pen around the desk with his index finger. Finally he looked up. "Can I ask you a question?"

"Sure."

"You somehow feel responsible for what's happened to your mom?"

"Responsible? For her cancer?" Gregg tugged at his collar, unhappy with the turn this conversation had taken.

"Well, not just the cancer. I mean the way her life has turned out. The fact that she's in her early sixties and living alone."

"Ah." Gregg didn't answer for a minute. He needed time to think about what Dave had said. "I guess I do in some ways. I was always the man of the house, you know?"

"Right."

"Had to practically raise Josh. There was no dad around to do it. And I always took care of everything for my mom. I thought I could save the day. You know?"

"I know. I'm an oldest son, too."

"As a kid, I prayed every day for a dad. And when Mom married Steve—my brother's father—I thought I'd finally found one. But then. . .well, anyway, that didn't pan out. But I guess there's some truth to the idea that I somehow feel responsible for my mom. That's why this cancer thing has been so hard."

"You can't fix it."

"R–right." Gregg sucked in a breath, willing the lump in his throat to dissolve. "I, um, I want to see her healed. Whole. And in church, going to those crazy teas and socials and stuff with the other ladies. She's all alone over there at that shop, and I feel so. . ."

"Responsible."

"Yeah. That's why I spend so much time with her and make sure I call her every day."

"Gregg, it's natural for the oldest son to feel responsible, especially one who had to be both father and son at the same time. But I want to free you up by telling you something. Only God can be God."

"W–what?"

"Only God can be God. You can't fill His shoes. They're too big. You've taken on the responsibility of looking after your mom, and that's a good thing. Especially during the chemo. But she's a feisty one. Independent."

"Always has been."

"Yes. And you can't change her now any more than you could when you were little, no matter how hard you try."

"I know." Gregg slumped down in his chair, thinking about Dave's words. "But that's never stopped me from trying."

"God has a plan, and it's bigger than anything you could concoct. He sees the whole stage of our lives. Knows whether we're going to move upstage or down. Knows if the next song is going to be a heart-wrenching melody or a song and dance number. So, go ahead and pray for her. Spend time with her. Make sure her needs are met. But don't overstep your bounds, and don't take on guilt that isn't yours. You were never intended to save your mother's soul."

"W–what?"

"You heard me. You can plant the seeds. You've already done it, in fact. You've lived your life in front of her, expressed your faith, and not held anything back. She's been watching those things, I guarantee you. But, Gregg, it's not your fault she hasn't come to know the Lord yet."

At this point, the dam broke. In one sentence, Dave had freed him from the guilt he'd carried for years. He'd never admitted it to anyone but himself, of course, but that's exactly what he'd believed. . .that he had somehow been responsible, even for his mother's very soul.

Dave rose from his chair and came to Gregg's side of the desk. He laid his hand on his shoulder and spoke in a gentler voice than before. "Witnessing to someone isn't like writing one of your songs."

"What do you mean?"

"I mean, when you write a song, you control where the notes go. Whether the melody moves up or down. When you witness to someone, it's like throwing a few notes out into space and then handing the melody off to that person and to God. It's up to them how the song turns out. Not you."

Gregg thought about Dave's words as he left the office. In fact, he couldn't get them off his mind for the rest of the evening. By the time he rolled into bed that night, he'd made up his mind to let the Lord write the song that was his mother's life.

Chapter 17

The following Saturday, rehearsals for the play moved forward. This time, things were even more chaotic than before. For one thing, Josh didn't show up. Tangie asked Gregg about him about five minutes after two, the projected start time.

"Have you heard from your brother?"

Gregg shook his head. "I know he's been staying at Mom's place, but I don't have a clue why he's not here."

"Ah. I'll try your mom's phone then." Tangie punched in the number, but there was no answer. She turned back to Gregg with a sigh. "Do you think we made a mistake casting him in such a large part? What if he doesn't show?"

"Hmm. I don't have a clue. But I'll try him on his cell." Gregg did just that, but Josh didn't answer. Looked like Tangie would have to read the lines of the Good Shepherd from off-stage. Not that it really mattered. Nothing today seemed to be going according to plan. A couple of the kids were missing, due to the stomach flu. And the ones who attended were rowdier than usual. Take Cody, for instance. Tangie hardly knew what to do with him. As the rehearsal blazed forward, he ran from one side of the stage to the other, making airplane noises, disrupting the work at hand.

Finally, Tangie snapped. "Cody, I'm trying to block this scene, but it's difficult with you moving all over the stage."

That stopped him in his tracks. He froze like a statue, then turned to her in slow motion, an inquisitive look on his face. "What does *block* mean?"

"To block a scene means I tell the players where to stand and where to move. When I say 'Move downstage left,' you go here." She pointed. "And when I say, 'Move to center stage,' you go here." She pointed to the center of the stage and the kids responded with a few "Ah's" and "Oh's."

Oh, if only she could block the kids in real life. Tell them where and when to move. Then they would surely be more obedient. Unfortunately, the characters in her play were better behaved than the kids performing the parts. Over that, she had no control.

Control. Hmm. Seemed she'd lost it completely over the past couple of weeks. And with the Easter production just a month away, Tangie felt like throwing in the towel. But every time she reached that point, the Lord whispered a few words of encouragement in her ear, usually through someone like Gran-Gran or Gregg. Then determination would settle in once again. Tangie would stick with this, no matter what.

Thankfully, there was one piece of good news. A humbled Margaret had come to her during the second rehearsal, asking if she could still play the role of the narrator. Tangie wasn't sure what was behind Margaret's change of heart, but had smiled and responded with, "Of course, honey."

Looked like the Lord was up to something in the child's life. Could it be the result of Tangie's and Gregg's prayers, perhaps? Surely faith really did move mountains.

She watched from the edge of the stage as Margaret delivered each line with rehearsed perfection. Then Tangie turned to Annabelle, listening carefully as the youngster sang her first solo. The precious little girl, though shy, proved to be a great lead character, in spite of her inexperience.

About halfway into the final scene, Gregg's phone rang. "Sorry," he called out. He sprinted to the far side of the stage. From where she stood, Tangie could see him talking to someone, with a look of concern in his eyes. Glancing at her watch, she took note of the time. Three fifteen. The parents would be arriving soon, and she needed to update them on costume requirements. Still, she couldn't focus on that right now. No, she couldn't see past Gregg's wrinkled brow to think of anything else. Something had happened, but what?

When he ended the call, he took a few steps her way and whispered in her ear. "That was Josh. He's taken Mom to the hospital in Trenton. She's had a really bad reaction to her latest round of chemo."

"Oh, no."

Up on the stage, the kids began to recite lines on top of each other, most of them standing in the wrong places or facing the wrong way. Tangie would have to correct them later. Right now she needed to hear the rest of the story about Penny.

Gregg sighed. "She's been having trouble keeping anything down since her last treatment. She's a little dehydrated, is all. They've got her hooked up to IVs."

"Do you need to go? I can handle the kids."

"No, Josh said they're just keeping her on fluids another hour or so and then releasing her. He, um. . .he asked if I would read his lines for him." Gregg smiled. "Actually, he told me how much he missed being with the kids and how much he's looking forward to being in the show."

"Aw, I'm so glad. Maybe God is working on him."

"No doubt. He's also using this situation with Mom—and the play—to accomplish something pretty amazing."

"Sounds like it." Tangie turned her attention back to the kids, who were now scattered every which way across the stage. "Boys and girls, we need to run though that scene again," she called out. "I noticed that some of you weren't standing in the right places and a few of you need to work on your projection skills. Give it your best. Okay?"

They hollered out a resounding, "Okay!" and she began again. Still, as the rehearsal plowed forward, Tangie's thoughts were a hundred miles away.

With a heavy heart, she did her best to focus on the kids.

❧

After the children departed, Gregg and Tangie spent some time cleaning up the mess the kids had left behind in the sanctuary. Then she headed to the office to use the copier. Gregg retreated to the choir room, taking a seat at the piano. Before touching his fingers to the keys, he made another quick call to Josh, and was grateful to hear his mom was now on her way home from the hospital.

Gregg's fingers pressed down on the ivory keys, and he felt instant relief. As the melody to one of his most recent compositions poured out of his fingertips, he reflected on the conversation he'd had with Dave about his mother less than a week ago. "Lord, I don't understand." He pounded out a few more notes. "Why don't you just reach down and touch her? Heal her? Why does she have to go through all of this?"

A few more notes rose and fell from the keys, and then he stopped. Gregg stared at his trembling hands, realizing just how worked up he was. He shook his head, feeling anger rise to the surface like the foam on top of his coffee.

"What is it, Gregg?"

He turned as he heard Tangie's voice. She stood behind him, holding a stack of papers in her hand. When he shook his head again, she placed the papers on the top of the piano, then reached out and put her hands on his shoulders. He relaxed at her touch. Tangie offered a gentle massage as he returned to the keys once more. When he finally stopped playing, she whispered, "What has you so upset? The news about your mom, or something to do with the play?"

"Both." He played a few more notes, finally pausing again.

"I'm ready to listen whenever you want to talk."

This time, Gregg pulled his hands away from the keys. His thoughts shifted to the kids, then back to his mom.

"Might sound crazy," he said at last, "but when I see Cody, I see myself at that age." He turned to face Tangie, emotion welling inside of him.

"You were rowdy and unmanageable and sang in twelve keys at once?" The laugh lines around her eyes told him she didn't quite believe his story. "I'm sorry, but after getting to know you, I'd have to say that's a pretty tough sell. Not buying it."

"No. Just the opposite. But I was the kid from the single family home with the mother who never seemed to fit in." He paused a moment, then whispered, "Did you hear about his mom?"

"Brenna?" Tangie took a seat on the piano bench next to Gregg. "What about her?"

"You know about her wedding and all that."

"Right." Tangie smiled. "Your mom is doing the wedding cake."

Gregg sighed. "Not anymore. Cody took me aside after the rehearsal and told me the wedding is off. Phillip took off to Minnesota without so much as a word of warning to either of them. He sent Brenna an e-mail after he arrived."

"Oh, that poor woman." Tangie rested her head against Gregg's. "And Cody. I can't even imagine how he must feel."

"I can." He drew in a deep, calculated breath as the memories flooded over him. "I grew up in the same situation basically, but back then, people in churches weren't always as kind to single moms. I'm not sure you would believe me if I told you some of the stuff we went through."

"Surely that didn't happen here. . .in Harmony?"

"No, I grew up in a small town called Wallisville, not far from here. Just small enough for everyone to know everyone's business, if you know what I mean."

Tangie laughed. "Harmony feels like that to me, after living in Atlantic City, then the Big Apple."

"Well, I'm talking about a group of people who weren't as kind as the people from Harmony. Instead of befriending my mother, they judged her. They were pretty harsh, actually."

"Whoa." After pausing for a moment, she added, "I know what it feels like to be judged, trust me. Been through my share of that."

A pang of guilt shot through him, and for good reason. Hadn't he once made assumptions about her, based on her appearance?

"Here's the thing. . ." He rested his palms against the edge of the piano bench and peered into her eyes. "My mom wasn't married when she had me."

"Right, I know. She told me all about that." Tangie nodded. "But that's not so uncommon these days, and it's certainly not the fault of the child."

"Oh, that's not what I was getting at. It's just that I was always looking for a father figure. Kind of like Cody." Gregg leaned back in his seat to finish the story. "My mom married Josh's dad when I was three. My dad never even stuck around to see me born. To my knowledge, he has no idea who I am or where I am."

"I–I'm sorry, Gregg."

He shrugged it off. "Anyway, when Mom married Steve, she was already pregnant with Josh. They had him a few months later, but the marriage ended before his first birthday, so it was a double slam dunk. I *finally* had someone to play a fatherly role, and he didn't stick around. That's why. . ." He groaned. "That's why I empathize so much with Cody. It has nothing to do with his ability to sing, or the lack thereof. It's just his situation."

"Well, let me ask you a question," Tangie said, the tenderness in her voice expressing her concern. "Your mom told me a little of this, but she mentioned a couple of specific people who took an interest in you."

"What do you mean?"

"I mean, you eventually got your life on the right track. And you figured out you could sing. Who were those people who took the time to pour into your life? Who led you to the Lord? Who stirred up your gifts?"

"Oh, that's easy. One of the men in our church always treated me kindly. Mr. Jackson. It was through his witness that I came to know Jesus as my Savior. And as for the music, I have my sixth grade choir teacher, Mrs. Anderson, to credit with that. She went to our church, too." As he spoke her name, a rush of feelings swept over him. He hadn't thought about her in years. "To this day, I still remember the joy in her eyes as she talked to me about music and the tenderness in her voice as she responded to my never-ending questions."

Tangie looked at him with interest. "Okay. So, she saw a spark of something in you and fanned it into a flame."

"Right. I remember the day she asked my mother to come to one of those parent-teacher meetings. She told my mom that I was born to sing, that I'd been given a gift."

"Sounds like she and Mr. Jackson played a pretty big role in your life."

"Actually. . . ," Gregg felt tears well up in his eyes as he thought about it, "I used to credit them with saving my life. I was at a crossroads that year. I was going to go one way or the other. And they caught me just in time to point me down the right road. The right road for me, I mean."

"Wow. That's pretty amazing. God's timing is perfect."

"It is." *Thank You, Lord. How often I forget.*

"Okay, well let's go back to talking about Cody, then," Tangie said, her eyes now glowing. "We just need to figure out what his real gift is, so we can begin to stir it."

"Well, he's not a singer, that's for sure." Gregg groaned. "Not even close."

"He does have some minor acting ability."

"Acting up, you mean." Gregg grinned.

"Well, that, too. I could probably turn him into an actor if I could just keep him focused, but I haven't been able to do that," Tangie admitted. "Have you ever heard him talk about anything else?"

"I know he wanted to play baseball last year, but his mom couldn't afford to sign him up. I heard all about it."

"Really?" Tangie's eyes widened in surprise. "Well, I'm not a huge sports fan—haven't really had time to focus on any of them—but it might be fun to test the waters with Cody. When does the season start?"

"Oh. This coming week, I think. I saw a poster at the grocery store just last night."

"Well, here's an idea. If his mom can't afford to sign him up, why don't we raise the funds through the church's benevolence ministry and do it ourselves?"

"Baseball?" Gregg groaned. "I'm terrible at baseball. Don't even like to watch it. It's so. . .slow."

"I know. I feel the same way, but we're probably biased. Besides, I'm not asking you to *play* baseball, just to watch Cody do it. Help him discover his dream. If it is his dream, I mean." Tangie laughed. "It's so hard for me, as an artist, to understand the love of sports. But I suppose some people are as passionate about baseball and basketball as I am about acting and singing."

Gregg shook his head. "Crazy, right?"

"Very. But I definitely think this is something we can do. His mom is probably plenty distracted right now, and I know her finances are probably tapped out, like so many other single moms. We can do this for her. Don't you think?"

Gregg didn't have to think about it very long. "It's the perfect idea. We should do it. And when we do. . ." He looked at her with a smile. "He's going to need someone in the crowd, cheering him on. Want to come to a few practices with me?"

Tangie paused. "If. . .if I'm still here."

Gregg's heart hit the floor. "Are you still thinking of leaving?"

She released a sigh as she gazed at him with pain in her eyes. "I don't know, Gregg. If you'd asked me a couple weeks ago, I would've said yes in a heartbeat. I have so many opportunities waiting for me in New York. But now. . ." She shrugged. "Now I'm not sure which way to turn. But I promise to pray about it."

"Me, too." In his heart, Gregg wanted to add, "I'll pray that God keeps you here, in Harmony." However, he knew better. Tangie needed to chase after her dreams, too.

Even if they didn't include him.

Chapter 18

The week before the Easter performance, the kids met with Tangie and Gregg for their first dress rehearsal. Although Gramps had worked long and hard on building the set pieces, he hadn't quite finished several of them. And though the kids had been told to have all their costumes ready, many did not. Tangie ran around like a chicken with her head cut off—ironic, in light of the many chicken costumes—looking for feathers, rabbit ears, and so forth. She tried to keep her cool, but found it difficult.

In fact, she couldn't think of one thing that had gone as planned, and now that the performance date was approaching, Tangie had to wonder if she'd made a mistake in promising she could pull this off.

As she paused to pin a tiny microphone on a little girl, her thoughts gravitated to a call she'd received just this morning from Marti in New York, urging her to come back for auditions for *A Woman in Love*. Tangie's heart twisted within her as she contemplated the possibilities.

"Vincent says he's had his eye on you for two years," Marti had said. "He thought you did a great job in *Brigadoon* and wants to see you audition for the role of Gina in his new play. You're coming, right? This is the opportunity of a lifetime, Tangie. It's what you've waited for—the lead in a Broadway show."

"I don't know." Tangie's response had been hesitant, at best.

It sounded wonderful, of course, especially in light of the chaos she was facing with the kids. But every time she thought about leaving Gregg. . .well, the lump that rose in her throat grew harder and harder to swallow. She'd fallen for him, from his schoolboy haircut to his geeky tennis shoes. She loved him, and there was no denying it.

Of course, they hadn't really had time to develop their relationship. Who had time to date with a show underway? But if she stayed in Harmony after the production, there would be plenty of time to see where life—and love—might take them. Right?

Oh, Lord, show me what to do. I don't want to miss You this time. If this opportunity on Broadway is what You have for me, then speak clearly, Lord. But if I'm supposed to stay here. . .

The road back to New York might not be a long one, but from where she stood, it seemed like a million miles.

"Miss Tangie!" Cody's scream startled Tangie back to reality.

"W—what, honey?"

"I can't go out there wearing this costume." He pointed to his chicken suit, and a sour expression crossed his face.

Tangie tried to hide her smile as she responded. "Why not?"

"My friends will make fun of me." He plopped down on his bottom on the stage. "Besides, I think I'm getting sick. I have the flu." He sneezed, but she could tell it was forced.

"Well, I'll tell you what," she said, "if you will do this one show dressed as a chicken, I promise never to cast you in a part like this again."

"I don't want to be in any show again," he muttered, pulling at his feathers. "When will people get that?"

Oh, she got it all right. And she had a wonderful surprise for him as soon as the rehearsal ended—a full scholarship to play baseball. She could hardly wait to tell him. And if he chose not to do another show, that would be fine by her, as long as he got to do the things he longed to do, develop the gifts he wanted to develop. But, for now, the boy was going to play a chicken, whether the idea settled well with him or not.

Minutes later, Tangie and Gregg prayed with the kids. Then it was time for the rehearsal to begin. Darla, who'd been looking a little pale today, sat at the piano, ready to play the intro music. The song sounded great. At the end of it, Tangie turned to Gregg and gave him a thumbs-up. He responded with a smile.

At this point, Margaret Sanderson moved to center stage, dressed as a baby chick, ready to deliver her opening lines. Her expression was clean, and her lines were flawless. However, a couple of the kids who followed bumbled theirs pretty badly. Tangie stopped the rehearsal to say something to the cast.

"Kids, I told you we would be *lines off* today."

Cody raised his hand. "What does lines off mean?"

Tangie groaned. "It means you can't use your scripts anymore. The lines are supposed to be memorized."

A round of "Oooh's" went up from the cast, and Tangie slapped herself in the head. She should've explained the term.

"How many of you know your lines?" she asked.

Annabelle and Margaret raised their hands.

"Anyone else?"

A couple of others half-raised theirs. Tangie sighed, then went back to directing the rehearsal. When it came time for Annabelle to sing her solo, Tangie breathed a sigh of relief. Surely this would redeem the day. Or not. Ironically, Annabelle sounded a little. . .strange.

"Everything okay, honey?" Tangie asked, trying not to overreact.

The child pointed to her throat. "I feel a little scratchy, and it hurts when I swallow."

"Oh no." Tangie shook her head. "Well, have your mom talk with me after the rehearsal." She would tell her to have Annabelle gargle with warm salt water and drink hot tea with lemon. Tricks of the trade for actors who'd over-used their voices. In the meantime, they'd better get back to work. The show must go on, after all!

❧

Gregg watched Tangie at work, his heart heavy. With just one week till the production, he had to face the inevitable. She would be leaving him soon, going back to New York. Every fiber of his being cried out for her to stay, but he would never suggest it. No, he of all people understood what it meant to respond to the call of God. If the Lord was calling Tangie to New York, she had to go.

On the other hand, the whole New York thing might just be a distraction, right? Should he mention that? Maybe if he told her that he loved her. . .

No. He wouldn't do that. If she stayed, he wanted it to be because the Lord had spoken, not because Gregg had spoken.

But I do love her.

As he watched her work with the children, he realized his feelings—once small—had grown into a wildfire. Listening to the sound in her voice as she soothed Cody's ruffled feathers. Watching her as she diligently poured into Margaret's life, in spite of the youngster's attitude. Observing the way she continued to nurture the gifts in little Annabelle's life.

Yes, Tangie was truly one of the most amazing women he'd ever met, and easy to love.

But he couldn't tell her. Not yet, anyway.

Chapter 19

Two days before the show, Tangie received a phone call from Annabelle's mother. She could tell by the sound of her voice that something was amiss.

"I'm afraid our little lamb is really sick," Annabelle's mom explained.

"No! What's happened?"

"I don't know. It started out as some sort of virus, I guess. I did everything you said. She gargled with warm salt water and drank hot tea. We've been loading her up on vitamin C and even making her drink orange juice, which she doesn't like. But every day is worse than the day before. What started out as a scratchy throat is now full-blown laryngitis. She can't speak a word."

"Yikes." Tangie wanted to dive into one of those, "Oh, man! What are we going to do now?" speeches, but stopped herself short of doing so. *It's not about the show,* she reminded herself. *It's about the kids.*

Instead of saying too much, she simply offered up a few kind words. "Please tell Annabelle how sorry I am. I hope she feels better."

"I will. And please don't give her part away just yet. We're going to keep her home from school for the next two days, so I'm hoping that will help," Mrs. Lawrence said. "But I wanted to let you know so that you can begin to look for an understudy. . .just in case."

"Right. Good idea."

As she ended the phone conversation, Tangie's mind reeled. An understudy? At this late date? Which of the children was savvy enough to pick up the role this late in the game?

Really, only one person made sense. But Tangie would have to eat a little crow to make this work. She picked up the phone and punched in Margaret Sanderson's number. The child's mother answered on the third ring.

"Mrs. Sanderson, this is Tangie Carini from the church."

"Yes?"

"I, um, have a little problem, and I'm hoping you and Margaret can help me with it."

"Oh?" She could read the curiosity in the woman's voice. "What's happened?"

Tangie went on to explain the predicament, finally asking to speak to Margaret. When the child came on the phone, she listened quietly, and then responded with words that stunned Tangie. "But Annabelle needs to do her art! She's the best at it. Her song is bee-*you*-tee-ful!"

Tangie laughed. "You're right. It is."

"How can I be the narrator and the littlest sheep, too?" Margaret asked.

"Oh, that's easy. The narrator costume covers you from head to toe. It's also ery tall, so you look bigger in it. The little sheep costume is completely dif-rent. I don't think the audience will even realize it's the same person."

"So, you're saying I get to do both parts?" Margaret's voice began to tremble. Both? Not just one?"

"If Annabelle can't be there, yes."

"Mom! Guess what!" Margaret hollered. "They want me to do two different arts." She returned to the phone, sounding a little breathless. "But I don't now Annabelle's song. Not very well, I mean."

"Can you meet me at the church in an hour? We'll go over it then."

"Okay. I'll ask my mom." The youngster hollered once again, finally return-ng to the phone with, "She says it's fine. We'll see you in an hour." After a ause, Margaret said, "Oh, and Miss Tangie. . ."

"Yes, honey?"

"I hope Annabelle gets to do her part. I'm fine with the narrator. Really I m."

Tangie smiled all the way to her toes. "Oh, honey, I'm so proud of you. And have to tell you, you're doing an awesome job with your part. I couldn't be rouder."

As she ended the call, Tangie realized just how true those words were. Mar-aret had come such a long way. Then again, they'd all come a long way.

Oh, but what a great distance they had left to go!

⁂

regg sat on a barstool at the bakery, chatting with his mom as she made ome of her famous homemade cinnamon rolls.

"Mom, can I ask you a question?"

"Sure, son." She continued her work, but glanced up at him with a smile. What's up?"

"I love you so much, but I'm worried about you."

"I know you are, but I'm going to be just fine."

"Still, with all you're going through, why don't you just sell off this place? ick back and relax a little? You deserve it."

"W—what?" She looked at him, a horrified expression on her face. "Close own Sweet Harmony? But why?"

"The shop has brought in all of the money you could need to retire in yle." He shrugged. "You could live stress-free for the rest of your life. I think would be good for you. All of this work is. . .well, it's work. And Josh and want you to be able to take it easy."

"But honey, I'm only sixty-one. I'm not ready to retire yet. Besides. . ."

Her eyes filled with tears. "Coming here every morning gives me a reason
get out of bed. People need me. And I need this shop. It's. . ." She shook h
head. "It's keeping me going. I'm surprised you can't see that."

Immediately, shame washed over Gregg. He'd never considered the fa
that his mom would respond with such passion. "Ah. I'm sorry I brought it u
We just want the best for you, I promise."

"I know you do, honey, but this *is* the best for me. If I keep my body bu
then my mind stays busy, too. If my mind stays busy, then there's no time le
over to. . ."

"To worry?"

"Yes." She nodded, then stretched out the dough for the cinnamon ro
adding cinnamon, sugar, and butter before rolling them. "It's all part
this great plan I've got for getting through this. Keep working. That's t
answer."

"Working helps keep your mind occupied," he said. "But Mom, there's rea
only one answer to getting through this, and it has nothing to do with wor
It's—"

"No lectures, Greggy." She turned to him with a warning look in her ey
"We've been through this. I don't mind hearing you talk about all of the thin
this God of yours has done for you, but I've managed pretty well without Hi
for the first sixty years of my life, and I'll do just fine for the next sixty."

She gave him a wink, but it didn't ease the pain in his heart. What could
do to get through to her?

Just love her, Gregg. Just keep on loving her.

Chapter 20

The afternoon of the final dress rehearsal, Tangie's nerves were a jumbled mess. The kids somehow made it through the show, but there were problems all over the place. Margaret seemed really unsure of herself in Annabelle's part, so she dropped quite a few lines. Darla wasn't feeling well, so Gregg had to play the piano in her place. The set was still incomplete, and some of the costumes still needed work. Tangie didn't know when she'd ever been more stressed or *less* ready to pull off a show.

As the rehearsal continued, Tangie offered up a plea to the Lord for both His mercies and His favor. She also spent a lot of time muttering "The show must go on" under her breath.

The rehearsal ended soon enough and Tangie prayed with the children, then handed out flyers with instructions for tomorrow's curtain call. She went over her notes one last time before releasing them. "Be here an hour before curtain. Have your hair and makeup done ahead of time. Get into costume immediately upon arrival. Meet in the choir room for vocal warm-up and prayer. Do everything you're told to do when you're told to do it."

"I'm never gonna remember all of that stuff," Cody muttered.

"That's why I've given you the flyer," Tangie explained. "Just make sure your parents read it. Oh, and kids. . .spend some time praying for our performance and for the people who will come to see it. That's the most important thing we can do."

That last part hit her especially hard. There would be people in the audience who didn't normally attend church. Some who had never heard the gospel message before. Would they really see the heart of the Good Shepherd shining through in her little play? Could a silly production about bunnies and baby chicks touch people's lives?

Suddenly, she wasn't so sure. All her confidence faded away, leaving behind only doubt.

As they rose from their places on the stage, Tangie used her most animated stage voice to holler, "Break a leg!"

Cody, who'd taken off running the other direction, turned back to look at her with a questioning look on his face. "Huh?"

Tangie hollered out, "Cody, be careful! The set pieces still aren't finished, and I don't want you to—" She never got to say the words "hurt yourself." Cody tripped over a piece of wood behind one of the flats and down it came on top of him, the canvas ripping straight in half.

He stood silent and still in the middle of the torn piece, his eyes as wide as saucers. All around the other children froze in place.

"I'm sorry, Miss Tangie." He groaned and slapped himself in the head. "But I told you I'm no good at this. I don't belong on the stage." He rubbed his ankle. "Besides, you *told* me to break my leg."

Tangie groaned, then rushed to his side to make sure he was okay. Convinced he was, she finally dismissed him. Ready to turn her attention to the ripped backdrop, she switched gears. With Gramps's help, they would get the rest of the set pieces ready before the show.

Less than a minute into the process, she heard her grandmother's voice ring out.

"Tangerine! Yoo-hoo!"

She looked up as Gran-Gran approached the stage, carrying a small box. "I, um, need to talk with you about these programs, honey." She handed one to Tangie, who looked at the cover and smiled.

"Oh, they turned out great."

"Yes and no."

"Yes and no?" Tangie looked at the cover again.

"Well, open one and see what I mean."

Tangie opened the program, realizing right away the text on the inside was upside-down. "Oh, yikes."

"The printer sends his apologies," Gran-Gran said with a shrug.

"Can't he redo them?"

"Unfortunately, he has a big order for another church in town and doesn't have time. But there's some good news."

Tangie handed the program back to her grandmother. "I could use some good news, trust me."

"He gave them to us for half price."

"Well, yippee." Tangie sighed. "I guess we don't have much choice, do we?"

"Look at the bright side. . ." Gran-Gran paused for a few seconds, her brow wrinkled.

"What's that?" Tangie asked.

"I'm trying to think of one." Her grandmother laughed. "But nothing's coming to me."

Tangie knelt to fix the torn backdrop, seaming the backside with heavy tape. However, just a few minutes into it, she heard Gregg's voice ring out from the auditorium. "Tangie, I hate to tell you this. You have no idea how much I hate to tell you this." He climbed the steps to the stage.

With exhaustion eking from every pore, Tangie looked up at him. "What's happened now?"

"It's Darla."

Tangie's heart quickened. "Darla?" She put down the roll of tape and looked into Gregg's eyes. "What's happened to her? She hasn't been in an accident or anything, has she?"

"No, nothing like that." Gregg shook his head. "It's her appendix. They've taken her to surgery to remove it. Doctor says if they'd waited another day it could've been deadly."

"No! Oh, Gregg." Tangie crumpled onto the floor, and the tears started. "What are we going to do? How in the world can we pull this off without Darla? We can't have live music without a musician." On and on she went, bemoaning the fact that the show couldn't possibly go on without the pianist.

Finally, when she regained control of her senses, Tangie sighed. "I'm so sorry. That was completely heartless. I should be saying how bad I feel for Darla, and instead I'm thinking only of myself."

"Well, not only of yourself." Gregg gave her a sympathetic look. "You're thinking of the kids. And the parents. And the other musicians. And the audience. And then, maybe, at the bottom of the list, yourself."

"Right." Tangie shook her head, then whispered, "I give up."

"W–what?"

"You heard me." She looked at him, determination setting in. "I give up. I can't do this. I'm not cut out to handle this much pressure."

"B–but. . .whatever happened to 'The show must go on'? Doesn't that stand for anything?"

"There's a time to admit defeat, Gregg, and this is it. Our leading lady has laryngitis, our set is in pieces, Cody very nearly broke his leg when he tripped earlier, the programs are upside-down, and now Darla can't be here to play the piano for the show."

"Anything else?"

"Yes." She stared at him with tears now flowing. "The drama director is having a nervous breakdown!"

He joined her on the floor and opened his arms to comfort her, but she wasn't having any of it. No, sir. Not today. Today she just wanted everyone to go away and leave her alone.

&

Gregg watched all of this, completely mesmerized. First of all, he'd never seen a grown woman throw a tantrum like this before. He found it almost comical. Entertaining, at the very least. Still, he did his best to hide any hint of a smile. Might just send Tangie over the edge. Looked like she was pretty close already.

Chapter 21

On the Saturday of the big show, Tangie was a nervous wreck. Before she left for the church, she spent some time praying. Only the Lord could pull this off.

She rode to the church with her grandparents, script in hand. Nestled beside her on the back car seat, the box holding the football-sized chocolate egg. Taffie had sent it, along with a note reading, BREAK A LEG. Tangie was half tempted to pick up the phone and tell her about Cody's mishap. Maybe she'd have time for that later. Right now, they had a show to put on.

After the Easter egg hunt, anyway.

She arrived at the church to find Ashley and other children's workers hard at work, putting out Easter eggs in designated areas, according to the ages of the children. Tangie looked at her with a smile. "How's it going?"

Ashley smiled. "Great!" She drew near and whispered, "Have you heard my news?"

"News?" Tangie shifted her script to the other arm and shook her head. "What is it?"

Ashley displayed her left hand, wiggling her ring finger so that there would be no doubt. A sparkling diamond adorned that finger, nestled into a beautiful white-gold setting.

"Oh, Ashley! You're engaged?"

When she nodded, Tangie's joy turned to sorrow. "Does. . .does that mean you're leaving?"

"Nah. Paul and I have talked about it. He has his own Web-design business. He can do that here, in Harmony. So, it looks like we'll settle in here, raise a family. You know." She gave Tangie a wink.

Tangie's stomach tumbled to her toes. *She's assuming that's what Gregg and I will do, too. But I'll be in New York, not Harmony.*

Tangie forced her thoughts back to the present. "I'm thrilled for you!" After a few more words of congratulations, she heard Gregg's voice sound from behind her. Tangie turned around, smiling as she caught a glimpse of him.

"Ready for the big day?" he asked, drawing near.

"As ready as I'll ever be." She sighed, and he gave her an inquisitive look. "What?"

"Well, I guess I should just admit that you were right all along. Doing a play with kids is a lot tougher than it looks. And all of the Broadway experience

350

n the world didn't prepare me for this."

Ashley laughed. "Nothing can prepare you for the chaos of kids, but they're worth it."

"They are."

"And I heard there's some good news where Annabelle's concerned," Gregg said.

"Yes." Tangie grinned. "Her mom called this morning and said she's got her voice back. Said it was a miracle. When Annabelle went to bed last night things weren't any better. But this morning. . ."

"Was a brand-new day." Ashley laughed. "Oh, God is good, isn't He?"

"He is." Tangie smiled—and all the more as guests started arriving. Within the hour, the whole church property was alive with activity. She had never seen so many children. And the Easter baskets! Nearly every child held one.

Except the kids in the production, of course. They hadn't come to hunt for Easter eggs. They were here to do a show.

Tangie glanced at her watch. One o'clock. Time to meet with the cast and crew in the choir room for final instructions. She and Gregg made their way inside, finding a lively crowd waiting for them. She managed to get the kids quieted down, and Gregg opened in prayer. Then he nodded for Tangie to begin.

"Kids, I know you've missed out on some of the activities outside," she told them with a playful smile, "but it will be worth it when that auditorium fills up with neighborhood kids."

Cody raised his hand. "My best friend is here. I already told him I'm wearing a chicken suit and he didn't laugh, so I don't think I'll have to give him a black eye or anything."

"Well, that's nice." Tangie stifled a laugh.

Annabelle's hand went up, too. "My aunt came and she brought my cousins. They've never been in a church before. My mom says it's kind of like a miracle."

Tangie's heart swelled with joy. "It is like a miracle." *Lord, You're proving what I've said all along. . .the arts* are *a great way to reach out to people who don't know You. Use this production, Father. Reach those who haven't heard the gospel message before.*

"Kids, let's pray before we do the show." Tangie instructed them to stand and get into a circle. Some of the boys were a little hesitant to join hands, but eventually they formed a large, unified ring. At this point, she encouraged the children to pray, not just for the show, but also for those in attendance. By the end of the prayer time, Tangie had tears in her eyes. For that matter, Gregg did, too. From across the room, she gave him a wink, then mouthed the words,

"Break a leg." He nodded, then ushered the children toward the stage.

❧

Gregg took his seat at the piano, stretched his arms, and then whispered a prayer that all would go well. He could take Darla's place as chief musician, ensuring the show would go on, but that was where his role ended. Everything from this point forth was up to the Lord. Would He take the little bit they'd given Him and use it to His glory? Only time would tell.

The lights went down in the auditorium, but not before Gregg saw his mother slip in the back door. He whispered a quiet, "Thank You, Lord," then began to play the opening number.

The stage lights came up, and the colorful set came alive. The colors had seemed bright before, but not like this. Maybe it was the energy of the crowd. There were, after all, over three hundred elementary aged children in the room. Everything seemed brighter and happier.

In the center of the stage, the spotlight hit the giant Easter egg. Then, as the music progressed, the egg began to crack from the inside out. "Good girl, Margaret," he whispered. "Come on out of that protective shell of pride you've been wearing. Show 'em what you've got."

She did just that. As she emerged dressed as a baby chick, the audience came alive with laughter and joy. "It's a chicken!" one little girl hollered.

Not swayed, Margaret delivered her line with perfection. Then Annabelle entered the stage. Oh, how cute she looked in that little lamb costume. Tangie had been right. The kids loved this sort of thing. Annabelle opened her mouth to sing, and a holy hush fell over the audience. In fact, by the end of the song, Gregg could hardly see the keys. His eyes were, after all, filled with tears.

❧

When the show ended, Tangie rushed around backstage, congratulating the children and thanking them for doing such a terrific job. When the last of the kids had finally gone, she plopped down into a chair, completely dumbfounded. "You did it, Lord. You pulled it off." And, with the exception of a couple of minor glitches, the show had been as close to perfect as any show could be. "Lord, I believe in miracles. I've just witnessed one." She paused for a moment to think of all He had done. More than anything else, the Lord had convinced Tangie that she did, indeed, have a call on her life to work with kids. Maybe it hadn't always been easy. . .but it had been worth it. No doubt about that.

"A penny for your thoughts." Tangie looked up as she heard a familiar voice. Gregg's mom stood in front of her, a broad smile on her face. "I liked your bunny show."

Tangie laughed. "Seriously?"

"Seriously. Lots to chew on. I'll have to get back with you on all of that. But I wanted you to know I think you and Gregg did an awesome job." Penny leaned down and whispered, "And didn't he sound great on the piano?"

"He sure did. You should hear him on Sundays. He's the best." Tangie stopped herself from saying more. Didn't want to push the envelope. Still, Penny was right. Gregg had saved the day by stepping into the role of pianist.

Penny glanced at her watch. "Well, I've got to scoot. Thank goodness Sarah was home from school and could babysit the store for me this afternoon."

"I'm so glad." Tangie smiled.

"You coming in on Monday?" Penny asked. "There's going to be a lot of cleanup."

Tangie gave a hesitant nod. "M–maybe. I'll get back to you on that."

Penny nodded, but took off in a hurry.

Tangie rose and started cleaning up the stage area. As she reached the farthest corner, a couple of familiar voices rang out.

"Tangerine!"

She turned, stunned to see her sisters and their husbands standing there. "Taffie? Candy!" Tangie sprinted their way, her heart now beating double-time as she saw her little niece squirming in Taffie's arms. "What are you doing here?"

"You didn't think Gran-Gran would let us get away with not seeing the show, did you?" Candy said, her words framed in laughter.

"And besides, I wanted Maddy to see her Aunt Tangie in her first church performance," Taffie added, passing the toddler off to Tangie.

She held the beautiful youngster, her heart suddenly quite full. "Did you come alone, or. . ."

"Oh, you mean Mom and Dad?" Candy shrugged. "They're in Texas this week. But Mom sends her love. And Dad says—"

"Break a leg!" they all shouted in unison.

"So, you saw the show?" Tangie gave her sisters a hesitant look. When they nodded, she asked, "W–what did you think?"

"You're kidding, right?" Candy shook her head. "It was amazing, Tangie. I got it. Every bit of symbolism. Every nuance. It was all there. And the kids were amazing."

"So was their director," Taffie added with a wink.

"Yes, you're a natural," Candy agreed as she reached to give her a hug. "You were born for the theater." She said the word *theater* in an exaggerated British accent, making everyone laugh.

Tangie wanted to ask her sisters' opinion, whether she should—or shouldn't—go to New York to audition for *A Woman in Love*. But this wasn't the time. No, this was the time to cuddle her niece, chat with her sisters. . .and introduce everyone to one very special music director.

Chapter 22

The Monday after the big show, Tangie received a call from a very hyper Marti.

"You're coming home, right? Vincent called again, and he said to tell you to be at the Marlowe Theater at two o'clock on Wednesday afternoon. That's the final day of the auditions. In my opinion, it's better to go last than first. You'll leave a lasting impression on him that way."

"I guess." Tangie sighed. "I've been praying about it, Marti, but I'm just not sure." Every time she prayed, images of Gregg's face popped up in front of her. And the children. . .she would miss them something fierce. She would miss Penny, too. And her grandparents. Would it really be worth it—to trade in the people she now loved. . .for a production?

"We're not talking forever," Marti reminded her. "It's just one show. And what can it hurt to audition? You don't have to bring all of your stuff when you come. Just bring a bag or two. Come tomorrow and stay at my place for a few days. You can make your decision after you get here. If you get the part, maybe that will be a sign you're supposed to be back here. If you don't. . ." Marti paused. "Well, I don't want to think about that because I really want you back in New York. But you can decide for yourself, okay?"

"Okay." Tangie realized this was really the only thing that made sense. If she didn't go back to New York and audition for this role, she'd never know for sure whether she belonged in the Big Apple or in Harmony. And, if she didn't at least give this a shot, she'd never know if she had what it took to be a leading lady.

Tangie settled down onto the bed, reaching for one of the programs from the children's musical. The kids had signed it—using their childish scribbles to offer up their thanks for the role she'd played. She grinned as she saw Cody's signature, followed by, *Break a Leg!* And then there was Annabelle's childish script, followed by, *Thank you for believing in me.* Her favorite, however, was Margaret's. After the beautiful, well-placed signature, the tempestuous little girl had written, *This was the best play ever! Thanks for letting me be the narrator!*

"Lord, I'm going to miss these kids. And my grandparents. And. . ."

She sighed. Most of all, she would miss Gregg. She'd miss the look of disbelief in his eyes when she said something outlandish. She'd miss the way they harmonized together. Most of all, she'd miss the way he looked deep into her soul, challenging her to be a better person.

Determined to get through this, Tangie made her way to the living room. She found her grandparents watching TV.

"I, um, I need to talk to you."

"Not now, honey." Her grandmother shooed her away with the wave of a hand. "We're watching *The Price is Right*."

"Yes, but. . .I need to tell you something."

Gran-Gran looked up, and for the first time Tangie noticed the tears in her eyes. "We know you do, honey. But not right now." The way her grandmother emphasized the last four words stopped Tangie cold.

Ah ha. She just doesn't want to face the fact that I'm leaving. Well, fine. I'll talk to them later. Right now, she needed to head over to Sweet Harmony to let Penny know about her decision. Then, of course, she had to talk to Gregg.

Every time she thought about telling him, Tangie felt a lump in her throat. The sting of tears burned her eyes. She'd fallen for him. No doubt about that. But then again, she always fell for the leading man. Right? What made this one different from the others?

She drove to town, noticing, for the first time, the green leaves bursting through on the trees. "Oh, Lord! I've been so busy with the show I almost missed it! Spring!"

Yes, everywhere she looked, the radiant colors of spring greeted her. They were in the blue waters of the little creek on the outskirts of town. They were in the tender white blossoms in the now-budding pear trees. Even the cars seemed more colorful than before, now that they weren't covered in dirty snow.

Yes, color had come to Harmony at the very time she had to leave.

"Stop it, Tangie. It's springtime in New York, too." She forced her thoughts to Manhattan as she pulled her car into the parking lot at Sweet Harmony. By the time she climbed out of the car, Tangie had a new resolve. "I can do this. What's the big deal, anyway?"

She pushed open the front door of the bakery, the bell jangling its usual welcome. Tangie drew in a deep breath and approached Penny, who was working behind the counter.

"Well, hey, kiddo. I wondered if you might come in today. Made up your mind yet? Are you staying or going?"

Talk about cutting to the chase. Penny was never one to mince words. Well, fine. She wouldn't either. "Penny, I hate to tell you this, but. . ."

"You're leaving for New York."

"Yes."

Penny set down the mound of dough she'd been kneading and gave Tangie a pensive look. "Well, look, kid, I've been preparing myself for it for weeks. I'll just put a sign in the window, and—"

"No, please don't do that. Not yet anyway." Tangie's nerves kicked in. "I'm going to New York, but I don't know if I'm going to stay. Auditions are on Wednesday, so I need to leave tomorrow. I should know something a few days later. Can you give me a week, Penny? I'll call if I'm not coming back."

"Sure." With the wave of a hand, Penny dismissed the idea. "I'll get Josh to help me till then. It won't hurt the boy to work with his mama. Go on and go to that audition. Might do you some good." She went to work washing out one of the mixing bowls. " 'Course, if you stay in New York it'll break our hearts, but don't fret over that." She turned back and gave Tangie a wink. "Kidding, kiddo. You chase after your dreams."

"Thank you for understanding, Penny. I'm praying about what to do, but God hasn't really given me a clear answer." She glanced down at the tattoo on her wrist, pondering the little star. *Is this really where I'm supposed to go, God? To follow* that *star? To see where it leads me?*

Everything in Penny's demeanor changed at the mention of the word *God*. Her happy-go-lucky smile faded, and she exhaled. Loudly.

"What?" Tangie approached with a bit of hesitation.

"Well, since you brought up God and all. . ." Penny began to fidget.

"What about Him?"

"I just wanted to tell you something. I've been thinking a lot about this. That play you and Gregg put on with the kids. . .it was, well, it was great."

"Really?" Tangie's heart wanted to burst into song with this news.

Penny's eyes filled with tears. "This is going to sound nuts, but that scene where the little sheep has the conversation with the shepherd about wandering away from the fold. . ." Penny's eyes misted over. "I got it, Tangie. I understood what you were trying to say. I'm that little sheep."

"Yes." A lump rose in Tangie's throat, and she could hardly contain her emotions. "T–that's right."

"Let me ask you a question. Did you write that play with me in mind?"

Tangie smiled. "To be completely honest, no. I just wrote it with *people* in mind. God loves people, Penny. All people. And He desires that we love Him back. It's really pretty simple. That's why I used such a childlike platform to get that message across."

"So childlike an old fool like me could get it." Penny smiled as she gazed into Tangie's eyes. "Oh, by the way, thanks for letting Josh play the role of the shepherd. I haven't seen him this excited since I gave him that *Star Wars* lunch box in the second grade."

Tangie laughed. "He did a great job. And I think memorizing those lines about how much God loves His kids really did something to him."

"I think you're right." After a moment, Penny's brow wrinkled. "Seeing God as a shepherd really messed up my thinking, I'll have you know."

"It did?"

"Yes." Penny exhaled, pursed her lips, then said, "I never saw Him as kind-hearted or loving before. I guess I always figured God was as mean-spirited as some of the people who say they represent Him."

"He's not." Tangie shook her head. "And I'm sorry your experience with the church was painful. I can only tell you that the people I know who love the Lord are just the opposite of what you've described. They're loving and giving, and they accept people, no matter what." She gestured to her bright red hair, her tattoos, and then the tiny diamond stud in her nose. "I speak from experience. No one there has ever judged me."

"Except me."

The male voice sounded behind her, and Tangie turned to find Gregg standing there. He must've slipped in the back door, but when?

"W—what?" Tangie turned to face him.

"I judged you." He sighed. "I don't think I did it on purpose, but I'm pretty sure I didn't give you a fair shake in the beginning. I'm not sure why."

"My appearance?" she asked.

"I don't know. I think it's just that we're so opposite. It took me a while to adjust to the fact that I'd be working with someone who's my polar opposite."

"You two are about as different as singing rabbits and dancing chickens," his mother threw in. "But that's what makes relationships so interesting."

"Yes, opposites do attract." He took Tangie's hands in his and stared into her eyes. "But the real question is, can this relationship stand the test of time?"

❧

Gregg's heart thump-thumped so loudly, he could hear it in his ears. He'd walked in at just the right moment—or maybe just the wrong moment, depending on how you looked at it. Tangie was leaving. She'd confirmed it. And he wouldn't stop her, though everything within him rebelled at the idea of losing her.

And all that stuff his mom had said to Tangie about the play. Had she really come face-to-face with the Good Shepherd, thanks to a kids' Easter production? If so, then God had truly worked a miracle.

His mom gave him a wink, then disappeared into the back room. Gregg took this as his cue. He wrapped Tangie in his arms, thankful there were no customers in the store.

"So, you're leaving tomorrow?" he whispered, leaning in to press a kiss onto her cheek.

"I am." She lingered in his arms, giving him hope.

He reached to brush a loose hair from her face.

"I'll never know what might've happened if I don't go."

"I understand. And I support you. It's killing me, but I support you."

Tangie gave him a playful pout. "You'll wait for me?"

"Wait for you? Hmm." He paused a moment, just to make her wonder, then grinned. "Till the end of time."

"Very dramatic. Spoken like a true theater person." Tangie winked, then kissed the tip of his nose.

He wanted to grab her and give her a kiss convincing enough to stay put, but the bell above the bakery door jangled. A customer walked in. At that same moment, Gregg's mother reappeared from the back room.

"You two lovebirds need to go build your nest elsewhere." His mom snapped a dish towel at him. "I'm trying to run a business here."

"Mm-hmm." He nodded, gingerly letting go of Tangie's hands.

"I need to get to work, anyway," Tangie said, reaching for an apron. "This is going to be my last day. . .for a while, anyway."

"Last day." Gregg swallowed hard and settled onto a barstool. If this was her last day, he wanted to spend every minute of it with her.

"Oh, but, Gregg, before I go." She turned to him with a winning smile. "There is one little thing you need to do."

"Oh?"

"Yes." She nodded, a hint of laughter in her eyes. "I seem to remember someone once promising he would eat a whole plateful of artichokes in front of the kids if the performance went well."

Gregg groaned, remembering. "You're going to hold me to that?"

"I am." Tangie nodded. "And, in fact, it might just be the thing that woos me back to Harmony. I'd pay money to see you eat artichokes."

"What? Artichokes?" Penny laughed. "This boy of mine can't stand artichokes."

"I know, I know." Gregg sighed. Still, he had promised. And Tangie had given him hope with her last statement, anyway. Maybe she would come back to Harmony. When the time was right. For that, he would eat all the artichokes in the state of New Jersey.

Chapter 23

Tangie made the drive to New York, her mind going a hundred different directions. She arrived in short order, marveling at the noise and fast-paced chaos she found. Had it always been this crazy?

Seeing Marti was such a thrill. They spent Tuesday afternoon visiting all their favorite places—Hanson's Deli, the art museum, FAO Schwarz, and Macy's, of course.

On Wednesday morning, Tangie shifted gears. Before she even climbed out of bed, she ushered up a lengthy prayer, asking for God's will. She wouldn't dare make a move outside of it, not with so much at stake.

At one thirty, she caught a cab to the Marlowe Theater. At a quarter of two, she walked through the back doors into the familiar auditorium. At once, her heart came alive. Oh, how she'd missed this place! It captivated her, set something aflame inside her.

She filled out an audition form, reached into her bag for her music and rèsumè, and passed everything off to Vincent's assistant, a girl named Catherine. Then, when her name was called, Tangie walked to the center of the stage, ready to audition. She drew in a deep breath and sent one last silent prayer heavenward. Then the music began.

With as much confidence as she could muster, she sang the first few lines from "On My Own," one of her personal favorites. Closing her eyes, she allowed the melody to consume her. It felt so good to be back on the stage. And that Vincent hadn't cut the song short yet. That was a good sign.

Not only did he *not* cut her short, she actually sang the entire piece. When the music drew to a close, Tangie smiled in his direction. Even with the stage lights in her eyes, she could see the contented look in his eye. So far, so good.

"We'd like to hear you read, please," he said.

Catherine crossed the stage with a script in hand, which she passed off to Tangie.

"Start at the top of page four and read for Gina," Vincent said. "We're going to bring in one of the guys to read against you."

He looked around the empty auditorium and then shrugged. "What happened to our guys?"

Catherine gasped. "I'm sorry, Vincent. I really thought you said you were done with the guys until callbacks."

"Did I? I can't remember."

Tangie shrugged. "I can just read both parts if you like. Or maybe you could call out Harrison's lines."

Just then, a noise at the back of the auditorium startled her. With the stage lights in her eyes, she could barely make out the figure of a man walking down the aisle toward the stage.

Vincent rose and greeted him. "Perfect timing. You'll need to stand center stage next to this beautiful young woman to read for Harrison."

The man stopped, and Tangie squinted to see him better. Was. . .was that. . .? No, it couldn't possibly be.

Just then, a familiar voice rang out. "You. . .you want me to read for a part?" *Gregg!*

"Isn't that what you're here for?" The director sounded a little perturbed.

His voice rang out loud and clear. "Oh, well, actually I. . ." He climbed the steps leading to the stage and for the first time, came into full view.

Tangie gasped as she saw him. "Gregg, w–what are you doing here?"

"I. . ." He squinted against the bright lights, then put his hand over his eyes.

"He's here to audition for Harrison," the director said, the impatience evident in his voice. The older man climbed the steps to the stage and pressed a script into Gregg's hand. "Top of page four. Read Harrison's lines. We'll listen to you sing afterward."

"E–Excuse me?" Gregg's face paled, and the script now bobbed up and down in his trembling hand.

"Just do what he says," Tangie whispered. "Please."

Gregg looked down at the script, then began to read the lines, sounding a little stilted " 'Gina, I don't know any other way to say it. I've told you a hundred times in a hundred different ways. I love you.'" He looked up from the script, his eyes wide.

Tears filled Tangie's eyes as she took his hand in hers and read her line. " 'Sometimes we only see what we want to see. It's so hard to crack through that protective shell we all wear. So, maybe you've been saying it, but I didn't hear it. Does that make sense?'"

" 'Perfect sense.'" Gregg looked up from the script as he continued. " 'Sometimes we resist the very thing that's meant to be because it's different from what we're used to, or because we're afraid.'"

Tangie almost laughed aloud at the words. *Lord, what are You doing here?* Her hand trembled in Gregg's, but it had nothing to do with the audition.

He tossed the script on the stage and stared at her. "Tangie, I've been the world's biggest fool."

"Wait, that's not in the script!" the director hollered out.

"I should have told you that I loved you before you left. I drove all the way here just to say it." Gregg spoke with deeper passion than Tangie had ever heard before. Tears covered his lashes as the words poured out. "I don't know what took me so long. Guess I let fear get in the way."

"That makes two of us," she whispered, her voice filled with emotion. "I've been afraid to say it, too." The script slipped out of her hands and clattered to the floor.

"We're as different as night and day, just like my mom said. But, you are who you were born to be," he responded, taking both of her hands in his. "And so am I. But being without you these past two days has almost killed me. I can't eat. I can't sleep. I can't even play the piano anymore. Everything in me stopped functioning when you left, and I don't know what I can do to make things normal again."

Tangie smiled and squeezed his hand. "Oh, we're halfway to normal already, trust me."

He took her in his arms and cupped her chin in his palm. Such tenderness poured out of his eyes. She'd never known such powerful emotions.

"I love you, Tangie. I love every quirky, wonderful, unique thing about you. I love that you're different."

"Hey, now—"

"In a wonderful, glorious sort of way. And I love that you love me, even though I'm just a boring, predictable guy." He leaned into her, a passionate kiss following his words.

For a moment, time seemed to hang suspended. All that mattered was this man. *He loves me!* Tangie whispered the words, "*That* wasn't boring," in his ear, then giggled.

They lingered in each other's arms, whispering words of sweetness. Until a voice rang out.

"Best version of that scene I've seen all day. Where have you two been all my life?"

Tangie opened her eyes, suddenly blinded by the stage lights. Squinting, she made out the face of the director. "Oh my goodness." How could she possibly make Vincent understand. . .they weren't acting!

"I love the way you took the lines and made them your own." The older man spoke in a gravelly voice. "Brilliant. No one else has taken the time to do it. And there's a chemistry between the two of you that's. . .well, wowza! We don't see a lot of that. People can act like they're in love, of course, but to actually pull off a convincing love scene? Almost impossible."

Tangie laughed until she couldn't see straight. Gregg joined her, of course. The only one who wasn't laughing was Vincent.

"I'm glad you think this is so funny," he said. "You're going to have to clue me in on whatever I've missed. But in the meantime, you've got the part." He looked at Tangie, then shifted his gaze to Gregg. "And if this guy can sing half as well as he can act, he's got the part, too!"

Tangie's head began to swim, and the laughter continued. Then, quite suddenly, she stopped and looked Gregg in the eye. "Let me ask you a question."

"Shoot."

"You once said that I had issues with leading ladies, that I was secretly jealous of them."

Gregg groaned. "I wish I could take that back. I'm so sorry."

"No, you're missing my point." She grinned at him. "I just need to know one thing, Gregg Burke. Do you think I'm leading lady material?"

"Always have been and always will be."

"Okay, then." She turned back to the director with a smile. "In that case forget the play." Tangie looked at Gregg with her heart overflowing as she spoke the only words that made sense.

"This girl's going back to Harmony."

Chapter 24

Tangie finished painting the set piece and stepped back to have a look at the stage. She smiled as she looked at the road sign she'd just put in place. One arrow pointed to Broadway, the other to Harmony, New Jersey. Perfect.

Gramps entered, covered in paint. "Do you think we'll get it done in time for the show? We're on at two, right?"

"Yes. Still not sure about the backdrop, though. Do you think it will be dry?"

"Won't make any difference if it's dry or not. The show must go on, honey." He walked out backstage, muttering all the while. "You're a theater person. I would think you'd know that. Doesn't matter if the set isn't built, if the costumes aren't ready, if the lines aren't memorized. The show goes on, regardless."

Tangie laughed until she couldn't see straight. *Thank You, Lord, for the reminder.*

"Honey, what are you doing in here?" Her mother's voice rang out.

"Yeah, don't you have a wedding to go to or something?" her older sister Taffie said with a laugh.

"Yes, I do." Tangie looked down at her hands and sighed as she realized they were still covered in paint. "I don't exactly look like a bride, though, do I?"

"You will soon enough," Candy said, drawing near. "But first we've got to get you into costume."

"Oh, it's no costume, trust me." Tangie sighed as she thought about the blissfully beautiful wedding dress her sisters had helped her choose. "This is one time I'm going with something traditional."

"Well, it's going to be the only thing traditional at this wedding," Candy said, coming up the aisle. "I've never known anyone who got married at a community theater before."

"You're a fine one to talk!" Tangie laughed. "You got married on an airstrip." She turned to Taffie. "And you got married on the beach."

"I guess all of the Carini girls went a different direction on their wedding day," Candy said with a giggle. "But I still think getting married in a theater—especially one this beautiful—tops them all."

"It's the perfect way to christen the building!" Tangie looked around the theater, marveling at the changes that had occurred over the last six months. The whole thing had been Penny's doing. She'd hung posters around town, asking for the community's support. And, once the funds started rolling in, the old Bijou movie house had morphed into the most beautiful community theater ever.

The artichoke thing had been a big hit, too. Tangie didn't mind taking the credit for that one. Folks had contributed up to a hundred dollars per artichoke. Gregg had downed nearly two dozen of them, all funds going to the new theater, of course. Then again, the artichokes didn't stay down long, but that part didn't matter. The money had come in, and the old movie house was now a fabulous place for folks in the town of Harmony to put on productions.

Tangie still marveled at the transformation.

Of course, she marveled at a good many transformations, of late. Take Penny, for instance. Now that her chemo treatments were behind her, she was feeling better. So much better, in fact, that she'd joined the church. She now thrived on providing sweets for the monthly women's tea. And Tangie had it on good authority that Penny also slipped Gramps free donuts for the Prime Timers. He wasn't complaining.

No, these days Gramps had little to complain about. He was too busy working on the theater and celebrating the fact that Tangie had come back. Well, that and driving Gran-Gran back and forth to auditions. She'd reluctantly agreed to be in the community theater's first performance of *The Sound of Music*. Tangie hadn't shared the news yet, but she'd be casting her grandmother in the role of the Mother Superior. What havoc that would wreak at home!

But no time to think about productions now! Only the one at two o'clock mattered today.

Tangie stepped back, looking at the fabulous decor on the stage. "All things bright. . ."

"And beautiful," her grandmother whispered, stepping alongside her. "It's fabulous, Tangerine. You've done a great job, and this is going to be the best wedding ever."

"I do believe you're right." Tangie turned with tears in her eyes. "I do believe you're right."

❧

Gregg left the ball field at one fifteen, racing toward the theater. He hadn't wanted to miss Cody's game, of course, but there were more important things on his schedule today. His wedding, for instance.

Gregg pulled up to the theater, amazed to find so many cars out front. "Oh no. I hope I'm not later than I think." He leaped from the car, pausing to open the back door and grab his tuxedo and shoes.

When had his life become so chaotic? Where had all the organization and structure gone? And then there was the wardrobe! These days, he was more likely to wind up wearing a chicken suit than a suit and tie.

Not that he was complaining. Oh no. Falling in love with Tangie meant falling in love with theater—lock, stock, and barrel. And there was no turning back, especially today, when he faced the performance of a lifetime.

Still, there would be no funny costumes on today's stage. They'd agreed to that. She would wear a white wedding gown—one he looked forward to seeing—and he would look top-notch in coat and tails. Bridesmaids and groomsmen would wear traditional garb, as well. No, nothing to take away from the beauty of their marriage vows or the amazing work God had done in their lives. Besides, there were sure to be costumes in abundance over the years to come.

Gregg sprinted into the theater, pausing only for a moment to look at the stage. "Whoa." Talk about a transformation. Tangie and her grandfather had done it again. Then again, she always managed to pull rabbits out of hats. Sometimes symbolically, other times for real.

Gregg reached the men's dressing area backstage, finding Josh inside, already dressed.

"You had me worried, man." Josh grinned as he ushered Gregg inside, then closed the door behind him.

"Sorry. Didn't want to miss Cody's game. You should see him, Josh. He's incredible. I think we've really discovered his true gifting."

Scrambling into his tux was the easy part. Getting the tie on was another matter. Thankfully, his mother rapped on the door just as he gave up. After he hollered, "Come in," she entered the room, her eyes filling with tears at once.

"Oh, Greggy." She shook her head. "You're quite dashing."

"Very theatrical response." He gave her a wink, and she drew near to fix his tie. "I need you, Mom."

"It feels good to be needed." She worked her magic, then stepped back and sighed. "That Tangie is a lucky girl."

"No, I'm the lucky one." Gregg paused, thinking of just how blessed he felt right now. In such a short time, the Lord had brought him his perfect match—someone who also turned out to be his polar opposite. What was it Tangie had said again? That God was always at work behind the scenes, doing things they couldn't see or understand?

Lord, it's true. You saw beyond my stiff, outward appearance to my heart, and You knew I needed someone like Tangie. She's perfect for me.

He allowed his thoughts to shift to the day they'd met. . .how she looked. What she was wearing. Then his thoughts shifted once again to that day in the diner when she'd shown up in that crazy hat. Funny, how he'd grown to love that hat over the months.

"Look at the time!"

Gregg snapped to attention at his mother's words. This was not the time for daydreams. Right now, he had a wedding to attend!

Tangie stood at the back of the theater, mesmerized by the crowd, the beauty of the stage, and the look of pure joy in her future husband's eyes. She thought back to her first impression of Gregg. What was it she'd told Gran-Gran, again? How had she described him over the phone that day? *"Sort of a geeky looking guy? Short hair. Looks like his mother dressed him?"*

Oh, how her impressions had changed. Then again, the Lord had changed a great many things, hadn't He? He'd washed away any preconceived ideas of how a person should look or dress and dug much deeper—to the heart of the matter. And just as she'd predicted, He'd been working in the backstage areas of her life, fine-tuning both her career and her personal life.

And what a personal life! The familiar music cued up—the theme song from *A Woman in Love*, of course—she accepted her father's arm, taking steps up the long aisle toward her husband-to-be. *Just stay focused. Just stay focused.*

Somehow they made it through the ceremony, though the whole thing flew by at warp speed. She spent the time in a beautiful whirlwind of emotions.

Finally, the moment came, one she and Gregg had kept secret from their friends and family for weeks. Darla took her seat at the piano and the familiar music for *Embraceable You* began. Tangie looked at her amazing husband with a grin. She mouthed the words, "You ready?" and he nodded.

Then, the two of them joined heart, mind, and voice. . .for a harmony sweeter than the town itself.

Epilogue

Ten Years Later

Tangie tucked her daughter, Guinevere, into bed and gave her a kiss on the forehead.

"So, is that the whole story, Mommy?" Gwen asked with an exaggerated sigh. "You met Daddy doing a play at the church?"

"That's right. We met doing a play, and we've done dozens of them since. . . at the church and the community theater."

"I love it when you and Daddy sing together. You sound bee-*you*-tee-ful! And your plays are so much fun. But"—the youngster's angelic face contorted into a pout—"when can *I* be in one of them?"

"Hmm, let's see." Tangie thought for a moment. "You're nearly seven now. I guess that's old enough to start acting. But only if you want to. Mommy and Daddy want you to be whatever you feel God is calling you to be."

The youngster's face lit up, and her brown eyes sparkled as she made her announcement. "I'm going to be an actress and a singer, just like Margaret Anderson!"

Tangie had to laugh at that one. Her daughter had fallen head over heels for the community theater's newest drama director. Then again, Margaret had come a long way from that stubborn little girl who'd insisted upon getting the lead in the shows. These days, she was happier to see others promoted while she worked behind the scenes. Funny how life turned out.

"Honey, just promise me this." Tangie looked her daughter in the eye. "Promise you'll use whatever gifts God gives you to tell others about Him."

"Oh, I promise, Mommy. I'll sing about Him. . .and I'll act for Him, too." Gwen giggled.

"And if you decide you want to be a softball player or something like that. . . well, that's okay, too."

"Softball?" Gwen wrinkled her nose. "But I don't know anything about sports."

"You are your mother's daughter, for sure." Tangie laughed.

"And her father's daughter," Gregg called out as he entered the room.

Tangie looked up as her husband drew near. Her heart still did that crazy flip-flop thing, even after all these years. Oh, how she loved this man! He sat on the edge of the bed and kissed their daughter on the forehead.

"So, your mom's been telling you a bedtime story?" he asked.

"Mm-hmm." Gwen yawned. "It was the best ever, about a singing rabbit and a dancing chicken."

"I know that story well." Gregg laughed. "Did she tell you that they live happily ever after?"

Gwen shook her head and yawned once more. "No, I think she left that part out."

Tangie smiled as she watched her daughter doze off.

Gregg rose from the bed and swept his wife into his arms. Brushing a loose hair from her face, he whispered, "You left out the happily ever after part?"

Tangie chuckled. "Well, the show's not over yet, silly. How can I give away the ending?"

"This one's a given." He kissed the end of her nose, then held her close.

As she melted into his embrace, Tangie reflected back on that day when Gregg had come to the theater in New York to tell her he loved her. On that magnificent Broadway stage—with the lights shining in their eyes—they tossed all scripts aside and created lines of their own, lines better than any playwright could manufacture. They were straight from the heart, words that set the rest of her life in motion. They'd sent her reeling. . .all the way back to Harmony.

And now, as she gazed into her husband's loving eyes, Tangie had to admit the truth. She knew exactly how this story would end. The singing rabbit and the dancing chicken. . .well, they would live happily ever after. Of course.